TRAFFIC AND LAUGHTER

TRAFFIC

TED MOONEY

AND

ALFRED A. KNOPF

LAUGHTER

NEW YORK 1990

THIS IS A BORZOI BOOK
PUBLISHED BY ALFRED A. KNOPF, INC.

Library of Congress Cataloging-in-Publication Data
Mooney, Ted.
Traffic and laughter/Ted Mooney.—1st ed.
p.   cm.
"Borzoi book"—
ISBN 0-394-58478-3
I. Title.
PS3563.0567T74   1990
813'.54—dc20   90-52959   CIP
Manufactured in the United States of America
First Edition

For my mother, Elizabeth;
for my father, Booth.

They rest.

"If it were not true, I would have told you."

ACKNOWLEDGMENTS

The author would like to express his profound gratitude to both the John Simon Guggenheim Memorial Foundation and the Ingram Merrill Foundation, without whose faith and financial support this novel might not have reached completion. The support of friends and acquaintances remains, as always, of a different order—hardly less crucial, in no way repayable, constantly something to live up to.

TRAFFIC AND LAUGHTER

On a certain day in Southern California, beneath a sky that held nothing of emergency or love, a lilac-eyed woman in the middle of life's youth dragged a garden hose across the lawn by its sprinkler; dropped it, without breaking stride, squarely in front of her house; and as she threw the spigot open, shaking her hair impatiently back from her face to see the trajectory of the teeming droplets, she cleared her throat, grimaced, and helplessly reinvented, while the whole shimmering world revolved, *everything*.

"Sylvie?"

Without answering, she hurried into the house. There was a four-speaker stereo system in the living room, and passing distractedly by, she flicked on the radio component. A trickle of sweat ran from her armpit to her waist. She thought: *I must remember not to leave anything open.*

"Sylvie, is there another hose for the back?"

The kitchen's sliding glass door was open, and the man who had brought her here was standing by the artichoke garden, looking at her. She had not till now noticed the unusual length of his hands, even though, in a sense, it was their ingenuity that had been the subject of her questions for the past four hours.

"In the garage, Michael. Thanks."

A hummingbird shot into the air between them then, but Michael had already turned toward the garage, and she went back into the house.

The suitcases were stored on the top shelf of a walk-in closet off the hall, and Sylvia had to stand on her toes to reach them, levering them off the shelf one by one with her fingertips. This gesture reminded her of her marriage, which, along with many other things, had begun and ended in this house. She had lived here half as many years as there were suitcases, and of the latter she now found it impossible to say if six was too many or too few. Hurrying down the hall with a pair of them, she remembered once kissing her husband's fingertips. Her heart had been racing, racing, racing, exactly as now, but regret of any kind—this is all true—was alien to her. She laid the two suitcases open on the bed and abandoned them at once.

In the garage, Michael hoisted a coil of garden hose onto one shoulder and looked around for a suitable nozzle or sprinkler attachment. He himself, he recalled, already had a suitable attachment: he was getting married, in the fall, to a carbon-haired beauty of unswerving self-absorption. And he was here in Sylvia's garage, breathing in the mixed scents of cut grass and gasoline, purely by happenstance. When he located the second sprinkler, wedged behind a birdbath pedestal, he caught sight of something else, a clear point of light sparkling amid the cobwebs and cicada husks.

He hesitated, then reached gingerly down for it.

Sylvia carried a third suitcase into the study. Opening the bottom drawer of her desk, she began tossing packets of letters into the suitcase, each packet bound with a rubber band in a primary color. *But I know all this*, she thought upon opening the second drawer of letters. Without closing either drawer, she abandoned the desk too.

The radio said: "Take me to the river; drop me in the water." Sylvia threw three photograph albums into the suitcase.

When the spatter of droplets on the roof grew suddenly louder, shifting from a shower to a torrent, Sylvia glanced automatically out the window, as if to see the effect of rain on her universe, but there was no rain, nothing to consider—only her ardent cypresses and cedars, tossing like sleepers in the heat.

She had feared the phone would be dead. Lifting the handset, however, she got a dial tone immediately, an answer on the second ring.

"Hi. It's Sylvia."

"Sylvie. What's up?"

"You in touch with the traffic chopper?"

"But of course. It's times like these our Charlie earns his pay. You wanna talk to him or what?"

"Well, I'm at home. I need to know which roads are still open."

"Sure, sweetheart, no problem. Only, things are a little crazy right now. Okay if I call you back? When I get hold of him, I mean?"

"That'd be great. I'll be here."

She hung up and for a moment was loath to take her hand from the phone. After a time she opened a cream-colored file cabinet and began transferring its contents to the suitcase.

"Tell me what I can do," said Michael, from the doorway of the study. "It's time to cut corners."

"How long do we have?" she said, sorting file folders, avoiding his gaze.

"They're saying two hours, but I'd say less."

"Two hours," she repeated, rising slowly, an armload of folded manila pressed against her chest. The quality of her voice, full yet slightly raspy, had the unsettling effect, purely physical in origin, of suggesting both deep emotion and barely contained amusement. While half a million cars in supernatural colors shot up and down the surrounding freeways, Michael remembered listening to Sylvia's voice at a stoplight, in a convertible, next to another convertible. He saw now, though, by the way she had of raising her face a little as she spoke, that he had been wrong about her. She was anything but the slave of effect.

"You know what?" she said, meeting his gaze. "I'm not ready for this."

"Well, of course not," he replied. In the context, the notion of preparedness made him indignant. "Who's ready to see the world go up in a puff of smoke?"

It seemed to Michael that she was smiling at him. "I wasn't talking," she said, "about the world."

She put the folders on the floor beside the open suitcase, where they slid into disarray. Michael had once seen the geological plates of the adjacent canyon slide apart in exactly this fashion, and stepping through the study door toward Sylvia, he felt something of the dreadful fascination he had felt then. Her back was to him; with one hand she was twisting her hair up off her shoulders and neck, with the other she groped through her desk drawer for a clip.

When Michael placed a hand on her waist she turned around without surprise, but also without the clip, so that she stood before him in an inadvertent parody of coquettishness. She blushed and let her hair fall: a quick blond blur over the ear.

From the living room her voice spoke to them. It said: "You're listening to the sound of the city of angels." From the driveway came an annunciatory crunch of gravel. Sylvie's voice said: "On KBZT-FM." But Sylvie herself was listening to the gravel and turning away from Michael, her breasts brushing his chest, her hip rolling free of his hand.

"I knew it," she said. And two miles away a palm tree exploded in flames.

Michael waited until he did not hear the front door slam shut, then he walked out of the house after Sylvia. A tall man in a khaki suit was getting out of a white convertible, and he was looking at Michael's pickup with an expression of mild curiosity; he looked at Michael the same way, but for a shorter time; he looked at Sylvia, running toward him in the dry wind.

"Zack," she said or shouted. "Zack, what in the world are you doing here?"

It was immediately obvious to Michael that neither Sylvia nor the man she now stood before, arms akimbo, believed for an instant that her question required an answer.

"Are you packed?" Zack asked. "They're already talking about closing the road."

"We just got here." She peered at him, engaging, out of her heart's habit, the concern she saw gathered at the corners of his mouth and eyes, but after a moment she looked away. "I was at the station," she said, taking him by an elbow. A helicopter shot across the ridges above them and vanished into the adjacent canyon.

"Michael, this is Zack, my erstwhile husband," she said against the wind. "Zack, Michael."

They shook hands. Looking at the sky, very black now to the north and west, Zack said, "Michael-the-special-effects-artist?"

People in Michael's profession were not usually recognized by strangers, and he gave Zack a closer look. "That's right."

"We were taping the interview when we heard," Sylvia explained. "Michael gave me a lift."

Zack turned to survey the house, a miracle of glass and redwood. "I forget what we did about the insurance."

"It's okay. In my name, in the safe-deposit vault."

Michael heard sirens downcanyon and realized he had been hearing them for some time now. Zack, too, appeared to be listening to something distant.

"How come you needed a lift?" he asked.

Sylvia looked down. A gust of wind had left her blue dress sprinkler-spattered, and her fingers began ineffectually to smooth over the water-darkened spots.

"Sylvia," Zack repeated, "how come you needed a lift?"

She glanced sidewise at him. "My tires were slashed."

Zack nodded thoughtfully, as if this bit of intelligence would prove handy at some later date. From the north came the first faint drone of the bombers, low and graceless. "Okay," said Zack.

She found herself staring at him again. "Okay what?"

"Okay let's just get you out of here."

There was, in the set of Zack's features, something as accidentally damaged as her dress, and for a moment Sylvia fancied she could see her own feelings in the effort with which her former husband was trying to relax the muscles of his face. But the moment passed. "Right," she said, glancing at Michael, making up her mind. She slipped between the two men and ran into the house.

Flinging open her bedroom closet, she gathered up an armload of dresses, then hurried down the hall with them still on their hangers. She thrust them into Zack's arms, and he retreated. She met Michael at the bedroom door with a stack of skirts, blouses, slacks.

The radio said: "Driving in my car, turn on the radio."

Zack, entering the bedroom, said: "Can't we get some news out of that thing?"

Sylvia handed him an overnight bag full of shoes.

There was a blur of stations, and then the radio said: ". . . attempts at containment on three sides." Michael bumped into Zack. Sylvia handed Michael another overnight bag full of shoes.

The water evaporating from Sylvia's dress surveyed the scene with the elemental indifference of its vaporous state, while a mile and a half to the north, bits of burning debris blew across the ridgetop road and, landing in a stand of manzanita, set it instantly ablaze with flames as high and fast as a running man.

"Okay," said Zack, putting the key in the lock of the convertible's trunk. "I'll leave all the clothes there in the back seat, where they won't get dirty. What else?"

Sylvia laid a restraining hand on the trunk just as it popped open. "Nothing else."

Michael swung the bag of shoes into the car, looked from Sylvia to Zack, and walked back into the house.

"Don't be silly, Sylvia. I've got a lot more room."

"I know. It's very sweet of you. But nothing else."

Straightening slowly, Zack looked then into her eyes, to see what she meant. At the same time, his fingertips closed the trunk. "We lived here together, Sylvie."

"Yes, we did. And I loved you." She saw him notice the hint of tears in the lilac. "I'll take whatever else out of here in the pickup."

The other houses visible from where they stood seemed long abandoned, the cars stampeded from their driveways.

"Right," said Zack. "Whatever else." As he withdrew the key from the lock and started around the car to the driver's side, she caught him by the elbow. Her lips, when he kissed her, were unexpectedly soft, wide and lingering. It seemed that it was he who broke the kiss, though an instant later neither of them was certain. Shaking his head, Zack opened the car door and slid in.

"Oh, hey," he said from behind the wheel. "Your father's been trying to get hold of you."

"From Geneva?"

"Yes, but he says not to call him. He'll call you at the station tonight. When he can get a line secured."

She nodded.

He started the engine. "I have to say, Syl. You're very good at it."

"Good at what?"

"At whatever the fuck it is you're doing." He released the hand brake and smiled. "Call me if you need a place to stay."

"Okay, Zack. Thanks." She watched him pull out of the driveway onto the twisting canyon road.

"And tell the police about your tires," he shouted.

She waved. She was still watching when, two switchbacks down-canyon, one of her dresses blew out of the back seat of his convertible and tumbled halfway across the ridge, finally snagging in a bit of chaparral. It fluttered and popped there like a flag.

If God had wanted people to live here, thought Michael, peering over the backyard fence, *man wouldn't have had to bring water two hundred fifty miles south just to survive.* But probably it was stupid to speculate about divine intent at moments like this. Water had, after all, gathered from the earth's every corner to hang temporarily suspended in the swimming pool behind Michael, in the forty-odd turquoise variations on it visible down the hillside, in the tissues of Michael's own body, the ice cubes in Sylvie's refrigerator, the air above Sylvie's roof, the mushroom cloud of vapor now forming high above the spreading fire—and in the dark basin of the dark ocean beyond.

The radio's tuner reeled again and said: "That's what I want."

Michael turned to see Sylvia arriving at the pool's opposite edge, trying to light a cigarette in the wind. "Are you okay?" he said when he stood beside her.

"It was hitting him too hard." She threw the cigarette unlit into the pool. "I couldn't let him stay."

At the shallow end, the pool cleaner's flagellant tail broke the surface with a tiny splash and slipped back under.

"We can't stay either," said Michael.

"No." She looked over her shoulder at the house, and Michael turned also. "I guess what I should do is . . ."

Her gaze swung back toward him, and as their eyes met she saw a quickly drawn breath ripple past his nostrils.

"I mean, I'll just . . ."

But perhaps it is she who has inhaled so deeply, and he who now places a hand upon her cheek, smoothing the skin across her cheekbone, the hair above her convoluted ear.

"I'll just . . ." She swallows, and he, feeling her temple flex, swallows also. "Oh, God."

Later, Michael will be unable to remember this moment in any precise way because it will seem that it must have involved a decision—an agreement with himself—to relinquish the person he has till now been. Sylvia is still holding the matches, and as flames break over the mountains to the north—bright orange puffs seemingly dissociated from sound—she has the impression that these matches have become too dangerous to relinquish, and her fist closes upon them.

Her eyes close upon him. Upon his.

They kiss at first without embracing, quick kisses, quickly deep, that savor the depth of their mutual reluctance—a reluctance renewed with every second and as quickly overcome. In his mind's eye he sees a woman in a slit skirt walking down a long street, the intermittence of thigh and clothing, of skin and fabric, growing more and more rapid as she passes. The woman stops and turns to look back at him. His eyes flutter open. The woman is Sylvia.

He says her name.

Their bodies have pressed gradually closer as they kiss, and at the sound of her name, she lifts a hand, the one that is not a fist, and places it on the small of his back.

"There's no time," she murmurs. "There just isn't any time at all." It is completely unclear to either of them what she means by this.

He kisses her throat. Lifting her face skyward in response, Sylvia sees one of the bombers, a mile to the north, release a long red stream of borate over the fire. The borate slides sideways in the wind, and she laughs.

In Michael's mind, this laugh becomes a word, the word an exhortation. He draws back to look at her. She, steadying herself against him, removes first one shoe, then the other, laughing foolishly at the marvelous irrelevance of the shoes' red toes. Michael thinks: *How can I get closer to that sound?* And his hands, from either side of her waist, set out on a long caress down the outside of her skirted thighs, to the edge of the fabric and slowly back up again.

For a moment the two of them stand looking at each other, she with her dress hiked up above her waist, he with his thumbs at the waistband of her cotton underwear. Blue police flashers are playing faintly upon the rimrock across canyon, flames billow in a broken semicircle distantly above, and yet: threat of every kind seems miraculously transformed.

With a shudder she lifts her dress still higher. He lowers her underwear, stooping to do so, and as the garment turns soundlessly inside out, a single thread of silver is flung back upward into the soft amber hair that is revealed. He kisses the spot. She moves against him. For a moment it seems she will fall forward over his shoulder, into the pool. Then she backs off, steps out of her underwear, and the two of them hurry, like giddy, griefless thieves, into the house.

There is an enormous bunch of Peruvian lilies on the coffee table in the living room. Michael does not remember seeing them before.

There is a house burning down in splendid off-primaries on the living room television. Sylvia does not remember turning it on.

There is music in all four of the radio's tireless speakers as Michael undresses, as he watches her watching him, but neither of them hears it—and neither thinks to turn it off.

When he stands naked before her, she reaches down in a cross-armed gesture, plucks her dress off over her head, and is, with a simplicity that for a moment surprises both of them, naked also.

They kiss, move closer, and his cock is pressed up between their two bellies like all that they have discovered themselves capable of.

"Should you—" he begins, but she shakes her head. And it is then that she puts her arms around him.

His hands slide down her back, beneath her buttocks. Slowly he lifts her. She has the sensation of growing lighter, lighter, still lighter and, as her feet leave the ground, weightless. She is not quite unaware that acres of chaparral are being consumed all around her in a way that frees them equally from gravity. As she descends, his erect cock is caught between her legs, and the downward pressure exerted upon it by her gradually resumed weight is an imperative that causes them to sink together toward the several-valued salmon-colored rug.

She is very wet; he enters her at once.

There are few motorists left on the ridgetop road, the north side of which is already ash, the south side still ablaze, but those remaining now find their speed abruptly diminished, as if they have driven into sand or mud. The muffled explosions that ensue confirm what some of the drivers have already suspected: their tires are melting. One by one they abandon their cars and flee on foot.

Sylvia abandons herself to Michael thrust by thrust, bracing her feet beneath his for leverage, meeting his movements with a force equal to his but with a slight syncopation that makes everything about her seem faintly interrogative.

Silently, he answers a question she has not asked. The world is not ending.

"Michael?" Her eyes open, her lips swell, and as her first climax sweeps over her, the rug they have dragged into a V behind them pulls free of one leg of the coffee table, and the crystal vase of lilies falls crashing, shattering, splintering—in what seems to be slow motion—to the floor.

He believes he smells smoke, but a second later is unsure. There are magenta-streaked flowers all over the floor and a puddle of water advancing across it. He lifts his head, flinging it up from the base of his neck as if surfacing for breath, and thinks: *Where?*

The smoke alarm in the kitchen begins to shriek. He identifies the noise without finding any use for it.

"Sylvie," he says.

She opens her eyes upon him. He realizes he has been waiting some time for this moment—for the sight of her surprised—and simultaneously realizes he is also waiting for something else. But nothing about their lovemaking has yet told him what.

She opens her fist. Memory, thought, consciousness itself, are swept consecutively aside in her by a second shuddering wave of warmth, which reaches past the limits of the first to deposit her, him, them—*where?* The matches slide off his sweat-slick back to the floor.

The water from the toppled vase continues to move across the floor, touching first the heel of Michael's hand where it supports his weight, then the muscles of Sylvia's back, the flesh of her buttocks, his knees. The water's temperature is so nearly theirs that they are scarcely aware of the spillage.

She lifts her legs into the air on either side of him. He moves more deeply in. And the liquescent sound of him in her, so exquisitely obvious, reminds him suddenly of her laughter by the poolside, of the great first joke of which the two of them have now become the subject. All amazement converges upon what has always been known: that together they can make this sound.

Through all sound, he hears her heartbeat. It fills the room, seeming to shift the space first one way, then the other. He kisses her throat's throb and begins, as dirt starts to fly against the glass door at the other end of the room, to come.

"Michael!" Her voice slides across the two syllables of his name till it has made them into five, each matched to a shudder, then it veers into a curiously pitched, damped-down shout. Her nails go into his back. "Michael, *what* is going *on?*"

In truth, for what seems the longest time, he does not know.

Dirt, cut grass, small pebbles, and bits of torn flower strike the glass door with the swarming urgency of live things blindly driven. Their number and velocity double, redouble, and Michael, lifting himself half off Sylvia, glances involuntarily in the direction of the kitchen, whose door to the yard still stands open. The sound from in there is of a room being undone in a hundred thousand tiny ways—furiously animated bits of matter caroming around the stove, sink, refrigerator, walls. A single pebble shoots around the corner into the living room, as if trying to work its way to the center of the house. Absurdly, Michael stares at it. When he looks to Sylvia, her expression of puzzled concentration invites him to listen more discriminatingly to the sound that only moments ago he managed to mistake for her heartbeat. It is coming from outside the house, getting louder and louder, addressing them.

"Oh, God, it can't be." Her eyes seize his. "Oh, no. Michael, quick. It is! It's them!"

"Them?" And he is out of her, off her, standing, dressing.

She throws her dress on over her head as she moves toward the door; the fabric sticks to her back and buttocks where the water has touched her. "It must be bad," she is saying. "They wouldn't be here if it weren't." He buckles his belt and sprints past her to the glass door.

A helicopter is landing in her backyard. It has the call letters of her radio station painted on its side.

"Shit!" Sylvia spins around to face him, the fingers of one hand clapped to her mouth. "Your pickup!" Michael, barefoot and but-toning his shirt, is already heading out the front of the house.

The heat strikes him with an intensity that registers as a sudden puckering of the flesh, a theft of its moisture, and he is aware at once that the helicopter has almost certainly saved their lives. There are things smoking and smoldering on every side: patches of grass, pieces of lawn furniture. Not two hundred yards from where he stands, a star-shaped house blazes festively from its several facets, all its windows blown out, its garage half-collapsed, the dwarf oaks that line the driveway seething like traffic flares. *So much faster than you ever think,* he thinks, and pulling the keys from the pickup's ignition, he feels a swift faint shame at the loss and waste, at the necessity for rescue, but the feeling turns softly in upon itself, a cascade of embers. He takes a briefcase from behind the driver's seat and reenters the house without regret.

Sylvia is in the kitchen, yelling excitedly into the ear of a man wearing sunglasses, snake boots, and an expression of alert detach-ment. He waves Michael forward with an urgent roll of one hand while with the other forcing Sylvia's head down and propelling her through the door toward the helicopter. Michael hesitates, remem-bering that he has left his shoes in the living room, but the man shakes his head.

"This place is ashes, Jack."

Michael looks once about the house and nods. Then the two men sprint out after Sylvia to the helicopter, which has come to perch poolside, one skid half out over the water. At the controls: a man in a billed hat and a headset.

Strapping herself into the back seat, Sylvia wonders briefly who's at her own controls. From between her legs, love's soft leakage darkens her dress, wetting it where the water has already soaked it. Michael slides into the seat beside her. The helicopter—hum-mingbird that was and dragonfly to be—rises into the air, thun-derously, perfectly, casually.

The air.

It is her medium.

"I'm sorry we couldn't get you out," Michael shouts. But Sylvie cannot hear him. She is watching her house, yard, life, disappear beneath her, and to her shy astonishment, she is thrilled.

Two arcs of garden spray meeting at the roof, a cannonball of burning brush borne down upon the wind to her garage, a spreading ring of fire upon her front lawn. She finds she is able without effort to see through solid matter, that every object in her home is aglow to her sight: each misplaced book, each familiar chair, each dish. The part of the house that is still the kitchen begins to smoke. The part of the lawn that might have been an extra bedroom begins to burn.

I left everything open, she thinks. She marvels.

A soft burst. Flames. And by the pool, as the underwater cleaner continues heedlessly to patrol its aqueous precinct, two red-toed spectator pumps hold down against the rotor's diminishing wash the spotless, crumpled bloom of her cotton panties.

"We're out of here," says the pilot. He hits the cyclic, the helicopter surges forward, and—incredibly—they are.

Sylvia's body goes small in her seat. Lodged there, she sighs— so deep and unexpected a sigh that it leaves her somehow wary. She turns to stare at Michael.

He puts a hand on her knee, slightly embarrassed. "What a look," he says, after a moment.

But the helicopter's churn sweeps his words mercifully aside; she does not hear. And he understands at once that he has just negotiated something as delicate and urgent and nearly serendipitous as their rescue. So he lets her look, holds her gaze, tests its weight.

"Poof," she says.

"What?" he answers.

"Everything," she explains.

It is then he remembers. Pleased to contradict her loss, he lifts his hips, gropes through his pants pocket, and produces the single artifact he has rescued, so purely by chance, from her garage. Still looking at her, he puts it, glittering, into her hand.

She wonders for a moment why he has bothered to give her a shard of ice, but even after she has recognized the transparent crystal for what it is—a diamond earring, triangular in cut, set as a stud—she cannot think what it has to do with her. Then—and it is as though a door has opened in the sky before them—she does.

Nomanzi stood in the bath, turned off the water, and frowned. She had never bathed in a rose-colored tub before; the combined effect of skin, suds, and tub struck her as coloristically interesting in an especially overseas sort of way. She watched herself shake her head in the mirror: the sight made her laugh, the laughter made her see virtue in hurry. She drained the tub and dressed.

There had for some time been a drought in Southern Africa, her native land.

Chentula and Johnny sat in the largest of the hotel suite's several rooms. At the moment they saw virtue in nothing—they were too tired—but nonetheless they watched what was in front of them: a house was burning down in splendid off-primaries.

"As I live, you boys make me mad," said Nomanzi, turning off the television as she passed. "Here you are overseas for the first time, all the way in California, and you don't want to do anything but watch that box."

Chentula sighed, stood, and walked over to the grand piano behind her. "It wasn't you in the studio all day, was it?" Although his half-sister had spoken to him and his friend in Xhosa, he used English, to sharpen his point. He hit a few strange-sounding chords, then retracted his hands from the keyboard as if he had been burned.

"All right," said Johnny, who had at last been persuaded that the piano was no longer extrinsic to the interests of Gondwanaland. "Why not ring in for some beer, then."

"And maybe some mealie meal to go with it?" taunted Nomanzi, squeezing his pale pink neck from behind. It was always the sympathetic whites who made the harder time of adjustment, since the persuasiveness of their position began not in their skins but in their wills. "What's a Zombie?" Nomanzi asked room service.

When the three tall drinks arrived, so did three unordered bottles of mineral water, but Chentula signed for them anyway; the recording company was paying.

"I'd still like it better if they'd flown the rest of the boys over," said Johnny. "I mean, these studio musicians! Tits on a bull."

"It will work," said Chentula. "It will work." He was wearing a melon-colored bathrobe with the name of the hotel written in appliqué across the back. "If not," he added, surveying the effect in one of the room's several mirrors, "I will become a—what do you call it?—prizefighter." He glared menacingly at himself and began shadowboxing his way around the room. Since arriving in California he had had three pencil-thin lines shaved horizontally across each of his temples. "Here, it is supposed to be a free country."

"Right," said Johnny. "Land of opportunity, anyone can be anything."

"Or read anything," said Nomanzi, scooping a paperback book from his lap. " 'On the Beach,' " she read aloud from its cover. She arched her eyebrows at Johnny, who even standing was fully a head shorter than she, then flipped the helpless volume belly-up and continued her recitation. " 'The celebrated novel of forbidden love: A middle-aged European man of letters, a twelve-year-old American nymphet—and a passion kindled in time's fugitive shadow . . . On the Beach.' "

"She's got talent, that one," Johnny told Chentula, who, with one last flurry of punches, had collapsed on the sofa. "Think she could make it in the bioscope?"

"Her?" He regarded Nomanzi with a mixture of weary affection and bewilderment. Then his gaze sharpened, his voice deepened. "Let me tell you: not a week ago at this time she was giving the walls of her father's hut a good fresh smear of cow dung, so what, I would like to know, can she tell us about town life?"

The paperback flew from Nomanzi's hand, but it bounced without effect off Chentula's chest, and the three of them dissolved in laughter. Nomanzi was the star of a TV soap opera produced in Southern Africa. The show was broadcast entirely in Xhosa—it was the story of a country girl trying to make her way in the city—and the cow dung line came from the intro that ran with every episode.

"Really, though," said Nomanzi when she had caught her breath. "It might as well be true, for anything these agency people can understand." She made a face and fished the orange slice from her drink. "One of them today—I was just going to leave off my tape, you know, photos, all that—and he comes in from lunch while I'm there. Of course, he walks right past me into his office and slams the door. So I'm set to go—hand on the doorknob; I mean it— when I hear him buzz his secretary and say"—she closed her eyes, actress at work—" 'Who's *she?*' "

Both men laughed—her imitation of American flagrancy was flawless—but Chentula fell the more quickly silent: because of the question, because of the problem it proposed, because of the elusiveness of the answer.

"Well, all right," Nomanzi said, biting into the slice of orange. "It's my first 'town' interview, I know: learn the game. So his secretary shows me into this man's office—he's wearing these fancy pretend-tennis clothes or something, I hadn't noticed, feet up on this big curvy desk he has—and I sit down. He looks at me. I let him—a minute, maybe more. Then I get up, walk to the window— deciding on a monologue, you know, anything to show him *who she is*—and walk back. He's still watching, and he has a pad of paper out now, so I think, fine, here we go. But just as I open my mouth, he asks me—"

She looked from Johnny to Chentula, aware of their attention as something entrusted to her as much out of natural fraternity as of need for entertainment. "He asks me"—she smiled and in compensatory understatement quickly dipped her voice—"am I African on both sides."

"Oh, Christ," said Johnny, standing up.

"I mean, what can you do with a man like that? Tell him about blacks and whites and coloreds and passbooks? I just laughed. I just laughed and told him: 'Yes, yes. I'm African on both sides, front and back; you were watching, so you know. Front and back. That's what I am. That's exactly what I am.' "

"*And* he loved it." Johnny drained his glass, the crushed ice striking his teeth with a crystalline click.

"Yes, he loved it." She laughed again. "It wasn't in the script; it made him nervous. He loved it."

Chentula held his drink untouched on one knee and frowned, his spine very straight now. "Did he have some work to give you, then?"

She waved a hand dismissively. "Oh, he'll look at the tape. I'm to call him in three days. The usual. I've just begun looking."

"Just begun," Johnny repeated. There was an electric-guitar case stretched like a plank across the arms of the easy chair beside him; he set his glass down upon it. "It's a funny country, ay. I know I've just been here one day and, compared to you . . . well, how long was it you lived in Washington, Nomanzi? I mean, before you came back home again. Nine years, something like that?"

"Ten," she corrected, in a tone of voice meant to be noticeably even.

"Ten, then." He glanced at Chentula, who with these words had put straw to mouth and had begun drawing his Zombie evenly down. "But still. I look around this place and I'm amazed. It's like with those studio musicians—play your licks, pick up your check, back to the beach. Life is great, right? Getting better, right? Live forever, right?"

"Johnny, man, you take it too seriously." But Chentula had once again been thinking about the ten years; his words sounded like a question, directed at his sister, and he looked at her.

"Well, if I *am* taking it too seriously," Johnny continued, leaning over to pick up a bottle of mineral water from the table, "then I'm bloody well in the minority around here, aren't I?"

Nomanzi reached quickly for the bottle opener, trying to hide her smile in movement, but Johnny saw it anyway and blushed. "No, I mean it," he said, pointing the bottle at her, his white skin turning redder as he did so. "When you get down to what's really going on around here—when you really get down to the *facts*, I mean—I'm not so bloody sure it's any fucking better than home."

For a long silent moment everyone simply continued to live.

Then from the hotel pool came the sound of an enormous splash, its billion flung soundlets blossoming as unexpectedly as life in their ears, and as slowly fading. Nomanzi said, "Johnny?"

He was trembling slightly.

"Did you see your Surveillance man today? The one that's almost like a friend after all these years. As *you* say. Did you see him?"

Johnny let out a breath.

"Did you see *any* Surveillance men today? Any at all?"

Johnny said nothing. Nomanzi walked deliberately over to him, holding out the bottle opener. He studied her, then, after a time, took what she offered.

"Sorry, Nomanzi. As Chenny said, it was a long day."

"Yeh, and you two must have spent most of it thinking up ways to make it longer for an honest gardener, overseas at last." Chentula stood as he spoke; this reference to the trivial job that was stamped in his passbook, in his file, in the official history of his heart and skin, reminded them at once of the future, which was theirs, and of their lives, from which they thriftlessly fed it.

Johnny grinned. The mineral water sighed quickly open in his hands.

And when Chentula saw in the night flash of his sister's gaze that he had indeed been understood, he wrapped the robe more closely about him, pursed his lips in mock capitulation, and shrugged. "Yeh. So let's go out. I'll get dressed."

Nomanzi was the only one among them with a driver's license valid in California, so it was she who, by unspoken agreement, slipped behind the wheel of the rental car the recording company had provided. By the time she thought of bringing the demo cassette along, the three of them were already halfway down the hotel's palm-lined drive. "I forgot something," she said, looping back around to the entrance. Just past the canopy, she stopped the car and put it in park. "Back in a sec."

The evening air smelled strongly of smoke. During Nomanzi's absence neither man felt inclined to talk, but Chentula turned on the radio. "What's cruise control?" Johnny wondered aloud, peering at the dashboard from the back seat. Then Nomanzi returned, spraying herself with perfume. The radio said that the fire was officially contained now, pretty much out now, extremely costly. Sylvia's voice told them they were listening to the sound of the city of angels, and Nomanzi nosed the car out into traffic.

There were floodlit signs up and down the boulevard. Advertisements. None of the cars that surged alongside their own appeared to hold more than a single person, but Nomanzi was as exhilarated as if she had just stepped into a party. "Where do you think they're all going?" she asked.

Johnny couldn't hear anything with the top down, but Chentula laughed and pointed to the brilliant billboard landscape looming up at left—verdant, rolling hills in several shades that receded beneath a sunset, into the distance, toward the sea. "That's good," he said.

"Yes," she said when she saw that the advertisement was for leotards, and the landscape composed of interlacing, variegated legs. "It really is."

Driving, Nomanzi felt herself set loose upon a river of casual intentions casually intermeshed and by degrees transformed—it was this that touched her—into matters of life and death. She changed lanes. She felt wonderful. The frivolous look of the cars she passed encouraged her to aspire to a reality in which a musician with an audience of millions did not have to work as a gardener simply to avoid being relocated to a mud hut. And what must their mother think, she who had raised them both on the daily promise of a better world? Nomanzi glanced furtively at Chentula, the faintly mutinous lift of his chin hardly concealing his pleasure now—pleasure in the cooling wind, the speed, the promise of the still-tossing palms—and in her mind's eye she saw her mother too, chin lifted as she splashed the burlap ceiling of the two-room family house with a lime-soaked mop: there was no plastic; she used to wrap cloth around a piece of glass to protect her eyes from the burning specks of white that spattered down upon her face like heaven's fire.

"The satellites are out tonight," said the radio.

"I haven't seen any stars," said Johnny, leaning forward. "Isn't this supposed to be the 'home of the stars'?"

The windshield wipers came on, and Nomanzi turned them off again. "I still can't find the turn signal on this terrible—" She thrust her bangled left arm out the window and pulled into the parking lot of a small boxy building with topiary hedges in place of windows. "Well, anyway, here we are," she said, cruising gamely around the building to the back, where the lot was all but empty.

" 'Here we are,' you say?" said Chentula. "But what is this place?"

"Tire shop, by the looks of that one." Johnny pointed to a cerulean sports car too firmly settled in its space. "Careful, Nomanzi; maybe there's glass."

"Well, it's just an idea I had," she said to Chentula, pulling up anyway beside the sports car. She cut the ignition and toyed with the keys but made no move to get out. "You see, well, Father has a friend whose daughter—"

"They've been cut," said Johnny, peering thoughtfully down at the sports car's tires. "All four of them, looks like. Slashed to bloody hell."

"—whose daughter works in the music business." She glanced at Chentula; his face had begun to close at this news, that there was a purpose to their outing, and Nomanzi found herself talking very quickly. "Well, she's a disc jockey, really, but she's very well known, and I thought, you know, since we have the demo, and since from what Father said she—"

Chentula's hand reached out to where her own was flickering nervously at the key ring's trinket telescope, the record company's logo. "*Your* father," he said, enveloping both hand and keys.

Nomanzi stared at him. "Yes. My father." She made no attempt to remove her hand.

"And when he left the country—with you—he left our mother."

Chentula's switch from English to Xhosa registered in Nomanzi at a place lost to consciousness, down by the river, at the tip of her tongue. "But we have talked about these things; you know what the plan was; everybody suffered!" Chentula made as if to withdraw his hand, but she seized it and continued. "Our mother, our mother herself holds no bitterness! You know this is so! You know it! And yet you would refuse to let me do this thing for you because it is through my father? How can you be so crazy? I don't believe it."

His eyes were moist. "I don't believe it," she repeated, letting go his hand, reaching for her bag, opening the door. From the yellow darkness far overhead came the sound of a helicopter. "I don't believe it." She turned away and Johnny said her name, but she left without closing the car door.

African on both sides, she thought as she crossed the lot. The staccato clack of her heels against the asphalt laid claim in radiating circles to the night's space.

"Hi," said the young woman at the switchboard. "Can I help you?"

The reception area of the station was a glowing place, green and terra-cotta colored, with carpet even on the walls. "Yes, I've come to see someone, if I can just . . . remember her . . ." The receptionist, a fair-skinned girl with a nimbus of red hair, looked placidly on as Nomanzi rummaged through her purse. "I think it's Olivia something, but I'm not quite . . . Ah, here it is," she said, and handed the girl a square of paper with Sylvia's name on it.

"Oh, gee," said the receptionist, glancing first at the paper, then at the digital clock built into her desk. "I'm afraid Sylvie's just about to go on the air; her show starts at ten, you know, and . . . I mean, do you have an appointment?"

"Well, no, I don't." Nomanzi blinked once and let her eyes go very big. For the first time since entering the building she thought of the boys outside in the car. Maybe it had been pettish of her to leave the door open like that. "But she does know who I am. I'm sure if you—"

"I'm sorry, but we get so many people coming in here who just want to see her for one reason or another." The red-haired girl held her elbows and made a moue of service-industry sympathy. "You understand."

"Well, maybe I could leave her a note, then," Nomanzi said, throwing a quick glance at the door behind her.

"Oh, for sure. No problem." Her relief was palpable. "Here's a pen. And some paper. And I'll make certain she—"

The glass door to the right of the reception desk swung open and two men came striding through, the older one tanned and attired for sport of no clear nature, the younger one holding a clipboard under his arm as he propped open the door.

"I *know* she hasn't said anything," he said, "because that's the way she is. But I'm telling you, George, she gets these calls every night. And now this business with the car."

Nomanzi said: "I'd like to leave something off with the note. Do you have an envelope?"

"A what?" The telephone console began to warble.

"Of course, none of us *want* to think there's a maniac out there, but supposing there is? You know as well as I do that no one's around when she leaves but her engineer, and we can't really expect *him* to—"

"Good evening," said the receptionist. "KBZT-FM."

"All right," said the older man, "all right. I'll talk to her to-morrow." He began with both hands to massage the muscles at the base of his neck. "If she wants a guard, we'll get a guard. If she wants a Doberman, we'll get a Doberman. But I have to hear it from her, okay?"

"An envelope," said the receptionist, opening drawers. "You wanted an envelope."

"Okay, George. Thanks. See you tomorrow."

"Thank you," said Nomanzi, when the envelope had been produced.

"Thank you for holding, sir," said the receptionist. "I'll transfer you."

In the low-level glow of the station's anteroom, beneath stainless-steel call letters joined in the form of a lightning bolt and affixed to the carpeted wall, Nomanzi sat to write a note that would explain herself to this woman whom people were always wanting to see, for one reason or another, or write notes to, for one reason or another, or have whisper sweet somethings into the air's electronic ear so they might hear it from *her*—okay? Okay. Nomanzi took the cassette from her bag and wrapped the note around it. " 'Maniac'?" said the receptionist to herself. Nomanzi unfolded the note again, read it over, and added a line at the bottom: "P.S. I hope you will not think me too bold, but I wonder if you know of any places to live around here? This time I am asking just for myself. Many thanks." Glancing again at the door, she sealed both note and cassette quickly up with two broad strokes of her tongue. The taste of glue can be as surprising as a kiss, to which it is precisely opposite. "I wonder if I could use the ladies' room," said Nomanzi, handing over the envelope.

In the coral-colored stall, she drew a finger up between her legs;

it came away splotched with blood. *I'll suggest a movie,* she thought vaguely, as she took a tampon from her purse. The onset of her period, together with the quarrel in the parking lot, had left her feeling suddenly bereft, becalmed, conciliatory. *Or maybe a nightclub.* She reached behind her and flushed the toilet.

Before the mirror Nomanzi searched her face for signs of her mother's. She washed her hands. The water that fell tenderly through her fingers spun counterclockwise down the immaculate drain—while in all the drains of her native country, and of every country in all the earth's south, it spun away the other way, flung opposingly by the turn of the world, by time's transit north and south, by the laws and bylaws of stuff. *Lipstick,* thought Nomanzi, and put some carefully on.

"Excuse me," she called in the corridor, disoriented not ten yards out the bathroom door. "Could you tell me how I get out?"

The woman rushing past her turned on one naked heel—she was barefoot, and smelled of smoke, and had lilac eyes. But Nomanzi and Sylvie had never met, and there was no reason at all why they should recognize each other. "Two rights and a left," said Sylvie, walking backward as she spoke. She carried a stack of envelopes and recordings. She was worrying about the time.

"Thank you," said Nomanzi.

Brother or lover? wondered Sylvie, watching her go but thinking of Chentula, whom she had seen politely asking a question in the reception area.

"Five minutes, Syl!" called a voice down the hall.

"All *right*, I'm here," she said, and hurried around the corner into the studio.

She closed the padded door softly behind her. Mack, whose show preceded hers, was emptying his ashtray. The mike was off, the music on. "Bonsoir, Tristesse," called the engineer through the intercom.

Sylvia blew the man a kiss. His name was Wayne. She wheeled back around to Mack, and he embraced her. "I heard about your house," he said. "I'm really sorry," he said.

"Well," she said, feeling suddenly as if she had been asked a question. "It leaves everything open, doesn't it?"

The one thing that wasn't open was her sister Kristen's phone line in New York—it was busy, off the hook, out of order—so Sylvia had been able neither to burst into tears nor to reproach her sweet and feckless sibling with Michael's unexpected discovery of the diamond earring. It belonged to Petra, Sylvia's friend, who, having lent it to Kristen, had said nothing whatsoever about its failure to reappear in her jewelry box. Stepping before the console, with its twin turntables, tape deck, microphone, Sylvia examined the log printout.

"You'll notice I slipped in a few of our special favorites," said Wayne from his glass booth. "Right there at the beginning."

She smiled. "Right there at the beginning," she repeated. There was a bowl of peaches beside the log, and she bit into one, causing juice to spurt in a beaded trail diagonally across the page. Without looking up, she tossed the rest of the peach in Mack's direction. He caught it. *Home at last*, she thought, and the simple truth of the reflection so startled her that she almost laughed. *I must really be tired*, she thought.

Taking a bite from the peach without diverting his gaze from Sylvia, Mack said, "I don't *believe* George wouldn't give you the night off."

"I didn't ask," she said. She did laugh. "All dressed up with no place to go," she explained, pointing to her naked feet.

"I'll do your show for you."

"No, really. I need the distraction." She twisted her hair up off her neck and secured it with a clip from the console before her. "But you're wonderful, Mack. Thanks."

Cueing up a cassette and waiting to do her intro, Sylvie felt what she always felt at this prefatory moment: gathering exhilaration, an acute sense of inevitability, the palpable quickening of her life's flesh and sense as they composed themselves—second by second by second—to become, on cue, pure voice. *It's why I do it*, she thought, swinging the mike toward her. She glanced at Mack, who was gathering his things, preparing to leave. *It's how I am*. To her left, the steady unfurling of the cassette described a spiral in whose measured curl Sylvia imagined she could see, read, hear . . . a countdown. Hers. She took a sip from the glass of water before her and ran her tongue across her lips. She sensed every revolution of the deck's spindle as a number bringing her closer to the zero point of her own sensuous disembodiment.

Then—and it happened so all at once that later she would try to recall the moment by holding her hand palm up and just as simply turning it over—she felt herself split open by a premonition of the same abrupt disembodiment perfectly inverted: slaughterous in tenor; vastly—frighteningly—public in scale. She saw a place on the earth simply cease to be. There had been people in this place, and trees, and dogs, and buildings, and potted flowers. The things that could move had been moving. There had been shadows. She had observed a woman with a bucket, walking in the sunshine, swinging her load in a lazy arc that finally had become a full circle. Then there was nothing. Exactly nothing. Sylvia blinked.

"Knock 'em dead, Syl," said Mack, giving her the thumbs-up sign from the doorway.

"You know me," she answered, when she saw he was waiting for a response. "I wouldn't have it any other way." The engineer threw the switches, the red lights went on, the LED beside her mike flashed. Through the plate-glass partition Sylvia saw Wayne, her engineer, standing with his arms spread and a pen in one hand. As she began to speak, he, with considerable enthusiasm, began to conduct.

"You're listening," she said, "to the sound of the city of angels." She turned the volume switch down just long enough to take a quick sip of water. "The smell you smell is the smell of smoke, my name is Sylvia, and I'm here with you till two." She threw the cue and let the first record fade in under her intro. "I don't know what you did with your day today, but what I did was watch my house burn down from very . . . very . . . close up. We think I'm in a mood. But I can stand it if you can—this night is ours—and I can also promise you one thing: there'll be no mood music played around here while I have anything to say about it. Okay?" She brought the volume up to level. "Okay." The phone before her, wired to flash a light rather than ring, was lit on all three lines by the time she cut the mike.

"George say anything about last night's show?" she asked, staring at the phone, thinking not at all about last night's show.

"George?" came the voice of the engineer through the intercom. "He doesn't mess with success." They were referring to the special favorites the engineer had mentioned earlier, none of which were on the station's play list, all of which they'd played anyway the night before. Then he saw her staring at the phone. "Hey, you want me to run interference, Syl?" he said, pointing at his own extension, which was flashing like fireflies on a summer night in synchrony with hers.

"No," she answered, making the decision, punching a button, lifting the receiver.

It was a fan, someone sympathetic; he said he was in love with the sound of her voice. He offered her a place to stay; she thanked him and declined. He sounded relieved, avoided introducing himself. He said he was a fan.

And so, as every night, did nearly all the others. Such declarations were part of why she had never allowed her photograph to be published, despite the periodic pleas and pressures of station management; freedom of movement had always been very important to her. A boy called to say his mother had a house to let in an oceanfront neighborhood; Sylvie took down the address. A man called to say he was sending flowers; a woman called to recommend tequila; two teenagers called to request a record. And Sylvie sent ribbon after ribbon of hopeful new music unwinding at the speed of broadcast into the night, over the freeways, out toward the desert and the sea.

"The night time," she said, "is the right time," she said, "to believe that the morning's going to be too good to much matter worrying about. All the songs are long in the dark, and all the little words; so change your lane but not your station, settle back and drive. I know where we're going, I've been there before, I read all the signs. And you can believe me, they all of them say the same thing." She paused, half went for the cough button, then shrugged and let her laughter spill out onto the air. "They all say the little words. Do you do the little words? This is KBZT-FM," she said, and brought up the sound on the left-hand console.

"I do the little words," said the engineer as soon as the song was on and the mike safely off. "I shit from pure fear when you talk like that. I mean, four slashed tires is hardly a bouquet of roses."

"Well, I'm trying not to let him intimidate me." She lit a cigarette
and put it out. She was feeling intimidated. "Anyway, I could recite
nursery rhymes all night long and that guy—he'd still call."

"Yeah," agreed the engineer. "He'd still call. You got the public
service announcement ready for after this set?"

It was not much later, hard upon the end of her first hour, that
her phone began to blink with an insistence—invisible, of course;
imaginary, of course—that seemed to Sylvie to separate this caller
from the others, and she realized, to her shame and irritation, how
rapidly this unknown person had made a place for himself in her
mind. She waited until, through the plate-glass partition, she had
the engineer's eye. He nodded. Then she answered. The caller
hesitated, then hung up. That was all. He would do it three more
times in rapid succession. Sylvie kept her hand on the phone,
waiting for the flash. Each time she answered with the same neutral
phrase, her gaze locked with the engineer's; each time the caller
hung up. That was all. The sequence would be repeated at the end
of her third hour. Sylvie sank back in her chair and lit a cigarette.

"You'd think he could have given me a night off," she said to
herself.

"News in ten, Syl," said the engineer.

"Right," she said. And pulled herself together.

One thing about the studio was that time turned into numbers,
and another thing was that the natural world, in which everything
was either down by the river or about to burn up, existed elsewhere,
in another place, not here. Sylvia thought for a moment about the
woman swinging the bucket, but there was something of which she
was absolutely certain, even with her house and possessions blowing
faintly through the universe in the form of fine ash: the world
remained intact, the world would always be intact, nothing disappeared. She took a great long drink of water, and the bits and
sub-bits of its substance busily set about becoming temporarily part
of hers. *We can't stay either*, Michael had said. She touched the
golden buckle in her hair and announced a few records, a few
intentions. Nothing that is solid ever really melts into air.

Her father's call from Geneva was being put through. A voice
was asking if she was she. She said yes. The voice asked her to
wait.

Being the daughter of a career diplomat had taught her a variety of things that she had discovered other people were not particularly interested in knowing, although they always thought they were. One such thing was that the phone lines were seldom secure unless actively secured. It required about twenty-five minutes to clear a line from Geneva, and another five to run the check back the other way, as an extra precaution. Slipping the next cassette out of its case as she waited, Sylvie was reminded of all the little five-minute waits she had watched her mother fill by the side of the phone in their house in Washington: all the bits of needlepoint, all the patiently turned library book pages, all the cups of tea. "Maybe once," said the record that was playing, "Maybe twice." Without thinking about it, Sylvie turned the studio speakers down.

"Sylvie?"

"Hi, Daddy." She pressed the phone hard against her ear. "You sound as if you're on Mars."

"Odd. I can hear you perfectly."

"No, wait. That's better." She glanced at the turntable to see how much of the song was left to spin. "Am I allowed to ask how it's going? Or is this one of those back-channel missions that are so secret I don't even—"

"Your former husband tells me there are fires in the state of California," said her father. He left a little invitational pause, then cleared his throat. "There are fires?"

Sylvia discovered herself staring at the phone. One of the other lines had begun to blink. "I lost the house," she said. "It all went. Everything." The engineer was looking at her, but she shook her head and swiveled so that she could no longer see the flash. "I guess I'm still sort of in shock."

"But you're not hurt, are you? You're okay?"

"No, I'm fine, Daddy. Really I am." She gave a nervous laugh. "I mean, that house was a little haunted for me anyway; I'm just as happy to start again."

"Big fire or little fire?"

"I'm sorry, you're fading out again, Daddy. I can't hear you."

"I said, 'Big fire or little fire?'"

"Oh. Big. What do you think? The whole canyon burned. We've had two solid weeks of desert wind." She switched the phone to her other ear. "Daddy, you don't sound so good yourself. What have they got you up to, round-the-clocks or something?"

The silence that ensued had so little of the character of considered exchange, and was thus so atypical of her father, that Sylvia thought for a moment he had not heard her. "Hello?" she was about to say, but instead he spoke: "You mean the world to me, Sylvia—you and your sister. I can't tell you how literally that's become true over the last few days." He paused, but she saw it was not a pause she was meant to fill, and she glanced then at the recording.

"When your mother was alive," her father continued, "she and I used to have a private language for talking about my . . . little jaunts. Over the phone, I mean. You girls weren't supposed to know about it, and I'm quite sure Kristen still doesn't, but a few years ago I got the impression—maybe I'm wrong—that you did. *Am* I wrong?"

Sylvie touched thumb and middle finger to the two wings of her collarbone, and then, remembering how Zack had interpreted and named this gesture—The Posture of Small Resentment—immediately removed them. "Of course I knew," she said. "How would I not? Diplomats' daughters are to sneakiness born."

"Good," said her father. "Wonderful. Now, do you actually know any of it? The language, I mean."

She left a pause. "Well, no." Feeling she'd failed a test. "That is to say, I pretty much got so I could tell when there was more to what Mother was saying than met the ear, but . . ."

"Okay," he said. "It was a long shot." He took a deep breath. "I'm going to have to gloss over a lot for now, but I think you'll get the idea when I tell you I'm not in Geneva."

"You're not."

"Back-channel, as you said. And of course won't repeat. I wouldn't even bother you with it if it didn't have some bearing—maybe more than I realized—on why I called. The fact is—"

But Sylvie's eye fell upon the recording, now in its final furls. "Daddy, wait just a sec, would you? I've got to do my deejay bit." She swiveled back to face the phone and saw that the flashing had stopped. She put her father on hold. "You're listening," she said, and said the rest. The engineer was watching her discreetly as she threw the switch. *What in the world did that mean about "big fire or little fire*? she wondered. One of the other lines began to flash again, and for a moment Sylvie couldn't remember which line her father was on. Then she did.

"If I wake up later this morning," she said, "and read that you guys have been up all night redesigning my atlas, I'm going to feel left out, Daddy; I really am."

There was a silence.

"Daddy?" She threw the phone a panicked look. "Hello, with whom am I—"

"Sylvia," he said, "in moments like these, the comfort I take is that if I were a bad man, I couldn't keep doing what I'm doing."

"No," she said faintly. "Of course not."

It seemed to her that he sighed then, but perhaps it was the connection.

"The reason I called—originally, I mean, before I heard about the fires—is that I'm worried about your sister."

"Kristen?" Instinctively, Sylvia felt around for her purse, whose soft leather recesses now contained the diamond earring Michael had rescued from her garage. "Is there cause for worry?" she asked, fingers coming quickly to leather. "I mean, Kristen seems fine to me."

"You've talked to her lately?"

"Actually, I've been trying to get ahold of her, but—"

"So you know her phone's been off the hook for nearly two days. And before that, she wasn't returning her messages."

"Daddy, she lives in New York. New Yorkers are unreachable. Especially Kristen. Come on, this isn't like you. What's going on?"

"I have other reasons to worry. And not just about her."

"Hello? Daddy, are you there? Hello? Hello?"

"Still here, Sylvia. Shall I call you back?"

"Oh, shit, now I've lost him completely. Daddy, I can't hear you at all. You'll have to call back." She glanced at the clock. "But wait. Don't call me here at the station. Damn these phones." She struck the handset sharply against her chair. Is that at all better? God, this is frustrating. Anyway, if you *can* hear me, call me after my show, okay? About three, my time? I'll be at—" She stopped; it was the one thing she'd put off considering: where she'd be after the show, about three her time and forever after. Her engineer was moving about his booth, flicking switches, and Sylvie decided once again that the reason her tires had been slashed the night before, the reason for the violence, was that she had allowed this man, in every sense a bystander, to answer her phone for her toward the end of her show's first hour.

"I'll be at Zack's," she heard herself say, although half a dozen friends had offered her beds. "Just for tonight," she added. "If you can hear me," she added. The phone's acoustic space was eloquently chambered with static, a mansion of lost signals. "I'm hanging up now," she said. She did.

The world was a place that was getting bigger and bigger all the time, in a way—even allowing for the number of listeners who had, during the last song, fallen off to sleep or into one another's arms, or had simply driven their combustion-warmed automobiles into their homes' garages and turned off everything but the lamps that lit the places they wished to be in next—the bedroom, for example, or the kitchen, or the bathroom. When next the phone flashed, Sylvie knew, because of the time, that it was her silent caller. "Hello," she said, and when there was no answer she said, before he could hang up, "Goodbye." He did not call back, although she kept her hand on the phone for nearly a minute, and she wondered if this variation of the routine constituted a triumph for her or simply harassment's further elaboration. "When I was young," said the record that was playing.

"Got those commercial cassettes ready?" asked Wayne.

She stared at him as if she had just noticed his existence. "Why is it," she replied over the intercom, "that every night about this time I look up at you, there in your booth, and, God help me, I find myself thinking, 'This man understands life. He knows the deeper textures.' "

The engineer's face expanded in a smile of the purest pleasure. He began to laugh. "It's the glass," he said at last, when he had caught his breath. "You think I'm TV."

The final hour of her show passed in a series of seamless segues. Sylvia finished her windup, then threw the cue on her exit theme. "You want me to walk you to the car?" asked the precocious long-limbed boy whose show followed hers and whose eyes, whenever they had the chance, worshipfully followed hers.

Sylvia slowly withdrew the pencil from the flap of the envelope she'd been given by the receptionist and threw him a quick smile. "No, Glen. I'll be okay." She put the imcompletely opened envelope into her purse. "But thanks. You're sweet to offer." On her way out she kissed the glass of the engineer's booth, leaving a lip print. "Time to see what else is on," she said.

What was on in the parking lot was fear's streetlamp hum, but she'd left the rental car right up against the topiary hedges, right by the door, and as soon as she'd unlocked it she felt fine. *I'll deal with tires tomorrow,* she thought, pirouetting past her own hobbled car; the idea of tomorrow was beginning to be gratifying. She pulled out into what traffic there was, and simultaneously plucked the blue fabric of her dress from between her thighs, where it had become twisted.

But maybe he's got someone with him, she thought. *I should have called.* The radio implored her in an undertone to sample the glory of Royal Air's express service from San Francisco to Paris, but she turned it off. *I can always look to see if there's another car in the driveway,* she decided. Her naked foot was light on the accelerator; she loosed her hair and, with a convulsive yawn, tossed the clip into the back seat. Not once in all her life's mornings had she ever imagined herself to be a woman who would one day go to bed owning absolutely no underwear.

Zack lived six blocks from the ocean, in a refurbished bungalow, and as Sylvie watched it swing into view through the windshield, she began, for the first time, to experience misgivings at having come. *I shouldn't have decided all this on the phone,* she thought. But of course there'd been no real help for that. She pulled up behind Zack's white convertible and killed the engine. The sound of cicadas came to her ears, an unexpected deepening of the night's expanse and, with it, of her doubts. She knew she'd never really believed Zack might have someone with him tonight.

The house, but for the single lamp in the living room, was dark. When she saw, through the door's glass pane, that the living room was unoccupied, she let herself in.

Listening to the gravel, turning away from Michael, her breasts brushing his chest, her hip rolling free of his hand . . .

Her hand reached out and turned off the radio: Glen's voice, tuned so low she hadn't noticed it at first, trailed off into silence. Zack had been listening to her show.

She walked twice around the room, clutching her elbows, wondering if she should leave. It was always strange to see the ghost of her taste haunting the house Zack had made for himself: the bleached-out colors, the indirect lighting, the abundance of houseplants. Sitting on the sofa's edge, lighting a cigarette, she noticed her hand was trembling. She held it out palm up and turned it over. The trembling stopped. Just like . . . that. *Trees, dogs, buildings, potted flowers: there are places like that everywhere.* She in no way believed in the woman with the bucket, not in the least, not for a moment. Putting the cigarette between her lips, Sylvie rummaged through her bag until she found the envelope with her name on it. She tore it open at one end; the cassette and note slid into her hand.

> You do not know me, but my father, Joseph Lolombela, worked with yours through many difficult meetings to negotiate separate diplomatic status for the "non-white" peoples of my country (Azania). They are both great men! Also, they are friends, so perhaps you have met my father after all. Anyway, it is at their suggestion that I am contacting you.
>
> My brother Chentula and his friend Johnny Greer are the leaders of Tsotsi, a controversial musical group that is very popular in my country and—if it is not too much to say—all through the African subcontinent. They are here for three weeks to record their first record on an American label (it is TDA), and we are all very excited. (I am not a member of the group but an actress looking for work—this story I will spare you.) Of course, what I want is to ask a favor: do you think you could find the time to listen to the demo cassette I have enclosed? It is hard for us to know what your listeners might think of these songs, and we would love—

Sylvia skipped to the signature and P.S., then reread the first paragraph. When she looked up, Zack was in the doorway, drawing his robe about him. His cheek was pillow-creased.

"I've gotten sensitive to smoke," he said.

She stubbed out the cigarette. "Sorry. I didn't want to wake you."

"It's all right; I'm not awake. How are you?"

"Okay." She looked at him. "How about you?"

"Extra bed's made up. You know where everything is." He yawned. "Sure, I'm okay."

"I should have called."

"You bet you should have." He walked to where she sat and, taking a great slow handful of her hair in his fingers, pulled her head gently back until she was looking no longer at her toes but up, and distinctly, at him. "You're alive," he said. "And it's much too late not to be satisfied with that."

She smiled. "Okay."

He kissed the corner of her mouth and let go her hair. Halfway to the door, he turned around again. "Too late at night, I mean."

"I know," she said. She'd forgotten how sweetly sleep transformed him, and as she watched him turn back toward the door, nodding to himself, she realized she was crying. "Zack?" she said, trying to keep the tears from her voice.

"Mmm."

"We really had it there for a while. Don't think I don't know that."

He sighed. "I thought you didn't want to wake me up."

"No, I—" She wiped her eyes. "Okay. Right." She was still crying, and the sheer silent volume of her tears confused her. "Sorry. I didn't think I was going to say that. What I meant to say was"— she took a deep breath—"I meant to say that I told Daddy it would be okay if he called me here later."

"It is. I'll just turn off the bedroom phone. Stop worrying."

She stopped crying. "All right."

When the phone in the kitchen rang, fifteen minutes later, she was still sitting on the sofa, still holding Nomanzi's note and cassette, but she was quite composed: she'd stopped worrying.

Her father said: "This will have to be quick. I didn't secure the line."

"So I noticed." Sylvia opened the refrigerator speculatively—it was bright, cold, nearly empty—then she shut it. "Does that mean the world is suddenly safe for democracy?"

"On the contrary. It means the world is suddenly a place in which I feel more secure using a public telephone than I do going through our own people on something like this."

She sat. "You're on a public telephone?"

"We were talking about Kristen. I'm aware that my concern probably sounds . . . silly to you. But at the same time, you deserve to know, and Kristen does too, that the issues being negotiated here . . . well, they go beyond redesigning the atlas." He paused. "To be quite blunt, they go beyond anything I'd ever thought could actually be negotiated by men."

Sylvia shifted in her seat, in the dark, until her elbows were resting securely on the kitchen table, her chin on one palm. "Now you *are* scaring me," she said.

"Of course . . ." he said, and paused again in such a way that she was unsure whether he was responding to what she'd said or was simply going on. "Of course," he went on, "there is a school of thought that sees this . . . development as quite possibly positive: maybe in the long run it really *will* redefine our concepts of war and peace; just maybe, in the very long run, it will even bring an end to the sovereignty system itself—though who knows if *that* would be a good thing. God knows I don't. Anyway, except insofar as we're all citizens of the world, none of this need trouble you at the moment. What matters most immediately is that you and Kristen understand that the pressures being called into play here—on all sides—are extraordinary, and that I want to know they're not being extended to you." He took a deep breath. "I need to know you're safe."

"Daddy, we're safe. We really are." Sylvia began to wish she'd turned on the lights. "I mean, what do you think—we're going to be kidnapped or something? I don't even have any place to be kidnapped *from* anymore."

"Exactly. You say your house burned down. There isn't any chance someone burned it down for you?"

"Dad*dy*! No! No chance. *Pas possible.*" She realized that throughout their conversation she'd been hearing two women speaking just-audible French on a line distantly crossed with their own. "The fire started all the way over in the next canyon—supposedly some jerks were using tracer bullets for target ammo. I live in California, remember? Anyway, even the CD people didn't know which way the fire was headed, so how could anyone else?"

"And Kristen? Where do you suppose she is?"

Sylvia sighed. "Come on, Daddy, you know keeping up with Kristen is a full-time job even on the best of days. Honestly, I'm sure she's okay."

"Sorry, Sylvie, but I've got to ask you to humor your old man on this. Isn't there a friend or somebody you could call? One of her waiters, maybe?"

A passing car threw a sheaf of yellow bars rippling over her, the table, and a corner of the nearby maple counter. "I guess so," she said, extending an arm into the chance illumination. "Sure."

"Because I'd leave these talks in a second if I thought either of you was being threatened." Yet he already sounded relieved. "Personally, I mean."

"I'll track her down, Daddy."

There was a silence. Then one of the French women said either *"Tu as raison"* or *"tour d'horizon,"* but Sylvie didn't hear the rest because she . . . "wanted to know what you meant by that 'literally.' You remember? You said you couldn't tell me how 'literally' Kristen and I had come to mean the world to you."

Another car passed, and Sylvie held her fingers up to the rippling yellow bars.

"I meant," said her father, "that the things being decided here—" But having said these words, he became confused by the diversity of explanation to which he had laid the conversation open. He paused an instant, sniffing the air, deciding which way to turn. Then he hurried on. "The things being decided here," he said, "are far too important," he said, "to be left in the hands of tired old men fond of power."

"You're only sixty-five."

"And tired."

"But not tired enough to have forgotten I don't know any secret languages."

Sylvia's father looked up and down the sunny little street from which he was phoning. It was midmorning, late summer. Except for a slightly overfed bull terrier lifting its leg against a nearby lamppost, the inhabitants of this place were nowhere to be seen. "It's a weapon," he said then. "A bomb. It could literally—which is why I used the word before—extinguish life on this planet." He turned back around to the phone. "In April some damn fools figured out that if you could split the atom, you'd release this tremendous amount of energy—'the power of a thousand suns,' as the goddamn briefing books keep saying—and by July they'd figured out how to do it. Needless to say, by July-and-a-half some other damn fools had figured out how to get a bomb out of it, and now, of course, nothing will do but we all get together, all the allies, and try one out. As a kind of lecture-demonstration on the futility of war, you see—with the added bonus, I guess, of a sudden suntan for everyone." He laughed abruptly. "A thousand sudden suntans. Excuse me." Closed his eyes. "My darling girl. Excuse me."

"Daddy."

He looked around again. Even the dog was gone. "Well, it's not at all certain any of this will happen. That's why we're here."

Sylvia was crying and did not know why. She made no effort to stop. "Are we for or against this demonstration?"

"Officially, for it."

"And you?"

"Conflicted." He watched nervously as a tiny blue car barreled through the intersection without stopping. "Sylvie . . ."

"State secrets; I know." She swiveled in the chair, knocking over something with her elbow. With the wick of her tongue she flicked a tear from a corner of her mouth; with her hand she discovered and righted the salt grinder. "Don't worry about Kristen. I'll see she's okay."

"The least threat. Harassment of any kind."

"Right."

"Either of you." He removed a key ring from his pocket. "And I can always be reached via the Geneva number or through—"

"Daddy?"

"What is it, Sylvie?"

She stood in the dark and walked to where the telephone receiver was fastened to the wall. "I—" But then, gently, and as if of its own volition, her palm came to cover the numbered key pads. "Nothing," she said, and she rested her forehead against the wall. "I love you is all."

"I love you, Sylvie," she heard him say. "I know you know that." And it was only when she'd hung up that she began to wonder what it meant that she'd stopped crying at the same moment she'd decided not to tell her father about the hang-up calls, not to tell him about the slashed tires, not to tell him about the harassment and threat of any kind.

She switched the kitchen lights on. Everything in the room but the brightness against which she squinted was made of atoms. Shielding her eyes, she poured herself a glass of rum. *But I'll be bombed,* she thought, looking at it. The thought made her smile, and the smile made her aware of the tears that had dried to a thin salt crust upon her cheeks. She drank. Then she called Kristen and left a message on her answering machine, now apparently working, to get in touch as soon as possible. She left the kitchen.

Sylvia did not entirely believe in the bomb her father had described to her. Because she could see no advantage whatsoever in her knowing of its existence, she had already begun to think of it as little more than the circumstance by which two independently surprising events had taken place: her father had confided in her and, simultaneously, had apologized to her in a way that had made her cry. She sat again on the edge of the couch and, taking a boar-bristle brush from her handbag, began moving it through her blond and blonder hair with the patient gliding strokes of a woman for whom the world is constantly reexplaining itself. The cassette on the cushion next to her reminded her to call Nomanzi in the morning. Her bag open on the rug before her reminded her that until Michael had reached into his pocket in the helicopter, she had not even known that the diamond earring, which was not even hers, had been lost. Her bare feet, brown and quiescent by the bag, reminded her that today was already, as always, another day.

In the bathroom she washed her face. Zack kept half a dozen striped Italian toothbrushes in a jar by the sink, and Sylvia made bemused use of one of the fresher-looking ones. *He'll probably be at work by the time I get up,* she thought, looking in the cabinet for dental floss. The faucet, when she tried to turn it off, continued to drip, though she was almost certain it had been sound before.

The sound of the cicadas was louder from her bedroom because it faced the back. There were green-and-white-striped sheets on the bed and a scanty patch of sand before the closet mirror. She stood a bit unsteadily in the sand, turning the ball of one foot lightly in it and wondering what it meant to have an ex-husband whose guests took their bathing suits off in front of the mirror. She hesitated a moment, then smiled, and in a cross-armed gesture plucked her dress off over her head and turned, at not quite the same instant, away, as she had, at last, from Zack.

She left her dress on the floor where it had fallen. The sheets were fresh. She slept.

In her dream, she and her mother, who is no longer dead, are strolling hand in hand through the natural world. The intermittence of tree shade and sunlight stripes the path; a light breeze ripples the stripes. Sylvia is very happy to see her mother looking so well; indeed her mother looks closer to forty-five than to the sixty-two she'd just turned at her death. "You might want to take your shoes off now," Sylvia tells her. "It gets steeper from here on." And as her mother, smiling gamely, places a hand on Sylvie's shoulder for balance, as she begins removing her shoes, Sylvie realizes that the two of them are actually in a play or film of some sort; they seem to have been given lines. *That's okay*, she thinks. *I'll just act natural.* She accepts the high heels her mother hands her, and the two of them continue downhill, past a mustard-dusted meadow, past the sound of unseen rushing water.

MOTHER: That was quite a soiree last night.
SYLVIA: Housewarmings always turn out better than they sound when you get the invitation. [*Pauses.*] I don't know why.
MOTHER: I wish the dinner seating had been better, though; I really got caught in a bad stripe.
SYLVIA [*Trying to remember who had been sitting with her mother but not really wanting to pursue the topic*]: Yes.

The lighting has become increasingly even, the colors multiple but flat, and Sylvia finds herself wondering if the scenery through which they are walking might not in fact be computer-generated.

I should have asked Michael, she thinks, but without regret, since she can see no advantage in knowing the answer. She is still holding her mother's hand, but because the grade has become steeper and the path narrower, her mother is preceding her.

SYLVIA [*Conversationally*]: I hear they've split the atom.
MOTHER [*Amused*]: My darling girl, wherever did you get such nonsense? [*She stops, looks up at her.*] They only took one of his ribs! [*Turning, continuing to make her way down the slope*] And besides, that's just a story.

Because she can think of nothing to say to this, Sylvia again focuses her attention on the mechanics of descent. She is not surprised when she feels her mother's hand leave her own. Nor is she surprised when, looking up, she sees her mother has disappeared altogether and that Michael is standing on a rock below, pointing at what seems at first to be the sky—perfectly barred in yellow, pink, and blue—but then appears to be a suitcase in the trees, although it is a radio.

MICHAEL: You get that. I've got the other hose.
SYLVIA: [*Approaching the tree in which the radio hangs and gazing apprehensively up at it*]: Right.

Standing on her toes, she attempts to lever the radio off the limb with her fingertips, but she has trouble reaching it. She looks around for something to climb up on. To her surprise, she hears Mack's voice coming to her through an unseen intercom.

MACK'S VOICE: Right there. At the beginning.
SYLVIA [*Turning around, to discover an enormous pile of peach pits behind her*]: Oh. Thanks.

She glances toward Michael to reassure him that she's coming, then begins heaping the pits in hasty armloads beneath the tree limb.

RADIO [*Keening*]: Down by the river/I shot my babies.

SYLVIA [*To Michael, indignantly*]: That's not how it goes! [*Stepping atop the pile of peach pits, reaching the radio, turning it off*]: And anyway, where's my mother?

MICHAEL: Come on. We can't stay either.

He takes her hand, the one not holding the suitcase that is a radio, and they hurry down the incline.

In the next part of the dream, they have reached the river toward which they've been headed all this time. It is broad, it is variously blue and brown, it sparkles unpredictably as if woven here and there with glass ropes. She and Michael are strolling along the grassy bank; they've been joined by Kristen on Sylvia's side, by Sylvia's friend Petra on Michael's. Petra is a movie producer, and Sylvia finds herself wondering if it's her movie they're in, if that's why they have lines, but at the same time she realizes she can't inquire—the question isn't hers to ask. She turns to Kristen and asks the one that is.

SYLVIA: Why didn't you *tell* me you'd lost one of Petra's earrings?

KRISTEN [*With a moue of impatience*]: What good would it have done? [*Relenting a bit*] I felt terrible. But really, what good would it have done? [*Remembering now, resentful*] Besides, I thought *you* were the one who knew all the secret languages.

Kristen drops a few steps behind the others, then skips around to Petra's side. They whisper in each other's ears, laugh. Sylvia finds herself increasingly aware of Michael—aware that the two of them have recently come from lovemaking, aware that it is to love-making they will return. The thought stirs her, her nipples stir and tauten against her cotton dress, and at that moment she bumps lightly against Michael, her bare arm against his. She looks quickly at him, he at her, but the gaze holds and they drop hands. *It's not secret, really*, she thinks, and blushes. Michael reaches out as they walk and, still looking at her, runs the inside of his forearm down the small of her back, over her buttocks to the place where her thighs begin. When he draws his arm back across her thighs, she, as suddenly as she blushed, comes. *Further*, she says or thinks, *further*. The warmth spreads through her. *Further*, she insists, but she cannot tell to whom she is insisting. She is being pulled slightly away from Michael when she realizes that the suitcase that is a radio is actually a bucket, and that she has been swinging it through the air in progressively wider arcs. There is a commotion. Everybody stops as she sets the bucket down. Nomanzi streaks by at a supernatural speed and flings a photographer's color scale at their feet, the kind of scale meant to ensure fidelity in photographs of paintings. Sylvia picks it up.

MICHAEL: What is it?

SYLVIA: It's a color bar; everyone knows that.

MICHAEL: No, I mean in the bucket.

PETRA [*Looking*]: Ein stein. [*Looking up again at the others, as if waiting for a reply*] Ein stein.

KRISTEN [*Aside to Sylvia, who stands now at an angle to the lip of the bucket*]: Is that the secret language?

SYLVIA [*Confidently the older sister*]: No, it's German.

KRISTEN: Well, what does it mean, then?

SYLVIA: It means "a single stone." [*Pauses, looks at Michael, who is peering transfixed into the bucket.*] But don't ask me what *that's* supposed to mean.

MICHAEL [*Gazing now at Sylvia*]: Well, go ahead. Look. That was your last line.

Alarmed, she realizes this is true. She edges over to the bucket. Everybody is watching her. She looks around at them one by one, then leans over. The bucket is full of water, and at the bottom— glittering, beautiful, permanent—is Petra's diamond earring.

But I'm *not through speaking*.

There is a flash. No one moves. Another. No one moves. Another. Above them, a second sun has appeared, and it is flashing on and off with an insistence—invisible of course, imaginary of course— that seems to Sylvia to separate each instant from every other. She tries to move. She can't. No one can. There are no more lines. The phone lines are closed. The river is not a line. It is the only thing that moves.

Sylvia woke half off the bed with the sheet twisted around her. "Jesus," she said aloud, and switched on the light. She was shaking, and the sheet was wet where it had been between her legs. She squinted at it, touched a finger to her cunt. "Jesus," she said again, and got out of bed.

At first she could make no sense of the stillness surrounding her; she felt only—and uneasily—that something was missing. When she realized the absence was only the trill of the cicadas, exhausted now in the night's last hours, she experienced no relief; she'd been hearing another sound. Leaving her bedroom door slightly ajar to light her way, she walked down the hall to the bathroom and turned on the light.

The faucet was dripping with a hollow, rhythmic clop, its rhythm precisely that of the sun that had flashed in her dream. Shaking her hair back from her face, Sylvia cleared her throat, grimaced, and with both hands tried to turn the cold-water spigot enough past off to stop the leakage. It did not stop. She switched off the light and left the room, closing the door behind her.

In the hall, she paused. Zack's bedroom door was ajar, and from within came the sound of his breathing—untroubled and, as it seemed to her then, inexpressibly peaceful. She listened for a bit, torn and soothed by what she heard, moved against her will by this reprise of the formerly familiar. Then she returned to her room, picked her sheet up off the floor, and made her way quietly back across the hall, through the kitchen, out the back door.

There was a pair of chaise lounges set casually side by side on the grass, poised with the eloquent certainty of unconsidered things to receive the light of every next day's sun. Sylvia sat. The wind rattled through the palms. She sat there on the edge of the chaise for a time that might have been long or not, holding the sheet bunched beneath her breasts, feeling calm or not, waiting for everything, waiting for something, waiting in perfect patience for the rest. And then, at no particular time, she lay back, covered herself to the waist with the sheet, and slept.

She woke once, but briefly. Zack was standing beside her, and she realized it was the sound of the sliding glass door opening from his bedroom that had awakened her.

She smiled sleepily up at him. "Doesn't that faucet bother you?" she asked, wishing to explain herself.

"Is that what it is?" he said, wishing the same.

She laughed. In her sleep. She'd never seen him in pajamas before.

"Yes," she either said or didn't. The wind fell away. He did. She.

In the morning, in light that the night had miraculously cleansed of smoke, Michael examined the keys to the pickup he had rented the previous afternoon. There were green plastic casings around the heads of the keys; in the plastic, the name and logo of the rental agency were embossed to form three wavy white lines. Taking a clasp knife from his pocket, Michael carefully cut away the casings and threw them into the semistagnant salt canal on which his loft fronted.

When Sylvia had thrown the unlit cigarette into the pool, he had not known that her impatience had already discovered his.

The vehicle started right up—except for the upholstery, it was exactly like the one he had abandoned the previous day—and nosing it out of the driveway, over the little arched bridge that spanned the canal, he resisted the impulse to turn on the radio. The part of him that had been born or discovered on the floor of Sylvie's house reminded him that the only time he was ever really alone these days was in cars.

At the shopping mall, he had to park some distance from the entrance, and so he walked past many hundreds of other people's cars, each making some small sound of mechanical relaxation or self-adjustment. In the driver's seat of a no-color sedan, a woman was shrugging a dress on over her bathing suit, shifting her hips a little to do so, and as she shook her hair out, his eyes met hers. She smiled.

"No fires today," he offered.

"Hope not," she answered.

Everything about his morning seemed unusually vivid.

The toy department was jammed with women and children; Michael walked among them in glad sauntering espionage. Small dramas of acquisitiveness swirled about his legs in a flurry of pointing fingers, avid eyes, and excited appeals, while the mothers sailed on above, their half-distracted authority barely concealing all this evidence of their own desires grown consequential, of their own girlish selves grown ripe and womanly and one or more times pregnant, though of course every story is different.

"I'm interested in whatever World War II warships you've got, Japanese or American," Michael told the lady clerk with half-moon glasses. He had lived his own childhood entirely through without ever seeing a toy store—he had grown up in a trailer park in Los Alamos, New Mexico—but there had been lizards and television and small machines to take apart, so he had never actually felt deprived.

"That'll be a hundred forty-six dollars and twenty-nine cents," said the clerk, stacking up the boxes on the counter before Michael. But Michael didn't hear. He was watching a small boy buzz his brother with a tiny, radio-controlled helicopter.

"I'll take one of those too," he said.

"It's not World War II," said the clerk. "And besides, it's a different scale."

"Doesn't matter," answered Michael. He took a credit card from his wallet. "You only live once, right?"

Back at the loft, Jabez, Michael's chief assistant, was building a sky. "I think we're going to need more cotton," he said to Michael. The two of them studied the waist-high, table-sized glass plate on which Jabez had placed several teased-out balls of cotton, their bottoms darkened nearly black with smoke.

"Probably have some upstairs," said Michael, sliding onto his back under the glass. Putting eye to camera, he surveyed the sky, beyond which Jabez's face hovered proprietarily. "Yeah. Good. We'll use the strobe for lightning and maybe throw in the fog machine too. More ominous that way."

"We like ominous." Jabez took a couple of steps back from the sky and squinted at it. "The question is, do we like more cotton?"

"Wouldn't hurt." Michael got to his feet. "Try upstairs, top shelf of the bathroom closet."

At first Michael had been nervous about living and working in the same building, but he now found the arrangement ideal. Whenever he had an idea, he could come right downstairs and try it out.

"I thought I'd get everything set up today," said Jabez, "and then we can go ahead and shoot the whole brouhaha on Monday."

"Fine. I've got to play around with these damn gunboats today anyway."

Michael took his purchases into the half-finished Sheetrock-walled room that served as his office. On his desk was a slip of paper with a telephone number on it; he studied the number for some seconds before recognizing it as the one Sylvia had given him a week earlier, when he had first agreed to the interview. "Just name the day," she'd said.

"Do you have a place to stay?" he'd said at the end of the day he'd named, as they parted barefoot in the lot of the car rental agency.

"I'll be all right," she'd said, eyeing him with something very like irritation, and he'd seen then that she wasn't thinking at all about where she'd stay. "I'll call you when we set an airtime for the interview. I'll—"

When he'd turned on the radio later, to see where she was, she'd said that the night time was the right time to believe, and it was, and he had turned the glowing tuner off and slept.

Now, this morning, he owned thirteen authentically detailed, action-ready, end-of-the-war battleships. He began removing them from their packages, pushing a thumb through each cellophane window in turn, reading what was printed on the cardboard backings. " 'Ships of Two Empires,' " he said aloud. Then he said it again. There was shortly a great deal of crumpled cellophane on the desktop, chair, and floor.

"Mikey," said one of his production assistants over the intercom. "I've got your intended on 2309."

"My 'intended'?"

She giggled. "Sorry. It's this book I'm reading."

"End of Western civilization," he told her, and punched the flashing button. "Hello, my intended. Are we having lunch?"

"Well," said Laurel, "if my cast of Peruvian-lily thousands can stand two more takes, I should be out of here by noon." Laurel made her living as a florist—or "floral designer," as she was usually listed in screen credits—and since dawn she had been on set supervising the death-by-photoflood of her sweetly meticulous arrangements.

"Perfect. Want to come here, or shall I meet you at Eden on the Boulevard." His name for her place.

"I'll come there. Hey, what's that burning sound?"

"Burning?" said Michael, blanching.

"I hear it."

He looked wildly about the room, knowing there was no need but unable to stop himself. Then he heard it too, and laughed. He was standing in a pile of crumpled cellophane that, in blind obedience to its own substance, was steadfastly uncrumpling. "War games," he said, crumpling another fistful right by the mouthpiece.

"God," said Laurel. "The man is a walking special effect."

"The man," he said, "loves you."

There was a pause. "I love you, my life," said Laurel. "I'll see you at one."

When he had unwrapped all thirteen warships, Michael ran a hose into his office from the industrial sink outside. Removing the nozzle, watching the water spill into light, he filled the miniature model basin he had improvised atop Jabez's Ping-Pong table. It was four inches deep, painted blue. *Just the sort of day,* thought Michael, *on which a peaceful man wakes up engaged.* Nuptially, he meant, navally, he meant, and unexpectedly otherwise. He remembered looking over Sylvia's fence at the hillside of unpeopled swimming pools. He saw now that he would have to attach little anchors to the fore and aft of the ships if they were to hold their places in battle. Taking some fishing line and lead weights from his desk drawer, he set about doing this.

What he began wondering about next was the private thoughts and inclinations of several thousand old or dead young men as, buttoning buttons and swearing sailorly oaths, they scrambled to their battle stations on yet another vivid South Pacific morning, decades before, hard upon dawn. Michael had long believed that it was pointless to design a special effect for movie characters unless you have at least tried to imagine them as human beings. He knew that this sort of literalism had led the film industry to regard him first as an eccentric, then, when the box office dollars had begun to roll in, as a genius. It was actually kind of nice to be part of an industry that so constantly nourished your sense of humor.

Michael peered at the pom-pom guns on his aircraft carriers. Retrieving his copy of *Jane's Fighting Ships* from the floor, he ran a finger down a table of artillery specs. When he found what he'd been looking for, he snapped the book shut again. *Well,* he thought, *okay.* And launched his ships.

There were fans at two corners of the basin. He turned them on. He focused the two video cameras he had set up, then moved one of the fans closer. There was still not much of a swell, and Michael wrote the word "calm" on his blackboard, which hung on the wall behind him.

He did not expect the word "calm" to figure prominently in a film about the last days of World War II, but it seemed a useful reference point. When you were designing your first naval battle and knew nothing of war, you took your reference points where you found them. *At least there are no spaceships in this picture,* Michael thought. *No humanoids, no dinosaurs, no entities of supernatural evil.*

Referring to his script, Michael saw that the American destroyer *Catawba* was to sustain the first casualties of this, the last naval battle before the invasion of Japan. He positioned it accordingly. The film's protagonist was on another ship, the *Roanoke*, but there was a complicated subplot involving the hero's half-brother, who was commander of the *Catawba*, and Michael anticipated that accordingly several extra sets would have to be built. He dimmed the lights to a predawn glow.

Part of what was interesting about the battle of the Cape of Bō was that the last five ships of the Japanese navy had been able to inflict an impressive amount of damage upon the American fleet before finally succumbing. Another interesting part was that the battle virtually ensured the Allied invasion of Japan in November of 1945. Michael's father had taken part in that invasion and, thirty-six days after landing, had found himself in a hospital in Russian-occupied Nagasaki, shrapnel in a leg and an arm, an imperious teenage nurse from Stalingrad by his bedside. Since he had later married this nurse and taken her with him back to New Mexico, where she had shortly given birth to Michael, yet another interesting part of the battle of the Cape of Bō was that Michael could be said to owe his life to it.

In the viewfinder of one of the video cameras, Michael studied the *Catawba*. A proud ship in calm waters. Just visible beyond: the enemy fleet steaming ahead in standard diamond formation, its sole surviving carrier at rear point. The sun flared at the horizon; the Japanese admiral lowered his binoculars. And when he gave the order to launch, when the carrier turned grandly into the wind, its flight deck humming with dive-bombers revved and ready, did he still believe in the "divine strategy" argued over by admirals whose cheeks were streaming even then with tears?

Michael tightened the focus. Two American seamen were conversing by the *Catawba*'s number four turret.

FIRST SEAMAN: I thought this fuckin' war was supposed to be over.
SECOND SEAMAN: Surprise, sucker butt. It ain't.
FIRST SEAMAN: Hey, you're here too, asshole. Tell me you like it. I mean you should fuckin' see yourself.
SECOND SEAMAN: Ah, war's all politics anyway. And if I told you once I told you a million times: in politics everything's relative. Even *your* sorry ass.
FIRST SEAMAN: Shit. You tell me how fucking relative you'd feel about taking a kamikaze up the turret right about now.
SECOND SEAMAN: Shut up. I'm thinkin'.
FIRST SEAMAN: Man, I just hope I don't get it in the balls. I'm not ready for this. I been through shit an' fire, but I'm *not* ready for this.
SECOND SEAMAN [*Softly, to himself*]: There's no time. [*Pauses.*] There just isn't any time at all.
FIRST SEAMAN: All I ask is I don't get it in the balls. I mean, a man's balls are his *life*, right? [*Leans over, places both hands on*

his crotch, and speaks with sweet urgency into it.] I love you, my life.

SECOND SEAMAN: [*Contemplating* FIRST SEAMAN *with sad distaste*]: Kid, don't you got a girlfriend to think about?

Michael straightened abruptly and walked over to the blackboard. His memory of Sylvia's body against his was suddenly so intense, so exact, that he had trouble catching his breath. *Business first*, thought Michael, but it was some seconds before he took up the chalk that dangled by a string from the blackboard.

He would use titanium garniture for the burning-metal effects at the *Catawba*'s number four turret, gelignite for the actual explosion.

By the time he had blocked out the sinking of the first American carrier, he could hear the metronomic thump of his golden retriever's tail against the floor outside his office. He unplugged the video cameras and covered them. Laurel had arrived upstairs.

"Come on, Boris. Come on." Michael used his foot to prop open the door while he fiddled with the controls of the toy helicopter. "Look what I got here, boy," he said when he had it airborne. He maneuvered the device to within a foot of the dog's grizzled muzzle. Boris stared intently at it, snapped once in its general direction, then subsided into a contented pant.

"You always were a total cynic, Boris."

On the way through the open area of the shop, Michael landed the helicopter atop Jabez's sky. Jabez, who, amid tufts of teased and darkened cotton, lay stretched out underneath, didn't even bother to take his eye from the camera. "Michael," he said, "I just hope that's you."

"Deus ex machina," said Michael, and tossed the remote-control box onto Jabez's chest as he passed.

Upstairs, the door was open. Michael's pleasure at entering this vast, sun-washed space was a constant. Nothing could diminish it, not even the half-formed thought that in the six months since he had asked Laurel to marry him, he had not till now walked toward her still dizzied with the bodily memory of another woman's embrace. What he liked was the light; he liked the space. Sooner or later everyone who knew him commented: he was the creature of his desert childhood.

Laurel stood with her back to him, in culottes and an off-the-shoulder blouse. The blouse was black, her hair black lacquer. As she leaned over the dining table, one ear emerged and went translucent in the light.

"I had this awful craving for sushi," she said. "I mean, you know, the really disgusting stuff—eel, abalone, sea urchin. I got everything."

"Memories of the primordial tide pool," he said, kissing the back of her neck.

"Who needs memories? I work for sharks." She opened the takeout containers and began transferring the sushi to a large blue platter. "Absolutely no movies ever again. Remind me if I forget."

"Bad morning, huh."

"Ridiculous. And on top of that, the monsters have hired away my beautiful, industrious, and wholly irreplaceable shop attendant."

"Oh, that's right. Rhonda's an actress."

"Lousy with hidden talents. Anyway, she's off tomorrow for Paris, and they start shooting the day after that. I gave her the afternoon off."

Michael put one hand on Laurel's waist and reached around in front of her for a tekka maki. "Me," he said, "I try to stay away from the creative end of the business. Absolute nest of vipers there."

She turned to him, smiling. Often, she allowed her eye to dwell upon the swirl of his nostrils, whose porcelain-thin definition she thought of as somehow Russian.

"I missed you last night," he said, made awkward by her attention.

"I also gave myself the afternoon off," she said. There were chopsticks in her hand, and she tapped them lightly against one corner of his mouth. "Want salad too?"

They sat side by side at the oblong dining table, eating and talking, while Michael attempted to ignore the Peruvian lilies she had placed in a vase before them. Laurel announced that her parents, who lived an hour's drive up the coast, had called to invite them for the weekend. But she and Michael had other plans, Michael pointed out. They were going to the desert, where they were building a house, where Laurel that very Saturday was to start a garden in which desert species of every variety were to thrive and bear subtle witness to the passing of conjugal time.

"It was the fires, I think." Laurel lifted the last lettuce leaf to her mouth and cast a greedy glance at the sushi awaiting their attention on the sea-blue platter. "They were terrified for us. Mom especially."

"Oh, come on. The fires were way back in the canyons. Your parents know where we live."

She shrugged. "I noticed *you* got a little jumpy when I said that on the phone about something burning."

"Because I didn't know what you were talking about." He poured them soy sauce and, abruptly, found himself sick with love for her. In his mind's eye, he saw a child of theirs, coming out of a house of theirs, into a desert wind. "I was at sea."

"Well, you have to admit it was scary. Did you see the news last night? That one house, they actually showed the glass melting out of the doorframe." She watched the wasabe melt into her soy sauce as she stirred it. "Oh, by the way, the yellowtail's for you, cowboy. Think of it as chicken."

He met her glance and seized a mackerel morsel with his chopsticks. "I never think of anything as chicken."

"So much the worse," she said, and chose a bit of fluke. "Who's the one who calls you Mikey?"

"They all call me Mikey. I run a nonhierarchical establishment."

She eyed him with amusement. He felt life had been generous in bringing under his hands a woman who so easily took his measure, and he had not shied when he had become aware she wished him to ask her to marry.

"Have I suggested eloping?" he said. "For some reason it keeps occurring to me."

"Okay, okay. We'll worry about the weekend later." She pointed with her chopsticks to what he held between his. "That's octopus there, though, fella."

He chewed. Tiny bubbles rose through his beer. Light fell through the skylight and bounced off the fender of a sculpture attached to the north wall—it was a car, or much of a car, crushed by a hydraulic press into an unaccountably beautiful configuration. Laurel didn't see its beauty. Her red plastic bracelet clicked against the table. There were several aloe plants set here and there about the loft, and some mornings, while still naked, she would break open a single pale-green stalk and rub the gel into her skin. Doing so, she invariably closed her eyes. The earth now turned just enough more to cause the light reflected from the Buick's fender to strike Michael's face. He blinked and sat back in his chair.

"When Rhonda was breaking up with her boyfriend," said Laurel, reaching with her chopsticks for a morsel of raw tuna and rice, "she served him a dinner of squid stuffed with its own tentacles. They were halfway through the meal before he asked what it was. I mean, that girl is pure instinct. Where, really *where* in the world, am I ever going to find another shop attendant like—"

At that instant the tuna leapt from the tips of her chopsticks to the bit of blond table between her and Michael. Laurel looked down at it: flesh the color and translucency of a ruby, ruby the texture of a lip. She looked at Michael. "Did I say anything about missing you last night?"

"No, I don't believe you did," he answered. The steadiness of her gaze seemed to deepen her brown eyes nearly to black. Michael picked up the dropped tuna with his fingers—it had come free of its rice—and for a moment he held it.

"I guess I must be shy, then." Her lips composed themselves into a half-smile; her bare left shoulder pressed against his. "Is that one of my qualities? Shyness?"

"I don't think so," he said. "But you have an awful lot of qualities. It's hard to tell." Then, finding the fish in his fingers, he lifted it to her lips as if to confirm the color match—the match was exact—and with it traced their contour, flesh to flesh, until she opened her mouth and took it in.

He laughed a small laugh. "The blushing bride."

"You know, I like that stuff a lot," she said, chewing it and hooking her sleek black hair back over one ear with her fingers, "but what I *really* like is that sea urchin roll—the cone-shaped, seaweed-wrapped . . . yeah."

As he picked the roll off the platter, he breathed in the mingled scents of her perfume, barely floral, and of the raw fish. *But he was young! And life was long! And the sea, like the desert, is a place where you sometimes are!* He offered her the first bite; she took it; and he bit into what remained.

Rice and pink paste. Taste of the tidepool.

They kissed.

He loved the always unforeseeable heat of her hair, a heat that stemmed, it seemed to him, neither from the hair's blackness nor from its fine, practically liquid density, but somehow—and it was this that stirred him now—from all that she ordinarily and without thinking withheld of herself from the world. His kiss slid across her lips, cheek, temple.

It was his restlessness she loved. The hand she now placed against his chest measured only provisionally the chance she felt in his heartbeat that his return belonged to her; the fingers that undid the buttons of his shirt counted nothing. But she knew:

That his cock would be by now absurdly canted out of the brief black cotton underwear he favored.

That his lip had not been recently enough shaved to keep hers from growing quickly burned by their kiss.

That their legs had begun like plants in the sun to align themselves according to the congeniality of need.

She drew back and removed her blouse.

They kissed again, and without breaking the kiss she stood. He unfastened her culottes at the waist and unzipped them, twisting his mouth off hers in order to see. A flair of red rose across her upper lip like a birthmark or a minor celestial event. She said that it hurt. She said that she hurt. He said that he loved her. And she knew:

That the truth of what he had just said depended, subtly but inalterably, on her believing him. Because she believed his declaration of love to be true, it once again became so. In this exhilarating power, mysteriously bestowed upon her and constantly renewed, lay the source of her equanimity. She moved forward and pressed her belly to his lips, a soft moan issuing from hers, escaping everything.

Her open culottes were caught diagonally across her hips. In love, he drew the garment down. He seized her underwear as well, and gently lowered it. There was sunlight everywhere. He drew his finger upward through her cunt, and from it, her, them, released a furl of crystal larval web. It trembled briefly in the air between them like a slung kiss, and broke that way. He touched a finger to her nipple, then kissed what glistened there. He said that he loved her.

"Yes," she said or didn't, easing back against the table, resting on the heels of her hands, lifting one energetic leg. She and Michael understood each other perfectly. They saw a child of theirs, coming out of a house of theirs, into a desert wind. I love you, she meant. And he bent to the taste of her, with every sense.

But does she move then slightly back onto the table, causing a small clatter of crockery as she renegotiates balance and need, balance and breath, the future and her body?

And does Michael, adjusting to her movement, himself experience the vertigo of "renegotiation"—a word he saw that morning in the newspaper, in an article on Geneva that led him to utter Sylvia's surname aloud because it was not until then that he had even half hit upon her father's identity?

And when Laurel drops her lifted leg slowly down upon his shoulder, shaping in her throat the small unmeasured sounds of yielding, is it not the case that something of their slippery lips' topography suggests the slow sliding of all that is inside to everything out, so that Michael, against his will, begins for the first time to feel how much, in fact, has happened between him and Sylvia?

Ships of two empires. Blackboard calm.

Lifting his head from between Laurel's legs, he lifts her to her feet, rising to his as well. They kiss. She says that it hurts. He remembers and apologizes. They walk together down the length of his loft to the bed.

The coverlet is white. The slatted wood partition casts bars of light diagonally across the bed and, as she sits down on the edge of it, across her.

Michael undresses, dropping his clothes to the floor. He sees that Laurel, before his arrival, has removed the phone from its hook. A loud recorded voice recommends that they rejoin the tele-communications network immediately or soon, and for a reason opaque to them both, the suggestion makes them laugh. He hangs up the phone. He moves toward her across a great distance of stripes.

For a moment, they are anywhere.

He enters her.

The scent of their kisses, of the skin at her hairline, of his fresh sweat, of her perfume and the times associated with her perfume, of the fish they have eaten and the beer—all seem subsumed, at heart's heat, by the pungent depth of their exchange. He stays very close up in her—in a moment she will wrap her legs around his back—and she . . . she is reminded of the first night they spent together, of the unexpected complexity with which their bodies then read and pursued each other, of the tenaciousness of that pursuit, of her irritation that it should be that way, of his less complicated irritation, of the rest. It was his restlessness she loved.

The noise that has begun in her throat veers from vowel to consonant to become his name. He is moved and—at the same time—fixed. Their fucking begins to seem a kind of unchecked streaming, composed, like the edge of a waterfall, of both pure movement and utter fixity: last things, lovely precipice. She gives way to his thrusts and follows his withdrawals, so that his cock moves no more than a wish's inch inside her, and the wetness, which begins as hers, becomes theirs, a drenching mutuality—churned, like all else they are aware of or care about, from inside to out, from possible to actual, into the world.

"Oh," she says—and on this they agree so thoroughly that only by dint of a sudden fishlike flip of her sweat-specked body is she able now to defer the shudder that has too quickly been summoned up in her—"Oh," she says again, atop him now, but laughing softly, bent very close. "You *love* me."

It is, again, the truth.

He says her name.

"This can never stop," she says, and calmly closes her eyes.

There is a sound below—but really below, in the street, the canal—of a large object falling into water. Improbably, Michael is reminded of last year's Olympics as he saw them on TV, of the large (and, as it turned out, triumphant) Russian diver: his body displacing this planet's water just a bit, just enough—*how odd*, thinks Michael.

"Did *you* do that?" says Laurel, her eyes still closed, and it is more than half reproach, though she is no longer hearing what she says. "It was you?" Her forgetful mouth drifts languorously toward his, but he remembers at the last instant and runs the heels of his hands hard down her back so that, startled, she sits upright upon him and avoids further abrading her upper lip's upper tuck upon his. She opens her eyes.

"I was at sea," he finds that he has said. "I love you," he says—as if in simultaneous translation.

She lifts herself nearly off him, then shivers and sinks slowly down upon him until her hair's bright sheen becomes darkness purely, cutting off both his peripheral vision and hers, giving up its heat at last, contributing it to theirs.

There is no particular moment at which they become aware of the sounds in their throats as they come, no particular moment at which either feels the other to have finished, even when the sounds are done.

It is likely that time, in its fashion, passes.

The light stripes their bodies.

"I wonder what—" Laurel begins. But there is then another splash—as loud as the first—and she stops.

Michael kisses her forehead, then gently disengages himself and goes to the window. The phone rings. Laurel rolls over to the edge of the bed and stares at the phone without answering it.

What Michael sees out the window: two fiberglass rowboats, each holding two not quite teenaged boys. Because none of the boys is very wet, Michael deduces that it is the boats themselves that upon hitting the canal produced the splashes, and he watches for a moment as the boys do battle: standing, shouting, trying to ram one another, using the oars to unfurl the fouled water in long arcs.

What Laurel sees beside the bed: Michael's keys, half-fallen from the pocket of his pants.

The phone stops ringing. Laurel picks up the keys. "Hey, Mikey!" she calls, rolling onto her back.

"Still here," he says, and comes back around the partition. She has lifted her knees up above her breasts and is kicking idly at the air. He, in silhouette, sees the keys in her hands.

"How come you changed the upholstery in your pickup?" she asks. "I saw it on my way in and I wondered, 'How come?' "

It is only now he realizes that when he that morning cut the casings from the rental truck's keys, he was already anticipating this moment. He finds also that he is grateful to her for proposing, in her choice of question, the lie with which to answer it— not because he couldn't have otherwise managed the deception, but because in casting its terms, inadvertently or not, she has instantly reminded him of what he is most certain of: that nothing is replaceable—not people, not things, not anything that happens.

"Oh, some friends of Jabez's wanted to use it in a made-for-TV." He moves back to the bed and stretches out beside her. "Upholstery had to be striped, don't ask me why. Studio pays."

"Nice of you," she says, turning her face to his.

"I'm a nice guy."

They consider this. "Could be," she allows. He runs a thumb lightly across her still-inflamed lip and she laughs. "Not that you know what you're talking about."

In the street below, a radio rolls by, woofing and tweeting in the arms of an unseen roller skater. Michael's own arms are haunted by what they have embraced: love, a lie, and bright, feckless belief. "You really taking the afternoon off?" he asks, shifting closer to her.

"Well, I was thinking of going to the beach," she says. "But maybe," she says, kissing him a shade perfunctorily on the corner of the mouth, "I should go look at wedding cake designs or something with my doting mom." She curtsies the corners of her mouth at him. "I mean, if we're really not going up there this weekend."

"Choosing on the basis of sheer sense pleasure," he says, stretching, "I'd vote for the beach."

"Bastard," she says. "You come too. Take the afternoon off."

But before he can answer, the phone rings. They lie for a moment looking at each other. The mirror over the dresser frames their hesitation; it considers them. The calla-lily-shaped bedside lamps consider them. Boris, who has arrived at the doorway in hope of more inclusive activities, considers them. "I'm not home," says Michael at last, and Laurel, cocking an eyebrow at him, rolls onto her stomach to lift the phone from its cradle.

It's Rhonda, Laurel's shop attendant. She has to rent her house before she leaves for Paris the following day and wonders if they know anyone who might be interested.

"As a matter of fact," Michael says. Laurel hands him the phone. "I think I do," he tells Rhonda. "Yeah." When he realizes he has inadvertently memorized Sylvia's phone number at the station, he goes out of his way to make an effective show of looking it up.

"I feel I can say this now," said Sylvia, sitting on the edge of a garage jack, in the KBZT parking lot, lighting a cigarette. "I can say I have never fully appreciated air before."

Her car rested on cinder blocks. All its wheels were off. There were new tires on all four wheels and new air in the tires.

"Shit, Glen," said Mack. "I was just plain positive she was going to say she'd never fully appreciated *us* before. Roll one of those suckers over here, will you?"

"What I *think* she means," said Sylvia's engineer, Wayne, collecting from Glen the lug nuts for the front right, "is she never fully appreciated being *on* the air before."

"Honestly, you guys." Sylvia stood up. "I mean why is it that in any number larger than two, men automatically form a football team?" She inhaled deeply on her cigarette, then threw it away. "Hut one, hut two, hut three."

"Ah, the football," said Mack. "Without air—"

"Much as I love you," Sylvia warned.

There was a brief hiatus during which Glen blushed furiously and everyone else fell again to considering what sort of misplaced aggressions or desires might cause someone to drive out to the station in the dead of night and slash four perfectly good radials to threads.

"Speaking of huts, though," said Wayne, "we're all of us a bit concerned about your real estate situation. I mean, where you going to park your car in between slashings?"

Sylvia folded her arms across her chest. "Park? What's that?" But all three men gave her the same look, so she relented. "Well, you know, I'm trying to find a place, but first you have to imagine a life. I let a lot of things go yesterday. And I have strong feelings about . . . where I live."

Glen gave a spin to the wheel he'd just bolted on. There was pride in the gesture, and it moved Sylvia in a way she recognized as maternal.

"Or I don't know. Maybe I should just move back to Washington and try on the role of dutiful daughter." She glanced at the sky, where three small planes were writing the name of a pop music group esteemed by no one present despite the frequency with which free enterprise obliged them all to play its records.

"Air pollution," observed Mack, following her gaze.

"But it's funny," she said. "I grew up in a place that wasn't any place—playmates coming and going with every change of headline, every election year—and now I live in a place that's no place either: shifting ground, piped-in water, rising stars, and burning houses."

"Don't you love it?" said her engineer.

Sylvia smiled and, taking off her sunglasses, tried to clean them on her jeans. "Paradise," she said, "is a very high-maintenance neighborhood."

When the station manager called to Sylvia from the building's back door, the opening bars of "The Mexican Hat Dance" were ringing repeatedly out over the boulevard at something more than the legal speed limit. Everyone looked up in time to see the car itself—a rebuilt Chevy covered entirely in Mexican ceramic tile. It had all the jaunty prestressed presence of a small tank.

"Close the door behind you, sweetheart." George sat at his desk doing wrist curls with one glinty gold-toned weight and leafing through a logbook with his free hand. "Just dump all that crap on the floor. It's okay."

She did, and sat. She liked George.

"Looks like you have some car trouble out there," he said, letting go both weight and logbook, leaning back in his chair.

"Flat," she said.

"Four flats," he said.

There was a moment of charged bonhomie. Sylvia asked if he minded her smoking, then shook out a cigarette and lit it.

"I've been listening to your tapes," said George. He rested his head against the back of his chair and stared with conspicuous tolerance at the ceiling. It was well known that Sylvia was the only person he would allow to smoke in his presence. "I listened to them twice, actually, and you know, I gotta say: they came as something of a surprise to me, Sylvie."

She laughed and flicked a bit of ash into an empty orange juice carton at her feet. "Oh, come on, George. What's the matter with adding some yeast to the mix? I mean, if we didn't play a *little* of the real stuff, all we'd get is the schoolteachers."

He waved a hand back and forth as if to disperse her smoke, though it was in fact blowing the other way. "Forget the play list. I'm talking about you." He folded his hands in his lap and rocked just noticeably in his chair. "I'm talking about my experience with deejays who are getting harassment calls. Usually it makes them— you know . . . jumpy? Distracted? A little unreliable, maybe? With you, nothing. You sound fine. Supergood. I mean it." His gaze grew softly speculative. "I ask myself how you manage it."

"It's my sense of concentration. Absolutely pathological. Everyone says."

"And the tires?"

A level look passed between them. Sylvia felt she was being offered the opportunity to confess to something, but she had no idea what it might be.

SYLVIA: They're made of atoms.

"What?"

"I said, somebody had *at* them. I don't know." With one hand she lifted her hair off the back of her neck to expose it to the cool conditioned air. "That's life, I guess. Or it's life on the radio anyway. What do you think? A jilted listener? I'm just trying to get by."

"I want you to tell me what you want to tell me."

She sighed with controlled impatience and put out her cigarette. "Oh, come on, George. There's a time to talk about feelings and a time to try to—"

The dumbbell George had placed on his desk shifted slightly as she spoke, then it began rolling off the logbook. When Sylvia's hand shot out to steady it, George had not moved.

"Frightened?" he asked, putting his hand atop hers as it rested on the weight.

"I try not to let it get to me." She wouldn't look at him.

"Could it be someone you know?" He leaned slowly back again in his chair. "Don't take this the wrong way, but sometimes, after a divorce, there's a certain amount of bad feeling."

She shook her head. "Zack's still in love with me, but he's not bitter."

George's watch beeped; neither of them acknowledged it.

"Sylvia," he said, "may I speak frankly?"

"Of course."

"I go out a lot. I'm that kind of guy and it's that kind of town, right?"

She smiled.

"And you know, as soon as I tell people what I do, the next question's almost automatic. People want to know what you look like. Men and women both."

"And what do you tell them?"

"I say you look the way you sound." He laughed and for a moment appeared as young as he clearly wished to be, though he wasn't old. "Really, all bullshit aside, that's the beauty of the medium: everybody gets to make up his own picture. The way things are, we could stand a little bit more of that, if you ask me, but . . ." He made a gesture to indicate no one had.

"George," she said, "this story has a moral. I sense it."

"Probably it does." For a moment he looked thoughtful. "But let's skip ahead, okay? Do you want me to hire a guard for you till this blows over?"

Sylvia hesitated, then shook her head almost imperceptibly.

"The voice that knows no fear?" asked George.

"Hardly."

"What, then?"

Sometimes, when Sylvia thought of her father, she saw the two of them as engaged, since her mother's death, in a struggle of mutual protectiveness—a struggle that could have no outcome: it was too serious; nor any forgetful little surcease: it was too serious.

She put her cigarettes back in her purse. "I don't know, George; it's just my instinct." She stood. "Don't think I'm ungrateful, but I'd like to hold off doing anything like that until—" She shrugged. "Until it feels right, I guess."

"Up to you," he said.

"Thanks." She kissed him on the temple and headed for the door.

"Oh, but, Sylvie, one more thing." He grimaced in the manner of one discharging a mildly disagreeable obligation. "Don't go out of your way to irritate our esteemed program director."

She stared at him.

"As far as play lists, that is."

She stared at him. "I know," she said then, "I know: you'd hate to have to fire me."

The moment in which she might smile almost escaped before her features caught up with it, and George smiled back.

"Sylvie!" called the receptionist as Sylvia swung past the front desk. She accepted the bouquet of pink phone messages being waved at her. The one from Rhonda explained that her house was for rent, named a price, mentioned Michael's name. Would it be possible to come look at it around four? Sylvia inquired over the phone from a brightly lit little room with no windows. Then she reread the note Nomanzi had left her the night before. The part about their fathers seemed touched with new meaning now, after the phone call of the previous night, but in her rational mind Sylvia knew that it was the nature of coincidence to generate apparent meaning.

"Nomanzi Lolombela, please."

"Yes," said the voice on the other end of the line. "It is me."

"Hi. It's Sylvia Walters. Listen, I got your brother's tape, and I—" When she had listened to the tape that morning, while she was straightening up the house, after Zack had left, Sylvia had wondered how she was in fact going to explain the effect it had had on her. She'd been unable, for that matter, to explain it to herself. The tape had made Sylvia cry, and the tears, along with the lack of explanation, were another thing that had linked it with her father's call. "Well, I . . . really loved what I heard. Much tougher stuff— musically, I mean—than I'm used to from that part of the world. Very informed. Very moving." She was aware of the distance in her voice, but she couldn't help herself. "Anyway, I hope they're treating you right at TDA."

"Oh, yes. Johnny and Chentula have never been overseas before, you see, and—" Nomanzi laughed. "Well, you should hear the talk—decadent this, amazing that. If they were treated any better than they are now—in *that* way anyhow—I think they'd pack their bags and run home." She laughed again. "But you really did like it? Would it go in the States?"

Sylvia heard the awkward fit of the word "home" on Nomanzi's tongue and was at once ashamed of her own reserve.

"If I knew ahead of time what records would go in the States," she said, "I'd not only be a millionaire, I'd be worshiped in this town as a divine messenger." She stood and ran a finger absently across the spines of the tapes shelved before her. "But. But, but, but. I do think that what Tsotsi is doing is terrific, maybe even commercial, and I'll try to get you guys a little airplay. Okay?"

"Oh, could you really? I'd be so—"

"It won't be much, but it'll be a start." Sylvia's eye fell upon a bucket of water that had been left in one corner of the little room, an unused sponge mop abandoned beside it. "As for a place to stay," she quickly continued, "I'd love to help, but I have to tell you, your timing is supernaturally bad: see, my own house burned to the ground yesterday, and I'm supposed to be looking for a place myself." Despite everything, she laughed. "Homeless in paradise."

There was a tiny shocked pause.

"Oh, please excuse me. I didn't know you had such trouble." Nomanzi's voice rose in musical self-rebuke. "And me asking you all these favors!"

"Don't be silly. Besides, it makes me feel better to think I've got something left to offer. My swimming pool isn't the drawing card it used to be." She hesitated. Nomanzi's apology had reminded Sylvia of her father's more complicated one the night before, and now, without the least warning, she felt herself possessed by the desire to see this woman, to talk to her face-to-unknown-face. "Listen, I'll tell you what. I've got to go up and take a look around what we laughingly call my house, but then I'm going to see this rental deal a friend dug up for me. It's cheap, a good location, all that. Now, if you don't mind coming along for the more morbid half of this expedition, then we can go out to see the new place together. If I don't like it, maybe you will."

"Oh, that would be . . . are you sure?"

"Why not? I'll pick you up at the hotel."

"You're very kind. But how will I recognize you?"

"I'll be the decadent one."

"No, I want to be the decadent one. You be the amazing one."

They both laughed.

"We'll recognize each other," said Sylvia. "Twenty minutes?"

"Yes. I'll be waiting out front."

Then Sylvia called Petra's office. Petra was taking a meeting, but could a message be taken as well? Sylvia said yes, that it was Sylvia and she was calling about the diamond earrings her sister Kristen had borrowed from Petra a geological age ago. A what ago? Sylvia said she'd call back.

In the parking lot, the sunlight made everything temporarily perfect, and when Sylvia saw that her car was back on its tires and ready to roll, she felt that way herself. So she kissed the three men seriatim—Glen, Mack, and Wayne—and though they looked a little competitive, standing there with their arms hanging at the ready, they looked a little companionable too. "I told him no bodyguards," she said to them, but before anyone could respond, a pickup truck came careening into the lot like something out of a made-for-TV.

Sylvia felt a little leap of the gut. Michael pulled the truck to a halt twenty feet away. The billed hat and sunglasses he wore made him feel unpleasantly conscious, under the circumstances, of look- ing a bit too much like yesterday's helicopter pilot. Beside him, Boris breathed in the world's vapors, trusting everything.

Sylvia hastened to excuse herself, and she gave the knot in her T-shirt's tail an extra tuck for luck.

"I'm interrupting," said Michael, stepping down out of the truck's cab.

"Sure," she said. "But interruption's all we know, isn't it? We interrupt each other." She glanced behind her at Glen, Mack, and Wayne, and the three began to disperse. "Who's *your* friend?"

"Boris, meet Sylvia," Michael said. "Sylvia, Boris." At the men- tion of his name, Boris lifted an ear, then jumped dutifully out of the truck. He thought they were going for a walk. "Did Rhonda call you about her house?"

"Yes. I'm going over at four."

Michael kept seeing Sylvia in freeze-frame increments, each more distinctly *she* than the last. "I was just passing by"—he gestured toward the noisy boulevard—"and some inner voice said to me,

'Okay, you're a real estate agent, check in on your client.' I always obey my inner voices because they're so goddamn insistent. And responsible. And clear." He was almost shouting at her. "You know?"

She was nodding. She was almost nodding. She dropped her sunglasses.

What she knew was:

Neither of them moved to pick up her sunglasses.

Not everything that had burned had burned away.

And, as she stepped toward him and he took her elbows in his hands, it became evident that there was nothing left to be smart about.

Their kiss was sudden, as brief and clumsy as a slap, and like a slap it impelled them away from each other at the very moment of touching.

"This is ridiculous," said Sylvia, turning her back on him, circling him. "I don't have time for this."

"I know," said Michael, wandering irritably away from her. "Me either. Me either."

"I'm completely out of control. What is going *on*?" She turned around in what might have been accusation, and he veered blindly into her: a collision, an embrace. They kissed.

"I didn't expect this to happen," said Michael. "In fact, I—"

"We have to talk."

"Yes. When?"

They stood breathless in the parking lot's bright nowhere.

Not now, she decided. "Not now," she said. "I have a meeting now."

"Tomorrow?" He kept hearing himself. His voice.

"Tomorrow." Hers. "Yeah, tomorrow's Saturday. I'm off." She blushed. "I'm *off*!" She laughed. "The Mexican Hat Dance" clattered back up the boulevard in the other direction.

"Okay. Call me at the work number?" He was smiling.

"I sleep late."

"Of course."

They kissed. "We can't do this," she said.

"We're not," he answered. Their bodies were pressed together from her breasts on down.

"I know." They kissed again. Boris climbed back in the pickup truck, then Michael did, and the engine started.

"I'm off," he said through the window, and they laughed; he was. She waved.

"Jesus," she said when he was gone. She looked down and noticed her sunglasses.

Nomanzi Lolombela, leaning against a palm. She adjusted the volume on her Walkman.

"Take me to the river; drop me in the water."

It was wonderful to be in a place where you could make everything up, even if it never happened. You were always about to meet someone, always about to go someplace new.

"Nomanzi?" Sylvia called, maneuvering her little blue sports car curbside without quite stopping. Invisible sprinklers cast their canopies of water softly upon the hotel lawn, and Nomanzi had to skip softly through a knee-high rainbow to reach the car.

"Well, you were right," said Nomanzi, slipping into her seat. "I knew right away it was you."

"How? Don't tell me I look the way I sound."

The two women examined each other with good-natured curiosity, and each was fleetingly aware of the other as sometimes possessed of beauty: Sylvia's stemming from the fidgetless presentation of what most people perceived as her ferocity (so often attributed to the color of her eyes), Nomanzi's from the obvious amusement with which she allowed her body to announce itself— her upturned breasts, her ample rear, her sardonically set mouth ("a born actress," women frequently said of her).

The Bavarian car behind them honked discreetly, and Sylvia let out the clutch.

"Well, yes, you do look the way you sound," Nomanzi answered. "Now that you put it that way. But really what I meant was that you look just like someone whose father my father would know."

Sylvia smiled. Darting another look at Nomanzi before pulling into traffic, she said, "I think we saw each other last night. At the station."

Perfect lips, pursed and painted. "Yes!" Nomanzi laughed, a

blooming of her mouth, and pointed at Sylvia's feet without looking at them. "You were barefoot!"

"And you were lost."

"Only a little." She frowned. "There are no windows in that place! Besides"—leaning confidentially toward Sylvia—"I was hiding from my brother."

"Hiding!"

Nomanzi nodded with mock gravity. "He was behaving badly."

"*My* sister's hiding from *me*," said Sylvia, shifting gears, "but I think she's the one who's behaving badly."

"You have a sister here?"

"She lives in New York." Sylvia became aware that she was grateful to this long-legged black woman with the flashing manner and jiggling earrings. But for what exactly? "We grew up in Washington," she added, "so sometimes I still think of Washington as my home." And there it was: that word again, like a catch in her voice. "But I love this place. I remember seeing a TV show when I was a kid. This scientist was looking through his microscope at a piece of L.A.—you know, a molecule or something—and he looks up and says, in this very solemn voice"—she assumed it—" 'It's alive.' " She switched into a faster lane. "It turns out L.A. is a creature from another planet, slowly taking over the earth." She laughed quickly, surprising herself. "It *is*." She looked. Home. Is.

"Well, I lived in Washington for ten years," said Nomanzi. "And what I do not understand is this." She turned entirely toward Sylvia. *"Where do the men go for lunch?"*

Sylvia whooped. It was indeed a Washington kind of joke. "Our fathers know," she said.

"But they'll never *tell*."

"Violates the mysteries."

"Yes, yes. The mysteries." Mock resentful, mock dismissive. Nomanzi Lolombela adjusted the bind of her brassiere. "But, Sylvia, these are *great men*. They *believe* in things; they have made our future with their hands and words; they've changed *history*." She wrinkled her nose, exposing in consternation her even white teeth. "Is it possible these men don't *eat*?"

There was a glazier's truck immediately ahead of them, and Sylvia passed it, the wind and sun striking flash from her hair as the car accelerated. "*Eat?* Nomanzi, these are superheroes we're talking about. Every day another secret mission, each detail more secret than the last: plane tickets, briefing books, scrambled telephone calls, steady stares across weirdly shaped tables. I mean, come on, girl, you can't expect these men to *eat*."

Nomanzi clapped her hands and threw her head back in amusement. The headphones, a silver band against her red-brown neck, were not a necklace.

"No," she said. "After all, it really is the secrecy that keeps them alive, isn't it?"

She'd been laughing when she'd said it, but even as the unexpected levity had so quickly spun a bond between the two women, the unexpected truth of her last utterance drew it tight, and each was momentarily aware of being seen through by the other.

"Not the food," Nomanzi added, settling back in her seat.

They crossed the place where the Los Angeles River used to be.

At the canyon turnoff, a police roadblock had been set up, and there was some confusion as to whether Sylvia's former neighborhood was among the ones the fire department had declared safe to enter. One cop tried to raise an authoritative voice on his walkie-talkie, while the other inspected Sylvia's driver's license. She was considering tears when the one with her license asked her if it was she, the sound of the city of angels. Swinging back the roadblock's striped slat, his partner looked with distaste at the walkie, which chattered unintelligibly at his side. "Where do they buy this shit anyway?" he asked. "Formosa?"

The smell of burn grew richer as the two women ascended, and like a wine in whose taste can be read the exact topography of the land that fed it, this scent compounded of charred chaparral, melted shower curtains, incinerated beds and kitchen counters spoke sadly of lives lived in the necessary confidence that *this* could never happen again.

"Why are there soldiers?" Nomanzi asked.

"It's the National Guard. I guess they're supposed to prevent looting." They rounded a switchback, passed a yellow tanker truck. "But don't ask me what's left to loot."

Bulldozers were abandoned here and there at improbable angles;

tired young men in orange hard hats leaned on their shovels, having a smoke. The sites of houses were marked by scorched chimneys and the tangle of melted plumbing. Farther upcanyon, there were swimming pools: brilliant blue, their brightness barely dimmed by the film of ash that had settled over everything. And by the larger swimming pools, there were pumps: yellow, grease-sludged units whose angry every-which-way drone seemed a constantly renewed announcement.

This is my house.

This was my kitchen.

This was my bedroom.

I'll draw you a picture.

Sylvia could see the level semicircle of her driveway despite the dusting of ash, and when she asked a guardsman standing nearby if she could park there, he said yes.

"It is a hard thing to lose a home," Nomanzi said.

SYLVIA [*Reaching across Nomanzi to open the glove compartment*]: I needed a witness.

"Sorry?"

"I said I needed to quit this." She rummaged among the maps, owner's manuals, gasoline charge slips. "The life up here, my used-to-be marriage; all that stuff." She removed the camera and her spare pair of sunglasses from the glove compartment. "It was time to soldier on, you know? And I just kept delaying and delaying and delaying. So what we got here"—she closed the glove compartment with a snap—"*this* is just a sort of forced march in the direction I probably should have been headed anyway."

Because she was trying not to look at anything that used to be familiar, her eyes settled on Nomanzi. "As my father would say," she added, ashamed of her tone. But Nomanzi's steady look offered a sympathy that was more than merely polite, and Sylvia, to quell her own eyes' brimming, looked away. "Incredible, though, isn't it? Nobody ever really tells you it's all on loan around here. . . ." She put on the sunglasses.

"In my country," said Nomanzi, "nobody ever tells you it's yours." She had seized one of Sylvia's wrists, and it lived in her hand, just like that. "But" (and there'd been bulldozers that night too, a burning mattress, a little girl who cried and cried) "even so, you always know."

It was the sort of admonishment Sylvia understood. She found herself nodding. Address by indirection. She smiled.

They got out of the car.

"My attorney told me I should document everything," said Sylvia, taking a picture of the burned-out chassis of Michael's pickup. "For insurance purposes, I guess. But under the circumstances it seems a little ridiculous."

Nomanzi stepped gingerly through the ash. "Well, you know, everything is a little ridiculous when you have serious trouble. I remember how when my uncle first went to prison, my mother—" Nomanzi's sneakered foot sank suddenly to the ankle in bone-dry ash, and she let out a small cry.

"Oh, God! Did you burn yourself?" Sylvia was at Nomanzi's side in an instant, offering a shoulder, offering a steadying hand.

"Thank you. No, I was just startled." She shook out her grayed foot; a small puff of ash set off through the house's unwalled rooms.

"You were saying about your uncle?" Sylvia prompted, looking around for something to photograph.

"When my uncle went to prison, I was seven years old. He'd been caught in a raided building and tried with the others on the usual charges: membership in a banned organization, contributing to its funds, holding a meeting, distributing pamphlets . . . well, it's enough to make you sick, eh." She leaned over and picked what proved to be a twisted fork from the ruin. With the exaggerated delicacy of someone offering a stale but still tasty morsel, she held it out to Sylvia. Sylvia shrugged; Nomanzi, her arm still extended, let it drop. "Enough to make you sick. But me, hmm, I decided I must actually *be* sick, and the morning he was sent off to the Island, I decided I would not ever again leave my blanket. I had a headache, I had a stomachache, I couldn't breathe. These things I told my mother when she came to see why I had not filled the water buckets."

"And when you said them, you began to believe them," Sylvia added, staring through the viewfinder at the melted metal mess that had been her refrigerator.

"Of course! I was the first one I convinced. But there's more, you see, because for one whole day my mother pretended to believe me too."

Sylvia looked up. She lowered the camera, her fingertip still hovering at the shutter release.

"Oh, it was like being in heaven, I felt so important. All my aches and pains were for my uncle—I was a little in love with him, wasn't I? And with my mother for agreeing to believe me! I heard her talk about me to my father—not the words but the sounds—and from the way he was, after, I knew she'd explained, I don't know, me . . . explained *me* to him. Because by the end of the day that's who I was really in love with: me. Me for being so important." She laughed at herself, alive again to the memory. "Oh, it was quite a performance, I'll tell you."

"Your first starring role," said Sylvia.

Nomanzi nodded. "But"—she raised an index finger—"it was a limited engagement."

"The next morning you got up."

"Yes. Because it worked! I'd been given my day; no one told me, but I knew. And I felt too important—too in love with myself?— to ask for another. I didn't need *that*." She squatted and held her hands to the ash as if it were still fire. "Oh, but everyone made fun of me afterward because of how I walked." She threw a glance up at Sylvia and her camera, smiling. "Like this," she said, rising again. And, eyes lowered, head high, she mimed the walk of a seven-year-old princess. "I was terrible," she added appreciatively.

"You're close to your uncle?"

"I was, yes." A faint fading of her eyes' light. "He's dead now."

"What happened?"

"Oh, what they always say: he hanged himself in his cell."

Sylvia took a step forward in the ash. "But that's not what happened?"

Nomanzi watched the gray cloud raised by Sylvia's feet drift diagonally through the house's former terrain. "He's dead." She didn't shrug.

A splash.

"Did you hear that?" said Nomanzi.

"Hey, Sylvie!" called her neighbor from the adjacent lot. "How about you? You gonna rebuild?"

"Not here," she answered. The man was standing in his living room with a shovel in his hand. "I mean, this is the sort of open house you only want to have once, right?"

Her neighbor, who Sylvia recalled had made his money redesigning shower heads, shook his head vexedly and spat. "I don't know." He had his shirt off and was wearing cheerful red sweatbands at his wrists. "Gotta sit down and look at the numbers first."

Nomanzi looked into the swimming pool. *I could teach Chentula to swim, if he'd let me,* she thought.

"Isn't it amazing what survives," said Sylvia. In her hands she held the drawer pulls to a dresser that had utterly vanished. At her feet was a ceramic ashtray with the name of a formerly fashionable restaurant written across it. In her pool, the pool cleaner made its sinuous way up one side, broke water, and fell back like a dream fish.

"Yes. But it's *who* survives that matters." Nomanzi turned her head to look at Sylvia. "Isn't it."

Sylvia extended her arm fully before her and, mimicking Nomanzi's earlier gesture with the fork, loosened her fingers so that the dozen drawer pulls fell into her pool with a plop. "We'll both be the amazing ones," she said. And even though it never happened, for a moment they might have embraced, there by the melted ruin of the diving board.

Two chimneys to the east, a TV crew moved fitfully about, trying to keep its lenses clean. There were more people in her neighborhood than Sylvia had ever thought to see: former homeowners, insurance assessors, guardsmen, mop-up crews, reporters, contractors, and builders. "Maybe you could stand over there to give it some scale," she said to Nomanzi, then took a picture of the master bedroom.

"Excuse me, are you Sylvia Walters?" said a young man in a white hard hat.

"Not today," she answered.

"Well, of course I know this must be a very difficult time for you," he went on, "but I'm with the governor's office, and the governor wondered . . ." Lifting a chin that suggested only partially abandoned aspirations to be an actor, he gestured toward the television crew and another, taller man in another, whiter hard hat. "Well, we wondered whether you might be willing to share your thoughts, feelings, whatever, with the governor. For the cameras, okay? Good for you, good for us." He expertly let the angle of the sun be a glint in his eye. "I mean, sometimes you've just got to make the best of a situation like this, am I right?"

"Sure you are." She looked him up and down. "Sure you're right. But then again, sometimes you've just got to tell self-satisfied jerks in white hard hats to get out of your kitchen."

The man appeared confused.

"That's my refrigerator you're standing next to."

The man asked her to have a nice day.

"D'you know, Sylvia, what a man told me on the airplane coming over?" Nomanzi bent her head and stepped through a half-collapsed arch of plumbing. "He said, as if it were a piece of information I absolutely had to have before landing—you know, like which snakes are poisonous, where the water's safe, all that—he said that the strongest muscle in the body"—she emerged from the arch and drew herself up regally, again the princess—"is the tongue." And with that, she stuck her own tongue out at the retreating figure of the man who was with the governor's office.

Sylvia's laughter was like a handful of dimes flung into the air. "And I voted for him, too."

Next door the Forest Service pump missed, spluttered, failed.

"I actually *voted* for him."

The dimes didn't come down. Acoustic space opened up startlingly around the idled pump. Somewhere a shovel twice struck dull metal: chance, then intention.

"It's too ridiculous. Like you said."

But there was another sound, and Sylvia first heard it without making sense of it: lightly calibrated metallic tension released, sprung, rereleased, resprung: precision's zip, precisely repeated. She turned, froze. Freeze-frame.

"Hey!"

Freeze-frame. Freeze-frame.

She started toward the driveway. A man in a green sedan was leaning out the driver's window, photographing them.

"Hey, what do you think you're doing?"

The man revved the engine and, completing the driveway's arc, pulled away at a speed that might, from some points of view, have suggested expertise in avoiding undue attention.

The man had a crew cut.

There were wet ashes smeared across the license plate.

"That really makes me mad," said Sylvia, throwing a dinner plate into ash so fine the china didn't shatter. "The idea of privacy is extinct."

Nomanzi Lolombela, standing in the sunshine, standing in California, revised some of the things she'd said to her half-brother about Surveillance.

The place they'd come to see about renting was a renovated tract house in the flatlands of the city, just north of one of the freeways, not far from the ocean. It had a pale-blue entryway set back from the street, and a convex door across which improbably fluffy white clouds had been painted. The woman who opened it wore makeup and jogging shorts.

"Oh, you're Michael's friend," she said when Sylvia had introduced Nomanzi and herself. "Why don't you just look around, okay? We're in the kitchen having a last-minute frenzy."

An entire extra story had been added onto the house, giving it the comical aspect of a domestic plant that, though left to die, has flourished. There were bright plastic things here and there, mirrors everywhere. Nomanzi breathed on one and asked: "Is *she* an actress?" "Which bedroom is hers?" asked Sylvia when they'd been through the pleasant disarray of both. On the roof was a stagnant-looking whirlpool bath and a view of the freeway: in the distance, lights flashed the latest traffic conditions.

"I could live here," said Sylvia.

"Yes," said Nomanzi. "It's very . . . made up, isn't it?" She crinkled her nose, let her smile go slowly abstract over the traffic conditions.

"Do you want to share it with me?" said Sylvia.

And everything that Nomanzi had put off thinking about in her own language came suddenly to flesh, like her brother's hand over hers in a rented car, in a borrowed parking spot, in what was after all just another made-up land.

She had turned fully round to Sylvia. "Oh, but you see, I just don't know how long my money—"

"Not worrying about the money, I mean. Just playing it by ear?"

"No. I'd have to pay you." The rooftop was bordered by a tilted quartet of triangular panels, fiberglass and steel. "And my passport . . ."

There was a magnolia in the backyard below.

"But we should stick together, Sylvia." Nomanzi had walked a few measured steps away. "Find the lunch spots." She turned again, angry without acting. "Up there at your house, I felt . . . it's so terrible, the things that can always be taken away. Just *things,* but . . ."

"As long as you never get used to it," Sylvia answered.

"*Used* to it?"

With the toe of one shoe Sylvia drew an invisible arc across the roof's sun-bleached planks. She sighed. "It's probably just a line. But that's what my mother used to say when people asked her if it was really possible to be happy knowing your husband might at any second, you know, be taken away. On business, they meant, but—"

Nomanzi relaxed, walked back to Sylvie, and placed a hand gently on the white woman's elbow. "Okay," she said. "Let's do it."

"You want to live here?" Sylvia's mouth took one of the myriad shapes more interesting than the one lipstick is applied to offer. "Well, all right, then! It's a done deal."

"It's lunch."

Beneath the apex of one of the overly designed triangles, they embraced.

"I hope it's not too weird for you," said the woman in jogging shorts when they'd made their way downstairs to the kitchen. Her name was Rhonda, and she was sitting at a round plastic table with a dark-haired woman whom Sylvia could not possibly have recognized as Laurel, since the two had never met. "My ex-boyfriend was an architect," Rhonda went on, gesturing toward the corrugated plastic kitchen cabinets. " 'All the materials are cheap,' " she intoned, " 'yet each is used in a precious way.' " She lifted a pink invoice from the pile that lay before her. "Hey, are we gonna pay for that pachysandra? Half of it was dead when we got it."

"So let's pay for the dead half and take the live as reparations." Laurel shifted her blouse from off one shoulder to off the other. "You must be Sylvia," she said. "I'm Laurel."

"This is my friend Nomanzi."

"Did you see the roof?" asked Rhonda.

"A city landmark. 'Caution. Bear Left.' "

"I know, I know. Like I said, it's weird. But you really can't hear the traffic, except maybe a little in the mornings."

"No, I'm serious. We want it." Sylvia noticed that Laurel was looking a lot at Nomanzi—assessing little glances, each marginally longer than the last. "The two of us, if that's okay."

"Really?" Rhonda let her hands fall together on the receipts like a paperweight. "God, you don't know what a relief that is, not having to do the whole references-and-security-money number."

"Well, if you want to, I can—"

"No, no, no, no, no. Any friend of Laurel and Michael's is okay with me."

Sylvia sat down.

"Really, Laur. I ought to look at my chart. The cosmic tide has turned at last."

Laurel was now staring openly at Nomanzi. "What do you do, Nomanzi?"

"I'm an actress."

"Working?"

"Not right now. I've just finished shooting a television series in my own country."

Laurel continued to look. "Rhonda, is she perfect or what?"

Rhonda looked too. "Well, it's an idea." Catching sight of Sylvia, who was putting a cigarette a shade shakily to her lips, she said, "Oh, the one thing I ask, Sylvia: no smoking in the house, okay?"

"You're very unusual-looking," Laurel went on.

To Rhonda, Sylvia made the gesture of, of course, no problem, I don't really do this anyway.

"Yes. I'm African on both sides." Nomanzi folded her arms and let her lip rise slightly.

"No, no; I meant . . ." She picked up a handful of invoices. "I run a sort of glorified flower shop." She put them down. "We have the kind of clients you'd expect—a bunch of industry people, music; sometimes we do movies. Like everybody else around here, we run on image a lot. Rhonda has been working as my shop attendant, and now—well, now she isn't. So I'm looking *desperately* for someone—someone with the right look—who wouldn't mind answering phones, hauling calla lilies around, being nice to people who usually don't deserve it." She ran a hand through her hair. "I don't know what your situation is, but I think I'm offering you a job."

Nomanzi didn't know what her situation was either, because it was something she was still trying to make up. "I'm not a U.S. citizen," she said.

"How long are you here for?"

Her passport said ninety days. She said, "I don't know."

"Do you want to try it out for a couple of weeks? I don't mind paying you off the books—twelve an hour—and you could see how you like it."

"Oh, I'd like that." She glanced at Sylvia, then Rhonda. "D'you know what they charge for rents in this city?" After the briefest pause, everyone laughed: Sylvia last, Laurel longest. "I'm hoping for some auditions, though."

"Yeah, like who isn't." Laurel appeared to make some mental calculations. "I need two weeks' notice, minimum, if you leave."

"All right."

"No roses," said Rhonda. "Tell her no roses." She held her hands up before her like a surgeon after a scrub. "Once I went to audition for a dishwashing-liquid commercial, they took one look at my hands and . . ." Two beats: her timing. " 'All the materials are cheap,' " she repeated, " 'yet each is used in a precious way.' "

There was a plexiglass vase of half-dead, half-red roses on the sill behind her.

"You know, I should've figured it out: he kept saying that about the house, but all the time he was probably talking about me."

Sylvia drove Nomanzi back to her hotel. The title of Nomanzi's TV series was "Ilulwane," which in Xhosa meant "bat," or "half-creature." Nomanzi, who was the star of the series, played the half-creature. "Half-creature because I am from the locations but making my way in the city." Was the series going to be renewed? Yes, it was. Had Sylvia known Laurel and Rhonda and, what was his name, Michael, very long? No, she hadn't.

A silence ensued between these two event-dazed women as the day's sun faded to gold in their laps, in the little open car that bore them through arteries of traffic in which every automotive corpuscle propelled someone toward something.

There was a silence.

The hotel driveway's asphalt sweep was as long and slow as a late-breaking wave; the palms that lined it were still. Sylvia parked, and there, at the hem of the flawlessly invented lawn, the two women made a few last small plans together: keys to be duplicated, a check to be written, morning schedules to be somehow reconciled. Sylvia stretched. Nomanzi yawned. A swim, they said, a bath, a drink, hungry soon, a nap. They'd talk in the morning.

But after Nomanzi had opened the car door to leave, her legs already swung out into the what next, she turned back toward Sylvia, and her eyes glittered with unshed tears.

"I didn't finish my story up there. The one about my first starring performance?"

"Your day."

"Yes. Because the next night, after I'd gone back to doing my chores—and, you know, I was walking like a queen, I was so proud—that night the government men came with bulldozers and drip torches and all the proper papers, they came and—" A pause, but for breath, not timing. "And they pushed my home to the ground and burned it as it lay there."

She got out of the car and closed the door. "So I know about that."

There was some kind of music emanating from the hotel.

"I knew you did," said Sylvia, realizing it.

Nomanzi's face clarified, as a body does when the blanket covering it is thrown aside. "We'll see each other tomorrow, then."

"Yeah. We will."

"Okay." It might have been a smile. "Goodbye." She turned and headed up the lawn.

"Tell Tsotsi I'll be playing their tape around midnight," Sylvia shouted after.

Nomanzi waved.

Sylvia drove. She was halfway to Zack's—to thank him, to get her clothes—when, glancing in the rearview mirror before changing lanes, she caught sight of what seemed to be, three cars behind her, a green sedan. The man at the wheel had a crew cut. Because of the traffic, the license plate was not visible.

I'm having my first crazy thought, she thought.

But she changed lanes again and at the next traffic light turned left off the boulevard onto a residential side street.

The green sedan was caught at the light, and the driver appeared to be paying her no attention whatever. She drove slowly for a couple of blocks, trying to keep him framed in her rearview, but when a slight dip in the road grade rendered him briefly invisible, she made another right.

Not that she wasn't entitled to a crazy thought, she reflected. Now and then.

She turned on the radio, and the radio said: "We're having a party."

Sylvia began to calm down. "We certainly are," she told the radio.

The only other cars on this street were parked; the houses were bungalows, each with a face-lift carried out according to the varying dictates of beauty, whimsy, and pleasant misinformation. There was hollyhock on the lawns and no one behind her. If it wasn't quite a neighborhood, still it would certainly serve. She could smell smoke from a charcoal grill, a hibachi, somewhere out of sight.

A trickle of sweat ran from her armpit to her waist, but Sylvia was thinking about a barbecue party she'd given, the one to which Kristen had worn Petra's diamond earrings, the one at which Kristen had disappeared for a time that now seemed to suggest a sojourn in the garage, of all the world's places. I'll try her again when I get to Zack's, she decided, glancing at her watch.

She pulled up at a stop sign, where she glanced left, then right.

Right was a problem. Right was a place from which a green sedan with ashes smeared across its plates was headed toward her at a leisurely pace.

"Okay," she whispered amid her heart's sudden surge. "Certainly." She took a breath. "This we can do."

She headed across the intersection.

The sedan, after lingering implausibly long at the stop sign, turned to follow.

When there were three full blocks between them, Sylvia signaled left and made the turn.

There were people in these houses, and dogs, and on the steps there were potted flowers. Brilliant red geraniums would be an example. And the things that moved were moving. There were shadows. Sylvia pulled into a driveway, then shifted into reverse and backed quickly across the street into another. The change in momentum caused her purse to spill its contents on the floor. She'd left it open.

Her father's daughter.

She waited.

When her pursuer nosed around the corner, Sylvia found that what she felt was not fear but anger. She shifted into first. Her eyes suggested to her hands and feet a pair of paths, one of which—*because when she was angry she was furious, because regret of any kind was alien to her, because nothing is only a story*—would take a much more abrupt conclusion than the other.

Coming out of the driveway, she didn't know whether she intended to hit him or not, but she knew she had positioned herself purposefully on the driver's side of the car he was driving.

There was a small smash, a shared jerk against unshared seat belts, minor catastrophes of metal (his) and fiberglass (hers)—contact.

The driver, unhurt, turned to look at her. For several elongated seconds they stared at each other as if they had traveled from the ends of the earth to this quiet side street for no other purpose.

"My mistake," said Sylvia evenly. "I thought you were following me."

The man smiled. He appeared middle-aged but very fit. The safari shirt he was wearing stood a bit stiffly off his arms.

"No harm done, though," she said. "We're both insured, right?" She got out of the car. It seemed to her now that she detected a grain of admiration in the man's smile, and it was this that stirred her fury further. "Right, asshole?" She strode toward him. He had a mustache. She was screaming. "So all we have to do is exchange our fucking driver's licenses and—"

The impact of the collision had caused the two cars to rebound slightly, and it was by virtue of the space this rebound had afforded that the man, shifting smoothly into reverse, was able to escape.

At the intersection, he made a U-turn and headed back the way he'd come. He waved without looking at her.

Sylvia made no move to follow.

There was little damage to her car—a tear in the hood, a drooping headlight—but she parked curbside for a moment to collect herself. The radio was still on. After a while she tried to light a cigarette, but her hands were shaking. She took it out of her mouth and looked at the half-lit end.

What she thought was: Where is the end of it?

What she felt was: Half on fire.

What she knew was: When in the course of human events, it becomes necessary for one people to dissolve the political bands which have connected them with another, and to assume among the powers of the earth the separate and equal station to which the laws of Nature and of Nature's God entitle them, a decent respect to the opinions of mankind requires—

What she hoped, to the point of already believing it, was: This has nothing to do with my father.

She threw away the cigarette and drove, carefully, to Zack's.

P. WALTERS (U.S.A.): Gentlemen. I feel we have lost sight of our task here. The difficulty is not that we—as men representing the sovereign interests of our nations, as well as the conjoined interest of the alliance of those nations—have been suddenly given by some shotgun wedding of science and . . . [*Pause*] Translator? "Shotgun wedding"—does that . . . ? All right. What I in any case wish to say is that far from having been given too grand a mandate in this matter—the matter of the fission bomb—we have unavoidably been given too narrow a one. The single option not open to us is precisely, and sadly, the one we would, proceeding with sobriety and conscience, most gladly embrace: but we cannot uninvent what has already been invented. This is the simplest fact of human curiosity.

Even the most cursory review of military history will show that the mere existence of a weapon is enough to ensure its eventual use on what is still referred to, rather anachronistically, I'm afraid, as the battlefield. It is our great good fortune that the fission bomb has been developed at a time—one of the few since the Second World War—when none of the nations represented here is involved in active military conflict. Victory or defeat is not at issue. We have been given a grace period in which to consider exactly how we will present the future of military politics to its present. That is a luxury. What we do not have is the means to suppress the unfolding of that future. This is our constriction.

Acknowledging both, we may proceed—but only by acknowledging both.

H. BLOCH (Federated Republics of Germany): With your accustomed eloquence, Dr. Walters, you have stated precisely what most concerns my government and, I think it is not too much to add, the governments of many of our colleagues present. Of course it is true, as my countryman Herr Bismarck observed over a century ago, that a sentimental policy knows no reciprocity. Yet it must also be said that if Pandora's hand is presently upon the lid of the box, and our hand upon Pandora's, we nevertheless do not differ from Pandora in our ignorance of that box's contents.

Sylvia's father flipped ahead impatiently through the pages of that day's transcript. Reading his own words depressed him; every syllable seemed by its very reasonableness a cry of protest against the position he was obliged to represent. Under the little wooden dressing table that was serving tonight as his desk, he used the toe of one shoe to pry the other from his foot. And what of Bloch, upon whom he had counted to sense that protest and worry it open, make it into a negotiating position, into something? Bloch had heard his appeal and had done nothing.

Impulsively, Sylvia's father bent down to remove his other shoe, both socks.

The negotiators were meeting in Compiègne, the little French town where Hitler had danced his famous jig.

At the window, the curtains, which had the leaves of plants embroidered upon them in a thread whiter and more opaque than the fabric of which they themselves were made, began to flutter like improvised flags, important things. Sylvia and Kristen had throughout their adolescence complained that he always and unthinkingly kept the windows shut in the rooms he inhabited. Now, wherever he went, he found himself just as unthinkingly leaving them open.

He forced his gaze back to the transcript before him.

G. BOCCERINI (Italy): The Swiss research teams have warned that the detonation of a fission bomb could cause the atmosphere itself to ignite.

Z. VÉCSEY (Hungary): No more quickly than the rhetoric of the Soviet bloc would cause it to ignite, once such a detonation had been accomplished.

S. BATAILLARD (France): Rhetoric: that is something whose effects we understand. Radiation . . . perhaps not. But the introduction into world politics of a weapon capable of destroying human civilization . . . that is something the full effect of which we are, by definition, *absolutely* ignorant.

J. LOLOMBELA (Azania): In ignorance we are all immodest. The sovereignty of my nation, Azania, or, if you prefer, black Southern Africa, is for the time being purely rhetorical. It exists as a nation because it is agreed to exist. And yet the distinguished M. Bataillard will forgive me if I observe that the effects of that rhetorical sovereignty have been much more far-reaching than even he could have foreseen, as my presence here among you testifies.

It goes without saying that I intend to see this rhetorical sovereignty made actual within my lifetime. However, the case of Azania at present nonetheless points to a different way of looking at the fission bomb. I believe this weapon's power is *purely* rhetorical. It is a weapon whose enormous power can only be fully realized *if it is never used.* [*Pause.*]

Paul? Are you awake? [*Pause.*] It is Lolombela.

Sylvia's father looked up with a start at the door, which was hung, he now noticed, a fraction crookedly in its frame. He padded barefoot across the floor and opened it: Joseph Lolombela, his moody features resolving into a smile.

"Your State Department should be more generous in its clothing allowance, Dr. Walters."

"None of your guff, Joseph. Sit and have an Armagnac with me."

"A rhetorical Armagnac?" But he had already accepted, and Sylvia's father was already pouring it, the door safely shut behind them.

"You were good today, Joseph." They sat simultaneously upon the use-burnished maple settee. " 'In ignorance we are all immodest.' I've been meaning to point that out to Bataillard for years." He stretched his legs out before him and wiggled his toes. "Guy's a living refutation of Descartes."

"A fool, yes. It is so." He stared through the amber liquid to the pale of his palm beneath. "On the right side about Algeria, though. Long ago."

"He's aged badly. I've known him."

"A man without children always ages badly." It was the first full look he had given Paul Walters since entering the little room. Sylvia's father met this gaze and at the same moment became aware, as if he had not till then noticed them, of the stag horns mounted improbably above the stone fireplace.

"In that case, we are fortunate men, Lolombela." He clinked his glass gently against his friend's: a tender rebuke.

"Of course." During the little space he left before answering, Lolombela's words of agreement became equally a reassurance. When both men had noticed this, they drank: a moment of personal diplomacy. Lolombela set his glass on his knee and surveyed the room.

"I am told," he said, "that stag hunts are still held in this part of France."

"Yes. There's one tomorrow, here in Compiègne."

"I would like to see this European custom. The hounds chasing the stag, the Guardians of the Forest chasing the hounds, the hunters chasing the Guardians, and the sports cars chasing everything. This is the history of Europe, I think."

They laughed.

"The hell of it is, Bataillard would be just the one to take us." Sylvia's father removed a pair of cigars from his jacket pocket. "If we were here, that is. I mean, me supposedly in Geneva, you supposedly in New York." He clipped the ends from the cigars and handed one to Lolombela. "God knows he's the first guy to think the stag hunt's the history of Europe. That you can be sure of."

"And the stag," said Nomanzi's father, rotating the cigar as he lit it, "the stag is still killed with a sword?"

The silence of a small town in Europe, at summer's end, when many insects have died in the cause of summer, and the embroidered curtains have fallen still in nothing like sympathy for summer's end, was a silence both men were comfortable inhabiting.

"Yes," said Sylvia's father. "At a stag hunt, firearms are purely rhetorical."

The two men smoked, each blue puff detailing, in this silence, their breaths' liveliness and limit.

"The Armistice was signed here," said Nomanzi's father. "Later, Hitler danced. Still later, now, we are here."

Sylvia's father drew his feet in. At his desk lamp, a moon-gray moth fluttered. "Joseph," he said, without looking at the man he was addressing. "We'll be done here before your daughter has to go back. You'll see her, I'm sure of it."

A sigh. "Ten years, man. It's hard."

"Her passport's good for ninety days."

"Yes, hers is. But these belly-over-the-waistband bastards in Security, they have nothing to do but think up stinking variations on their shitty games." He drew heavily on his cigar, its end a glowing eye, quickly dimmed. "They made sure her half-brother's papers are only good for two weeks. You understand."

"Your daughter will go back with him?"

"It's half of why she returned to Africa in the first place. To reclaim him, and through him her mother. To reclaim her country, where I cannot go. To be *there*."

There. It was a place in time—the long, dusky past on one side, the future on the other. Sylvia's father felt the bright dithery vertigo he always felt when made aware—as more and more frequently he was—of the confluence of public event and private circumstance. He himself missed his daughters, feared for them; missed his wife, mourned for her. With one hand he removed his necktie, already loose at his collar, and threw it not quite lightly across the room.

"We'll be out of here in under a week," he said. "Even we can't be kept secret longer than that."

"So we will have to work harder than we did today."

"Yes."

The two men looked at each other. Before them was a bench, meant as a footrest; on it was a transistor radio. Nomanzi's father leaned forward and, without taking his eyes from Sylvia's father, switched it on.

The radio said: something in French rock-and-roll.

Sylvia's father's eyes, scanning the room's walls theatrically, said: Turn it up a little louder.

Lolombela, increasing the volume of the music through which

he and Walters had already begun to work, said: "Bloch approached me after dinner. We talked for half an hour."

The shaped and ghostly ash of Lolombela's cigar fell through the air like a natural event, though neither man noticed.

Lolombela said: "I think he's ready to work with us."

Crossing a culvert that spanned the mostly theoretical Los Angeles River, Sylvia looked in synchrony with the two softly sounded horn beeps behind her into her rearview mirror: PETRA, said the retreating license plate; a few fingers wiggled at the lip of a hastily lowered window.

At the first opportunity, Sylvia turned around and joined her friend in the parking lot of the mall she herself had just left.

"Darling, I heard about the house." Chill tendrils of conditioned air spun off Petra like breath from a mirror as she and Sylvia embraced. "Thank God you're okay."

"Oh, I'm fine." And Sylvia saw, as she swung back from Petra, who wore her thick platinum hair in a fashionably asymmetrical bob, that at the lobe of her right ear there glittered a diamond earring, triangular in cut, set as a stud.

"I didn't know where to call—I tried at the station—but I'm sure I don't have to tell you your room with Max and me is always ready." This was a reference to the period when, during Sylvia's initial separation from Zack, she had lived with Petra and Petra's husband of twenty-two years.

"Thanks, Petra. You're the best." This was a reversion to the language of that period. Sylvia held her hair up off her neck because of the heat. "Actually, though, I've already found a place. A rental— until I know what I'm doing, I mean."

What she was doing was silently thanking Paris for the fashion that allowed Petra's hair to fall fully enough on the left to cover her other ear, and so to shield her, Sylvia, from the reproachful sight of its interim nakedness.

"But, lovie, you know what the custom of the country is. When your house burns down, you go out and charge a lot of clothes, then you join an exercise class you only go to once, and then you go on vacation, it doesn't matter where." Petra was rattling her car keys as if they were a ceremonial accessory. "The same charm works for divorce, but you do it in reverse order." They were standing next to a soldierly array of newspaper vending machines, and Sylvia distractedly noticed the word "Geneva" pressed against the scratched plastic vitrines of three of them. "Trust me, I'm your elder, I know about these things."

"Okay, but what's a vacation?"

"I think it's when you don't do business over breakfast," said Petra.

"Well, that's out. I don't eat breakfast."

"No," said Petra. "You don't. You're beginning to look a little spectral."

"And what's business?"

"I knew it. You need a vacation."

A tiny child, dressed in terry cloth and merrily startled by his own locomotion, raced stroboscopically between the two women, trickling orange soda from a can that he held both cherished and forgotten in his hands. After looking with conspicuous tolerance at the thin, fizzy trail across her sandaled toes, Petra stooped to wipe it away, and Sylvia—as in a dream, as in a film—watched the longer locks over Petra's left ear part to reveal a second diamond earring, triangular in cut, set as a stud.

"No, okay," Petra continued. "Forget vacation for now; you're not up to it. How about a little fishing?"

"What?" said Sylvia.

"You remember fishing; it's the business with the hook and the boat?"

"Oh, yeah." Sylvia was guiltily trying to calculate what it had cost Petra to replace the missing earring. "I didn't know you indulged."

"It's Max, lovie. I think he's staging a middle-life crisis for my benefit. He thinks I expect it." She looked at her sticky palm with faint distaste, then smiled. "Wouldn't that be pure Max?" Petra was rarely successful at concealing the fact that, whatever else, she adored her husband.

"Pure Max," Sylvie agreed.

"Anyway, he's rented a boat for this afternoon, and I'd just love it if you'd—"

"Petra?"

"What, darling?"

"Why didn't you tell me Kristen hadn't returned your earrings?"

Petra's smile, briefly frozen, broadened; she'd expected something else. "Oh, but, Sylvie, it was nothing. She mailed them to me as soon as she got back to New York."

"She did?"

"I do the same thing all the time. It's nothing to get upset about; they're only pos*sess*ions." A look of concern clouded Petra's brow. "Oh, lovie, you do know insurance will pay for everything you lost in the fire?"

"Sure. But the point is . . ." She, with a third diamond earring buried in her purse, was no longer certain what the point was.

"Come on, Sylvie, sail the seas with me and Max."

"I can't; I can't."

"But we don't have to *fish*; we'll leave that to the big strong men. And it's the cutest little boat; I saw a picture. The *Cassava*, it's called—or something like that."

"No, I mean I've just got a million errands."

"They'll *wait*."

They laughed. It was what Petra always said, in the middle of a movie deal, regarding those in the lesser bargaining position.

"Petra, why is it I get the feeling you're doing a deal on this cute little boat?"

"Oh, well. It's pretty much in the bag already, really." Her features hesitated between faint embarrassment and mirth. "Just a few fine points left." She grinned. "And, you know, you might like this director guy."

"Not today, lovie."

"Okay, okay." She glanced at her watch. "Who am I to interfere with industry?" And tilted her head. "Call me?"

"Sure." They exchanged blown kisses, and as Petra was turning from her, Sylvia added, "By the way, I love your hair."

Petra whirled around, pleased. "Do you? You don't think it's too . . ." She leaned down in front of one of the newspaper machines to seek her reflection in its plastic face. "Too . . ."

Sylvia drove into the shopping district of the enormous city. She had left Zack's house early that morning with what remained of her clothes, had met Nomanzi at the rental house, and had left there early too, wishing to avoid Laurel, who was coming to pick up Nomanzi and instruct her in the ways of the flower shop. Throughout the morning, Sylvia had made what she knew to be excessive use of the rearview mirror. Each glance behind her had proposed a world in which there were no green sedans driven by crew-cut men: a temporary happiness. Repeating the glance now, however, she realized that each time she had also half expected to see Michael in her wake, his relaxed but expectant gaze: a happy temporariness. And she realized as well, in light of Laurel's unexpected emergence, that she had somehow decided not to call Michael again after all.

There was a parking space directly in front of the jewelry store. Flanking the store's entrance were a pair of guards in cocoa-colored uniforms. Sylvia found it disconcerting to see security guards with suntans.

"I'd like," she said to the store's elderly manager, "your expert opinion on something."

"Of course," he answered. They stood surrounded by discreetly lit gems that had been torn from the gut of the earth to adorn temporarily the pulse points and earlobes of the women of California and other places.

"You see, I have this earring that I—" She stopped herself and, remembering what she'd once been told about jewelers, decided upon a different tack. "Well, I'd like to match it."

"We'll do our best. Let's have a look."

Sylvia fought down embarrassment and increasing panic as she rummaged through her bag for the earring. *Nothing that is solid ever really melts into air.* But then she felt it, one of its three points, and tossing back her hair, she laid the diamond quickly down upon the black velvet pad the man had slid across the counter toward her.

"Ah," he said, looking from it to her. "An heirloom?"

"Why do you ask?"

"It's the cut. Definitely nineteenth-century." He picked it up with respect, a folding loupe materializing in his other hand. "See that color play? That's what we call the stone's 'fire.' Now, 'brilliance,' that's the total light reflected from the stone. This one was cut for maximum fire, so you lose a little brilliance. The trend today of course is to do it the other way. Gives you a flashier stone."

"People like flashy," Sylvia offered.

The man raised an eyebrow and made a sour face. "Don't get me started." Immediately, he smiled; apparently the phrase constituted a sally of some sort. "Now, if you'll step over here," he said, indicating a small table beneath a north-tilted skylight.

Sylvia sat opposite him as he submitted the earring to greedy scrutiny.

"Yes," he said, "yes, indeed. Mmm."

Sylvia's heart sank. What she'd wanted him to say was: "And what cereal box did you find this one in, dearie?" She felt herself reduced to a desire for nicotine.

"It's . . . it's okay, then?" she said, reaching again into her bag.

"Oh, my goodness, yes. It's . . ." He looked some more, again oblivious of her.

When at last he dropped both loupe and diamond from his eye, she had smoked half her cigarette, and his face was as drained as if he'd spent an entire afternoon at strenuous love. "D-flawless; what we used to call River grade. Probably South African. A little over a carat, I'd say." He shook his head. "It's an exceptional stone. Reset, of course."

"How easy would it be to match?"

"Well." He set the earring down on the black velvet pad between them. "Matching is a relative thing, even if you're cutting a pair from the same stone."

"But just so you wouldn't notice, I mean. Just so you'd have a pair."

He stared down at the troublesome gem, its facets throwing points of fire out into the world according to the laws of physics.

"Do you ever get to New York?" he asked.

"Sure." She choked on her smoke and put out her cigarette. "I have a sister there."

"It's your best bet." He leaned back and crossed his legs beneath the table. "Most of the larger stones are cut on Broadway now. I could arrange it for you, but to be honest, you'd do better to see to it yourself, pricewise."

"I'd have to have it cut to order?"

"Almost certainly. It's the triangular make, you see. There's hardly any of it around these days—especially with fire like that. A stone this good, you practically always give it a round brilliant."

"Flashier."

He bowed his head briefly in an attitude of regretful agreement.

"But what if I just went for a fake match, a—what do you call it?—zircon or something."

A hand shot out to cover one of hers. "Don't even talk about it."

"It'd be obvious?"

He released the hand. "I could set it as a necklace for you."

"Thank you. I don't think so." She stood.

"Well, try New York, then." He rose as well. "And if you find that you want to sell it, for whatever reason, please come to me." His eyes seemed to have absorbed some of the stone's natural spark. "I'll top New York."

"Okay," she said. "I'll keep that in mind."

On the sidewalk outside, three impeccably dressed women were photographing the leather goods store across the street as if it were a national monument. Sylvia pulled out in front of them and slid smoothly into a U-turn.

The thought that her sister had likely been engaged in some sort of fraudulence involving Petra's earrings caused her to yawn convulsively. It had always pleased her that Kristen was so free with the truth, but the arrangement had often been inconvenient. Sylvia yawned again, covered her mouth with her hand. And why were people always seizing that hand lately: did they think it was going to escape?

She made a left turn, toward the rental house that she already regarded as home.

As the older sibling in this family of devious diplomats, Sylvia had early on made truth, an underpopulated place, her province. Accordingly, when she realized that what her hand was going to do next or soon was dial Michael's number, she was not really able to persuade herself that the sole reason for her call would be to ask him again precisely how and where he had found the earring. Although it would have been a convenient thought.

One school of opinion had it that civilization itself was based on convenient thoughts.

Insofar, her father had said, as we're all citizens of the world.

She accelerated to make the light and pulled hard into the parking lot of a famous department store. There, by signing her name, she bought fourteen pairs of underwear.

"I am elbows!" yelled Michael. "I'm feet!" He threw a fake to one side, an elbow to the other. Jabez caught it in the gut. Michael dribbled with his outside hand. Angle of incidence, angle of reflection.

"Who's tall?" said Jabez, slapping the ball out of his hands.

"*What's* tall?" Michael said, recovering. He drove around him, got off a shot. High bounce off the rim.

Sun off the surf.

Michael tipped it in.

Boris lay contentedly in the shade cast by the backboard.

"Hey, Jabez. I forget. Are we still young?" Michael was looking down at his own sweat-slick chest, wondering what beat there. Jabez, fifteen feet out and undefended, sank a skyhook that barely rippled the net.

"My honest impression," said Jabez, "is that we're not." The ball bounced untended beneath the basket. "But, you know, I've got a kid. It skews the perspective."

Michael had woken that morning from a dream of flowers—immense, long-stemmed purple flowers shaped like jungle hearts. Laurel and his mother had been sorting through them sadly, whispering in Russian. It had skewed his perspective.

"C'mon, Elbows. Let's swim." Jabez scooped up the ball and passed it to a place in space where Michael would be, if he ran, if he were young, if movement mattered enough to get there.

So he got there, and fired the ball out in turn in front of Jabez. Which is how, with each pass marking a less oblique leg of a zigzag straightening out toward the sea, they found their way into a footrace whose finish line Michael, pausing to heave the ball as far straight out upon the surf as he could, made abruptly aquatic. A wave curled, curtain falling. They dove.

Michael felt naked, then not naked enough. He tried to kick, but his shorts were down around his ankles. A few grains of sand swirled among his teeth. He surfaced.

A teenage girl bobbed beside him, belly-down on an abbreviated surfboard. She eyed him and giggled. "Hey, man. Better hang on to your britches."

"Nah," he said sourly. "I'm going native." But then he ducked under again and pulled them up.

Jabez was twenty feet away. "Yo, Michael."

"Right here."

"You got the ball?"

The girl paddled furiously after a promising wave, stood neatly as she caught it, and rode in a rush to shore.

"Well, don't look at me," said Jabez. "Christ."

The ball, it developed, was nowhere to be found. They swam methodically up and down the length of the beach, looking for it. The ball was lost at sea.

"Nothing to worry about," said Jabez as they walked from the water, their shoes squelching in the sand. "Just rent another one."

Michael stopped.

"Relax, Michael. I'm kidding."

Boris was watching them from the wrack line, wagging his tail. Michael let his features expand in a grin of weary amusement. He put an arm across Jabez's shoulders. "Yeah, the pickup. I was going to tell you about that."

"You're right. It's not my business."

"Did I say that?" They started up the beach. Michael sniffed the air. "What always amazes me is how a few perfect but misguided bodies can get this whole stretch of coast to smell like coconut oil."

"I just noticed the upholstery, is all. And I heard what happened to Sylvia Walters's house."

"But we do realize I did the interview *at the radio station*, don't we."

"Certainly," said Jabez soberly. "Perception coinciding with fact. A clear case."

"You talk to Laurel about this?"

He shook his head. Boris lumbered joyfully about, showering them with sand.

"Well, see, that's helpful," said Michael, as they continued up the beach toward the boardwalk. "It really is. Because I lied to Laurel about the truck, and I used your name in the lie."

He let go of Jabez. The sand being what it was, tiny and multiple to the point of infinity, both men staggered sideways a few steps. There were kites in the air—bright, plastic, tethered things.

"I told her some friends of yours wanted to use the truck in a made-for-TV. Upholstery had to be striped. I told her the studio paid."

Jabez listened.

"An abuse of friendship, Jabez, I agree. But I guarantee it'll never come up, not in a million years. Any doubts she has, she'll come to me. I'll owe you one."

Jabez waved aside the apology. "No abuse. These things happen." They stepped over the ash-gray piling that marked the beach's limits. On a concrete court nearby, a pair of trick bicyclists rode repeatedly up and off a wooden ramp, turning neatly parabolic somersaults over each other. "What I can't help wondering, though, and I know it's none of my business, is whether this has anything to do with the Japanese picture."

"The Japanese picture?" said Michael, realizing it must be so. "What in the world would it have to do with that?"

"Oh, I don't know. Nothing, I guess. I just saw you'd put your old man's Purple Heart on your bulletin board this morning, and I thought . . ." He rubbed the drying salt from his beard, then looked at Michael and clapped him on the shoulder. "Look. Play with fire if you want. You always have. Just be sure you know how far you want it to go."

"This is pretty far, I think."

"Obviously."

Michael and Jabez strolled together down the boardwalk, which was not made of boards. Jabez said what he had long been meaning to say: that their workplace was too easily open to unannounced assholes. But that was how he and Jabez had always operated and maintained, countered Michael, not without weariness, since this was an old argument, a personality difference, an issue that resurfaced in times of stress. Jabez bought a hot dog with some wet money. A spiky-haired man asked whether Michael would mind taking a picture of some Germans on vacation. Backing up to fill the frame, Michael collided with an interestingly underclad female roller skater. She embraced him for balance and called him a name.

Then she spun away, rolled in front of the Germans, and Michael took her picture. The Germans thanked him. Then he took their picture.

JABEZ: But this is different, I think.

"It's the mustard," said Michael. "Worst mustard in L.A."

A chop of the hand, indicating willful misunderstanding on Michael's part. "No, I mean it's different who's hanging around the premises. We're getting people from the industry now. I had to throw some producer type out of your office this morning."

"Oh? Anyone we know?"

"I didn't recognize the name. A crew-cut guy with a mustache, crypto-safari gear."

"Stranger to me."

"Well, he knew all about our problems on the Japanese picture—your fights with Dick, the budget screwups, everything." Dick was the director of the Japanese picture, *Steel Chrysanthemum*, and he had accused Michael of challenging his authority: the actors were not Michael's business, he'd said. Michael had expressed a different point of view.

"These are hardly state secrets, Jabez. They were all over the trades for a month."

"Yeah, but see, it didn't stop there. This guy implied he had some special knowledge of the project—that it might be going into turnaround, or that it was maybe about to be shelved completely. All this he communicated obliquely, no eye contact. Very disconcerting in a producer."

"He say what he wanted?"

"Oh, he had a project in mind. No details, but the gist was clear: if we found ourselves freed up, he wanted to be considered."

"Just another harmless jerk, Jabez."

"I threw him out. I told him to make an appointment like everybody else. It was outrageous."

People were eating ice cream cones in different colors. There were seagulls that seemed to be interested, but Michael was not comparing them in his mind to scavenging producers who hung about his studio uninvited. He was thinking about his parents, who had met in catastrophe. Jabez tossed his crumpled paper napkin ten feet into a wire basket. Michael hastened to reassure him that the movie was not going to be shelved. They discussed ways of improving security.

"It's the motion control system I'm most worried about," said Jabez. "We're way ahead of everybody on that."

"Patent pending," Michael reminded him.

"But we'll be using it all next week for the aerial battles. I've got planes to launch, flight patterns to shoot." What was good about the motion control system was that it allowed the camera to move in a precisely computed path, endowing a stationary model with not only the illusion of movement but also the "purposeful blur" that made it realistic. "It's one thing to have a few ex-girlfriends around for reinforcement, but these commando producers are something else."

What was good about Jabez was that he was a different kind of perfectionist from Michael.

"Okay," said Michael. "You got it. We'll close the shop to outsiders beginning Monday."

There was a crowd gathering ahead. Everybody was looking up. "Speaking of motion control," said Michael, also looking up.

To where, at the center of the crowd, atop eight stacked grocery crates, there stood a black man in minstrel garb: white shoes and gloves, black pants and tie, a red-and-white-striped jacket, wing collar, straw boater. He held his hands before him at chest level, lightly curled. In the crook of his arm, a cane. Everything about his dress and manner suggested a lively abundance, some sort of athletic imminence, but all the while he held himself perfectly still. Still as a map, still as a stopped watch, still as an event that has already happened forever.

"You ever seen this guy before?" Michael asked Jabez. Jabez shook his head. They worked their way around front.

Flanking the tower of crates were a pair of very large black men in polo shirts and sunglasses. Their arms were folded filmically across their chests in a manner at once comical and disconcerting. At the foot of the tower, propped up by a shoebox, was a hand-lettered sign:

IMMOBILITY ARTIST
(DONATIONS ACCEPTED)

The man did not blink. He did not appear to breathe. He towered above the eddying pedestrian traffic and the traffic of nonmotorized wheeled vehicles that filled the boardwalk, and he towered, too, above the continental plates upon which California itself rested, those two vast, unsettled masses grinding past each other at their accustomed rate of five careless centimeters a year, two quaking inches. The man was a still point.

It was only when Jabez nudged him that Michael noticed the man's other audience. Arranged in a semicircle at the edge of the boardwalk, drinking beer and staring sullenly upward, sat perhaps fifteen young men in wheelchairs. They had beards or mustaches to a man, they were dressed in fatigues and wore the insignia of America's recent foreign wars: Iran, Afghanistan, Hungary, Cuba.

"Jabez," said Michael at length, "we are in the presence of genius."

One of the windows of the restaurant Michael had named over the phone was being replaced, and Sylvia sat in a booth where she could watch the glaziers at work. In Washington, as a teenager, she'd once had a boyfriend who had driven her into the city's poshest suburb and hesitated outside a house they'd chosen at random while she'd hopped out and thrown a brick through its front window. The motivation, as she recalled it, had been somehow political.

Noticing the red half-moon she'd left on her wineglass at first sip, she reached into her bag, tore a leaf from her datebook, and carefully pressed it to her lips. She folded the paper neatly in half and put it under the ashtray. It was a bad sign that she'd overdone it with the lipstick.

The glaziers were busy removing the remnants of the old window, one holding on to the jagged edge with gloved hands, the other tapping gently at it with a hammer. With each shard that came away, a flash of midday sun struck Sylvia's eyes. The world seemed to her an enormously vast place and, at the same time, tiny. This thought reminded her of her father. And although Michael was not yet late, she contemplated leaving the restaurant.

"Look," said a man in the booth behind her. "There are only three categories of anything, am I right? More, Less, and It Doesn't Really Matter."

It came to Sylvia that the other reason she'd chosen this booth was so that she could see any crew-cut men with mustaches who might happen in. *If I were really smart*, she thought, *I wouldn't even be here.*

Michael arrived with a newspaper folded under his arm. "I'm late."

"No. And you're not interrupting either."

He slid in opposite her. She was wearing a red-and-white candy-striped dress. *This is quite far*, he thought. "I hear you've found a home," he said.

"Oh, it's perfect. All the materials are cheap, yet each is used in a precious way."

"How's that again?"

"Sorry, I'm being difficult." She shifted in her seat, all at once uncomfortably aware that the dress she wore had been a Valentine's Day gift from Zack in the halcyon days of their courtship. "The house really is perfect, and I think it's very clever of you to have come up with it. Thank you."

They were staring at each other. Michael put his newspaper down on the table. "Do I look strange to you?"

"No. I mean yes." She laughed. "We'd better order something. I'm starving."

"What I wanted to tell you was—"

"Now, do you suppose they're still serving brunch, because what I am exactly in the mood for is—"

"I wanted to tell you that I never meant to—"

"Hush," she said. "Just . . . hush." She scooped her hair behind one ear and considered him. There was a single stem of freesia in the bud vase by which he'd dropped his newspaper. "What you wanted to tell me is that you never meant to make a secret out of your girlfriend or wife or whatever she is—which is fine: we didn't really get around to life stories. Now, what I want to tell you is, whatever else you may have seen up there in my gloriously burning house, I am in fact a big girl who, believe it or not, can take care of herself." She glanced involuntarily over his shoulder as the door of the restaurant swung open. "So let's just have ourselves a civilized meal and, I don't know, talk about—what do you call it?—'purposeful blur' or something."

Neither of them touched a menu.

"Our life stories nearly *ended* up there at your house, Sylvia."

The waiter arrived and tried to recite some specials, but Sylvia ordered the eggs benedict and Michael the cold sturgeon. Michael also ordered a shot of vodka, iced and peppered in the Russian manner. Although he had never before shared a meal with Sylvia, he had already foreseen that she was a woman who in all circumstances took delight in her food. *Why did he know such a thing? What was he doing?*

"Besides," Sylvia went on, as if there had been no interruption, "I'm grateful to Laurel, really—is that her name: Laurel?"

He nodded.

"Grateful to her for hiring my friend. Nomanzi was in a tough spot, and Laurel was able to help her out. Not that it wasn't mutually beneficial—business is business, right? So all the better. A little serendipity, right here in the city of dream bubbles and dashed hopes."

"Neither girlfriend nor wife. Fiancée."

"What?"

"Laurel is my fiancée."

"Oh." Sylvia sought a cigarette in her bag. Michael lifted the matches from the ashtray. The headlines of the newspaper referred cautiously to the arms talks in Geneva.

"I say that not in the spirit of a wedding announcement," Michael added, lighting her cigarette with the little flame. "It just seemed to me maybe I ought to try a little experiment along the lines of . . . filling us in."

"Us." Two glasses of ice water arrived. "I thought it was me you were filling in." She sensed the conversation getting away from her. "Not that I asked you to, and not that I think you really want to sound as if your own wedding comes as a total surprise to you."

"But more and more it does," he said. "Over the last couple of days." And the despair contained in this truth flooded through him now for the first time. He stared down at his vodka, wanting to reach for it, but fearful at the same time of everything his reach implied. *And there were people all around him! Leading lives of normally contained acquisitiveness! In sports clothes!*

"Mi-*ch-ael*!"

He looked up in astonished recognition of her strangled tone, of the division of his name into more syllables than it had. Her face was twisted with anger.

"*Stop trying to have an effect on me.*"

Beneath the table, one of his knees was pressed tightly between the two of hers.

"Here you are, my friends," said the waiter. "Eggs benedict for the lady, our delectable sturgeon for you, sir. Enjoy."

"Damn," said Sylvia.

"What's the matter?"

"I've got a piece of cigarette ash in my eye." She dipped a corner of her napkin into the water glass and dabbed gently at her cornea.

"I thought," said Michael, moving his knee from side to side between hers to reestablish his presence, "that the problem here is we're having an effect on each other *without* trying."

At these words, Sylvia felt her anger, which had briefly abated, return. Had she found Michael's profession of surprise at his impending marriage truly incredible—or, as her outburst had implied, purely manipulative—she would have been relieved of the burden of their present encounter, and would have been quite happy to let it fall away into the near accidental realm of a postmortem. Had she, on the other hand, believed without reservation in that surprise—had she not seen the look of despair upon Michael's face as he gave voice to it—she would have left the restaurant at once. As it was, she was obliged to explore with him the nature of his astonishment, and from this circumstance flowed both her anger and the sudden moistening she now felt, to her shame and confusion, between her legs.

"I don't love you," she said, seizing her fork.

"It doesn't matter."

"And I hate the effect we have on each other. Because that's exactly all it is: a special effect, a clever little piece of camera magic that we haven't figured out the trick of yet." She ate ravenously, speaking around her food. "You shoot something small so it looks big, you shoot something dead so it looks alive. You set off a little charge under some dirt and talcum powder, photograph it right, and it looks like the end of the world." Again she glanced reflexively at the door of the restaurant. "These are things you told me." She swallowed. *"Why don't you know them?"*

"Because," he said, "when you're maybe about to love someone, it's only fair to act a little stupid about yourself."

"You are *not* about to—"

"So the person can see you for who you are."

Sylvia shook her head. The glaziers were attempting, a little nervously, to unload a new pane from the side of their truck. They had special tools for the task. "We'll walk away from this," said Sylvia.

"It's a pretty far walk," said Michael.

The newspaper said below the fold, "Death Toll Mounts in South African Drought; Thousands Displaced."

"Everything *simpatico?*" said the waiter.

Michael did not remember the exact moment at which his attention to Sylvia, across the table from him, had taken on a sexual acuteness, but he was aware now, as he used the heel of her shoe to pry one of his own from his otherwise naked foot, that the pressure on his captured knee had taken on a faintly swooning weakness.

He put the sole of his bare, sea-washed foot against her outer thigh, under her dress.

"Michael." She was flushed. She closed her eyes for a moment. "I *don't* see who you are."

"Then ask me simple questions. In simple factlike words and phrases." The smoothness of her thigh, though he recognized it instantly, had been impossible to foresee.

"Okay," she said, leaning back despite herself. "What did you tell Laurel about the pickup?"

"That a friend of mine wanted to use it in a shoot. That the studio redid the upholstery."

"And she believed you."

"Yes."

"What makes you think you know the first thing about women?"

"Nothing. Stick to simple questions."

"I am. Why did you come here?" Sylvia saw her left hand leave the table top and drift in hazy slow motion beneath.

"I wanted us to decide to meet—to make a date and keep it."
When he felt her hand come to rest on his foot, he left a little
involuntary pause. "It had to be a matter of choice."

"That's all?"

"Yes."

As she began to caress his foot, one of her knees, still gripping
his, began to tremble. "Aren't you afraid of . . . of what you might
do to your life? Probably for nothing?"

"Can't you tell?" he said.

She forced herself to shake her head, but even as she did so she
saw fear flicker across his face like the shadow of a small bird's wing.
The bird itself seemed to have come from, and returned to, her.
It settled in the place where her heart quickened. *Frightened?* the
station manager had asked, putting his hand atop hers.

"Yes," said Michael. "I'm afraid. That's part of it."

She felt her knees weaken and her hand together with his foot
lift so nearly simultaneously over her thigh's crest that, sliding
forward on the banquette to meet the soft pads of his toes with her
cunt, she was unable to tell who had initiated the movement.

"I don't love you," she said again.

"It doesn't matter," he said again.

She moved against him. The wet cotton of her underwear was
warm against his toes, and his toes, whenever they broke touch
with her, were cool against the air. She closed her eyes, then opened
them. He was leaning far back, against the wall of the booth, watching her.

"Michael," she said. "We're too theatrical, you and I. It's
ridiculous."

MICHAEL: Sylvie, Sylvie, look. When I said that in the interview
    about that guy Sabbattinni?

SYLVIA: I don't remember.

MICHAEL: Yes you do. Seventeenth-century stage designer? De-
    signed a stage flood so convincing that people ran from their seats
    when they saw it coming?

SYLVIA: Yes, okay. Wait. *No!* Don't . . . don't stop, just . . . [Glances
    around to see if anyone is looking, then slips her underwear down

beneath his foot to the tops of her knees.] There. Yes . . . that's
. . . Oh! . . . Oh, Michael, what are we—
MICHAEL: Is it ridiculous that the people in that audience ran out
  of the theater like that?
SYLVIA [Staring at him]: No. No, it's a beautiful story.
MICHAEL: Why?
SYLVIA: Because they . . . they must have believed in so much.
  [*Moves her hips an involuntary inch forward on the banquette.*]
  I know. [*A sharp intake of breath*] I know what you're saying.
  But—

"Michael!" she cried, removing him from her with both hands,
sitting bolt upright in the booth, staring at the door.

"What is it?" He didn't know whether to look at her or in the
direction she was looking.

"I—" But she saw that the crew-cut man who had just entered
the restaurant had a goatee as well as a mustache. And he was with
a group. And he was dressed in designer clothes.

Sylvia's body went suddenly small in her seat. "Sorry. I'm a little
jumpy."

"You thought you saw someone you know."

"No. I mean yes." Gazing down at the tabletop, her eye hit upon
Michael's still-untouched vodka. She downed it, choked a bit. "It's
a little hard to explain."

"Guilt, maybe?"

"You don't feel any?"

"But it's not that."

"No."

Amid the babble of the by now nearly filled restaurant, both of
them felt all at once undone in their small nakedness.

"Listen, would you excuse me for a moment?" asked Sylvia. "I'd
better use the ladies'."

Michael nodded. Glancing across the aisle, Sylvia noticed a
woman staring discreetly over the tops of her sunglasses at them.
She gave the woman a friendly little wave and, when she continued
to stare as Sylvia wriggled back into her panties, a blinding smile.
The woman looked away. "Be right back," Sylvia told Michael.

Why not? Michael reflected; anything was possible. Noticing the slip of paper pressed under the ashtray, he reached for it: Sylvia's lips, perfectly parted, perfectly printed. *Lundi 6 Août.* He put it back where he'd found it. The French datebook was no doubt worth some part of Michael's speculative attention, as was the discovery that Sylvia had been preening before his arrival, whether specifically for him or out of habit, but Michael found his mind sliding uselessly sideways toward a half-passive daze. When, some moments later, Sylvia glided back into the booth, he was startled.

"I know this sounds paranoid," she said. "But I think I'm being followed."

Looking her over a little harshly, he said, "Right now?"

"Well, no. I don't think so. But that's what made me jump that way." She reached across the table and helped herself to some of his sturgeon. He watched it disappear into her mouth.

"I wonder what I say to that," said Michael.

"You could try nothing."

"I don't think so." He began to eat. "Who might this person be, who's following you?"

"A fan?" she suggested, attempting a shrug. But it didn't come off, so she shook out another cigarette and told him about the harassment calls, reminded him about the slashed tires, told him in careful detail about the way she and Nomanzi had been photographed amid the ashy ruin of her former home.

The more she spoke about it, the more aware she became that she'd been waiting for something exactly like this from herself—a confession, a recital of her competence in the face of threat, a way of showing him through her outrage who she was—so that her story became a kind of total self-display: she was the sort of woman who kept a watchful eye turned to her rearview mirror but was able to pull into the driveway of a place where there were people, and trees, and dogs, and potted flowers, so as to ambush any green sedan that might be following her. It was an account of herself delivered for Michael's benefit; it was a performance. As with the crescent moon of lipstick she had earlier discovered on her glass, she recognized it at once as a warning signal. There were no secret languages.

"You must have talked to this guy, then," said Michael. "After the collision, I mean."

"Oh, I talked to him okay."

"Well?"

"He didn't say a word. He smiled and pulled out, I told you."

"But you have, as they say, informed the police?"

"No."

Michael cocked an eyebrow. When Sylvia reached with her fork for the last bite of sturgeon, he put a hand over the hand that reached. "Why not?"

"Because"—she met his gaze—"because I'm not ready for that."

The restaurant seemed to both of them to fall still as they considered for a second time the notion of readiness. Then Sylvia blushed and Michael released her hand, which, after a further hesitation, speared what it had sought.

"Next time I'll order twice," said Michael.

"I thought we were still discussing whether there should be a next time," said Sylvia.

"What does he look like?" said Michael.

"Blond crew cut; mustache, no beard; lots of muscles, but not in a California way, if that makes any sense—bulkier, maybe? Forty, forty-five years old, I'd guess." Sylvia grimaced, took a sip of ice water. "He was wearing some kind of safari getup, brand-new by the looks of it."

Once you have been startled from your seat by a staged flood in which you have helplessly believed, and thus abetted and made real, you can never return to the theater in the same way. After all, you can now envision the day when life will present you with a real flood.

"What's the matter, Michael?"

"This guy you're describing—he was in my studio this morning."

"Oh, God."

"I wasn't there, but my assistant found him nosing around. Said he was a producer. Apparently he knew all the industry gossip about the picture we've been working on. If I remember right, the man claimed"—Michael rubbed his eyes—"that he wanted to work with us."

"Did he give his name, leave a card?"

"I don't know. As I say, I wasn't there. Jabez threw him out."

Checks and plastic cards sailed by on little trays to the left and right of them, but neither Michael nor Sylvia made a move in the direction of departure or even coffee.

"He must have seen you come by the station yesterday," Sylvia said. "If he'd been up at my house during the fire, we'd have noticed."

"Maybe this is a different guy," said Michael. She raised her lilac eyes to his, and it hit him then with the force of a blow: if there was a different guy, and if they were speaking in a slightly different sense, the different guy could only be himself—him in the rearview mirror, him pursuing her uninvited to the radio station, him inviting himself into her life. He laid his large hand open across the table, and she immediately placed her fingers in his palm.

"You think I'm bad news."

"I didn't say that." Her nostrils flared. "Did I?"

He got up and came around the table. "No, you didn't." He slid onto the banquette beside her. "You didn't say that."

She looked at him resentfully. Without turning his eyes from hers, he slipped the folded paper from beneath the ashtray. When he had opened the discarded sheet and had seen her register its casual lipstick trace, he pushed the remnant still unfolded back where glass and ash might keep it flat.

She continued to direct her stare downward, her variously blond hair spilling in a slow swell over her shouldertop.

After a time as broad as a space, she said: "I want you to kiss me."

And when she turned back toward him, with a nervous shaking out of her hair, each saw in the other a submission to surprise so near to absolute as to rekindle surprise.

Reflected sunlight struck Michael's right eye a moment before he closed it. The glaziers tilted the new pane slowly vertical. Sylvia knocked over her water glass.

NEWSPAPER: Tomorrow—clear skies, continued sunny and hot.

In the motel room, as she braced the heels of her hands against the bed's headboard the better to meet his thrusts, all of what had happened between them up at her house came back to both of them in flashes of image and sensation.

The drenched sheet clung briefly to her buttocks each time she lifted them.

His arms on either side of her pressed her breasts together so that her nipples repeatedly grazed his sweat-soaked chest.

But this, too, is true: that it was the kiss in the restaurant—the kiss with which Sylvia was only just able to stifle the impulse to tell Michael about her father's phone calls—that marked the real beginning of their affair.

"We'll need a lemon and some lemon leaves," said Nomanzi, her eyes streaming. "There's a tree out back." She tossed the chopped onions into one of Rhonda's Brazilian frying pans. "*Hamba,*" she said. "Go."

Johnny got up from the kitchen table. Chentula hit the channel selector on the remote control.

"You'll like Sylvia," Nomanzi said, drying her false tears with the kitchen towel, measuring out the curry for the bobotie. "Did I tell you what she said about Tsotsi? 'Very tough stuff,' she said. 'Very moving.'"

The television said: "You are the light of my life."

Chentula hit the selector again and stretched. He was wearing a T-shirt with the name of an American motorcycle written across it. "So it is maybe true, what Johnny said. That things here are not so different from home, really."

"No. But it is maybe true that Americans are not as ignorant as they like to advertise themselves to be."

Johnny returned with the lemon cradled among leaves. "It's okay about the water, you think?" They were draining the rooftop whirlpool bath, siphoning it dry with a garden hose they'd hung over the side of the house. "It is spilling down the driveway and making a mess in the street, ay."

The man in the house next door had been practicing his stage laughter for the past half hour. It was an increasingly convincing effort: a deep, chambered sound that began in his throat, bloomed in his chest, trailed off in chuckles, then began again. A note on the refrigerator gave his name and phone number. He was the man to call in case of emergency.

"Water is not a mess," said Nomanzi. "It evaporates."

"As it has in our country," said Chentula in Xhosa.

"Yes."

The TV said: "Gradually, the unfocused but ambitious Dr. Freud began to discern connections between sexual frustrations and physical illnesses."

Chentula changed channels. "You have talked to your father?"

Nomanzi squeezed the soaked bread free of milk, saving the milk. "I can't reach him."

"He's not in New York?"

"Everyone is very vague: 'Mr. Lolombela is out of his office, Mr. Lolombela sends his love, Mr. Lolombela will call you as soon as he can.' "

"So he knows you are living here now. In this house."

"I left the number. But I think he is not in New York."

In the momentary silence, all three of them felt the argument beginning anew, gathering strength. The sound of water flowing down the driveway assumed its own momentum. The neighbor's laughter did also.

"You know they are trying to drive us apart," said Chentula. "You know how they work."

"But they don't know how we work."

"Two weeks for us, ninety days for you."

"Am I so simple? Are you?"

"My eyes see what they see."

"What, then? What do they see?" She flung the minced lamb into a mixing bowl and began kneading the pale meat with her fingers. The light in the kitchen was very bright, but the fixtures were recessed; the brightness seemed to have no source. "Tell me, Chentula."

His jaw worked grimly, as if to dislodge a bit of food from between his front teeth. Then he said: "You want to belong to this place, eh. Already you have a house, a job. Our land gets to be far away like that. Like Johnny says, in the studio here, things become just music: 'Suffering Land.' Okay. You add some keyboards, you pull the guitars up front; maybe you have a hit."

Johnny looked at the Japanese watch he'd bought at the airport; he shook it. It still said 8:16. Sighing, he leaned over to untie his shoes.

"And you think that's what I want to be," said Nomanzi. "A hit."

"Our work is not here."

"We are here." She threw mango chutney toward the bowl's lip. "That's all."

"No," said Chentula. "That is not all." He stood, and Nomanzi, against her will, became aware of their shared mother's features in his: the mouth set in false disdain; the cheekbones that sometimes, *back there*, had led others to guess at Khoi-Khoi blood mingled not so faintly with Xhosa; the finely sculpted ears, thickly lateral at the top; the jutting jaw.

She had an impulse to turn her back on him as he approached, but she could not.

The TV said: "You cannot *deliver* more potent relief to your nose."

Chentula gently lifted the single strand of cow hair that encircled her neck—hair from the tail of the cow (*ubulungu*, doer of good) that her mother's father had given his daughter when she was wed. It had been tied around Nomanzi's neck at birth; the cow by custom had been preserved from slaughter.

Chentula said: "We are here to make for us the protection that will be our new *ubulungu*. Is it? Is it?"

"Yes, the publicity," she answered. "We have talked about that."

"Because we cannot do our work from prison, eh." He saw her pulse beating in the dark cup of her collarbone—she was that still, mistress fully of her movement—and he once again became shyly aware that his half-sister was beautiful. He let go the strand of cow hair.

"Look, to be famous in our land, it is good. To be famous in America, yeh—we are here for that, Nomanzi. But there are plenty people would like to see us forget why that is important for us." He thrust a finger at his own chest. "We don't need T-shirts with our names on them, magazines with your picture. We need *them* to know—yes, them, the whites who hold our land, our lives—that they cannot hide us from the world in prison. Nothing more, no less. That's all." Breathing heavily, he felt the unfair charge of his own ferocity. "So we have gained nothing until"—with a grimace he registered the unfairness—"until we take what we get here, and bring it home."

Their faces were so close she could have but mouthed the words and been understood: "You think I'm going to stay."

"Ninety days! Ninety days!" He turned from her as she had wished to turn from him earlier.

"I! Me! As if I were a star-struck child!" She flung the chopped almonds at his back. "As if I could forget!"

Chentula whirled. "Yes!"

"Oh, Chenny, man. You go too far." Johnny stood, barefoot, abashed. The TV behind him was a flat, bright place of harshly shifting colors.

"Don't you think they know how long a time ten years is?" Chentula opened his palms to her as if presenting those years at the ends of his long fingers. "You grew up in this country. It is there on you—sweet-sweet, eh?" He offered the scent, two fingers beneath her nose; she slapped them away. "Pretty cars and houses. Polite whites who only care about the color of your money."

"You disgust me."

"Good, good. Now you say it. Now."

"The way you hate my father. Because it's that, isn't it? Him."

"What do you know? What do you know, eh?"

"It is. It's him. Say it." She took a half-step forward, her hands on her hips. "Because I *did* come back. He's the one who stayed."

"The famous Joseph Lolombela."

"Yes. Famous." She untied Rhonda's apron and threw it at Chentula's feet. "Because he did more to 'make protection' for our people than the rest of us put together."

"Diplomacy. What is that? A trick of words." Chentula appeared faintly embarrassed by the apron, which covered the toe of one of his red high-topped sneakers. "Nothing has changed."

"As the world does not change for one who was asleep and now is awake."

Through the open window came a gaspy sucking sound as the hose drew the last of the water from Jacuzzi to street. The laugher paused, cleared his throat, assayed a looser chuckle.

"Come on, you two. We're all on the same side." Johnny put a hand on Chentula's shoulder, then bent to retrieve the apron, which he hung over the back of a white wire chair. "None of us can forget that."

The TV said: "And the balloons are released, here at Candlestick Park."

"No," said Nomanzi. "None of us can."

Chentula rubbed the back of his neck with one hand, glaring at his shoe toes.

"Yesterday—" she said, "I was going to tell you this before—but yesterday I was photographed by a man from Special Branch." For a moment, everything stopped. "Well, you can always tell a *Gat*, even overseas, mmm? The big car, the arrogance. I was up at Sylvia's house that burned down; we were there together; I didn't explain."

Johnny turned up the volume of the TV, indicated the walls of the house with his eyes.

"Not yet, I think," Nomanzi answered.

Chentula stepped forward and took hold of her elbow. She shook it free, but almost gently. "As if I could forget," she repeated, staring back.

The back door opened, and Sylvia entered, groceries in either arm. The screen door slammed behind her. Johnny turned down the TV, and Sylvia stood motionlessly taking it all in, looking pleasantly awry with her unbrushed hair and scooting eyes. She was happy to be home.

"What," she said at length, "are all those nuts doing on the floor?"

And one by one—Chentula first, Sylvia last—they began to laugh. It was the moment for which the patiently practiced attempts from next door had been the reiterated cue; it was time out of time. Chentula bent over double, gasping for breath. Johnny let himself fall back in his chair, his head thrown farther back in full voice. "Yes," Nomanzi managed to wheeze, "that's it. That's it exactly." One of the grocery bags fell sideways on the floor, where Sylvia had been forced to set it. The two women embraced, weeping with nonspecific amusement. An avocado rolled in wobbly scallops across the immaculate white linoleum tile.

They ate in the kitchen. They left the television on but turned off the sound. They talked about music.

"I got at least a couple of dozen calls after I played your tape last night," Sylvia told the two men. "They wanted to know when the record would be out. They wanted to know who you are."

In the looks the three Africans exchanged, Sylvia could read the remnants of argument. "What did you tell them?" asked Johnny, helping himself to more stewed apricots.

"I said what I knew. Well, I guess it's not that much, is it?— what Nomanzi said in her note, a little bit I know about from my father." She swallowed what she was eating; what was she eating? "That you were stars in Azania, that you were going to be very big here." She grimaced, conscious of the casual promises and evasions built into the jargon of her trade. "Anyway, it played very well. I'll do it again."

"We are grateful," said Chentula. "To be known overseas, that is insurance for us."

"The acoustical quality of prisons is very bad," Johnny added.

"Even though," said Nomanzi, "the audiences are very good."

"Are you allowed to give concerts in your own country?" Sylvia inquired. She was trying not to notice the sprays of orchid Nomanzi had brought home from Laurel's shop: white, violet, palest lilac.

"So far, yes." Johnny wiped his mouth and leaned back in his chair. "So far they think we are less trouble running around loose than we would be in their hands."

Nomanzi pointed to the television. "Sylvie, look! It's our land-lady."

And it was: Rhonda, wearing makeup and jogging clothes, sur-rounded by cats. In each hand she held a different brand of cat food, trade names and logos clearly marked upon the plastic bowls. She gestured well. She mouthed words in close-up. Highly paid cats besieged her.

"And God said," said Sylvia, " 'let there be residuals.' "

After dinner, beneath the night's yellow-gray sky, the four diners stripped with a shyness that varied according to the dictates of sex, culture, and custom, then sank together into the refilled whirlpool bath: stamen of the flower that the house, with its exploded-petal roof, proposed itself to be.

"In my country," Nomanzi observed, staring at the moon, "this is an illegal act."

To the south, streams of cars poured across the elevated freeway in parallel lines. Sylvia pressed a plastic button by her elbow, and the water began to churn, startling everyone.

"We're like that old cartoon, eh, Chenny?" Johnny settled a little deeper in the tub. "You know, the one where the cannibals boil the missionaries in a big black pot?"

Chentula chuckled. "Yeah, Bra. But this time you got the cannibals in with you."

It was everybody's night.

FIRST SISTER [*Climbing out of the Jacuzzi to answer the phone, perhaps wrapping herself in a towel, perhaps not*]: Hello?

SECOND SISTER: Hi, Sylvie, it's me. Jesus God, I didn't realize what time it was. Did I wake you?

FIRST SISTER: Kristen! Daddy and I have been trying you for days! Where are you?

SECOND SISTER: I think I'm in Vermont. [*Muffled sounds of inquiry*] Right, northern Vermont. I'm having a romantic adventure.

FIRST SISTER: Should I be worried?

SECOND SISTER: No. I mean, love always has its worrisome side, but that's what makes it fun, right? Don't answer, I'll have to dissemble, since I'm not alone.

FIRST SISTER: We also associate not being alone with being kidnapped.

SECOND SISTER [*Laughter*]: And with being a member of a family.

FIRST SISTER: Sorry. Daddy asked me to check up on you; he's . . . he says he's worried about us. That we quite literally—

SECOND SISTER: I'm worried about *you*. I saw the papers, and this isn't your phone number. Is your house—

FIRST SISTER: Yes, it did. Burn down. But I've got insurance, it's okay. I'm having an adventure too, I guess.

SECOND SISTER: Oh, Sylvie. I'm so sorry.

FIRST SISTER [*Rolling her eyes*]: Sibling rivalry. [*Pause*] An adventure of the kind you're having, I mean.

SECOND SISTER: Sylvie! And you always say *I'm* the one who does everything at once. That's great.

FIRST SISTER: Maybe. [*A pause while she wanders with the phone to the roof's edge and, looking out past the freeway, sees what*

*we've seen from the beginning: a brilliant blue neon sign, simply
but artfully limning a kitchen faucet from which staccato dash-
shaped drips fall in endlessly repeated sequence—a hardware
store's advertisement*]: Listen, Kristie, there's something I
wanted to ask you. Besides whether you're all right—which you
are, right?

SECOND SISTER: Right. What?

FIRST SISTER: How come you didn't tell me you'd lost one of Petra's
earrings in my garage?

SECOND SISTER: But I didn't! [*Pause*] Oh, shit. [*Putting a muffling
hand not entirely effectively over the phone's mouthpiece*]: Darling, I think we're out of ice. Could you . . . [*Giggles.*] Yes, girl
talk. Just a minute or two. [*Addressing herself again to Sylvia*]
That was too easy; it'll never last. [*A deep breath*] So. I take it
the dark-eyed stud confessed to his wife. That's why you're
calling.

FIRST SISTER: Dark-eyed stud?

SECOND SISTER: Wyatt. The actor? He came with Petra and Max
to your party, then with me in the garage. We were supposed
to be going for more charcoal, remember? [*Laughs.*] It probably
wouldn't have happened if it weren't for that obscene artificial
turf you California degenerates insist on putting down everywhere. Anyway, it was just one of those sometime, one-time
things. [*Pause*] I hope I didn't mess things up for you.

FIRST SISTER: No, this is all news to me. But . . . is that how you
lost the earring?

SECOND SISTER: I told you, Sylvie: if I lost something, it wasn't an
earring. [*Pause*] Actually, now that I think of it, one of them *did*
come off when he first kissed me, but it went right down the
front of my dress, and we—ha! "We!"—the slime found it right
away. Ask Petra. I sent them back as soon as I got to New York.
Okay?

FIRST SISTER: Sure, I guess. But . . . you wouldn't mislead your
poor homeless sister about something like this, would you?

SECOND SISTER: Sylvie! No! *Pas possible.* [*Pause*] Listen, I have to
cut this a little short: the iceman cometh. [*Indistinct sounds of
arrival*] Pa's in Geneva, huh? When did you talk to him?

FIRST SISTER: Day before yesterday. I think he'd feel better if he talked to you himself. You know how he's gotten since Mother's death.

SECOND SISTER: Protective.

FIRST SISTER: Yes. Protective. [*Holds her hand out before her, palm up, and, as if deliberately spilling a handful of sand or salt, turns it over. A jetliner passes overhead at an ascending angle, lights flashing.*] Well, it's all relative, I guess, but he seemed particularly anxious this time. There's something very big in the works, more than headlines. [*Turns to survey what she feels to be her household, parts of Africa's future, talking quietly among themselves in a language of which she knows nothing.*] Which reminds me: you don't know any secret languages, do you?

SECOND SISTER: Ig-pay atin-lay?

FIRST SISTER: I guess not.

SECOND SISTER: Are you in love with him?

FIRST SISTER [*Startled*]: Who?

SECOND SISTER: Your adventure.

FIRST SISTER: Wrong question.

SECOND SISTER: Right answer.

[*They laugh.* PETRA *and* MAX *pull into the driveway. The* SISTERS *promise to speak soon. The ambient sound—freeway traffic, cicadas, a garage door on a slow electric pulley—comes slowly full; the dialogue grows gradually indistinguishable from it.* MAX, *arriving on the roof, says something about catching a marlin—but we can't hear it clearly.* PETRA *says something about losing her movie deal—but we can't hear it at all. The* FIRST SISTER *takes a stem of freesia from an impromptu wine-bottle vase,* NOMANZI's *invention, and holds it ravishingly aloft; its blooms resemble a bout of studied long division, perfectly accomplished.*

[*And then, below: a car goes by, its left front wheel hitting* A SINGLE STONE *that has been dropped there by a child. The headlights' beam is thrown just enough off kilter to travel through the kitchen window, strike the television's remote system, and turn it on: minimal volume, phosphorescent dots swarming into never constant place.*]

Five tiny fighter jets flew horizonward in diamond formation. When with a great crack they accelerated and peeled off in different directions, the festoon of contrails they left against the dawn sky indeed suggested an explosion.

Michael and Laurel were driving to the desert house. Sand extended from the highway's either side in waves and ripples. It was Sunday.

"Boris okay?" Michael asked. "He just hates sonic booms."

Laurel peered through the rear window into the bed of the pickup. She was wearing a purple scarf folded in a band across her forehead and looked, not quite without knowing it, like a perfectly beautiful Hollywood version of the Indian princess. "Asleep," she said.

"Old," he said.

They drove. Michael talked to her about the origin of diamonds. Diamonds, he said, were one of the few substances to reach the earth's surface from its remote depths, borne up to the eyes of men by the volcanic rock kimberlite.

"You mean it came out of a volcano?" she said, holding her hand out before her where the breaking light might strike the diamond ring she wore.

"Shot from the earth like a speeding bullet." He had given it to her some six months previously. She looked pleased at the thought of such violent manufacture.

The creation of diamonds, Michael continued, swerving to avoid a jackrabbit, had coincided with the beginning of continental drift, the great shake that had split apart each of the two primal continents: Gondwanaland, which was now South America, Africa, South Asia, parts of Australia, and Antarctica; and, to the north, Laurentia, which once extended from North America to the high latitudes of the Far East, by way of Europe and northern Siberia. "And that's how God invented the Atlantic Ocean," Michael concluded.

"I always wondered how He did that," said Laurel. She shook her head in admiration. "And diamonds at the same time. What a guy."

"Best effects in the business," Michael said.

"Plus which"—she shook her finger at him—"no Oscars to spoil Him." Giggling, she put her arms around Michael, and he swerved briefly into the empty left lane. A dust devil blew up over the far sands, then disappeared. "You know what?" Laurel's whisper came loud and warm in his ear. "I really like that name: Kimberley."

"Kimberlite."

"No, I mean if we have a girl."

He kissed her quickly—no, automatically; no, defensively—on the cheek. *Why was he talking about diamonds?* "We'll see," he said.

"You don't like it." She moved away.

"No, I do, I do." Huge boulders rose up on either side of the road; Joshua trees, cactus. "Kimberley," he said, and put a hand on Laurel's knee. "A name to conjure with." After a while she put her hand atop his.

They stopped at the hardware store for a bag of cement before turning off the highway onto the little dirt ribbon that ran thirty lunar miles out into the desert. Boris was awake, breathing the breeze. There were tension-wire gates every few miles.

On the morning after Laurel and Michael had first slept together, he had made a discovery for them both. They had been sitting naked at his table, surveying the sunny space of his loft together as she read it aloud for him: the sense of this salvaged chair, the legible history of that seductive corner. Some industrial shelving caught her eye—a fashion of a few years earlier—and she had launched into an explication, using the adjective "gray" to describe it. The first time she'd said it he'd let it pass, but the second time he'd been unable to stop himself: "Laurel, sweet," he'd said, "you're color-blind. The shelves are green."

After a tiny shocked pause, she had accepted his observation completely—it was clearly true—but she was at the same time so manifestly hurt and perplexed at having had to be told something so essential about herself that they had both become embarrassed. She had asked for a robe, he had produced one, and in all the time since—though, as now, they often thought of it at the same moment—neither had mentioned her green/gray blindness again. Michael, for his part, had accepted her judgment about the shelves— they were no longer stylish in the way he had intended—but more than that: he felt lastingly regretful at having told her that a small part of the spectrum that was live to the world's eye was dead to hers. It was distinctly murderous. He had had the shelves removed the following day.

And now the desert, with its countless shades of gray and dusty green, sometimes seemed to Michael—however peculiarly—to be Laurel's natural birthright: an indemnity, a promised land.

"How are we on gas?" she asked. "Maybe we should stop at the desert rat's." This was their name for the gray-bearded rabbit-raiser who was their only real neighbor. He had a horse, a gas pump, a telephone, and he called the city "Lost Angles."

"We're fine on gas. Are we fine on rabbits?"

They waved as they passed the old man's cluttered yard. He had the engine out of his truck on a chain hoist, and he gave them a more than usually knowing look.

"Old fart's gonna get friendly if he doesn't watch out."

"Oh, come on, Michael. He's crazy about us. You know that." She wriggled happily in her seat. Cranky old men inspired in her a fondness derived from television, where their gruff exteriors never failed to disguise hearts of pure gold. Her own father was a retired software salesman who told complicated knock-knock jokes.

Michael strong-armed the truck around a small geological insult in the road.

"Last time I got gas at his place, the old guy asked me if we'd ordered our—what did he call it?—our 'shit-ass salad bowl from outer space.' You weren't with me. I had to interpret on my own."

Laurel laughed. "A TV dish. He's thinking of getting one—not that he'd ever let on."

"I said we were off space salad. Dietary considerations."

"Did he like it?"

"He spat. Highest form of rejoinder in a desert situation."

She put her arms around him and kissed him on the mouth. They swerved.

"Second highest," Michael said, recovering direction. The sun now appeared fully before them. He put on his dark glasses and cast a nervous glance at her hand, which had come to rest on the radio's controls.

"Okay," she said. "This is it. In or out?"

It was a game they played, a variable measurement of proximity and distance. Somewhere within the seven miles between the home of the desert rat and the crooked tension-wire fence that set off their property, radio signals from the city frittered finally off to static. Exactly where depended on the weather, air pressure, time of day, but the point of passage had become for them a private locale, as other couples had a favorite restaurant or hotel.

"Me, I'd say it's too soon." He gazed out guiltily at the terrain, where here and there tumbleweed tangles lay lodged in bright stillness.

"Conservative!" she cried gleefully. Then followed it up with a look. "That's not like you."

"I'm thinking of Kimberley," he said, adjusting the rearview mirror. "Having kids changes your perspective, you know?"

Her own facial expression changed craftily—her eyes going bigger and darker, her mouth finding its set at the corners, as if there were a director off-camera feeding her cues.

She turned the knob.

Static.

"Okay, I do dinner," Michael said.

"For once," Laurel said.

Tufts of panic grass cast shadows in the slant light.

They reached the last wire fence, and Laurel got out of the truck to let them through. For a mile behind them, their dust had not settled, but overhead the jet contrails had dispersed, and the sky was flawless. Laurel remembered something Nomanzi had told her:

that in Xhosa the word for "blue" was the same as that for "green." Michael had green eyes. Getting back into the truck, she avoided them—they were behind sunglasses; they knew too easily what she was thinking.

Michael steered the pickup around a big red boulder, and their house came into view: an L-shaped stucco structure with a red tile roof. There was a long balcony on the south side. There were shelves stacked with soothingly packaged food products within.

"Ah," said Michael. "Rest at last." When he turned off the engine, it was all at once so quiet that the two of them could hear the blood buzzing in their veins. Boris leapt neatly over the truck's rear gate.

"Soon I'll want to be naked," Laurel said. She removed his sunglasses. He had closed his eyes.

"Soon we will be," he answered. He was relieved to notice that other things, other people, Sylvia, seemed far away. When he opened his eyes he saw Laurel and, on the well's pump beyond, a cactus wren watching them warily.

Laurel unlocked the front door; Michael took the cement around back to where he was sinking piles for a sundeck. When she opened the back door to him, she stood framed there for a moment, touching nothing with her hands. She was fragile-looking, luminous with fear.

"Michael," she said, "I think someone's been inside."

He drew her back out into the sun and went in himself. Boris was plunging from one spot to another, snuffling interestedly. A window in the kitchen was open, but otherwise nothing seemed amiss.

Laurel had followed him back in. "I don't know what it is. Just a feeling. And we're always so careful about the windows." She hugged herself against the night chill that the house in its desert dignity still held. "Oh, but probably it's nothing. I'm just being silly." She followed him very closely, a step behind, talking to herself. "I mean, now I'm getting embarrassed. This is ridiculous. Another episode of premenstrual doo-dah."

He stopped beside the kitchen sink, and she ran into him, rested her forehead against the back of his shoulder. "But we did take all the trash out with us last time, didn't we?" Michael asked.

"Yes. I'm positive."

Michael moved on. There were two beer cans in the bottom of the wastebasket. Laurel skipped after him to catch up, ran into him again.

"And I don't play solitaire; do you?"

"Solitaire?"

He stepped aside. A pack of playing cards lay spread upon the dining table in the orderly overlapping scales, alternated by color, of a game of patience. The play was blocked, the game at an unsuccessful end: of the cards freed and laid out above the rest, none of the suits had accumulated beyond its five; indeed, of the diamonds, only the ace had been released by the draw.

"Laurel, go out to the truck and wait there." It appeared they had decided to whisper.

"No. I'm terrified."

"Don't argue. Go."

She went, glaring at him in a way that signified he would later pay for this banishment.

The light streaming in through the brand-new east windows struck a red glow from all straight edges. Michael removed the handgun that Laurel didn't know about from the drawer where it still resided and began systematically to search the house.

Line of sight. Line of fire. Line of least resistance.

He looked behind the rattan couch. He opened the closet, the pantry. Boris snuffled at the broom closet, and Michael opened that too. He reversed his path and started up the stairs.

Halfway up the redwood steps, he caught his breath and stopped—struck unexpectedly by a premonition of a day in which this place, this house, this invented structure whose protection he was manfully miming, would simply cease to be. It was a place with people in it, a dog, potted flowers. Things would move about in it for a while; there would be shadows, sighs, carefully cooked meals, and water measured out. Then, all at once: nothing. Desert, sun, silence. Exactly nothing.

Michael looked at his watch. It had stopped hours before. Or maybe was it fast? He shook his wrist out once in the shadowed air before him, but the squared-off numbers still said 8:16.

Michael knew then that he was alone in the house—realized he had known it from the start. Abandoning caution, he continued up the stairs and completed his inspection, rote and thorough: the bedroom closet, the study, the crawl space beneath the bed. Nothing seemed to be missing, nothing disarranged.

He hid the gun behind some books in the bedroom before going out on the balcony. Laurel was leaning against the pickup's fender, her arms still folded over her breasts. She seemed shiny with resentment, fear, addled unease. She had to shade her eyes with one hand to see him where he stood.

He let her look for a moment, then whispered: "Just us chickens, baby." And she stalked into the house.

She wanted to leave, she wanted to stay, she wanted to call the police. Michael sat semidazed in the middle of the rattan couch, an arm outstretched on either side, watching her pace. He removed his watch and set it on the whitewashed bench that served as a coffee table.

It became apparent to him that watching Laurel work herself into a frenzy had a mildly erotic content lost upon neither of them: she was performing a sort of cognitive striptease. It also had begun to dawn on him that something was missing from the house after all, although he couldn't yet say what. He began to cast his eye systematically about the room.

"It's worse than burglary," Laurel was saying. "It's violation. Like rape. They could be back at any time."

"Solitaire is a game normally played by a single individual," he offered.

"Still worse. The guy was waiting. Passing time." She tore the scarf from her forehead and threw it onto the couch next to him. "I grew up in this state. I know."

"Waiting," said Michael, examining the walls.

"For the rest of the guys. A motorcycle gang, maybe."

"No, I mean you. You grew up waiting." He studied the placement of the chairs, the potted plants, the hook-hung skillets. "In the state of waiting."

"Don't be an idiot."

"Probably I can't help it."

"They'll be back. That's what the message is." She was half unbuttoning her blouse, fumbling at its fastenings as she paced. "The message is: Never relax, no peace, this is not your home."

"But it is. We know that. Because we make the rules around here."

She whirled upon him. "*Rules?* In the *des*ert?" At one of the windows a beetle made a melancholy clicking sound, stirred to life by the quickly gathering heat. "This is the wisdom of a man who grew up in Los Alamos?"

"So I'll buy you a gun. Something exotic and ladylike—Belgian, maybe."

"Idiot." She pulled her blouse over her head without undoing the lower buttons, tossed the garment onto the couch. "Lovely fucking idiot."

Stalking into the kitchen, she banged some pots and pans around to indicate the difficulty of coffeemaking in a desert climate. Michael continued his silent inventory.

"There's only one set of tire tracks besides ours out there," he said. "A rear-wheel-drive vehicle. No motorcycles."

"I want you to sell this place on Monday. I'm through with it."

"And I have this feeling that something actually *is* missing. Something subtle but important. Only I can't for the life of me figure out what it is."

"We'll get a good price with the new well and everything, the building clearance. Anyway, *I'm* never coming out here again." She returned dressed in nothing but panties. She carried an espresso pot in one hand, two raku mugs in the other. "Never." She sat down on the couch and gave him a look, black and spiky-eyed. Her hair had gone a little which-way. "It's hoodlum heaven. We could be killed."

He smiled, not necessarily at her. "Not on your life," he said.

She threw the mugs across the room, where they shattered against stucco. "You're not even *lis*tening!" They were her mugs anyway. What's more, she already knew what was missing—though she was too angry to tell him. She drew her knees up before her on the couch and, resting her head sideways upon them, cried—briefly, bitterly, rushing through her tears. She was too hurt on his behalf to tell him.

"Laurel, love, I'm sorry." He put his arm around her. "I'm just as upset as you are, but I'm trying to think this through."

Boris sniffed at the shards of mug, then drank noisily from his water dish.

"I'll finish changing," said Laurel, wiping her eyes, starting for the stairs.

Michael caught her hand, and they looked at each other a long moment before she leaned over to kiss him.

"Yes," he said, letting her go, getting up himself. "Before we do anything else, I think we ought to drop in on our neighbor the desert rat."

He approached the fireplace as she hurried so nearly naked up the stairs. The hearth smelled strongly of mesquite smoke, a smell Michael had come, over the course of many lengthy evenings, to associate with his love for Laurel. Reaching impulsively out, he touched the place atop the stone mantel where his father's samurai sword habitually rested—the war souvenir with which Michael had been entrusted since the morning of his twenty-first birthday. His fingers read the stone's rough braille in a single unimpeded sweep.

It took Laurel and Michael a full forty minutes beneath the bald desert sun to extract from the desert rat a description of the discriminating interloper, the particulars of the green sedan he drove.

"I will be blunt, Dr. Walters," said Bloch. They were walking side by side along a forest path. There was the slightest of breezes. It was late afternoon.

"I count on it," responded Sylvia's father.

"Good." Bloch took the older man's arm near the elbow and cast his gaze over the faintly bellying leaves above—light green, dark green, light green nearly gray. "It is of course well known that you enjoy the special confidence of your President, a popular man."

"A Texan," Walters said, apparently to himself.

"Exactly." They exchanged smiles, and Bloch, giving the arm an appreciative squeeze, let it go again. "But my government is troubled by the sense that your State Department and Department of Defense do not appear to vouchsafe you a similar confidence."

Removing pipe and pouch from his jacket pocket, Walters silently congratulated Lolombela. In the course of his career he had had many an occasion to note that Africans were natural diplomats, and of the Africans with whom he had worked, Lolombela was far and away the most talented. "As you know, Heinrich, from time to time we find it expedient to encourage a little competition between State and Defense. But we do it for strictly internal reasons—management principles, if you will—and to conclude at any point that Defense conducts our foreign policy would be . . . I'm sure that's not the conclusion your government draws."

Block let a polite silence indicate that neither was it the answer to the question he had by implication raised. The light, now entering the forest so obliquely as to exaggerate with gold and shadow the forest's already considerable depths, momentarily caught the like-dappled breasts of a pair of thrushes soaring down the path ahead of the two men.

Walters fired up his pipe and pocketed the match without looking at it. "The President will decide personally the disposition of the fission bomb. His mind is not made up. A lot depends on what I relay to him concerning any . . . creative options afforded by my consultations here in Compiègne."

"So it is not a matter of the messenger bearing bad news?"

"I feel that certain of us may be able to work together."

Bloch smiled and again took the American's arm. "Good," he said. "I've been counting on it."

After an abrupt descent, the path opened up into a small clearing, a meadow of tall grass interspersed with wild carrot and toadflax. The weedy white and orange blossoms reminded Walters of the year he had courted his wife, and he was forced to reflect upon how much of what he'd done in life—hundreds of thousands of miles of clandestine travel; countless hours of negotiation and assessment; severe decisions inflecting history for better or worse—he had done, at bottom, out of love for her. It seemed surprising, supremely so. And now he would see this last, largest matter through for his daughters, whose ways seemed both strange and sad to him, whose world he wished, however fruitlessly, to make sound. He began to be glad he'd lived out most of his own life and would not know that world. He saw he had decided to retire after this last embassy.

The two men's legs made scything sounds as they strode through the meadow grass.

"Europe," Bloch was saying, "will side with the United States against the Soviets in any instance of ultimate confrontation. Yet it should also be understood that we cannot thrive tied to your apron strings. For all the differences among individual nations, there is a European commonality, just as, for all the differences among the German states, there is a German commonality, *nicht wahr?*"

Walters grunted his half-assent. It was one of Bloch's conceits that the loosely federated republics into which Germany had been divided after World War II were in fact a microcosm of Europe. Walters knew further that Bloch harbored a dream of a Europe united by Germany, perhaps of a Germany united by Bloch. In a life lived mostly among ambitious men, Walters found Bloch one of the most ambitious and engaging he had encountered.

"And of course, as you are aware," Bloch continued, "it is the understandable fear of this commonality that we are being informed of, rather than consulted about, your country's plans for this new weapon."

From the rim of his vision, Walters watched a ladybug alight upon his lapel. "I have already told you that as far as you and I are concerned at present, that need not be the case."

"Yes," said Bloch. "That is true." Both men paused, turning as one to survey the open ground they had traversed, a terrain of slant sun that had left them both slightly sweaty and light-dazed. Several swallows had descended in their wake to feed upon the insects their steps had raised.

Bloch thought: *It is time to be satisfied with what I have stirred up and to seize what I can of it on the wing; he is beginning to think I am a fool.*

Walters thought: *All my life! All my life I have worked among men to lay open at twilight my love of a woman.*

As they reentered the forest, Bloch picked a branch of dead alder from the path. He allowed it to strike successively the trunks of the living trees they passed, the way a small boy might run a ruler along a picket fence on his way home from school.

"What is it people say in America, Paul, when they feel their lives are—how should I put it?—lifted out of the ordinary, into something . . . momentarily grander?"

Walters smiled; he had begun to see where Bloch was headed. "They say, 'It's like a movie.' "

"Ah." Bloch touched his companion's shoulder, immensely pleased. "Yes. Like a movie. How wonderful." A hunter's trumpet sounded in the distance off to their left.

"But sentimental," prompted Walters.

"Yes, yes. Sentimental, I agree." Bloch peered in the direction from which the horn's treble note had come. "By the way, did you know that our esteemed colleague Mr. Lolombela has a daughter who is an actress?"

"Of course. But I've known Joseph a long time."

"Ah. Well, I myself just discovered this." Bloch shook his head ruefully as if to acknowledge a slowness on his own part. "But it occurred to me to wonder whether, extrapolating backward genealogically, it does not in fact explain Mr. Lolombela's talents as a diplomat. In some sense?"

Walters gave him the quizzical look he felt was being elicited.

"Because I would put it to you this way: that the nature of our work, its true aim—"

But he broke off suddenly as, to the right, the sound of many hoofbeats swelled to claim their ears' attention. Both men turned.

A firebreak ran through the forest where they stood, affording them an unimpeded view to either side. This open space followed the faintly womanish heave and roll of the land's contours, and running through its center, perhaps every hundred meters or so, lay like vertebrae the trunks of the trees, piled in tight fasces of seven or eight, that had lately been felled to create it. As Bloch and Walters watched, a portion of the hunt party went thundering by, jumping their horses three abreast over the logs amid a storm of turned earth and sound. They were decked out in full hunt dress—blue coats, buff britches, black boots—and there was froth upon the horses' flanks. One of the women in the party, by far the eldest among them, actually bared her teeth at the two men as she passed. She was riding sidesaddle.

"*Quelle grande dame!*" said Bloch as they rumbled out of sight. "Did you see her?"

Walters bent to remove a clod of flung earth from his trouser cuff. "Lolombela says this is the history of Europe," he offered.

"The hunt?" Bloch laughed. "Possibly so. Our friend has a unique perspective."

They resumed their stroll.

"You were speaking of the nature of our profession."

"Yes. I hope you won't think it fatuous of me, but I, too, would like to propose a metaphor. It seems to me that in an age in which people describe the sense of their deepest hopes' and dreads' imminent fulfillment as being 'like a movie,' we could ourselves do worse than to think of our own peculiar profession—and here, agreed, sentiment does not pertain—as being like *making* a movie. *Nein?*"

"Heinrich," said Walters, who frequently bestowed compliments when stalling for time, "I'm always discovering new sides to you. Unexpected facets."

"I mean something quite specific," said Bloch.

The skeleton of a small animal lay in the path—a fox, perhaps a mole—and without comment the two men parted to pass it on either side. An irregular cone of skin, dry and weathered, flared round the neck like a torn evening glove.

"We shoot our movie in many scenes, each scene in many takes. There is a shooting schedule and, if you will, a kind of budget." Bloch looked at Walters to judge the extent of his attention, then continued. "We reshoot each scene until we have a take that, within the parameters of budget and schedule, seems the best we are likely to get. We report our progress regularly to our backers. Most important, we shoot our movie not in the sequence it will ultimately be viewed but in the sequence most congenial to its making."

"To us," said Walters, "this film is imaginary; its making, real."

"Exactly."

They rounded a jagged outcropping of rock whose moss blanketing seemed to dampen the suddenly audible sound of automobile engines. Bloch was walking with his hands clasped behind him, in an attitude of savored possibility, and Walters felt a pang of the deepest fondness for this man, for what he saw in him of his own younger self. He knew also that such feeling always presaged the onset of his own most professional engagement. He was a veteran of such moments—perhaps even a connoisseur—and he had learned to save his energies. Sentiment always flooded in on him instructively just before draining finally to purest purpose: the knife at the bottom of the fountain. It was upon the certainty of this sequence—

and of the knife's eventual emergence—that he had come, both as a diplomat and as a man, most truly to depend.

"Now, let us say," Bloch went on, "that in the present matter we decide to shoot the ending first."

"A scene we have yet to rehearse."

"True. But I think I am not mistaken in sensing your agreement with Lolombela's view? That the fission bomb's enormous power can best be realized if it is never used, that its strength is fundamentally rhetorical?"

"Joseph and I agree on this. Yes."

"Good." Bloch's pace grew brisker. The throaty baying of hounds, of which both men had for some time been subliminally aware, now tattered the space ahead of them. "So leaving aside for a moment the question of a test detonation, let me say I am confident we can shoot a satisfactory ending for our film. Provided"—he thrust a finger into the air and shook it twice for emphasis—"provided that afterward we block out and shoot some middle sequences. Sequences that in the film itself would precede the ending without changing it."

Walters said: "You are proposing to guarantee Europe's support, and in return asking me to guarantee Europe the appearance of dictating the terms of that support."

"In the film of which we speak," said Bloch, "appearance is everything."

"You'll have to be more specific."

"Of course." The grade ahead sloped gently down, and the path itself, partially obstructed by a fallen tree, momentarily narrowed. There was a squirrel's nest in the branches of a birch before them, and despite the sloppiness of its weave, it reminded Walters fleetingly of a radio speaker. Bloch gestured for the older man to precede him down the path. When they were again side by side, he said: "Has your government chosen a site for the bomb's detonation?"

"Present arrangements are for a desert in the American Southwest."

"I see. And is it technically feasible to shift the apparatus to another locale?"

"Awkward, but possible, yes. There's a lot of equipment involved."

"In your opinion, would the clandestine transport and reassembly of this equipment be . . . out of the question?"

Walters blinked. "Naturally it depends on the circumstances and what we mean by 'clandestine.' " He paused. "But no, I wouldn't say out of the question." As the slight declivity into which they had descended leveled out, it dawned on Walters that he had known, from the moment of his own last surge of feeling for Bloch, that Bloch was afraid. Fear was frequently the fruit of personal ambition exercised in the name of a polity, but Bloch's case was different. It was the extent of Bloch's fear, not the man's obvious mastery of it, that was impressive.

"Europe's colonial period," Bloch continued, as if bestowing a mildly comical confidence, "is long behind us now. Our future strength must lie in a cohesiveness born of mutual self-interest, and in alliances judiciously chosen." There were flies in this part of the forest, but they were logy with autumn's imminence, and Walters's pipe smoke was sufficient to keep them at bay. "We will look increasingly to the developing nations. It is something Europe is uniquely equipped to do."

"Television has redefined colonialism," said Walters.

"I meant something else."

"So did I."

Bloch, paling perceptibly, swiped at the flies, which still posed no nuisance. "If you will forgive the impertinence, it is in your country's interest to see us succeed. A strong Europe will be a more certain ally than one resentfully dependent on the U.S., whether economically *or* militarily."

"And the fission bomb upsets this strength."

"Can you doubt it?"

Amid the sound of car engines, much closer now, they heard a woman's cry—possibly a laugh, possibly of triumph—but it was quickly carried away by the leaves that tossed the late light to shadow.

Walters reflected that it was probably time to send his President an encouraging word, using the official channels.

"Suppose, Heinrich, that we do decide to look for a new location, a better set for our film's last sequences. What would you suggest?"

They walked for some time without speaking. Bloch's smile again suggested fear to Walters, fear and exhilarated ambition in equal measure, and it seemed oddly congruent with the mingled chorus of hound cry and hoofbeats that had now grown large among the near trees.

The odor of crushed fern was very strong.

"Lolombela," said Bloch, "has expressed to me his desire for a more substantive recognition of Azania's sovereignty."

"Lolombela!" cried Walters.

"There would be advantages for all of us."

"But has he forgotten who actually controls the borders within which Azania has its rhetorical existence?"

"I've put the idea first to you. He knows nothing of it. And I assure you I've forgotten neither the white minority government nor the extent of its power in that suffering land."

"There will be radiation. We don't know how much."

"The land to which the white government attempted to relocate its black majority was poor to begin with, and the drought has made it worse. You are aware of the migrations. There are stretches of Azania that are now as empty as the American Southwest."

A butterfly of iridescent blue fluttered crazily ahead of them, and Walters found himself thinking of the hundreds of thousands of young men who had died here or nearby, astonished victims of their leaders' ambitions. "To violate the sovereign borders of another nation, even one no longer recognized by us, must be considered an act of war."

"Under ordinary circumstances, yes," Bloch replied. "But suppose I outlined to you an alternative ending to our film, one dependent on shooting the middle sequences I've already mentioned to you. And suppose that in this alternative ending the actual detonation of the fission bomb would become completely . . . unnecessary."

Bloch gave Walters a long look, then stopped to prop a foot against a fallen tree while he tied his shoe.

They walked.

"I'd want to hear about it," said Walters.

When they reached the clearing where the members of the hunt party had gathered, the stag had already been killed, an eight-point buck, inert and huge amidst its blood. Two sports cars had poked their noses into the open space, and the hunters themselves had dismounted. Their horses heaved and tossed in panic at the nearness of death. With practiced motions the swordsman was eviscerating the kill so that the hounds, barking now in frenzied anticipation, might receive their traditional reward of entrails.

Medium shot of the downed stag, its head twisted to an unnatural angle by the prop of its antlers against the forest floor.

Close-up of its head, bathed in sunlight.

Extreme close-up, this close, a last thing: its eye, so lately live that the downing sun struck from it a single point of clear fire that grew gradually mineral in its flash until it filled one second of sight *completely*. No one moved.

Then everyone did.

Chentula was wearing Nomanzi's Walkman, and to communicate with him it was necessary to shout.

"I would like to try to roller-skate one time," Nomanzi communicated, observing with pleasure the musculature of the men and women gliding expertly by her on either side.

"You would like to fry *what*?" shouted Chentula in English. Half of the way he walked now was a little dance, and instead of answering, Nomanzi skipped ahead a few steps, whirled around, and with the flats of her hands beat the pavement before him, praising the dance. Chentula laughed and danced some more. Beside him, Johnny looked pointedly over his shoulder, as he had been doing ever since they'd left the house.

"Johnny, your face and neck are taking too much sun," she said, tucking a hand briefly between his belt and shirt at the back. "We must buy you a hat."

All three of them understood that it didn't really matter if they were being followed. In a crowd like this, there was no point in thinking about it.

Johnny decided upon an oversize cowboy hat in straw, paying for it with some of the American money the record company had given him. In the shade of the hat's brim he thought about all the things people did because of their skin.

" 'I cried me some rivers of tears,' " sang Chentula from between the earphones' acrylic sponges. He closed his eyes and executed a full turn as they walked.

The seaside air was dazzlingly bright.

Sometimes when Nomanzi dreamed she appeared to herself as the character she played on the TV series. This way of seeing herself irritated her because of its possibly unprofessional overtones, but it was also true that she was famous among the Xhosa of Southern Africa, the only tribe the Zulu had failed to conquer in the long period before the arrival of the Europeans, and she had come to understand that even the most sophisticated of her people expected her to resemble more than not the half-creature she played. At first she had been disappointed by this failure to appreciate the artfulness of her acting, but then she saw she had lent herself to a need.

Johnny said: "All the cowboy movies I saw as a boy." It was not a clear statement, but Nomanzi saw he was enjoying the hat. He was also rubbing one of his own overdeveloped biceps appreciatively.

"You look like the man on the beer commercial at home," she said. Then, switching to Xhosa: " 'After a long day on the veldt . . .' "

" 'I work up a man's thirst,' " finished Johnny, also in Xhosa. According to the laws of their country, it was all right for a white to appear on TV2, the black channel, if he spoke exclusively in the tongue of that particular broadcast—Zulu, Xhosa, Tswana, Sotho, Venda. Johnny put his arm around Nomanzi's waist.

Ahead of them there was applause, then cheering. Chentula raised his arms to the sky and did a little backward-forward step. The crowd before them parted.

A golden-skinned girl of no more than seventeen, her ponytail flying out behind her like a blond pennant, was skating up the oceanwalk at a terrific speed, naked except for a pair of black nylon running shorts. Thirty yards behind her, pedaling furiously and blowing a whistle, a mustached man on a bicycle was in close pursuit. He wore navy shorts, running shoes, a billed hat; only the gun at his waist identified him clearly as a policeman. In their wake, the crowd quickly closed.

Chentula removed his headphones to look. "The natives," Johnny said in deliberately deep-voiced English, "are restless."

The previous night's dispute over the visas had remained unsettled, suspended first by Sylvia's liquid presence in the kitchen, then by the rooftop nakedness they'd together undertaken, there by where the traffic was . . .

Where Chentula had seen his half-sister discreetly remove a tampon before easing into the Jacuzzi's warm waters, and had thought: *The fruit of Africa, my land.*

Where Johnny had seen, by the light of his own skin, inflamed just today by the sun, that the naked women were beautiful, and had thought: *Too much my fault, this quarrel.*

And where Nomanzi, easing into the tub's water, had seen what the two men were thinking and had thought: *I love these men, and tomorrow, on their day off and mine, we will go down by the ocean, the only place people walk in this city of cars, and I know right now we will have a day of peace.*

She stopped by the display board of a sidewalk vendor and asked to examine a lilac-dyed lizard belt, shining in the light as if wet.

"Is it really lizard skin?" she asked the vendor, a swarthy man who wore a bandanna over his head like a pirate.

"No," he said, handing it to her.

Chentula flipped the cassette and resumed his musical communion. Nomanzi held the belt at arm's length and let it unfurl. Johnny, watching, remembered a dream.

Lately, when Nomanzi entered his dreams, she appeared to him as the character she played on "Ilulwane"—a clever girl making up for country ignorance at every chance. In last night's dream—and this is why he remembered it now—she had held a thin sword out to him exactly as she was now holding the lizard belt that was not lizard. He had accepted it, had turned it upright, and somehow had understood that the sword was Japanese. (In his country, the Japanese were classified as whites, the Chinese as colored.) "What hour is it?" Nomanzi the half-creature had asked him, and looking at his watch, which he then remembered to be Japanese, he had answered, "Eight-sixteen," which he had then remembered to be the time at which it had stopped.

NOMANZI/ILULWANE [*Singing*]:

> *Lomtana akule*
> *Abemdala apike into azaziyo*
> (May this child grow.
> When it is old may it deny the thing it knows.)

JOHNNY [*Dreaming*]: But it can't deny that, don't you see? [*Looking down, realizing it is not a sword he is holding but his own cock, hugely erect and classified as white*] Morning is already here.

NOMANZI/ILULWANE [*Laughing*]: Oh, women have cleverness! It is in our skin, which is beautiful, beautiful. Night and morning. No ugliness anywhere! [*Drawing him toward her by his cock*] See how long it is!

The belt vendor explained that that was the style, that the belt was supposed to be draped twice around the waist.

"Well, so what do you think?" she asked Johnny and Chentula, when the belt hung properly furled around her African both sides. But even as she displayed herself to the two men, smiling and turning a quick pirouette, it was obvious she would buy the belt. It was the perfect shade of lilac.

Chentula's most secret, guilty wish: to attain through music, or the feelings he had when playing music, to titled political power in his country—his country as it would be transformed in his lifetime.

Johnny's most secret, guilty wish: (partially attained, but twice transformed by what he knew to be its pettiness): to own and eventually operate, in the defense of his country as it would be transformed and placed past the power of his race in his lifetime, a .45 caliber Ingram MAC-10, modified to the status of submachine gun, with silencer, so that it would fire 1,200 rounds a minute. He kept this weapon under the floorboards of his home.

Nomanzi's most secret, guilty wish: to begin and lead a dance—sometimes she thought of it as a procession—in which she and the beauty of her movements would be the center of everyone's attention. In these movements she would lead everyone out of a dry little dell to a stopping place that, when the last follower stopped, neat, quick, and very near, would be for everyone, in a world of misery and hope, a home.

Sometimes Nomanzi dreamed about this dance.

Three children ran past, holding plastic bags that bulged with water as clear as the lens of an eye, each bag containing at its center a stupidly bewildered goldfish with its own pair of unblinking eyes.

"How did you like my friend Sylvia?" Nomanzi asked. "She is pretty, I think, with her eyes and voice."

"I didn't notice her eyes," said Johnny, who did not wish to remember that in his dream Nomanzi, coyly refusing him, had led him instead to Sylvia's bedside.

"Yeah, yéah-yeah, yeah-yéah-yeah; yéah-yeah," sang Chentula. He had yesterday purchased a pair of golden-glazed sunglasses, which, all things considered, became him.

"So then you *know* she's pretty," said Nomanzi, laughing. "You looked at all the rest." When Johnny blushed, she laughed some more. "Pretty for a white woman, eh?" And kissed him passingly— she knew it was pushing the flirtation, but this was America—on the cheek.

"She handles herself well," said Johnny. "Yes."

The motionless man, whom they might have seen thirty strides earlier had the traffic on Ocean Front Walk and among the three of them not been so distracting, stood elegantly poised atop his stack of grocery crates, perfect in his minstrel garb, oblivious of all that passed beneath him.

Chentula removed his headphones in honor of this sight: a black man whose parody of dignity achieved a kind of universal rebuke that restored dignity to its deepest ground. He glanced at the polo-shirted guardians on either side. He read aloud the hand-lettered sign.

"What is it that this means?" he asked Nomanzi, turning fully to her. Johnny peered into the shoebox that held up the sign; it was filled with much-handled money in varying denominations.

" 'Immobility Artist'?" said Nomanzi. "Well, he is a street per-former, someone with an act." Shielding her gaze from the sun, she looked up at him. "His act is he doesn't move. At all. Everything else does, but not him."

The three of them looked up at the man who didn't move at all.

Chentula said: "We bring you greetings from Africa, our land." He paused with some confusion. "Possibly he does not speak either?" he asked Nomanzi. "To speak, he would have to move, I think." Chentula aligned his own body with what he had to say, as if the situation required especially attentive address. "So I tell you this: There are black people everywhere, singing the songs of our peoples and making our way. History will be with us, if we are with history. It is good to see you say what you say with your . . . dance. This is a dance, I think. We praise this dance; it is American." Chentula paused, but his pause was no longer one of confusion.

The earphones chattered on at his collarbone like tree frogs.

Someone tapped Nomanzi on the waist. Turning, she discovered a white man in a wheelchair looking up at her. She was puzzled less by the man's actual presence—he had a sunburn, he wore fatigues, he was long unshaven—than by the realization that during the past minute she had, for the first time in a very long time, completely forgotten about white people.

"Know who that guy really is?"

Nomanzi glanced a bit guiltily at Johnny before following the man's gaze back up to the Immobility Artist.

"He used to be the best damn fighter pilot in the whole U.S. Navy. Could fly an F-4 Phantom up his own ass at twenty thousand feet and sing like an angel the whole time. That's how he got that name. But he's retired now."

"What name?" said Johnny, who had sensed Nomanzi's emotional withdrawal.

Looking at Johnny's hat with some distaste, the white man ran the back of his hand over his mouth. "People still call him Angel—like in radar. But he's, you know, retired now." The man looked at each of the three in turn, nodding to himself. "Okay," he said at last. "Have a nice day." And wheeled off.

Momentarily embarrassed, Nomanzi cast her eyes down.

Chentula wanted to know what an angel-like-in-radar was.

"When there's a blip on the radar screen but nothing is really out there, I think," Johnny explained in a mixture of English and Xhosa.

A dog slept peacefully in the shadow cast by the man who didn't move at all.

.   .   .

Wheeling down out of the canyon's face, Sylvia made the fullest possible use of her brand-new tires, taking a small but consoling pleasure in their grip, and in the imperative they delivered to drive just a bit faster than usual. She had not enjoyed the band she had driven up to hear—she had made the trek as a favor for a friend of hers in the recording industry—and she had most especially not enjoyed the house in which they had played: a place without a single piece of furniture but equipped with improbably perfect sound insulation: egg crates and pink fiberglass staple-gunned to the walls.

It always worried her when she realized she was in her profession for reasons that had little to do with its ostensible substance. The insight had the effect of making her thirsty.

But the perfection of the day—all of this is true—was such that nearly all the inhabitants of the city were having second thoughts about one thing or another, although in this perfection, its absolute invitation, the day resembled many others.

Sylvia pulled into a gas station, bypassing the pumps in favor of a machine that dispensed carbonated beverages. When she cut the engine, she could hear the driver of the poison-green roadster that had turned into the station right behind her exchanging pleasantries with the attendant.

DRIVER: Hey, Carlos. What you doin' out here in the elements?
ATTENDANT [*Making no move to get out of the canvas beach chair in which, eyes closed, he lay peacefully slung*]: Is no fuckin' elements out here, man. This is fuckin' L.A. No elements, no weather, no nothin'. So fuck you.

Sylvia put two quarters in the machine and bought a Stripe. For a moment, the sight of the green-and-white-striped soft drink, vividly layered in its transparent plastic can, threatened to plunge her into despair—but the moment passed, and she popped the top. Carbonation was exactly what she needed.

A dirt path straggled out behind the gas station, through a puny growth of ponderosa, and Sylvia—always restless—found herself propelled precipitously down it, quenching her thirst.

Which is how she arrived, almost without realizing it, at what passed for the Los Angeles River bank—a dusty walkway, little walked upon, bordered at its far edge by a cyclone fence and below, in a sleeve of concrete, by the river itself: glassy without depth here, wide without discernible flow; most of its movement was underground, elsewhere.

She remembered: Take me to the river; drop me in the water. Finishing the soda, she had a sneaking impulse to toss the can into the river. *But enough jetsam,* she thought, and strolled impulsively on.

In the river's sparseness, at the far edge of its turn, a small deposit of silt had left a margin upon which stood a crew of college students. They were shooting a film with a small-format camera, and they were having trouble with the boom shadow. The girl who seemed to be the principal actress stood in an attitude of disgruntlement, holding under one arm a life-size photo cutout of herself in a swimsuit.

"So just shoot it from the other direction," she was saying. "I mean, it's not exactly a raging torrent." She turned her back on the others and in so doing caught sight of Sylvia, who gave her a sympathetic little wave. The girl smiled self-mockingly and shrugged.

Kristen's phone call, which had seemed reassuring enough the night before, had over the course of the morning settled badly with Sylvia, not because she disbelieved her sister—on the contrary, both the episode in the garage and the romantic flight to Vermont seemed perfectly in character for Kristen. Still, what had been left in the phone call's wake was the diamond earring, supernumerary and nearly perfect, beginning even in Sylvia's dreams to spin out scenarios, contradictory, complementary, that her daytime imagination had seized all the more firmly—prolific anecdotes of origin and end, molecular narratives to which she felt herself kin, as someone saved, as someone suddenly extra to a pair, as someone who had all her life been asked (and who in childhood had frequently passed the question on to her parents), "Where do *you* come from?"

On the drive down out of the canyon she had remembered reading that people's fascination with diamonds had its origin in the infant's alertness to the eye of the nursing mother.

"Okay," said the young man in the river gully, looking up from the camera with an awkwardness that loosed the tails of his aggressively patterned shirt. "So the sun is not on our side today. So what. This is not a union production. This is us."

"I mean, can't we matte-screen the river in later or something?" said the actress. Sensing she was about to get her way, she peered into a hand mirror, trying to decide whether to have a makeup crisis or not.

Sylvia did not flinch when the hand mirror's flash found her own unprotected eye for part of a second and left the sun's temporary trace upon her retina.

In one version, the diamond had been smuggled out of the mining compound by carrier pigeon, thus buying its possessor, a migrant Xhosa from the Ciskei, passage across the Limpopo to relative freedom. In another, it had been bought by a Memphis heiress, a self-bestowed gift of celebration prior to her trip down the Mississippi, to New Orleans, where she discovered her lover loving the maid and consequently fled to California to buy and occupy the house that Sylvia in her turn was to buy, and occupy, and divorce in, and flee for her life from, in that order.

Sylvia bent to take a pebble from her sandal: sharp, small pain of the lively flesh. And because she'd tied her hair back that morning, she at the same moment saw, coming at her from the direction that cut her off from her car, the scissoring khaki-clothed legs of the man whose steps she for some reason was unable to hear. He had a crew cut, a mustache; he wore a slightly wilted safari shirt.

Affecting a casual stroll, she turned away from him.

The film crew was near enough by.

It was always possible to run.

Fear was a feeling that stunned the *heart*. That this was so stunned her doubly, doubled her heartbeat and breath, halved her pace.

She turned.

And it came to her in a rush that this was what she had wanted. To face down and eat the distance that her voice created nightly on the radio. On the air.

She began, but slowly, to walk toward the man who apparently wished to trouble her life.

She found his gaze with her own, though he was still twenty-five meters away. His eyes were an oddly familiar blue-gray. She'd seen the color before. Before she'd ever seen him.

She dropped the soft-drink can but continued to walk.

He did not appear to be carrying a weapon. She wondered if she really knew anything at all about the kinds of weapons people might conceal.

Her voice said: "I think you've been looking for me."

He said: "Dear girl, I've found you."

That simply, they stood before each other, down by the river.

A surprising degree of intimacy had been established in the moment of her approach. *Matters were in this condition when—*

When Sylvia saw that she did not enjoy looking at the part of this man's face above his mustache because it seemed too familiar, and consequently she found herself addressing his mouth.

"What makes you think I'm not going to turn you over to the cops, mister?"

He laughed almost gently. "You can't," he said.

"I can't," she repeated. "Why not, I wonder."

"Because I *am* the cops, in a manner of speaking."

"I see," answered Sylvia, realizing she'd known it would have to be something like that. Her fear had not diminished, but her stunned heart insisted on speech. "Okay. Right. You harass me at work every night, you slash my tires, you follow me and photograph me and do me I-don't-even-want-to-know what other kinds of nastiness." The man smiled, almost apologetically to Sylvia. "On top of which," she continued, "you use weirdly un-American expressions like 'dear girl' and 'in a manner of speaking.' So." She thumbed the strap of her shoulder bag a bit more securely back up her collarbone's dip. "Well, see, I just can't help wanting to know what the point is."

"The point," said the man, not unkindly, "was to get your attention." Sylvia formed a look of disgusted impatience, but he cut her off before she could speak. "We thought it might be the fastest way to deal with . . . the particular situation we're concerned with. But now we've changed our minds."

" 'We.' " Sylvia looked quickly around her. In the far distance, out toward the desert, she could see the city's stolen water supply gushing down aerating spillways in an extremely stylized way. The man himself appeared to be alone.

"I use the word in its official sense," he said. "For the time being."

"What else," said Sylvia, attempting to inject a bored note into the terror she was experiencing as she watched this man who called himself "we" reach, staring at her all the while, slowly into his pocket. *I don't even have any place to be kidnapped from,* she wanted to tell him before she had to look at any weapons. But at the same time she was seized by the thought that these were very possibly the last moments of her life, and the notion made her willfully speechless. She was outraged that she might have to die without being given the chance, after so much airtime verbiage and off-the-record secret language, to say what she meant. So, in her anger and terror, it happened that she took one last step toward her tormentor exactly at the instant that he produced, not a pistol, but two one-hundred-dollar bills.

She stood before him stupidly. "What's that?"

"For the tires."

I'm having my second crazy thought, she thought.

Yet when she glanced down at the film crew in the riverbed, she could not avoid the impression that, because of the angle, the camera's field might well include her, the man, the money, the moment.

She stepped rapidly back, shaking her head in an exaggerated fashion.

"You think I'm trying to set you up?" he asked. "I'm not."

"I don't know what you're trying, and I don't know who you are." She forced herself to study his face, brow, hairline. "I know I've seen you before. Before all this, I mean." She knew also that she lied, lied as she said those words, because it wasn't *he* she'd seen before, but the features above his mouth, and in a place so near to her life that she couldn't bring herself to believe it.

The flesh beside the man's eyes crinkled, as he pushed the money back into his pocket's depths, audibly crinkling the fresh paper, collapsing between him and Sylvia its agreed-upon value.

"You have," he said. "You have seen me before. But you were much too young to remember."

"No!" she answered. Her hands wanted to cover her ears. Her ears wanted to cover the earth.

"I'm your father's half-brother," said the man, dropping his hands to his sides. "I'm William."

"No! He's dead. You're not him." She turned toward the river and saw, in her distraction, that the camera was really paying them no attention at all. After all. Before God.

"I know. William died. Where did William die?"

"Leave me alone."

"William died in a union dispute on a highway in Oklahoma. He was an organizer, a teamsters official, and he was shot in the chest with a thirty-aught-six when you were three, wasn't he?"

"I hate you."

"But it wasn't really that way. That was the story."

"Don't tell *me* the *story!*"

"Because things were a lot sleazier than that. William was a government informant, a spy. And when he realized the union was onto him, he called in his debts. You ever do that, call in your debts?"

"I'm not hearing this."

"I called in my debts. I told Washington to get me out of it. I wanted to *live*, and they knew they owed me. And they had to think about Paul, your father."

"He has no part in this!"

"No, he has no part in this. Except that one: they had to think about him.

"So they relocated me. That's the expression: 'relocate.' And they planted the story in the press; they took care of all the details, and I lived." He paused, as if to study her. "Live was all I knew—sometimes it's like that. Where and how don't matter when it's like that."

"What do you want from me? Why are you doing this?"

"Well, to begin with, I'd like you to believe me."

"Why?" She whirled upon him. "Something in it for you?"

He hesitated. "There's something in it for *all* of us." Turned toward the river himself. "I can't tell you how literally I mean that." And he seemed then for a moment half-convincingly half-oblivious of her.

"What? Where did you hear that? *Where?*" She actually ran him up against the fence.

"I didn't *hear* it," said the man. "I just said it." He appeared genuinely confused. "Come on, calm down now. Christ."

"That's right. I'll calm down. I'll calm down. Sure. Okay." She fumed, walked around a little. For a while, she tried to remember natural environments she had enjoyed as a child.

"Let's say you believe I'm William," said the man after a time.

"Okay." She nodded. "Fine. Then what?"

"Let's say Washington has called in its debts on me."

"On *you!*" She turned toward him, using her voice and eyes to their fullest effect. "So it *is* about my father."

"The things that are being negotiated . . ."

"You *did* hear that phone call!"

"I heard nothing." He appeared embarrassed. "I'm told only what I'm told." Wrapped himself with his arms. "That's the problem with debts, right? You don't get to call the shots."

She grimaced. "Like a thirty-aught-six-in-the-chest kind of shot, huh?"

"Yeah." He relaxed a little. "Like that."

"So. Getting back to the point. What do you want from me?"

They were both peering now through the fence at the river, a broken sheet of water headed for the sea. The actress with the cutout was wading out into it, swearing prettily. The camera was off duty.

"I'd like," said the supernumerary William, "for you to use your influence with your dad."

"My *influence?*" Despite herself, she laughed. "I guess you guys aren't what you used to be, are you?"

He shrugged. "Who is?"

She threw him a look more troubled than angry. "What *is* it I'm supposed to really want?"

"We know you know he's not in Geneva. We know you know what's really being negotiated. All we ask is that you think it through for yourself. Concerted opinion has it that a—what shall I call it?— demonstration of this thing could bring an end to war in our time. It just might put the body-bag people out of business, okay? We want you to have some idea of the stakes."

"I have some idea of the stakes," she said. "I also have some idea that they don't sic people like you on people like me just to recruit ambassadorial advisers."

From the freeway, faintly audible but audibly beyond the legal speed limit, the first few bars of "The Mexican Hat Dance" rang out—once, twice, then the third time swallowed in midphrase by traffic's semipurposeful hum.

"Cigarette?" said William, taking a pack from one of his unnecessarily abundant pockets.

"I don't smoke," said Sylvia, believing it for a moment.

William said, "I was her second son."

"What?" said Sylvia. She was thinking of the dream she'd had that night at Zack's, of the flashing second sun that had appeared in her dream's sky, there to put a freeze-frame on everything but the river, which was not a line.

"Oh," said Sylvia. "My grandmother, you mean." She turned impatiently from him. "You know I don't believe you. Everybody knows William is dead."

"You don't have any idea how much depends on what you, Sylvia, believe. In something like this."

"Right, right. Sure. And you can't tell me how literally you mean that." The urge to whirl around and strike him was so strong in her that she was able to refrain only by concentrating her gaze upon the increasingly disobliged actress, who was wading at the director's instruction through the thin waters below, cardboard twin still in hand.

"You're liable to hear and see a lot of things over the next few weeks," William went on. "You may be approached by parties less subtle than myself. Or"—and at this his mouth drew itself taut in a twitch of distaste—"for that matter, more subtle than myself. One opinion might be that you already have been."

"Fuck you," she said without turning around.

He shrugged. "I'm sorry I seem crude to you. It's not what I'd choose either, eh?"

And now, in what felt repugnantly to her like the widest, most elegantly cinematic slow motion, she wheeled round again to face him, the world passing in half an arc before her finely focused eyes. "You say you were relocated, 'William.' *Uncle* William." She peered into his familiar irises, pupils, hope-burned retinas. "*Where* were you relocated?"

William did not blink. He said: "*Lomtana akule / Abemdala apike into azaziyo.*"

She began immediately to walk away.

"Okay," said the concrete-riverbed director. "Mark."

The actress stopped. Sylvia stopped.

William said: "Not that it's really your business, but I'm trying to make up for all that now. It's more than a second chance; everything's been, well, in its way, reinvented. And this time I'm taking the long view." He exhaled smoke, crushed out the butt. "I know all about the sword outwearing the sheath, but Paul . . . Paul was always better at the long view than me."

Sylvia understood that, with every passing moment, there were fewer and fewer things she could really walk away from. So beneath the sun's seeing sky, she walked. But so also, not ten paces on, she stopped, turning one last time, and despite herself, half toward her tormentor.

"You know," she said, "if you really were William . . . I mean, if William really were alive . . ." She felt herself at nil, utterly without design, as if everything had indeed been reinvented. "Well, that'd be really disruptive, see. Because then I'd have to hate him even more"—she drew breath—"even more than I hate you."

The man smiled at her in a way that she thought at first was meant to be intimidating, but after staring at him for some time she was no longer certain what the expression was intended to communicate.

"But you're okay, then, aren't you?" said the man. "I'm dead."

When she slid back behind the wheel of her car she found his card tipped into the speedometer's casing.

"**C**an't we do something about these poopy ghosts?" said one of the production assistants, fiddling with a video monitor.

" 'Poopy'?" said someone else. "Christ. Don't we have child labor laws in this state?"

"Sure," said someone else. "You have to *be* a child to work here."

"Ready with those fog machines?"

"Ten-four on fog."

"Strobe One, could you move about two feet closer? I'm going to need a little variation here."

"Got you. That okay?"

"Fine, fine. Super." Michael eased a lever forward, and the dolly on which he lay supine began rolling soundlessly across the floor, beneath the tablelike strip of glass suspended above him. Two thirds of the way down its length, he stopped. He turned red. The whole crew was laughing.

"Very funny, Jabez." Through the camera, through a break in the clouds, Michael was looking at the face of Dick-the-director, decked out in the voluminous gray locks and beard of God, if God were a short-tempered guy from New Jersey.

"How many times do I have to tell you people, this is an agnostic picture." Michael was laughing despite himself. He was still at odds with Dick-the-director, who was elsewhere, not present, dealing, no doubt, with the animate aspects of the enterprise. "What we believe in on this picture is—"

"Lawyers," said someone else.

A second wave of laughter broke over the studio. Jabez removed the doctored photograph of Dick from the sky and restored the cotton cloud cover.

"Now I know why Jabez made me close the set,"Michael offered. "Guy's too polite to humiliate me in front of strangers." He finished his glide down the sky's length, then removed himself from the dolly. A union cameraman took his place.

"Okay, guys," Michael said, as the cameraman rode the dolly smoothly back to its original spot. "Now we make movies."

He squatted in front of a monitor. "Fog people, gimme fog." He peered into a video monitor for the better part of a minute. "Yeah. Okay. Good." He clapped his hands a couple of times like a football coach. "Lights to level."

The air turned silver-green, then pewter-green. "Level."

"Ready on camera?"

"Ready."

"Well, shit, then." Michael's voice went soft as the promise of love. "Let's do it."

And the heavens opened.

"Don't they smell heavenly?" Reaching into the back of her shop's station wagon, Laurel off-loaded a great gorgeous mess of cut verbena, white and pink. "Really this is the part I like best." She rolled the bunched flowers into Nomanzi's open arms, black and black and pale, and she stared at the array. "Once I came back from the market with a load of jasmine for a party and, no kidding, I really had to pull over to catch my breath." Standing before the shop in the dawn light, she sorted through her keys. "I was ready to pass out; God, I could have wrecked the car." She grimaced. "Now, *that* would've been a weird way to go."

The two women had been downtown at the wholesale flower market since shortly after its three A.M. opening.

"But it's why perfume is so expensive, I always think." Nomanzi buried her nose briefly in the verbena. "Because you remember it so long? And the flowers it comes from, d'you know, they're so much more, but gone in a week."

"I guess so. Sure."

They walked together to the storefront. A newspaper lay before it like a doormat. Laurel lifted the key toward the lock, her hand trembling.

NEWSPAPER: German Republics Announce Trade Embargo Against White South Africa; Azanian Leaders to Meet with German Industrialists

LAUREL [*Embarrassed, fumbling at the lock*]: Nomanzi, could you . . .

NEWSPAPER: 27 Azanians Killed in Water Rights Clashes

Laurel pressed the key into Nomanzi's palm, her own hand still shaking enough to make the transfer difficult.

"Oh, yes. I'm sorry. Here, I'll just—"

"I'll get the orchids," said Laurel, turning quickly back toward the car, hiding her embarrassment.

When she returned, with her arms full of scentless cymbidiums, oranda-vandas, cattleyas, Nomanzi had already unlocked the shop and turned on all the lights. It was a white and spotless place, with many surfaces and running water. Laurel laid the orchids on the counter.

"Boy oh boy." She ran the rebellious hand through her liquid black hair. "You must think I'm a real wackadoozie, huh?"

It was not a term Nomanzi had encountered before. "Oh, but, Laurel, with all the pots of coffee we had downtown, I'm s'prised we both don't have Saint Vitus's dance." She removed a vase from the shelf and began to fill it with water for the verbena. "Really, I feel like a whole chorus line of it myself." In her mind's eye she again saw the Immobility Artist, and she smiled. "How does that song go?" Holding another vase to the tap, she danced with her hips and sang with her lips. " 'Twitch and shout / Baby, twitch and shout.' " She moved like the ropy tap water. " 'Twitch a little closer now. . . .' "

Laurel shook her head and made a fluttering attempt to begin sorting out the sprays of orchid. "No, but I mean, when I can't even unlock my own place . . ."

And they both saw she really meant: I want to tell you what happened to me.

Nomanzi fell still.

"Oh, I don't know. . . ." Tossing a cymbidium back onto the heap. "It's stupid, probably. But Michael, my fiancé?"

Nomanzi nodded.

"He and I are building this house out in the desert, and when we went out there yesterday, the place had been broken into."

Walking over to one of the shop's three glass-faced refrigerators, she peered at the thermometer, then gave the thermostat a slight forward twist. "I guess I should be grateful there wasn't any damage, right? And nothing stolen except this Japanese sword that used to belong to Michael's father—lots of sentimental value, but hey, we can live with that. It's just—"

Something had shifted slightly in Nomanzi's bearing—a squaring perhaps of her negligently held hips, or a faintly more angular bend of her elbows at the paler outcome of her forearms—and Laurel, without quite realizing it, was encouraged by the display.

"It's just the violation. That we were *meant* to notice. He drank our beer, he played solitaire with our cards. Intimidation was the point. Like he wanted to say he'd be back, you know?"

"Did you call the police?"

"Sheriff. Out there it's a sheriff. Just to give you some idea."

"Idea?"

"Of the isolation." Laurel, moving back across the room, caught a glimpse of herself in the stainless-steel side of one of the refrigerators and, with an already calmer hand, automatically readjusted her hair. "Sure, we called the sheriff. But what are we supposed to say? The boogy-man came and took our sword when we weren't looking?"

A smile shot across Nomanzi's face.

"Oh, shit, I'm sorry. That's racist, isn't it?" Laurel struck herself lightly on the brow. "Great, Laurel. Just great: 'boogy-man.' "

Nomanzi struggled briefly with her own amusement. "No, no. Please don't apologize. It's—" Then matched her laugh with half a little knee bend. "I must tell you about my country sometime."

"I guess it's pretty different there."

"It's pretty different. In some ways." Collecting herself, Nomanzi began to clip the stem ends from the verbena. "But this man you're talking about—you did not even see him?"

"No. Which is all to the good, I guess." She allowed her glance to drift proprietarily around the shop. "But still, the way he filled the place; his presence: I kept wondering what he'd done there, what he'd seen. It was like having a ghost in the house. I changed the bedsheets. I touched the toothbrushes to see if they were wet. All the dishes in the dishrack—I washed them again. It was pitiful."

Outside, trash-eating trucks ranged up and down the boulevards, loosing Mesozoic yowls.

"It's a shame you didn't get a license plate number at least. Something for the sheriff."

"Our nearest neighbor is a rabbit farmer—one of those great old desert guys?—and he says he saw the car." Laurel began sorting the orchids in earnest. "There was mud or something all over the license plates."

"Mud?"

"It was a green Phoenix sedan, late model. The sheriff just laughed. 'Near to ten thousand of those in this county alone'—that's what he said."

"Police. They are the same everywhere." Nomanzi wielded the garden shears with false attention. "And there was no description of the driver, then, either."

"Ha! *He* looked like a hundred thousand other guys: crew cut, mustache, middle-aged but healthy-looking." Laurel sighted along the shelves for the vases she wanted, then levered them off their perches with her fingertips, catching them one by one in her arms. "I'll get over it, I guess. It's just that's why I was so weird with the key just now."

Nomanzi nodded.

"So anyway, that's how I do it: I hit the market Monday, Wednesday, and Friday mornings. Usually I'll go myself, but I may ask you to come along from time to time."

Nomanzi nodded. She divided the pink verbena into two large bunches and put them in the vases she had filled. "I'll go get the rest of the flowers out of the car?"

"Great. Thanks." Laurel was running a length of hose from the sink into an elaborate aluminum watering can on the floor. Nomanzi, on her way out, heard the water strike an elastic sliding note from the bottom of the can, then quickly swallow the note with its own weight.

She would, she realized, have to move faster than she had planned. Surveillance was making too much a point of itself.

The scent of the flowers in the car was very strong, and Nomanzi stood for a moment, breathing the sweetness. Then she leaned in over the car's rear gate and, reaching out with both arms, gathered the flowers to her breast. The shop behind her blazed with light. She turned to look at it through the flowers.

Clematis, pyracantha, cosmos.

"What do I *think*?" repeated Sylvia, tossing the script back onto the station manager's desk. "I think it's a cosmically bad idea. We're a *radio* station, right? Voice, music, invisible presence."

George looked pained. "It's a sixty-second video, Sylvie. One minute U.S. time." He popped a vitamin capsule. "You'd appear in maybe eighteen or twenty seconds of it."

"No. As in 'See my agent.' " She lit a cigarette. "Besides, aren't you the guy who believes in everybody making up his own picture? Don't I recall something about that being the beauty of radio as a medium?"

Baring his teeth in a rictus of discomfort, George with one finger drew the collar of his polo shirt away from his neck, as if the heat had become suddenly oppressive.

"Aha. Certain pressures."

"From certain quarters. I know you know how it is." He reached out for the acrylic hand-grip exerciser that lay upon his desk and began to work it absently, first with one hand, then with the other. "Which is why I think you ought to reconsider."

Sylvia was beginning to think she did know how it was. "George." She leaned forward to still his restless hand with her own. "Don't bullshit me. This is more than just a promo for the station, isn't it?"

The station's voice, piped into the office at a woman's near whisper, sang a few things about somebody's weather.

George disengaged himself and walked across his office to the water cooler. "Okay, look." He drew himself a cool drink and spilled a cool half of it on the carpet. "Don't ask me why it is, but you're the one person I deal with in this town who actually refuses to admit she's a star."

Sylvia sighed and rolled her eyes at him. "Heaven only knows how I could be so forgetful."

"*And* who really needs someone to tell her she's just operating in about second gear, with one foot on the brake to boot."

"I'm a defensive driver, George. You know that. Now please: just make your pitch."

He walked back over to his desk and stood with his hands upon his chairback. "Well, it's sudden but obvious; I'd like to say I saw it coming, but I didn't. The money boys have decided they want a cable TV outlet too—some visuals to go with the station. That way we could break a potential hit eight ways from sundown—run the video, hold the record; do it the other way around, anything. It could really open things up, I have to admit."

"So this promo is more like a screen test."

"No one thinks you need one."

"Good. We agree. I don't want anything to do with it." She put out the cigarette, half-smoked. "Do you?"

The station's voice, struck by the hour, began reciting *sotto voce* the facts of the day: German trade embargo against white South Africa; industrialists to meet with, etc.; twenty-seven fatalities in, etc., etc. Weather. Sports. Things you must buy.

George sat on the side of his desk. "Look, I'm not going to twist your arm, but this is the point in the conversation where I'm supposed to mention money."

"I thought that might come up."

"We're talking in the neighborhood of a forty-five-percent salary increase, details and benefits negotiable. That'd be if you switched to the prime-time video slot, five nights a week."

Sylvia tried to think about money, but instead, in her mind's eye, she kept seeing yesterday's actress, wading out into the river with a photo duplicate of herself under her arm. "George, if I wanted to be an actress, do you think I'd be *here*?"

"This has nothing to do with being an actress. All this is, is filling out the picture. Letting in your style, your presence." He looked her over. "Like that with the earrings, okay? I notice it. They don't match."

Sylvia looked shyly down. The earring business was something she'd done without really thinking about it: an onyx drop on the left, the unaccounted-for diamond stud on the right.

"You go on-camera like that, and in a week every kid in L.A. will be mixing her earrings. I guarantee it."

"Dearest George, I already told you: voice, music, invisible presence." His mention of the earring had made her self-conscious. "It's hard to believe, I know, but I'm not really interested in wielding unnatural fashion influence over my market share."

"Okay, sweetheart, okay. I got that. But I haven't heard you say you're not interested in the money."

George kept a couch in his office for the usual reasons, and on the table next to it were flowers. Asters. Sylvia tried to remember the motto of the day school she'd briefly attended in Washington, but all she could come up with was *Ad astra per asters*. The flowers were newly arrived, the wrapping paper still crumpled on the couch, and Sylvia calculated how she might contrive to read the accompanying card on her way out.

"Money," said George, "should always be of some consideration in these matters." He gave her a soulful look. "I speak to you now not as your boss but as your spiritual adviser."

Sylvia smiled. "I had no idea you were so deep."

"It's unpredictable." He shrugged. "I'll be going along normally, and suddenly—boom—*profondeurs*."

"*Profondeurs?*" She laughed outright. She stood. "Okay, George. Talk to my agent about the promo. I'll tell her I'll do it if the terms are right."

George nodded gravely, his lips pursed in what was presumably the further negotiation of spiritual matters. "And what about the cable station, Sylvie? Is it something I can get you to consider, or at least hold off saying no to?"

From its vantage point at her right earlobe, the triangular diamond earring, set as a stud, belonging to no one, whispered its sweet crystalline something into Sylvia's open ear.

"Not a ghost of a chance," Sylvia repeated, blowing George a kiss as she took her leave.

In the ladies' room, running warm water over her hands, she burst into tears.

. . .

When Jabez approached Michael to tell him they had a problem, Michael could see from his assistant's bearing, at once excessively casual and alert, that it was not the sort of problem they could discuss in front of the rest of the crew, which was currently engaged in the shooting of the shooting down of a Japanese suicide plane that was diving in frame-by-frame increments toward the gray plastic deck of the *Catawba.*

So he called a break.

"Might as well make it lunch," said the cameraman, looking at his watch.

"Okay," said Michael, glancing at Jabez. "It's lunch."

The lighting people killed the lights, and someone began an elaborate joke about C-ration sushi as the folk walked off in various directions, temporarily resuming their peacetime, real-time lives.

Michael shut the door of his office. "Don't tell me. Let me guess."

But Jabez, slumped at the room's far corner in the salvaged seat of an otherwise defunct Corvette, was already shaking his head. "Believe me, Michael. This one—"

"Artistic differences with our director. Right?"

"—you're not ready for."

The two men looked at each other, and for some reason Michael remembered the basketball.

Jabez expelled a breath and closed his eyes. "There's been a major restructuring at the studio. It'll be in the papers tomorrow."

Michael went for the refrigerator. "Well, how major can it be? I mean, the contract—"

" 'Major' 's maybe not exactly it. How about 'complete.' "

"Oh, no."

"Oh, yes. Our contractual president of creative development is out on his ass as of midnight last, along with his entire staff, and our picture has specifically—I emphasize 'specifically'—been scrapped."

"Scrapped." Michael was holding a bottle of French carbonated water.

"I understand that's the word they're going to be using. For the press."

"But Dick must be twelve or fifteen million into his budget. They're just going to take a tax write-off on it?"

"My impression, as I say, is that this picture has kind of been singled out. Not that a lot of other projects didn't get killed or put into turnaround, but *Chrysanthemum* is the only one already in principal photography, and—"

Michael realized that since watching Sylvia throw her unlit cigarette into her doomed swimming pool he had not once let pass his lips the floral name of the film—*Steel Chrysanthemum*—with which he had lately filled his working hours. He sat down hard on the edge of his desk. "Sorry, Jabez. Run that by me again."

"I just said that in these situations they like to have a sacrificial lamb. A sign of seriousness. This guy Avery—"

"It's Avery who's the new head?"

"Yeah. The money guy."

"Out of *Wash*ington?" Michael stood up again and walked around behind his desk. "Christ. What does he know about—"

"C'mon, amigo. Since when did that matter?" Jabez exercised his impatience by going to the refrigerator and from its nearly bare shelves selecting a can of Stripe. "Anyway." He popped the top and swallowed. "We're basically okay. I checked the contract: usual terms; paid for our work up through midnight tonight. But I think it'd be a good idea to make some kind of announcement to the crew. Before it hits the papers."

"Definitely." Michael had begun to pace. "And I think I'd better cool things out with Dick too. Diplomatically speaking."

"Good idea. Send him some chrysanthemums."

Michael looked at the place on his wrist where his watch used to be. "Listen, Jabez. What about that guy you told me about on Saturday, the one you caught snooping around?"

"Forget about him. I threw him out."

"No, I mean how did he know about the studio shake-up before we did?"

Jabez sank back into the seat of the missing Corvette, his free hand playing the lever that still adjusted the angle of inclination. "The guy had a lucky breakfast meeting; I don't know. Who cares? We've got a situation here. We deal with it."

Michael dealt with it. He phoned a congratulatory telegram into the office of the new studio head, careful that the time of day printed on it would precede all official announcements. He phoned the director of *Steel Chrysanthemum*, expressing regret that they would not be continuing their invasion of Japan together, confidence that Dick's talent and future could not be touched by professional politics, sorrow that he himself had let personal friction at times impede the picture. He made a short speech to his employees, explaining the situation. They would remain on the payroll at full salary, he said; they were to take a week off, he said; they were to leave all relevant phone numbers with his chief production assistant.

He called Sylvia's home number before and after each of these communiqués; it was each time busy.

Matters were in this condition when—

When he remembered that as a boy, maybe eight, maybe nine, he rode out with his daddy in the pickup truck one desert summer, burning up mile after mile of two-lane blacktop, watching the puddle mirages come and go, come and go, on the asphalt ahead, and a question had framed itself in his mind.

THE SON: Daddy, how many Japs did you kill before you met *Mamochka*?

THE FATHER: [*Easing up on the gas*]: Now what're you thinking like that for, huh? On a fine summer's day?

THE SON: I bet you blew their brains out. [*Making a rifle of his small hands*] Blat-a-data-dat-dat-dat-blam! Just like that diamondback you let me shoot over by the trailer yesterday. Blam! Blam!

THE FATHER: Hey, hold on, son. Killing a rattler is one thing. War is another.

THE SON: You said that about war and snakes to *Mamochka* last night right before she ran out of the trailer. Blam! Blam! Are we going to get her now? [*A silence, in which only the road hums*] Daddy? Is that where we're going?

THE FATHER [*Drinking up the road's white stripes and vanishing puddles with eyes whose thirsts lie elsewhere*]: Son, you're gettin' to be grown now—be a man before you know it, sure as water flows downhill.

THE SON: Will I get to go to war then?

THE FATHER: I hope not. But what you gotta do is kinda watch out for your mother's feelings. Women, they're stronger than us; got more feelings. That's why we gotta take care of them.

THE SON: I betcha *Mamochka* didn't kill any Japs, though. Blam!

THE FATHER: Damn it, son—

THE SON: Blam! Blam! Blam!

"Damn!" said Jabez, slowly easing the Corvette seatback to a near horizontal and staring at the ceiling. "It's incredible what we internalize."

Michael stared at the somnolent phone. "What do we internalize?"

"I always knew this was the driver's seat." Jabez slapped its leatherette side. "I never even thought about it."

"He's going to ask for a raise," Michael told the phone.

"But it's only now I figured out *how* I know. Simple, stupid, internalized. The levers are all on the left."

Wresting the phone from its cradle, Michael punched Sylvia's number. "Yeah. I got it from a junkyard."

"And what I can't help wondering . . . I mean, obviously the car was totaled, right? I can't help wondering what happened to the passenger. That's why you don't have both sides, right? Talk to me, Michael. I need some reassurance in this time of professional uncertainty."

Sylvia's line was busy. Michael still had the snakeskin belt he and his father had made from the hide of the controversially slaughtered diamondback. Jabez was looking at him.

"Listen, Jabez. I've been meaning for a long time to make you a full partner," said Michael, swiveling to face him. "If you don't mind my making the offer on a down day, I'd really like it if you accepted."

Jabez grinned in several directions, stroking his beard. "If you don't mind my laughing at you a little," he said, "on a down day, I do accept."

They laughed together, shaking hands, and Michael remembered the Corvette as he had found it at the junkyard, its tempered windshield a snow of fragments in which could still be read the foreheads of both driver and passenger, both lost. "I'll have the lawyer draw up the papers," he said. *But war is something else,* he thought. His shoelace was undone. "And there *was* no passenger," he said, bending to the tattered sneaker, "in that Corvette."

When Michael straightened up, his shoelace drawn taut again, he saw that Jabez had walked over to the bulletin board and was looking contemplatively at Michael's father's Purple Heart.

"A Corvette is actually a kind of ship," said Jabez. "Isn't it?"

Michael drove the rented pickup, with its striped upholstery, to Sylvia's house.

If you are a ghost, you are a place that has already been vacated by yourself but not yet occupied by someone else; what's more, you are exactly the difference between memory and history; which is to say you are, in short, the very stuff and substance of trouble.

There was no visible trouble on the street where Sylvie lived when Michael pulled up before her house, because exercise clothes in high-contrast colors make trouble look distant—that is their purpose. Sylvia's exercise class was to begin in thirty minutes, and she was walking around the front yard speaking energetically into a cordless phone. It was her agent she was speaking to. It was blue and magenta—nearly purple—that made up the heraldic mix of her exercise gear. It was love and foreboding that leapt through her heart's chambers at the sight of Michael's pickup. It was time, nearly time, too soon time, for her to go.

"Just no real trouble for George, okay?" she was saying. "We're going for self-protection here," she was saying, "not intimidation."

"Right. Perfect. Love you," she was saying.

Michael, who was familiar with the language in which one spoke to agents, moved to within a kiss's inch of her and stopped.

Sylvia telescoped the telephone's aerial back into its housing with the palm of one sun-touched hand.

The two of them looked for a moment at each other. Then they remembered.

"I love you," she was saying.

MICHAEL [*Running the inside of his forearm down the small of her
back, over her buttocks to the place where her thighs begin*]:
Everything that's matter.

"What," Sylvia indicated, holding the phone at arm's length as
if she were about to dance with it or him.

"Everything that matters," Michael was saying.

They were in each other's arms on a lawn in a city where little
else but longing lasts long enough even to talk about.

"You're tense," she said. "What's the matter?"

"So are you," he said. "Why?"

They laughed. The phone rang. She looked at it as if it were a
small mammal that had just ceased being a pet.

They parted. "Well, answer it."

Space grew to include the caller, even before Sylvia did answer,
and Michael turned away from her briefly to make room for the
petitioning voice.

Which belonged, at a flick of the switch, to Petra—her extrav-
agant inflections audible even ten feet away. Since Michael and
Petra had never met, he did not recognize her voice.

"I'm on the run, lovie, but I just *had* to thank you for Saturday
night and, well, you know me, I'm always putting a few things
together, and I just couldn't help wondering . . ."

Sylvia strode a tightened circle on the Bermuda grass. "Spare
me the previews, Petra; I'm your friend. Tell me what you want
to know."

"That African girl—can she really act?"

"Oh: Nomanzi. I'm told she's a big star at home. Maybe you
should look at her tapes."

"The face is perfect. And her presence—really super prime, a
lot to work with there."

"Give her a call. She's working days at Foxglove."

"Laurel Westfall's flower shop? Great. Okay, I will." She was
already mentally redialing. "Thanks so much, lovie. Call you."

"Sure, Petra."

"Kiss kiss."

And as Sylvia once again disengaged the phone, the diamond at her ear softly hummed its carboniferous rondelet as to what in this world was permanent and what was passing.

"The good news is," said Michael, "I've had a visit from your second-most-passionate admirer."

She allowed her head a slightly puzzled tilt, causing the lone onyx earring to dangle interrogatively.

"The one who drives a green sedan," he added.

She seized his forearm. "The bad news," he continued, sweeping aside the welter of questions she had obviously placed on hold, "is that I wasn't there to offer him my hospitality in person."

Michael explained about the break-in at the desert house, about the theft of the samurai sword, about the studio shake-up that had taken place exactly as the man in the green sedan had predicted. He paced the lawn in front of her as he spoke, and the bright intermittence of her image at the peripheries of his sunglasses kept reminding him of their fucking, opposed as it was to all that stood still, to all that was planned and all that the late-summer sun had parched. He felt his cock stir.

"So what you're saying," she said, "is that this guy knew ahead of time that *Steel Chrysanthemum* was going to be shelved? And that he stole that sword so that you'd know he knew?" Sylvia bent to pick a bit of foil from the grass. "Why would he do that?"

"Why would he slash your tires?"

"Well, if we knew that . . ." She stood. "Look. I've got to get to my exercise class."

She appeared exercised. Flushed.

"You're holding out on me," he said softly, stepping forward to touch the place where her throat throbbed. "I've sensed it before. But now I'm sure."

"Don't."

"I love you."

"Then leave it."

"I would." He began to pace again. "I would certainly fucking leave it, but every fucking time I leave something, it comes back to haunt me."

She managed not to flinch. " 'It' or 'she'?" She was feeling haunted.

"Sylvie, this is not a conversation about you and me and Laurel.

This is a conversation about . . ." An enormous iridescent green fly shot erratically between them. "Okay, look. I don't even know that. Maybe it does have to do with the three of us. Maybe there's even more than three of us. But here's what I do know: Some guy has been committing minor acts of criminal harassment against you for more than a little while, but you won't call the cops. And now, when he's doing it to me, you ask me to 'leave it.' Where I come from we're apt to call that strange."

"Try 'discreet.' "

"Try 'bullshit.' "

They were walking a figure eight around each other, and they stopped at its invisible waist, face-to-face.

"Okay, look." She shrugged her shoulders—a gesture of capitulation. "I'm a diplomat's daughter, right? I never told you Paul Walters is my father, but you've guessed it by now. I know you at least that well."

He nodded.

"So it's also probably crossed your mind more than once that I'm deceitful, manipulative, ruthless, mean. Well, friend, I learned that stuff at my father's knee, you better believe it. And he's the best. Now, me—"

Michael grabbed her by the arm and shook her. "Stop it."

I am very far from the province of truth today, thought Sylvia.

Michael considered the willfully blank expression on her face. "You do know who this guy is," he said. "Don't you."

The rubbed-grass smell of the lawn rose between them.

"I know," she said, "who he says he is."

The red plastic watch at her wrist emitted a triple chirp, and eight fine fountains of water, sprinklers connected to a timer, erupted in perfect synchrony across the lawn. Michael ran one way, Sylvia the other. The phone lay abandoned upon the ground. The ground lay at the mercy of the sky. Michael ran back the other way, retrieving the phone, retrieving Sylvia. They stood together in the driveway, wet from the waist down.

"Better than half an hour of aerobic exercise," Sylvia managed to gasp.

"Surprise is the thing," he began.

"Interruption is," she interrupted.

They stared at each other.

And then this house, with its water-blooming lawn and petaled roof, became yet another house into which they were hurrying together.

It would be a mistake to think that the sudden brilliant flush of love that has even now begun to unfold Michael and Sylvia to one another signifies in any way a retreat from her admission regarding William, or the person who has called himself William.

Walking through the kitchen, Sylvia slips one strap of her leotard off her shoulder.

Michael, abandoning his shirt, thinks: *I know who she says she is*.

At the foot of the staircase, she turns to face him, but he does not stop where she does, backing her instead gently yet with increasing pressure up against the immaculate wall.

"Are you going to fuck me?" she asks in a whisper. It is not a question, and the words are no longer language. He has slipped her leotard's other strap off her shoulder and pulled the garment down to her waist. "How truly are you going to fuck me? Tell me how truly. Tell me everything."

Michael finds that he, too, has a voice that speaks in words that are no longer language. It bathes itself in the warmth of her mouth before it speaks, and it knows things not otherwise vouchsafed him: "I can't help fucking you. I can't help telling you everything."

"It's this effect we have on each other," she seems to be saying. "For instance, I don't usually use the word 'truly,' do I?"

He pries his shoes off in a reprise of his last meeting with her. He steps out of his pants.

"I mean, being a diplomat's daughter. And all."

He draws her to him, and the voice that in interruption he has discovered says: "We know who we say we are."

And again, as at her burning house, he is surprised by the sudden depth of her wetness when, still standing, he lifts and enters her. She draws her sun-browned legs up on either side of him, knees almost to his armpits. He draws no conclusions and can no longer imagine a time in which conclusions would be necessary or reassuring.

"Why is it I—" She interrupts herself with a sharp gasp—a first stop—and she understands that she is possibly going to be too much for even the both of them. She shivers: the recognition is not without its component of fear. "Don't fuck me gently," she says. "Don't tell me gently." After a long-drawn breath alongside his ear, she says: "But for God's sake—tell me."

And so he begins.

They are in a wild place, far from the city, far from any place known to them. The light that falls upon them as they walk together naked among the trees is dappled and shifting—as fluid as warm water, but somehow, in touching them, more viscous. She spies something in their path, leans over to examine it. Discovering himself hugely erect, he enters her from behind. She pretends to take no notice and mutely hands back to him what she has found: a wristwatch, its crystal shattered, its hands arrested at 8:16. Her own hands seek the support of a tree trunk that is, as she touches it, no longer a tree trunk but Michael's cock, glistening before her; just as instantly, he himself stands facing her, still holding the watch.

"I'll let her lick it," Sylvia explains. "But it belongs to me now. Can't you see?"

"I was wearing my sunglasses," he says.

"But now you've taken them off?"

"They lost themselves," he says, "in the burning place."

"I *am* the burning place," she says. And he enters her again, unquenched.

There is, he tells her, a river in Southern Africa. In drought it is diminished but never staunched; it is not a ghost. The two of them, Michael and Sylvia—this is what he tells her as they fuck—are walking languidly toward it and toward the sun that has not yet quite risen, and they are both carrying buckets in their hands. The buckets collide from step to step, making a repeated clink, and this sound is the only sound to be heard within earshot—the only sound, he tells her, besides that of the water running its course through clay and rock.

"I'm going to come again," she says. And for a moment the arm that is not around his neck seems to graze the newel of the staircase she is being carried past. *This will hurt later*, she thinks, but for a long time it seems the last of thought. Then they are in the living room.

They are within sight of the river.

"Come back," he says. Or thinks.

"Mm-hmm," she thinks she says. And it is enough. He continues.

They are within sight of a place where the river bends, making a natural landfall, and in negotiating the slight descent to the bank itself they by their movements cause the buckets to clatter together like broken bells. The sound makes them laugh and hurry, hurry for the pleasure of their clattering laughter, hurry for pleasure, and they slide together—though without losing their footing—down the last of the clay embankment.

"I can't help telling you," he tells her again. And for a time there is only the sound of their fucking.

"Buckets, you say," she tells him. She is shaking her head in what might possibly pass for . . . amusement? But then he finds himself, insofar as it now remains possible, suddenly and truly astonished: she is weeping. "Why them?" she says. "Tell me why buckets."

He lays her down upon the sofa. They stand upon the riverbank. They fuck with concentration that has long since ceased to surprise either of them.

"I—"

Their eyes open simultaneously upon one another.

"Buckets," he says, closing his eyes before her elegantly demanding presence. She draws herself away from him, turns over, and places his cock inside her from behind. He says her word again, perhaps to himself, but he senses in it now their mutual uncertainty.

The river's water is the reason for their being here—*here*—together.

The telephone is warbling. Elsewhere, down by the river and forever invisible, a bird calls in wordless warning.

"The thing about buckets," he tells her, "the thing about them is . . ."

She gasps with a violence that suggests the purest indifference to breath. He realizes that he doesn't know a single reason why they might be carrying buckets, or where they might be doing it.

"Sylvia?" he says.

And she hits him.

It is, physically, a glancing blow, her fist awkwardly striking his temple, but the shock—to both of them—is enormous. They separate, face each other, and he enters her again almost immediately.

"Did I do that?" she says. "My love?"

They are on the floor. She weeps. "My love?"

Everything in their world is wet.

"I want to tell you what I know," he says. "But about buckets . . ."

She gasps, her eyes close, and for a moment she is gone to him. "About buckets . . ." He shakes his head sadly.

"Michael!" she cries, so close to his ear that for an instant, idiotically, he is unable to connect the sound with the woman who has uttered it.

"Right here," he says when he can. "Right here." He wonders for another moment to whom he thinks he's talking. Then, after all, he finds himself able to think. To speak.

"Okay," he says. "This is how it is. I mean, no buckets, right? But this is how it is."

"Yes. Okay."

She seems to him to have somehow begun another ascent, and though she is still weeping she is nonetheless assuaged.

There are, he tells her, in North America a pair of rivers: the Catawba, the Roanoke. They flow more or less from west to east, they spill into the Atlantic. They are near enough together that when the sun falls on them in a certain way, it is usually the same way, and the catfish hover near the surface, warming themselves and chewing water.

"Don't lie to me," she says. "You're a desert boy. Don't lie to me now."

He shivers, momentarily ashamed to have forgotten how instinctively—even viciously—she went for the unadorned core of things. As he holds her head in his cupped hands, protecting it from the floor, her tear-reddened eyes flutter briefly open. She seems inexpressibly beautiful to him, soaked and dangerous in what she has come to demand from herself and so from him. He moves forward on his elbows until his cock is as far inside her as her hips will allow; she raises her legs and locks her ankles together at the small of his back. "Okay," he hears himself say. "No catfish either."

In the version that will be the truth because it is the last resort of lovers who care first for last things, there is a country in North America that names certain of its warships after rivers—the *Roanoke*, the *Catawba*. There is a restless ocean whose name, in contrariety, is the Pacific. Among men there is more war than peace.

"Oh," says Sylvia, "I love you."

He has to pause. Across her breasts and throat there is a flush like a scatter of out-of-season sunburn, or shed chrysanthemum petals. He has not come; it occurs to him that he may never.

"Don't stop," she says, though their fucking has already, of its own accord, resumed. "Don't stop ever."

Locking the shop door behind her, folding the newspaper to her, Nomanzi stepped out into the afternoon sunshine. She'd put the prescribed late-lunch message on the flower shop's answering machine; she'd put a sign in the window saying when she'd be back, and now, as she peered back through the shop window to double-check that the answering machine was indeed on, she caught sight of her own reflection in the vitrine.

"Ilulwane," she said, under her breath, touching the glass.

Then she drove the record company car to Petra's office.

"You'll have to give me running subtitles," Petra was saying as she watched Nomanzi's tape unfurl upon the VCR.

"Oh. Well. 'Ilulwane'—that's the name of the show—and it means, well, it means 'bat,' or 'half-creature,' really. Because my character—"

"I love the intro."

Nomanzi settled back into the white cotton couch and sipped her French soda water. She wondered when she was going to be asked on which side she was African.

"How long have you been doing the series?"

"We have now finished our third season. And there's a renewal for the next one."

"Fantastic." Petra scooped her bias-cut hair back from the ear it hid and studied the video screen.

Nomanzi accepted the prompt. "In this episode"—she raised one long arm to stretch it, and her bracelets fell elbowward with a clatter—"in this episode, I discover that my brother is living at the other end of the township with a woman who is not his wife. See, that's him there. Anyway, his wife is still back in the raw place, the country place I have left behind, and there she was my best friend: it was she who told me not to go into the township but to marry among those of my people I knew." Nomanzi laughed. "My character does not take advice well."

They watched the tape together for a while, Nomanzi continuing her explication until she noticed that Petra had stopped watching the video screen and was watching her instead. When their eyes met, Petra smiled and flicked off the tape.

"Not only are you a natural actress, but the camera loves you. Loves you even better than I'd hoped." She stood and walked past Nomanzi to her desk, a bright and nearly void expanse of white Formica. "Have you had training?"

"In my country we've all had training. We all act." Nomanzi looked up from the cream-colored carpet she'd been staring at, then laughed, successfully implying that she'd been speaking in character of some sort. "No, I've had a little training—private stuff, y'know. I lived in the States for ten years."

One of the sleek white devices on Petra's desk proved, by its sudden gurgling, to be an espresso machine.

"Coffee?"

"No, thank you."

The other was a telephone of preternatural complexity.

"Well." Petra drew a cup for herself. "I guess what I'd like to do is tell you what I'm up to now and see"—she sipped—"if we might not be able to get a little something going."

"I'm flattered that you like my work so much. And yes, that would be lovely." From where she was sitting, Nomanzi could observe that the phone was lit up with winking red eyes: Petra had asked her secretary to hold all calls.

"*Wunderbar.*" A pad had materialized on Petra's desk, and she began doodling on it. "I'm sure you've got a sense by now about how things operate out here: you've got to put together a package that's attractive to everyone, and you've got to keep it that way.

There's no bad news, only deals that need repackaging and pictures that don't get made."

"Tinseltown," said Nomanzi, acting a little now, letting the light strike a flash of amusement from her eyes.

"That's it. Tinseltown and Heaven's back door. So I know you'll appreciate that I'm violating a town ordinance when I tell you that my deal of the year fell through on Saturday last." Petra looked down at the cubes and blocks she was doodling in axonometric projection upon her memo pad. "And did I weep? I certainly did."

"Oh, I'm very sorry."

"But you shouldn't be. Being in Tinseltown means never having to say you're sorry." She began to give the doodled blocks elongated human shadows. "For one thing, there's no time for it, and for another, nobody remembers what there is to be sorry about. Even me." She looked up brightly. "And I like to think I run an operation that's a little different from most."

"You do seem different from the operations . . . from the film people I've met so far." Nomanzi's hand went to the strand of cow hair that encircled her neck, then, appeased, drifted back to her lap. *We are here to make protection*, Chentula had said.

"I like to tailor my projects to a few people I believe in," Petra continued. "A lot of producers, they're like drunken fathers on Christmas Eve, tying all their presents up in pretty packages with lopsided bows. Then, come the morning, headache's all they know—can't even remember who gets which package. I'm not like that."

"I'm not like that either," said Nomanzi, looking at Petra but answering Chentula.

"Of course not." For the first time Petra sensed that the waters into which she was wading might after all be torn by riptides. She pursed her lips. "So it's fair to say you don't have any work commitments you can't get out of?"

"Yes. It's fair."

"And can I ask you to keep our conversation here—you know—confidential?"

"I assumed it." Her heart was pounding.

"Okay." Petra resumed her doodling, sketching a cartoon speech balloon above one of the axonometric blocks she'd already drawn, then filling it with paired letters—DM, DM, DM—as she spoke. "I got a call yesterday from a friend of my husband's, a European man of considerable means, and he has decided he wants to spend some of his considerable means on a picture that I'll put together for him. Isn't that sweet? I mean, the man trusts me."

"From what I've seen of things in this town," Nomanzi said, "trust is worth more than money."

Petra's face expanded in delight. "You better believe it. Absolutely." She paused, herself theatrical. "But both is best." She was watching Nomanzi very closely.

"So you have a script, then?"

"No. That's exactly it. I thought I might try a little intentional backwardness—assembling the personnel before the script."

A crystal hummingbird hung suspended from the window casement behind Petra, and the sunlight shining through it caused a slurred spectral bar to strike the corner of her desk.

It's all just movies out here anyway, Nomanzi thought.

Petra drew herself another espresso. "Let me ask you something else. You're a friend of Laurel Westfall's. How well do you know Michael, her fiancé?"

Nomanzi in no way needed to affect puzzlement, but once she was aware that that was what she felt, she could not quite keep from supplementing it with a blink, a pause, a two-beat stare. "Laurel is my employer, and I met her only on Friday, three days ago." She crossed her legs, making a slight fuss with her skirt as she did so. "She mentioned her fiancé to me once, and yes, I think she mentioned his name—but that's all, really." She herself began to wonder into what waters she was wading. "Why do you ask me this?"

"Because you see"—Petra swallowed coffee—"I've had this brainstorm." She picked one blond hair with unnecessary deliberation from her cup. "As it happens, Michael's just lost his pet project too. I don't know if you know who he is in the industry?"

Nomanzi tossed her chin in the nearly international motion of No.

"He's a special-effects designer, the best in the business. But I've always thought—and I've been hearing things, of course—I've always thought he'd be an even better director."

"So this man is part of the—what was the word you used?—personnel."

"He might be, yes." Glancing at her notepad, Petra felt with unpleasant swiftness the vulnerability of her position: how profoundly relative everything was. The patches of what she knew and didn't know about the very project she was proposing formed a pattern whose presumed coherence might easily, in the end, exclude her. *What the hell*, she concluded silently, *I'm a producer, so I'll produce.*

"What I'd like to do," Petra said, laying her pen neatly beside her pad, "is talk to Michael first. Then, if he's agreeable, we'll all three sit down and bat a few ideas around. How does that sound to you?"

Nomanzi smiled. "It makes me feel good to be overseas again."

"You have an agent?"

"Not yet."

"Okay. We'll work on that if and when." Petra gazed nonspecifically at her telephone console, with its field of little lights. "Oh, one other thing. You might give a little thought to the kind of character you'd like to play, maybe even the kind of story line you could see yourself in. I mean, nothing too elaborate—just catch it in the corner of your eye. That way we might get a better idea of where we want to go."

"Wonderful. Yes. I will." But what she'd caught in the corner of her eye just then was the visa stamped in her passport, purple-ink filigree allowing her only ninety days, of which six had already elapsed.

The two women stood at the same time.

"So I have both your numbers, and I'll be in touch sometime this week, okay?"

"Miranda," said Nomanzi.

Petra looked alarmed. "Sorry?"

"I thought we could do a *Tempest* and I play Miranda."

Nomanzi mimed obstinance, lifting her chin, meeting Petra's eyes, and for a moment the choreography of impasse drew them close to each other, although they had not moved. Nomanzi burst into laughter, doubling over with it, and Petra at the same time, or nearly so, did likewise.

When the two women had recovered themselves, they kissed each other goodbye on either cheek, and parted.

Petra seated herself again at her desk. She propped her chin on her outstretched fingers and stared at her phone until, as if in response, the intercom buzzed.

"Ambassador Bloch called about twenty minutes ago," came Petra's secretary's voice. "He said he'd call back in an hour."

"Super. Could you drop all my afternoon appointments back an hour—tell them I'm running late?"

"Sure. No problem."

"Thanks, Julie."

Petra smiled and sat back in her chair. Then she picked up her pen, leaned forward, and very slowly, thinking of nothing else, she drew a perfect oval on her notepad around the doodle that had been speaking in deutsche marks.

Although already a few minutes late, Nomanzi did not drive directly back to the flower shop. The excitement she had felt in Petra's office did not diminish—indeed it redoubled as she began to think about all that might now be possible—and although she checked the rearview mirror more than the traffic or her lane changes really required, she also had to keep an eye on the speedometer, an eye on herself.

To a woman who understands she is the instrument of history, the world's traffic can sometimes be cause for patient amusement, although a man with the same awareness might not be free to be amused or patient. And of course neither man nor woman might, strictly speaking, be free at all. Not to mention that freedom might itself, from several points of view, be only an absence of instrumentality.

Nomanzi kept her eyes on the world and accelerated until a smile came to her lips, the kind of smile that caused her to wriggle back and forth a bit in the driver's seat and say to herself, more than a few times, *Oh, absolutely, yes, certainly, yes. Absolutely.*

The shopping mall into whose parking lot she glided was a puzzle in perfect fit: brushed aluminum, green and terra-cotta-colored concrete, glass.

Nomanzi parked near the glass elevator and took it to the third floor. Citizens moved at different levels about the atrium's perimeter in the manner of expensively appointed ants.

Once, when visiting her grandmother in the raw place, Nomanzi had been bitten so badly by ants that she had taken fever. She remembered the taste of the grass infusions she had been given to break the fever. She remembered the red clay of the land in which the ants had made their home.

She walked into a glass-walled boutique that sold only sunglasses, and observing the style worn by the salesgirls, bought a similar pair, with white-checked frames.

"No, I'm serious," said the woman behind Nomanzi on the escalator. "That's what she does: walk from beach to beach, and when she comes to a lifeguard she asks if he has an extra swimming suit she can have."

"Then what?"

"Then nothing," said the woman irritably. "I told you, she *collects.*"

Nomanzi got off at the second floor and strolled the arcade until she came to a leather-goods shop. Peering through the glass door at the tiers of perfectly cured and shaped animal hides, each stamped with the same set of initials, she noticed there was, at the shop's other end, a duplicate door, giving onto a duplicate arcade. She walked briskly in.

"And what may we help you with today?" asked the salesman.

Enough so that she was able to kill a good ten or fifteen minutes inspecting handbags and keeping one watchful eye on the door by which she'd entered. When she was satisfied, she thanked the man, said she'd have to think about it, and quickly left by the rear door.

There was a bank of telephone booths not ten yards from the shop. She slipped into the half-shadowed one at the end and for a moment just sat there, very still, with the handset of the phone pressed to her heart.

"Yes," said the voice in the phone, when it was at her ear, the next time she was conscious of it.

"It's me," she said simply.

A long sigh, signifying impatience. "We were expecting your call two days ago."

She felt ashamed, but it was dream shame. Movie shame. "It wasn't possible."

"You're being followed."

"No. I've been careful."

A different sigh. Briefer.

"But more than that really: I've been lucky. Lots of contacts already, people who trust me." She heard in her own voice a surge of feeling, a desire to prove herself to the presence at the line's other end. It was widely understood in her circles that feelings of that order constituted a danger to all whom they touched. Nomanzi was careful to cleanse her voice of passion before she next spoke.

"I may have a part."

"It is not good news. Your part is with us, eh?"

Always this blunt suspicion of her motives, when she . . . she of all people . . . Nomanzi was aware that her sex, her beauty, and her relative political privilege somehow constituted a provocation to the cause, but she did not accept that provocation or its circumstances.

"I have called you," she said. "I have waited," she said. "I am above suspicion." She paused to strip the fury from her voice, and in doing so, she removed the earring that, pressed between her ear and the telephone, was physically mimicking the irritation she'd begun to feel throughout her being. "Now it is up to us to see what can be done." She waited for argument, put the earring down on the stainless-steel flange beneath the phone, and went on. "You have contacted our cousin?"

"Yes," came the voice, a bit more briskly. "The birds are safely nested. Twenty-six crates. More than we'd hoped."

"Good."

"But it makes a lot of weight and bulk. There is talk of taking only half of them home."

"No. Where is the worth of that?"

The voice laughed bitterly. "The worth is what you know. To keep us out of prison. To help our comrades instead of taking glory for ourselves. To keep you out of prison."

"Is there a plan?"

"We were waiting for you."

"But is there a plan?"

Silence of several kinds, some of them ironic, some of them furious.

"Okay." Nomanzi surveyed the view from the telephone booth, a fan-shaped scan of no immediate import. "Yes, okay. Where do I call you next?"

"Here. It's all right. Our cousin has a filter box on the phone."

"Good." She stood. "You think I have a plan? I don't have a plan." She met the eyes of a diminutive blond woman holding many shopping bags, and the woman looked away to speak to someone. "But you must listen to me: when a plan is needed, I have never failed to find one. Sometimes in my life my plans have failed. But not often."

"You have American ways. It is both good and bad. But we have waited for you."

"For my plans."

"Yeh, Cousin. For your plans."

Nomanzi became aware of vaguely instrumental music that, having lost its melodic direction, seemed to have become physically omnipresent, fed into the mall by countless invisible speakers. It reminded her of money.

"Okay, look, then. I'm following my instincts. I'm with people who transport lots of equipment. They wouldn't even notice if our twenty-six crates of birds nested with their baggage—for them it would be unimportant, just inventory error. But I have to do this my own way."

"It is dangerous to us that you may be a bioscope star."

"It is crucial to you that I am. Or might be."

" 'To you'?" He repeated her usage, giving edge to it.

"Don't."

"Even your brother, your half-brother—"

"He knows nothing of this."

A long silence, different from all the others.

"When will you call?"

She was shaking. "Two days."

"Okay." The voice seemed relieved. "Same time."

After she had hung up, she sat for a while in the phone booth, aware of nothing but the circulation of her blood.

. . .

"What are you thinking?" Sylvia asked Michael as they lay still naked together upon the love-dampened sheets. He turned his head so he could see her.

What Michael was thinking was that he would have liked to ask her now, while they were still extraordinary, what had compelled her to say what she had said in the final delirium of their lovemaking. She had said it several times, as though its repetition were the point. She had demanded, in as many words, and each time appending his name, that he kill her.

Yet he knew that this was not a question that could be asked in words, any more than what she had demanded of him had anything to do with the words she had chosen to express it—quite the contrary. And so he came to see that his desire to ask the question was in reality a desire to savor the answer, which he already knew: that he and Sylvia had so filled each other with life that for a certain set of moments death itself was something they together could have lived through without difficulty.

"I was thinking," he said, "about what kind of survivor you probably are."

"Same kind as you."

Her eyes were open very wide, and he found it hard to disbelieve anything they said. "Maybe," he said. "But even in the best of times, there's context."

"Always," she said soberly.

"I mean, we probably have to survive completely different things."

Sylvia sighed. The subject, without having been even remotely exhausted, was exhausting. "Are you going to tell her?" she asked.

"Of course. You and I, we've stopped being an interruption."

She shifted away from him in bed, she turned her back—but he understood it was acquiescence that animated her.

"I think I've always known," Michael said after a while.

Sylvia didn't move. "About me?" she asked. "Or about her?"

"About me," he answered, turning her to him again. "If I ever met anyone like you."

The bedroom was drenched in light, but their sense of what surrounded them, after all that had happened, was more nearly what people feel when they are enveloped in, and have grown used to, the dark.

"You said . . ." Michael was momentarily embarrassed to be making use of the lapse in their conversation to return to a lapse in what they knew of each other. "You said, 'I know who he says he is.' "

"Yes. He said he was my uncle, but my uncle is dead."

"I don't understand," said Michael.

"I meant to say half-uncle," Sylvia added.

"What?"

"Biologically speaking, this guy's my half-uncle."

Michael's hand set out, slowly tracing, from armpit to hip, her body's contour. "Not to be stupid, but it sounds like this guy's a ghost. Biologically speaking."

"No. Him, he's something else. Don't ask me what." She shivered, and Michael's hand stilled her. "He probably doesn't even know."

"Okay, but how about I ask you what he wants from you?"

"From me? I haven't the least idea." She threw him a quick look. "But I do have something else."

"Tell me."

Sylvia reached across the table where her earrings lay motionless and, retrieving the business card she had found tipped into her speedometer the day before, handed it to Michael. "I've got his number," she said.

"William Walters," Michael said. "So he's your *father's* half-brother."

"Was." Sylvia squirmed, but turned the squirm into a caress. "How did he die? I mean, he did die, right?"

"It's a long story."

"Ah."

"A lot of my stories are long."

"Ah."

"You can be sarcastic."

"Yes. It's a special effect."

"Well, it must be nice to know which of your effects are special."

"That's exactly what I *don't* know."

She said nothing.

He looked at the number on the card and began dialing.

"Wait, wait. What are you going to say?"

"I thought I'd rely on grand inspiration."

She ran her hand through her hair. "Do you think that's a good idea? I mean, how grand is your inspiration? This guy's a professional."

"A professional what?"

She said nothing. There were cigarettes on her side of the bed. Despite her landlady's genial prohibition, Sylvia lit one.

"Does the name Jonathan Avery mean anything to you?" he asked.

She shook her head. "What does it mean to you?"

"It means Washington. He's the new head of the studio I was working for. And I'm getting a lot of Washington ever since I started up with you."

"Started up?"

A smile worked its way across his face. "Started up loving you."

"If you love me," she said after a moment, "then you'll have to trust me."

He laughed. "Don't be ridiculous."

"Right." She blew smoke from the left corner of her mouth. "Okay." She took the phone from him and punched out the number William had given her. Her eyes never left Michael's. When the ringing began she hit the speakerphone button so they both could hear whatever there would be to hear. Then, because she knew exactly what trust was for, she handed the phone to him.

"Hello. William Walters, please."

"You got him."

"What a day. My luck just doesn't run out. This is Michael Bonner."

"Oh, yeah. Hi. How's it going?"

"You came to my place of work the other day—uninvited, like."

"I thought we might do business."

"With timing like that, why bother with business? Why not just take your timing out to Santa Anita and bet a year's worth of trifectas?"

The man sighed as if this sort of sally distinguished a personality type with which he was wearily familiar. "Okay. So I had word. I wasn't the only one in town who did."

"What town would that be?" said Michael, catching Sylvia's eye.

"What *town*?" said the man. "Christ. I'd ask if you were busy, except it was you called me, not the other way around. Plus which, with all due respect, the whole point of our having a conversation is I know you can't be *that* busy. So maybe we should talk another time?"

This man is not my relative, Sylvia thought, stubbing out her cigarette, certain she was wrong.

"Mr. Walters," Michael said. "I really have to tell you: I don't believe I'm familiar with your work. What with the industry having diversified and all, it gets a little hard to keep up—I'm sure you understand."

"Well, of course. Naturally I assumed you'd want to know about my credentials." The voice, tinny over the speakerphone, fell with these words into an intonation—just possibly an accent—that it had till now somehow swallowed. Sylvia threw a quick look at Michael to see if he had noticed, but he had not, and the voice at that moment paused with the deliberate intention, it seemed to her, of again swallowing what it had just possibly—but perhaps not—revealed.

"And shit," the voice went on, recovered. "What can I say: I know it's not my credits that'll get you. I mean, I've been producing low-budget documentaries out of Canada the last few years—*Dr. Strangelove*, *Hiroshima Mon Amour*, *The Clock on the Bedside Table*—nothing anyone's heard of."

"They don't exist," Sylvia soundlessly mouthed.

"So why should I be talking to you?" Michael asked.

"Because I can package you as a director," said the voice.

"Director?" said Michael. "I do special effects—smoke and car wrecks, right? Invisible deception."

"But you're a born director. I've seen all the pictures you've worked on."

Michael, caught short by the sense that this voice knew him, executed a visual survey of the room, of Sylvia in it with him, of himself in his life.

"So you got a project going or what?"

"I'd like," said the voice, "to have the chance to tell you about it over breakfast."

Sylvia rolled out of bed. She recalled that she had not yet telephoned her father to tell him Kristen was all right.

"Breakfast?" said Michael. It seemed to be a question, and he seemed to have directed it at Sylvia. She looked at him, then shrugged. "Yeah, okay," said Michael, turning back to the phone. "Breakfast. We can tell each other our life stories."

Sylvia kissed Michael lightly on the shoulder and left the room.

From the upstairs bathroom window she gazed down at the mimosa tree in the yard below and reflected that whatever unspoken betrayal of her father might be involved in the events to come, there probably were after all worse things to keep than secrets.

When Sylvia heard Michael coming after her, she went out into the hallway to meet him. She didn't want him to see her standing still.

No one whose business it was to notice such things could afterward remember the moment the silver Bavarian sedan had come to be parked outside the American consulate in Geneva, but when, shortly before dawn, it lifted abruptly off its tires and exploded in a lopsided ball of pure white flame, the relevant parking regulations temporarily assumed the quality of embarrassingly obsolete folk customs.

The wrought-iron fence that had fronted the consulate was down—broken and bent. All the building's windows were gone, and an alarmingly large part of its gingerbread facade had been transformed into a cloud of stone dust that drifted sideways through the night air. A few American men in boxer shorts or pajama bottoms wandered distractedly down the staircase, now exposed to the street like an elaborate stage set. A few other American men, fully clothed, were loping purposefully about the grounds with semiautomatic pistols in their hands.

"We all here?" asked the American Secretary of State. He was wearing underpants that bore a crocodile motif in three colors.

"Yes, sir," said a Secret Service man whose gray suit was slightly singed. He was trying not to stare at the crocodiles. "All accounted for."

Sirens began to converge on the building, on the men, on the burning automobile fragments that lay scattered about the street and lawn.

"Son of a bitch." The American Secretary of State shook his head in disgust as he surveyed the wreckage. "Not that it couldn't have been a hell of a lot worse." Clapping his naked shoulders with his hands like a man who has just come out of a snowstorm, he turned in resignation to the Secret Service agent beside him. "Okay. I guess you guys better get us out of here before the press come in and really mess things up."

At the wire services, newspaper offices, and TV stations of Geneva, men and women put the unmarked audiocassettes they had received into tiny tape recorders and bent earnestly over them.

The volume of international calls swelled, then ebbed, then swelled again.

In Compiègne, the decision was made to wake Paul Walters.

Sylvia's father struggled up from the domain of his dream (*where he had been waltzing with his wife on a construction scaffolding, of all places! and she had been beautiful, knowing-eyed, pregnant—with her arm looped through a basketful of mushrooms, of all things!*), and from that struggle he lifted himself up onto his elbows in bed. His chief aide stood silhouetted in the doorway.

"A car bomb?" Paul Walters realized that compared to his dream the man to whom he was speaking was a shadow. He turned on the bedside lamp. "How bad?"

There had been no one hurt, said the aide. No U.S. statement had yet been issued, he said. The man moved into the room's light.

Paul Walters remembered another part of the dream.

"Sit down," Paul Walters said.

The man thanked him and looked around the room; the burden of his news was such that he then forgot to sit down. "We do, ah, have a little more on this," he said, shuffling through a handful of diplomatic cables. "The group that took responsibility is something called, let's see, the Broederbond Front—some sort of white supremacist South African outfit."

"New to me."

"Right. We're checking into it. Anyway, these guys left tape cassettes with every news bureau in Geneva, and—"

Watching his aide push his horn-rimmed glasses nervously back up his nose, Paul Walters knew with an unpleasant certainty exactly what he was about to be told. "Okay. Just leave me the cables. I'll get dressed."

The man looked stunned. It was an expression of nearly unbearable clarity.

Seventeen years ago, when Paul Walters was informed of his half-brother's murder on an Oklahoma highway, he had been sunning himself on the beach at Three Mile Vineyard with his daughters, his wife, his mother. He had handed the telegram to his wife, who had read it in a glance, then handed it back. His mother—his and William's—was making her way down to the water with the ski poles she used as beach crutches: she had a brain tumor and was not expected to live out the month. "Darling?" his wife had said, trying to catch his eye. But he was absorbed in watching his mother's painful pilgrimage to the sea, in watching the seagull that waddled after her, in watching the play of light, sea foam, and sun off the smooth young bodies of his daughters, gamboling in the surf. Then—because it was his talent to know when news was best withheld—he had plunged the telegram into the gray sand beside him and, turning slowly around to face his wife, had discovered, to his enormous surprise, the very expression of stunned avidity that now had seized the features of his aide.

"Wait a minute," Paul Walters said. Throwing the sheets aside, he drew himself up into a sitting position on the side of the bed. "Sorry I cut you off."

"Oh, no problem." The aide had not moved. "It's just that—"

"It's just that the car bomb was meant for me, right?"

The man hesitated, as if some embarrassment were involved in this evocation, however circumspect, of the older man's death. "Yes, sir. It was."

"Because officially I'm *in* Geneva. You, too, for that matter. And since, as we know, I was involved in traitorous negotiations with the indigenous peoples of a sovereign land . . ."

"Uh, yeah. Actually, there's something in the tapes about you being an agent of 'state terrorism.' That Azanian business, I guess."

"Right." Walters ran a hand through his hair, which, thinned though it was, undoubtedly numbered more days than he himself would see, car bombs or not. Yet—because this, too, was his talent—his heart began to fill with unedged optimism. He found he wished to tell his aide, a man still in his thirties, about the splendors of life—about what it was to gaze out upon your daughters at dance with the sea. How the very clumsiness with which you continued to live and live was finally what let you attain any kind of grace, waltzing with your wife atop the scaffolding that towered, radiant, over the living and the dead.

Of course, it was no doubt a difficult point to make under the circumstances.

"We'll have to coordinate with State on this," he told his aide.

"The Secretary already has a call in to us."

"Otherwise, next thing we know, the press will be wanting me to do public calisthenics in Geneva to prove I'm still alive." Paul Walters stretched. He was still alive. "Anybody wake the President?"

"Not as far as I know."

"Shit sake." He yawned. "Okay, give me ten minutes."

Then, as his aide turned to leave, Walters added, "Oh, and I'll see you get to talk to your wife to tell her you're okay."

When he was again alone, Paul Walters found himself staring across the room at the oaken chest of drawers on which rested the two handleless silver-backed hairbrushes he carried with him wherever he traveled. They had been a birthday gift from his wife. One of them had a deep dent in its back.

Getting to his feet, Walters approached the chest of drawers. He took the brushes in either hand as if they were themselves hands.

The dent had been incurred one Sunday morning more than two decades ago, while he and his wife slept. He had left the brushes downstairs so that the maid might polish them the following day, and his early-rising daughters, frustrated in their attempts to turn the night latch on the front door, which stood between them and the Sunday newspaper, with its double complement of comics, had used one of the brushes as a jimmy.

He imagined his children banging away at the night latch, swinging open the door, hauling in the swollen newspaper.

He saw them side by side on the carpet, poring over the brightly colored pages.

In one strip, a car grew steadily larger from frame to frame.

When, in the last frame, it exploded, each nut and bolt was carefully delineated, and the whole was surrounded by a zigzag penumbra of stylized fire: white, orange, red.

Taking a step closer to the chest of drawers so that he could see his watch, Paul Walters began drawing the brushes across his scalp. Because of the time difference, it would be more than two hours before Sylvia could be reached, at the radio station in California.

"We're all three of us sincere men," said Bloch. "That is not the difficulty. The difficulty is that governments, by their very nature, are never sincere."

It had not escaped Paul Walters that the car bomb in Geneva could quite possibly have been the work of factions within his own government, an incident meant to exert pressure of a cruder and more personal kind upon his own decisions and dealings here in Compiègne. But Bloch, he knew, meant something else.

A small rain, light but steady, fell upon the roof of the little stone church where Lolombela, Walters, and Bloch had arranged to meet in secret before the general negotiations resumed, later that morning. Strolling together up the nave, they could feel cold air rising from the stones beneath their feet. Ahead, in the dim light, gold objects emerged without shine.

"Sincere men," Lolombela said, after a time. "Governments beyond sincerity." He frowned. "It is possible. But if so, perhaps out of that difficulty we may make an advantage."

"We must try." Bloch's agitation was apparent only in the deliberateness with which he controlled it: hands clasped behind his back, each footstep a measured event. "So I repeat: the car was German, the target our esteemed American colleague here, the perpetrators a white South African group that does not appear to exist."

When Paul Walters stopped to light a match, the two men flanking him were carried a few steps forward by their own momentum. In this way the three briefly became a triangle of men regarding, in near darkness, the sudden upward surge of flame. The fire was a thought, the thought was the oldest one:

Around this danger—this heat and light—we can be safe together.

Then Walters drew repeatedly on his pipe, coaxing the small flame into rhythmic submission, and the three men's considerations once again subsided into civilization, difference, suspicion usefully controlled.

"I have spoken to the President," he said.

"And?" Bloch now walked slightly ahead of the others.

"Nothing has changed."

"I find this hard to believe."

"If I may speak for Heinrich . . . ?" Lolombela kept his pace matched to Walters's.

Bloch gave a curt nod.

"The two of us feel that the plan we have discussed among us may now be doubly compromised by the Geneva incident. First, and most obviously, you yourself have, for a time, become the object of unusual press scrutiny. This could be a problem. But we are more concerned about a second possibility."

As they walked, Walters regarded Lolombela. As hard as he was to know, Joseph was nonetheless a man about whom it was impossible to be mistaken. The soft flashes of energy that crossed his features when he spoke were those of a man who understood his desires. He was a patriot. He believed that men without children aged badly. He was a dreamer, but a realistic dreamer. "Go on," Walters prompted.

The sound of the rain's gentle fall upon the church roof now interlaced itself with the more distant gurgle of water massed and draining through the stone waterheads outside.

"It is not hard to imagine that your government, upon learning of the role Heinrich has proposed for Europe in the matter of the fission bomb—"

"But I have not informed the President of the substance of our discussions. He knows only that I see promise in them."

"Still. Let us speculate. Would the U.S. not then try to expand its options?"

"As you know, Joseph, that is why I am here."

Having reached the chancel, with its intricately carved lattice-work screen, Bloch whirled round to face his colleagues. There was enough drama in the gesture for Walters suddenly to wonder if Bloch's apparent distrust was not at least partially staged.

"What is to prevent an intelligent observer," Bloch demanded, "from concluding that the U.S. itself detonated that car bomb?"

Walters allowed a small silence. His pipe smoke spread like incense. "To what purpose?"

"As a result of the German republics' trade embargo on white South Africa, we will lose over a billion deutsche marks in revenue this year alone."

"But since we all agree that the future of the white South African government is limited, this loss is an investment." Walters removed the pipe from his mouth. "To what purpose would my government terrorize itself?"

Bloch put one hand stiffly in his jacket pocket, and his anger seemed immediately to catch, like a pawl in a ratchet wheel. "What are you playing at? You know what is at stake for all of us. You cannot—you cannot hand us a line."

Walters dropped the spent match to the floor, regretting the necessity for gesture. The church was a treasure, twelfth century. It was said Jeanne d'Arc had been brought here.

"Heinrich," he said, "I'm not handing you anything but the ball. Just tell me what you've got."

"The ball. Yes." Bloch broke his stare long enough to glance at Lolombela—a gesture of inclusion, certainly, but also, as Walters had foreseen, a not quite voluntary assertion by the German of his own command of the American idiom. "It is interesting that of all the world's nations, only the U.S. plays a form of football in which the ball is mainly passed by hand." He extended his own hand, the one not sheathed in his jacket pocket, to invite the two men to precede him through the chancel arch and into the little side chapel beyond. "Having it both ways is a thing your country seems to enjoy."

"You are speaking about the car bomb."

They were in the chapel now. "That and everything else."

The two Westerners watched Lolombela approach the chapel's small stained-glass window, which time or craft had turned out in tortoiseshell tones. The scene depicted was familiar to none of them. When Lolombela turned back around, his features were swallowed in his companions' shadows.

"Later this morning," Bloch began, "the Prime Minister of white

South Africa will hold a press conference. He will deplore the bombing, he will announce an investigation. There will be the usual rhetoric, but only for"—he tossed his chin; he searched for the phrase—"only for domestic consumption."

In the two strict paces and the pause Bloch measured out for himself Walters read a resumption of theatricality. It calmed him. His attention grew expansive. His pipe smoke did.

"Then," Bloch continued, apparently addressing the barrel vault that arched over them, "the Prime Minister will suggest evidence that the car bomb was in actuality the work of black Azanians, a group seeking to undermine the white government's international ties. He will issue an invitation: that the U.S. be part of a joint investigation of the incident. Full cooperation, intelligence sharing, extradition agreements—whatever is necessary."

Contesting wills, absolute attention. In fact, Walters had already been extensively briefed on the white Prime Minister's plans for a press conference. He sat now in one of the chapel's side pews, twisting in it slightly so as to continue facing the two men.

"Heinrich," he said, "allow me once again to congratulate you on your nation's intelligence operations. One of the marvels of modern statecraft."

"And I in turn must warn you that if the U.S. intends to play both sides in Southern Africa, it will no longer be possible to organize the middle scenes we have discussed."

"I assure you: nothing has changed. Either in U.S. policy or in my charge here."

From the nave came a soft burst of panicked chirps and a flutter, barely grazing the men's sight, of mottled bird wing, breast, and beak. A sparrow had become trapped in the church.

Leaving the window, Lolombela began a slow circuit of the chapel, and Walters, while continuing to listen to Bloch, subtly shifted the larger portion of his awareness to the African.

"My instructions are to take nothing for granted," Bloch went on. "There are even those who believe your fission bomb to be only in the earliest stages of development—a ploy to gain military and trade concessions."

Walters emptied his dead pipe into his hand: ashes. He foresaw Lolombela's cheeks streaked matte where now they glistened:

ashes. He imagined his daughters' children's dreams purged of color, filled with fear. "Nothing," he said, "could be more dangerous. I have been frank to the point of treason."

"But if you are being used by your government—"

"You insult both my intelligence and your own."

"We have reports."

"Disregard them. The situation is as I have explained it."

"But your President's term expires in less than two years. After that—"

"The President will not leave office without resolving this matter."

"Time," said Bloch. "We need time."

"This is our time," said Walters.

Lolombela picked something from the seat of one of the back pews.

"It is up to us," Walters said, by way of a cue.

"Yes, yes. Three men far from our peoples." The rosary Lolombela had plucked from the pew seemed a marvelously irrelevant thing. He wove it around his knuckles as he walked. "But it is to them we are responsible, so we must be . . . cautious? Yes, that is the word I want."

He stopped before Walters, standing very close to him, in the African manner. "Today Ambassador Bloch and I will stall the talks until the U.S. issues its response to the white South African proposal. If it is satisfactory, we will proceed with the plan we've discussed. If not—" He puffed his cheeks.

Walters relaxed. "By noon you will have it. Is that agreeable, Heinrich?"

Bloch nodded.

They walked to the priest's door, its threshold worn concave by the passage of feet. Behind and above them the sparrow resumed its desperate cries. When Bloch pushed open the ancient oak door, the bird dipped in flight and shot out of the church ahead of them.

"An omen, let us hope," said Walters.

"Let us hope," said Bloch, and with a baleful look he dashed through the rain to his waiting car.

For a moment Lolombela and Walters remained in the doorway.

"You know," said the African, "our daughters are sharing a house in Los Angeles now."

"No. I had no idea."

"Bloch told me."

Walters fumbled with his pipe in dismay. "Heinrich? How would *he* know?"

Lolombela said nothing.

The light was pearlescent and the air soft as cloth. Much of what Bloch had said still unsettled Walters, but as he and Lolombela moved out into the rain he displaced his worries. They were useless. When he was far enough away from the church to see it whole, he turned back toward it, and the sight filled him unexpectedly with love, longing, and the greatest trepidation. He understood.

Seeing was Believing.

On the way to the hotel where he was to have breakfast with the man who called himself William Walters, Michael nearly caused a traffic accident.

Shortly after waking, he had loaded the bed of his pickup with a dozen boulders that had been promised to a client for later that day. None of them was smaller than four feet in diameter, and Michael had taken care to secure them beneath a tarpaulin, which he had then tied down with rope. Once out on the freeway, however, he saw to his horror that the pickup's own slipstream was working the tarp loose, and even as he looked for an opportunity to stop, the ropes came undone, the tarp flapped open, and three of the boulders were hurled out of the truck, to dash themselves against the windshield of the car behind him.

The man in the besieged car slammed on his brakes, causing the vehicle to spin a complete circle on the roadway, burned-tire smoke swirling up on all sides. Behind him, other drivers peeled off to the right and left, successfully avoiding both him and the now scattered boulders. The man gazed in stupefaction through his windshield. It was intact.

"You okay?" Michael asked him. Traffic had come to a halt. "I'm really sorry."

The man said he was okay. He got out of his car.

"Maybe we should exchange addresses and that stuff," Michael continued. "Just in case."

The way the man shook his head could have meant no but seemed more to indicate continued disbelief that he was not dead. He walked over to one of the boulders and stared at it. Horns were honking.

"Well, then we better get out of here." Michael picked up the boulder nearest him and tossed it back into the truck.

Looking from Michael to the boulder he himself had been staring at, the man stepped forward and gave it a tentative kick. It tumbled several yards. "Hey," he said. "They're not real."

Michael stopped. "Well, no, I guess. Not in that way." He threw another boulder into the bed of the pickup.

The man had begun to laugh—though whether out of relief at his reprieve or because of the incongruity of the foam rubber boulders, neither of them knew. He picked up the one he had kicked and tossed it to Michael.

"Weird," said the man.

"Every day in every way," said Michael. "Weirder."

Traffic had resumed, parentheses around them. They returned to their vehicles, and in departure Michael waved.

Things, he thought, *keep coming undone*. This was a form of speculative mourning. Laurel and Sylvia were constantly on his mind.

As he entered the hotel dining room, Michael realized that he had no idea what the man whom he'd come to meet looked like. An agreeably out-of-work actor serving as morning maître d' inquired whether Michael wished to be seated inside on a banquette or outdoors on the terrace. From the trees branching this way and that above the white mesh table Michael selected, a magenta petal fell into his orange juice.

"Michael Bonner," said a man who seemed to have arrived at Michael's table without approaching it. He was wearing a freshly pressed safari shirt. "I'm William."

Michael did not take the proffered hand. "Sit," he said.

They studied each other—William smiling, Michael not. The waiter brought a second glass of orange juice.

"Okay." William sighed. "So you're pissed off at me in at least

eight different ways. Do you think I blame you?" He took a sip of
his juice, then skimmed his upper lip with his tongue in the normal
manner of a man with a mustache. "All I ask is that you hear me
out."

"Hear you out, huh. I bet that'd be real interesting."

William gazed mildly across the table, and for a moment Michael
thought he could in fact see something of Sylvia in the set of the
man's nose, brow, hairline. But a fraction of a second later he was
again uncertain.

"I mean, I've never heard someone explain to me before why
he's been committing acts of vandalism, burglary, and criminal
harassment against me and the people I know."

William nodded sympathetically. "It's unusual."

"You fuck. I'll put the cops on you."

There were tufts of grass springing up among the flagstones. They
had been planted there, and watered, and carefully maintained, by
illegal aliens. No one liked to think about the desert.

"We've already discussed this cops business. I mean, my niece
and I did, but we both know she told you, right?"

Michael blinked and braced himself.

"Or maybe I'm wrong?"

It was too late to be prepared.

"I don't want to be indelicate, but I'm sure you've considered
the possibility that your new girlfriend isn't giving you the whole
story. Not that she'd have to lie, exactly; she could just leave out
a few central bits. Right?"

"There's nothing she doesn't tell me," said Michael, though even
as he spoke he realized he must be wrong. William shrugged and
raised the glass of orange juice to his lips. He took two measured
swallows and replaced it on the table.

"I want to know what your stake in all this is," Michael said.

"It's immaterial," William said.

"Not to Sylvia. She doesn't believe you are who you say you are."

"And you?"

Michael watched the man's features shimmer and shift again. He
rubbed his eyes wearily with his fists. "I'm withholding judgment,"
he said at last.

The waiter arrived and said a few things about specials. Michael and William ordered breakfast. People were cutting deals here and there beneath the spreading daydream trees, and Michael was thinking about his father's samurai sword, which might yet, it seemed to him, cut to the center of this matter, if there really was a center. He let his gaze become a stare, his silence grow bolder.

"Off and running, then," said William, who had begun turning his fork methodically over and over in its plateside place. "The interests I've been working for—those fellows had a plan."

"What fellows would those be, I wonder," Michael wondered aloud.

"And because I have a weakness for plans—it's my training—I went ahead and performed those unpleasant little acts of vandalism, burglary, and criminal harassment you mentioned a moment ago. Not nice, I agree. But no one was hurt."

"No one hurt!" Michael's outrage began on behalf of Sylvia but careened with a force that surprised him back into the realm of self-interest. *Not that he really believed she'd leave out a few central bits.*

"I see why you might not want to take my word on that, but for what it's worth to you, coming from me, you can." The ghost of a smile crossed William's face. Breakfast arrived. William ignored it.

"I'm sure you're one of the few people in this town who actually read the papers," William continued when the waiter had left. "And I'm sure you know who her father is."

"That sounds like a question."

"Only partially. No, the real question is whether you believe Paul Walters is in Geneva."

Michael swallowed a forkful of eggs benedict. Both William's hands were on the table, and Michael was in the process of noticing that the man must be left-handed, since he wore his watch on his right wrist, when the watch's second hand stopped. The face read 8:16.

"You're going to tell me I'm stupid to believe that," Michael said.

"I'm going to suggest you ask Sylvia about it," William said.

Michael looked away.

"In the meantime, there's the project I mentioned over the phone."

Michael's returning eye fell, for no particular reason, upon William's shoulder, where a tiny moth had come to rest.

"I thought we were going to listen to you explain yourself."

"Sure. But you know this is how we do it around here. In deal memos, contracts, my-people-in-touch-with-your-people sorts of arrangements. The lingua franca."

"Don't bullshit me. How much time do you spend in Washington?"

"Aha. Washington."

"As in our seat of government. Because it seems to me that's the project you'd better want to talk to me about just now, since I don't know what your relation to Sylvia is, but if you are what I'm starting to think you are, I'll see you burn."

William drank his orange juice halfway down; it seemed to Michael that as he did so the man grew paler. "Excuse my directness," William said, "but what is it you think I am?"

"I think you're a spook."

Another near smile. "In the sense of a restless soul returned to life?"

"In the sense of an undercover operative for government interests."

"A spy?"

"Bluntly put, yes."

A sadness passed across William's features. The moth on his shoulder fluttered into the air, then settled again where it had rested. William likewise drew himself up, heaved a sigh without breath, and, just like that, began.

"Okay, I won't deny I've lent my talents to a government agency or two in my time—we'll get to that—but now I work for myself. And it's me you need to know about.

"As it happens, I really am the half-brother of Paul Walters. Sylvia has some trouble believing this, but under the circumstances, she can't be blamed. Paul's father was a flamboyant man, a commodities speculator, as the story goes, and he married my mother late: he was forty, she was nineteen. They had Paul right away. When the country had the Depression, the old man had a stroke. Within a year, my mother remarried, a U.S. Army colonel this time. I was born the same year, twelve years after Paul. We lived in Washington."

Touching his napkin to his mouth, Michael tried to wipe away the anger and apprehension that were gathering there. He knew he could be hurt by what he might hear. He recalled that he had come here to listen. "I'm listening," he said, lifting his coffee to his lips.

"Well, Paul and me—with an age difference like that, of course I worshiped him. I went to his high school football games suited up just like him; I took his side in the political arguments he'd have with my father, even though I was too young to know a broken accord from the crack in my ass. He taught me chess; sometimes he let me win. Sometimes I used to imagine it was really Paul who was my father. You know how things can get."

In the distance, an automobile horn sounded the notes of "The Mexican Hat Dance." Michael wondered if he actually did know how things could get. For example, though he had purposely chosen the shady side of the table so that he could study William, the light seemed now to have reversed this arrangement. He leaned back in his chair; he contained his impatience.

"Anyway," William continued, "the war changed all that. Paul joined the Navy and was gone for five years. I contracted a finely honed sense of betrayal, which pretty soon developed into a full-blown, generalized piss-off. By the time Paul got back, I was in military school; after that, the Army. All pretty standard, all pretty boring. When I realized I'd decided to leave the service, I made the down payment on a used twelve-wheeler, and my short but happy life as a trucker began."

"I'll bet this is where the plot thickens," said Michael.

"Well, sir, you could say that; yes, you could. Because it's my death scene."

William's huevos rancheros were untouched, stone cold. His orange juice drank half of what remained of him before he put the glass back down. Michael stared at the paling man.

"Your death scene," Michael repeated. "I wonder what the effects budget was. For a sequence like that."

William smiled and stroked his mustache with his forefinger—once left, once right. "This is how it happened. I joined the union right away. Got very active, very close to the leadership. I liked the excitement. When certain government elements recruited me as an informer, I liked that even better—a life of intrigue, some extra cash. Then one morning on a highway in Oklahoma, a couple of rigs forced me over to the side of the road, and when I opened the door to find out what was up, I got a rifle blast in the chest. Horrible to see so much of your own blood. I was dead before I hit the pavement."

The ash-winged moth on William's shoulder had fallen motionless. The cup of coffee that had just then slid from a waiter's tray hung sideways in motionless spillage over the flagstones. Michael's right hand, fisting and unfisting beneath the table, stopped in mid-flex, midfist. Nothing was a motion picture.

"Everything okay, gentlemen?" inquired the waiter, above the clatter and breakage of the coffee cup.

And although okay wasn't quite the case, Michael dismissed the man with a nod and smile, then turned his gaze back upon William. "You know, Mr. Walters, I'm just an industry guy temporarily out of work, and I haven't met too many *completely* dead people yet, but it'd seem to me that someone in your condition would have more pressing things to do than bother the rest of us. Or, for that matter, make no-budget documentaries in Canada, although now that I think about it, maybe there I can see the connection. Still, I don't know whether you're telling me you're a ghost, an angel, or a liar. Do you?"

"Maybe it doesn't matter?"

"That depends on what else you have to say."

William smiled in the manner of someone who has learned the limits of other people's willingness to listen. "Right," he said in ambiguous preface.

Just then Johnny and Chentula strode diagonally across the shimmering field of Michael's vision. Johnny carried a guitar case and Chentula was gesticulating—they were arguing over whether or not to insert a guitar break in the song they were to record that day—but since they and Michael had never met, there was no reason he should recognize them, or they him.

"You know those guys?" said William.

Michael felt the hairs on the back of his neck bristle in animal surmise. The two men who had just passed had never entered William's line of sight. "What guys?" said Michael.

"That's okay. I know you don't know them yet."

"Listen." Michael backed his chair partway from the table and looked, purely theatrically, at the place on his wrist where his watch had once been. "I've got a lot of other appointments today, so if you'll excuse me . . ."

"And you know what I've got?" said William. "I've got a copy of the screenplay for *Steel Chrysanthemum*."

Michael froze. It had been an unshakable rule of the production that all such copies be strictly accounted for.

"Good stuff," William continued. "Wonderful, really. But for my money, the real story's buried in the subplot."

"The subplot."

"The *Catawba*, the *Roanoke*: sister battleships commanded by half-brothers. The younger guy worships the older one, then feels betrayed by him. Has to prove himself. Yeah, I know—it's a convention. But that's because it's enduring, a truth. Am I right?"

At that moment the hotel management saw fit to turn on an artificial waterfall near enough to Michael's ear to chill its tympanum, and though he continued to meet William's blue-gray gaze, he found himself unable to keep from wincing. A mind, he reflected, must be a terrible thing to read.

"So you're the one," said Michael, "who killed *Steel Chrysanthemum*. You and your Washington buddies."

"No. I knew about it. That's all. And the way it was handled was part of what changed my mind."

"Changed your mind?"

"I know it tarnishes the image a bit, but you don't always know right away in my line of work who you're supposed to be . . . haunting. Strategic damage can be an oddly free-floating sort of pursuit."

"That's your field? Strategic damage? Great." Yet Michael was feeling more kindly disposed toward William. There was a subtlety to the man. Moths liked him.

"I don't expect you to trust me. Just to keep in mind what I say."

Throughout this last exchange Michael had been toying with the salt shaker, a small domed object that he now held before him until

William delivered his attention to it. Michael gave it a short toss. William's hand shot out and plucked it from the air.

"Left-handed," Michael observed.

"Since Oklahoma," William answered. "Sure."

Because when you are a ghost, certain reversals occur, the effect of your having walked through the mirror, so to speak, to embrace your reflection—a thing of light, after all, as opposed to lovely, lumpish flesh.

"What is it you want me to keep in mind?"

"That I've changed sides," said William.

Momentarily at a loss, Michael decided, at the urging of his bladder and his self-esteem, to seek counsel in the hotel men's room. Even as he excused himself, he saw William raise the orange juice glass once more to his mercurial lips.

It was the practice of this hotel to enshrine in a plastic-faced frame above each of the men's room urinals the front page of the daily newspaper. Information-gathering during an otherwise idle moment. Michael was distracted as he unzipped his pants, unsettled as he pissed, so he read fully half an article on the newly imposed prohibition of public assembly that obtained in the rhetorical state of Azania before he noticed—

Before he saw—

Before he was able to absorb the purport of the captioned photograph of Paul Walters that accompanied the lead article, itself coupled with the one he had just read.

U.S. CONSULATE LEVELED BY CAR BOMB IN GENEVA
WHITE SOUTH AFRICAN EXTREMISTS CLAIM CREDIT,
NAME AMERICAN DIPLOMAT AS TARGET

For a while he read. The story broke to an absent page. He flushed the urinal and left.

By the time Michael got back to the table, William was gone.

Upon the table there now sat a full glass of orange juice. In it floated the moth. Beneath it: two hundred-dollar bills and a fold of paper.

Michael lifted the glass to open the paper, which, in an angular left-handed script, bore the message "For her tires."

As he examined the note, Michael negligently let the glass tilt to one side, causing it to produce an odd metallic clink from within. He shifted his attention from the note to the glass, then, after peering into it, poured its contents carefully through the white metal mesh of the tabletop.

The orange juice seeped immediately away into the desert that lay disguised among and beneath the terrace flagstones.

Upon the tabletop, perfectly dry: the dusty-winged moth and a thirty-aught-six slug.

There were video cameras all around her but none of them were yet aimed her way, so Sylvia persisted, as if to absent herself, in rereading James Joyce's last novel, *A Simple Tail*. That someone who had so purposefully reinvented language in *Finnegans Wake* could come around at the end of his life, at the end of his sight, to write so vivid, erotic, and loving a volume as the one she now held had always seemed to her exemplary, moving, instructive.

She closed the book.

"Sylvie?" said the director, a college-age man with a tufty haircut. "It's you next." He was looking at her in a way that seemed unnecessarily optical. "Of course, if you want to be carried *bodily* over to makeup, your wish is my . . ."

She kissed him on the cheek as she passed.

The first of her father's messages the night before had reached the station before she herself had, and the cryptic brevity of its reassurance had had the effect of alarming her thoroughly. However, by the time father and daughter had actually spoken on the phone, a third of the way through her show, she'd made a visit to the newsroom and knew what there was to know, at least publicly, about the car bomb.

She'd said: "So the whole incident was for show, it sounds like."

He'd said: "Speaking off every kind of record, yes—that's what I think."

"You've got terrific skin," the makeup girl told Sylvia. "I'll just give you a little foundation, do your eyes." She considered her charge. "And maybe just a tad of lip liner, okay? To keep those angles."

"Sure," said Sylvia. "Whatever."

At the other end of the huge swimming pool that was to be the set for the shoot, Johnny, Chentula, and their studio band were doing a sound check—tuning up, adjusting volumes, fixing the mix. It had been Sylvia's idea to include Tsotsi in the station's video promo, and now everyone was happy with the notion. The swimming pool sported unlit flares placed at strategic intervals. There were going to be fire effects.

"Okay," said the director. "You guys on felt, do your stuff." Their stuff consisted of stretching a sheet of green felt over semiperforated fiberboard, itself to be lodged over the water at drainage line so one could walk about upon the pool's surface without undue moisture. In short, a pool table.

It struck Sylvia that fire effects were excessively esteemed by those who had not experienced the real thing.

"Now, you don't have to do anything until Glen and Mack've almost finished," said the director, crouched before Sylvia, whose eyes, for receipt of eyeliner, were hugely open and motionless. "If we have to reshoot it, we'll just do that. No big deal."

"I want my engineer," she said, to be annoying. "Without him, I'm an infant."

"Him you get to see at work tonight. This is something else, right?"

She essayed a smile.

"Beautiful," said the director, already turning away.

When Sylvia had decided to tell her father about William, in some fashion, what she had found herself asking him was why she and Kristen had been kept in the dark so long regarding William's death.

"You with the reflector, we need a little more sunlight over there," said the director, pointing left. "Yeah, right," he said. "Let's go."

A pair of production assistants arrived, clutching fifteen twenty-two-and-a-half-inch billiard balls—exactly ten times regulation size—and racked them up at the foot spot, which Sylvia would shortly be occupying, on the table of the pool.

Chentula gave a nod, and Tsotsi launched into the intro to "Change Reaction," their newest song.

"This is going to be a bomb," the director's assistant said into the director's ear. "We should be using miniatures." The director took off his sunglasses, gave the man a withering look known to all assistants everywhere, and fired him.

A pair of enormous honeycomb-core cue sticks were brought on set, and after Mack and Glen had attempted a few preliminary strokes, so as not to look unnecessarily comical, Tsotsi hit the song's three-measure vamp, Mack said what he was supposed to say— "We came to play"—and, spotting the cue ball two thirds of the way across the head string, took aim and broke.

He sank the ten ball, the thirteen, the seven.

"Maybe we should try it with your hair up," the makeup girl said, cocking her head assessingly at Sylvia. "I like that with the unmatched earrings."

Sylvia wasn't listening. She was thinking instead about the semi-professional evasiveness of her father's answer regarding the hiatus between William's death, if death it was, and the imparting of that news to herself and Kristen. It was this evasiveness that had prompted her to tell her father how the current love of her life had arranged to have breakfast with someone who claimed to be, and looked disturbingly not unlike, her dead half-uncle, William.

Glen dropped the five ball in the corner pocket, the two in the side, then scratched. He looked sheepish.

> Now we have a change reaction,
> One thing leads to another.
> Now we have a change reaction,
> State of the heart,
> No change apart;
> The masses are critical, brother.

Switching out of the ostinato figure he had been spidering across the keyboard before him, Chentula began a short but emphatic solo. The artificiality of the scene before him annoyed him, and this annoyance gave his music a staccato quality new to the song, new to him. He was here in America to make things real, but the very things he was most certain of kept sliding away from him, as had, for instance, his argument with Nomanzi over their respective visas. Perhaps it didn't matter. But he wondered to what extent the blond woman who had arranged so much for him, for Nomanzi, for all of them, might—if only by class and nationality and parentage—be an undermining influence, a poison flower. He hit a chord, held it, and removed his gold-glazed sunglasses. He nodded to Johnny.

"Are these guys going to be around for a while or what?" whispered the director to Sylvia as she stripped down to her bathing suit. "If we have to do a retake and lip-synch it, I mean."

"Sure. They'll be around." She patted his knee. "Stop worrying."

Worrying, however, had lately become her own special province, and her father's reaction to the news of Michael's breakfast plans had done nothing to reassure her. "Don't let him go," Paul Walters had said. "William's been dead for years," he'd said. "Stay away." The tones of concern in his voice had seemed, in their multiplicity, to collide with one another like cars in a freeway pileup.

Mack drew a bead on the twelve ball and dropped it easily. He sank the nine ball. The four, three, fourteen.

Although Johnny had originally argued against even brief instrumental solos, seeing them as a sign of decadent bourgeois individualism, he had in the end allowed Chentula to convince him otherwise. Listening now to the stream of chiming notes that rushed with perfect clarity from the amplifiers lent them by the record company, Johnny felt that he had never heard his own music this well before. Video cameras circled him as he played; they singled him out, using the brim of his newly acquired cowboy hat as a horizon line to their view. *Because I am white,* he thought. *Because I am their market.*

It was then, while the cameras were pointed the other way, that the crew brought Sylvia out on her green-and-white-striped chaise longue. There were checkered sunglasses covering her eyes. Languor. As she rubbed pale sunscreen slowly into the skin of her naked legs, she seemed oblivious of the mock billiard game around her, to the band behind her. Leaning back, she put a set of miniature headphones over her ears.

The song fell back into theme. The video cameras descended smoothly upon her.

Sizing up the table, Glen dropped the eleven ball in the side pocket, the fifteen in the corner. Only the eight, the one, and the six remained. The director looked at his watch.

Matters were in this condition when—

When Sylvia thought, *A sudden suntan for everyone. A thousand sudden suntans.*

For a moment she was afraid she might cry again—because her father had confided in her; because he had then apologized to her; because of the light, in which she'd be seen. One of the cameramen was being drawn around her on a dolly—the start of a full circle whose completion would end that part of her life in which she was pure, disembodied voice.

Tsotsi's song fell once again open for three measures, Sylvia removed her sunglasses and, meeting the camera's transparent gaze, said what was hers to say about the voice of the city of angels made visible.

Okay, she thought, *fuck it. Let a hundred videocassettes unfurl.* She was aware of the cameraman zooming slowly in on her face, glaring at her and pulling at his own cheeks in an alarming way; just in time she remembered to smile for the camera.

> Now we are a change reaction,
> Fire burns the water, sister;
> Can't stop a change reaction:
> Sun twice in your eyes,
> Sleepers arise,
> See what you hear now, mister;
> Hear now, hear now,
> Hear what we see now, mister.

And then there were some things for her to do.

Sylvia sat slowly upright, swiveling her legs—knees together but calves splayed—out over the edge of the chaise. The flares fired up in brilliant red behind her, to her left and right, at the edges of the pool's table, like a curtain. She disengaged herself from the headphones that were just for looks. Peering over her shoulder, she watched the white ball fail to sink the black ball. She headed for the headspot.

She'd been asked if she wanted a body double for this part, for the athletic side of it, but it had seemed to her that since she'd agreed to become visible, she ought to feel the whole purport of it; there were enough doubled bodies in her life already.

The production assistants had used razor blades to score the felt before her in an invisible asterisk radiating from the headspot; a matching disk of fiberboard had been cut out underneath.

Drawing herself together in animal anticipation, she stood for a moment absolutely still. *If there's one thing I know about,* she reflected, *it's going in headfirst.* She stepped forward and dived flawlessly through the felt into the chlorinated waters beneath.

"Sylvie. It's me," said the voice in her ear when she was again poolside.

Switching up the volume on the cordless phone she'd been handed, Sylvia breathed what, to her alarm, she recognized to be a sigh of relief. "Kristen! Where are you?" Not that she'd be ready to hear from Michael when he did call.

"We're in the Bahamas. I'm in the hotel lobby with a *New York Times* in my lap. I'm confused."

"The Bahamas!" Sylvia shooed away the makeup girl, who was trying to dry her hair for a second take. "What are you doing *there?*"

"That's not what I'm confused about. The heart has its reasons of which reason knows about jackshit, right? But you see there's this story in the paper about Daddy, and—"

"Yes; he called. Things are not"—she bad-eyed the idle crew, who were standing collectively too close to her conversation—"not what they seem."

"When were they ever?" Kristen answered with an impatient rattle of static, or newsprint, or family history. "Some kids had piano lessons; we had lessons in deniability."

Then there was an acoustical moment, as if she'd switched the phone from one hand to the other. "He's okay, though, right? This car bomb stuff is just some brilliant tactical initiative—is that what you're telling me?"

"Daddy's fine. He called me at the station last night."

"And he's not really in Geneva—that's what you're telling me. Right, Sylvie?"

"Oh, Kristen." Sylvia left a little silence to remind her sister of what they'd been taught not to discuss on the phone. "He's worried about us. He'd call you himself if he knew where you were." The production assistants were stretching new felt over the part of the pool table that had been ruined by her dive. "Besides, that's quite a junket you're on; maybe you'll run into him at your next port of call."

"Jesus Christ—a little slack, please. I run a year-round catering business; I'm taking a vacation. It's not exactly as if I sold the family jewels to finance it, you know."

At which Sylvia's free hand rose with a birdlike flutter to adjust the diamond at her ear. "Sorry," she said.

It was not that she distrusted Kristen, really, and it was not that she had any idea what might lie in store for anyone in days like these—but she did quite suddenly imagine an afternoon in which Petra and herself would venture gaily out in their respective automobiles to have all their jewelry reappraised, the price of things having become so unpredictable, so volatile. And they could have dinner afterward. Trade secrets, trade time. "How's your beau?" her voice asked.

"He loves me," Kristen answered. She giggled.

"Well, at least he knows what's good for him."

Mack and Glen were gathering the oversize billiard balls, complaining as they did so. They looked like basketball coaches from Mars.

"Sylvia?"

"Yes?"

"Maybe when Daddy gets back, it would be fun for the three of us to get together."

"God, yes. I mean, it's been far too long, what with our various adventures and everything."

Chentula had put on Johnny's hat, and now, to amuse himself between takes, he was attempting an Africanized version of a country-and-western song on his guitar.

"No, I meant something more," said Kristen. "Hey. What's that weird music?"

"Oh, we're shooting a video promo for the station. I've decided to go visible."

"Gee, Sylvia. Do you think the world's ready for that?"

"Lately it's hard to tell who's ready for what, so I'm just taking it step by step. But thanks for the vote of confidence."

"Anytime." In the radiophone's static, an exchange faded in

through the police frequency, then as quickly faded out. "So. Anyway."

"Kristen, you know Daddy would call you himself if we ever knew where you were. Are you sure you're all right? It isn't like you to keep disappearing this way." Sylvia fluffed out her hair to hasten its drying. "Can't you leave a number? He's genuinely worried about you."

"About *me*? I'd say a car bomb is a little more life-threatening than a pink coral beach."

"I think . . . I think you and I've already communicated about the Geneva incident."

" 'The Geneva *incident*'? Come on, Sylvia—you can't just keep hanging your future on this cloak-and-dagger business. We both have our own lives to lead; in fact, what I was starting to say is that maybe it's time—"

"And you're in the Bahamas—outside direct U.S. jurisdiction."

"—time for Daddy to begin slowing down. Retire, even."

"Re*tire*? Kristen, don't you think you'd better leave that to him?" She watched Johnny execute a tribal dance that was part Xhosa, part Texas two-step, and part something funny of his own. "I mean, if anybody but Daddy decides when he ought to stop, when he ought to go home, when he ought to say 'I've done enough'—that would kill him. You know it."

"I guess."

"I think he's almost ready, but I know it's got to be up to him."

"Did you see the press conference?"

"Daddy gave a press conference?"

"No. I mean it was a statement, really—no questions. And it came out of the White House. I've only just seen something about it on TV, but the U.S. basically declined white South Africa's invitation for a joint inquiry. We said we'd launch our own investigation. Which must mean the President is still behind Daddy."

"Definitely." Sylvia watched Glen wandering across the felt with a last armful of oversize billiard balls. She sat up. Johnny and Chentula were looking at a newspaper they'd been given. "Listen, Kristen."

"Sister dearest?"

"You know Daddy would worry about your being out of the country at a time like this."

"I'll call him."

"That might be a little difficult now, but try the Washington office."

"I will."

"And if you know when you're going to be where, maybe you'd better give me your itinerary."

"Well, I would . . ." Kristen sounded suddenly distant. "But we're kind of improvising."

"Improvising." Sylvia swiveled half around, looking for her sunglasses. "That's a word I associate with risk."

"It's okay, Sylvie."

"You're sure this guy's okay? You're sure about being in the Bahamas?"

"It all feels right. Yes."

There was a short break in the exchange. Everyone on the crew was waving at Glen, who was stepping carefully across the felt, the pyramid of billiard balls still in his arms.

"Hey, Sylvie," said Kristen finally. "That's really great about the video. It's the right move."

"Yeah, well, I'm not sure how much visibility I—"

But just then Glen strayed over the newly repaired felt at the headspot and, to his obvious astonishment—billiard balls borne haphazardly skyward on a geyser of water—sank from sight.

Through shallow dream, in the blue twist of Michael's sheets, Laurel woke. Because it was a Tuesday, one of two weekday mornings that did not require her predawn presence at the wholesale flower market, she had allowed herself to sleep past noon. Bands of sun and shadow fell through the slatted bedroom partition and across her naked body in what seemed the most flattering of bonds. She imagined momentarily that these bonds were her impending marriage to Michael. This marriage, she believed, would complete what was unsurveyably beautiful in her, just as Michael's hands, mouth, cock constantly surprised and completed her more creaturely beauty. Running her own hands lightly over her breasts and the fronts of her thighs, Laurel felt a flicker of desire so intense she was unable to keep from crying out. She drew the fingers of one hand up between her legs, shuddered, and, a moment later, rose from the bed.

The window nearest her was half open. On its sill, two aloes, thriving in the sun. Breaking off one large stalk, its pale green an equal valued gray to her vision, she closed her eyes, crushed it in her hands, and rubbed the sweetly viscid gel over her nipples. From the canal below came the mild mutter of a duck and her ducklings at swim. Laurel opened her eyes. The aloe pulp, as she drew it away from her breasts, left twin strands of sap as clear in the sunlight as the single droplet of first sperm that sometimes broke over the head of Michael's cock just before he entered her.

She thought the Michael thought: *I love him because I allow him to be dangerous to me.* Originally, the terms of this proposition had been reversed—*Because I love him, I allow him to be dangerous to me*—but at some point the thought had taken on its present formulation. And now, as she turned toward the bed she had just vacated, she saw how far such a strategy might indeed take them.

When she had asked Michael why he had had his pickup's interior reupholstered in stripes, the truth—that it was the vehicle itself, not its appointments, that had been replaced—had long since been obvious to her: she had come across the truck's rental papers while searching the glove compartment for a hairpin. However, Michael's lie—that Jabez had borrowed the pickup and a TV studio had paid for the upholstery—had also immediately satisfied her. Having, in a sense, initiated the lie, she felt she had ensured that any future consequences it might have could only bind her and Michael more closely together.

From its carriage midway across the loft, Michael's video recorder emitted a sound of soft electronic commencement. An array of blue and red digits appeared across its browless face, and simultaneously the image of two men shaking hands materialized upon the several video monitors deployed here and there about the loft. The title on the screens read: "Geneva: A New Beginning?" A voice faded in over portentous music.

"Jesus Christ," Laurel said aloud, tossing the remote back onto the sofa.

Michael's sudden enthusiasms.

Laurel went to the refrigerator and poured herself a glass of mineral water.

It was true that when he had come to bed the previous night, to find her drowsing over an Italian fashion magazine, she had sensed in him an urgency to speak. It was true as well that she, lifting her nightgown's hem, lifting her hips to his mouth, had allowed her own urgencies to engulf and silence his. She finished the mineral water in one long series of swallows.

Now, suddenly, it was tomatoes she wanted, tomatoes she'd always wanted. She fetched from the crisper the largest one that came easily to hand, sliced it avidly, and spread it in an arc across a cobalt-blue plate. She chopped some fresh basil, sprinkled it on top. Breakfast.

Something was missing. Distraction was missing. So before she settled down with her meal at the dining table, she retrieved the Italian fashion magazine from its resting place on the bedside floor. She found its full-bleed color photographs soothing in their unnatural elegance; she found the seasonal line of clothes promoted in its pages completely improbable.

As she flipped through the magazine, though, she was unexpectedly arrested by this image: an elaborate gold-and-white harp, strung not with acoustic wire but with coiled telephone cable in colors arranged according to the spectrum. A black model in past-the-elbow white evening gloves was shown plucking the instrument, and on the succeeding page, a white man in black evening dress, the corresponding telephones burying him to the knees, held six handsets dexterously among his cared-for fingers and spoke, with apparent calm, into a green mouthpiece at right, a white mouthpiece at left.

Laurel closed the magazine.

She remembered.

In the middle of the night, she had woken to find Michael gone from their bed. After a while, she could hear him murmuring into the phone at the opposite end of the loft, and though she had meant to question him about the call—it was clearly he who had placed it, since the bedside phone had not rung—by the time he had returned to her she was again asleep.

Tomatoes? Laurel thought, looking down at her plate. Next she noticed the floor, half-bleached planks glossed sleek with poly-urethane, passing beneath her until she was standing next to the phone, the one Michael had used the night before, his private line.

For a moment she considered the gleaming black-and-white de-vice, with its ranks of accessory keys—memory, pulse/tone, pause. The number Michael had called the previous night was lodged there still, coiled into the telephone's circuits like an electronic snake. Laurel lifted the handset, punched the redial button, and as the jammed-together tones sprang into her ear, she once again closed her eyes.

Hi. This is Sylvia. Neither Nomanzi nor I can come to the phone right now, but if you leave a message, we'll call you back just as soon as we get home. Please don't forget to wait for—

Laurel did not wait for the beep, or for anything else.

Well, this is the silliest waste of time, Nomanzi thought petulantly. *And all for some Knightsbridge girl slumming it in the American sun.*

The woman who had phoned in for the floral arrangement had had an unmistakable patrician English accent. She had said her chauffeur would pick up the flowers within an hour.

Oh, but it shouldn't matter. Nomanzi stepped back to view her efforts, so specifically—and to her eye, so oddly—legislated by the caller: a large bouquet, white at its center (Nomanzi had used calla lilies), with radiating rings of orange anemones and brilliant red roses. *All jagged,* she thought. *Like a cartoon.* Impatiently she pulled the flowers from their vase and scattered them across the white tile surfaces that surrounded her.

The door swung open, and a pair of sunny-haired women in perfectly cut white tennis skirts entered the shop, their heads swiveling to take in the thrown blossoms. "I told you this place was high-concept," the taller one stage-whispered to her friend. "I mean, we're not talking flower shop here, we're talking *art.* Like Japanese or something."

Nomanzi sold them a hundred and forty-five dollars' worth of orchids. When the women left, she began assembling a new version of the white/orange/red arrangement.

It had disturbed her to find Sylvia's father the subject of a front-page story in the newspaper that morning. She had immediately perceived a connection between the bombing in Geneva and the suspension of public-assembly laws in Azania. She doubted Sylvia's father was in Geneva, and she was nearly certain that her own father was wherever Paul Walters was. This was not an issue she had felt free to discuss with Sylvia—there had been no telling where such a talk might lead—but she also understood that to avoid the subject now would be still riskier. As a diplomat's daughter, Sylvia was nothing if not fluent in the language of silences.

The phone rang twice. Nomanzi answered it. The caller hung up.

Imagining what Laurel might say about the flowers scattered haphazardly around the shop, Nomanzi was unable to suppress a smile. Perhaps she, Nomanzi, would pick them up soon; equally, she might scatter them farther. She laughed aloud. Unconscious illustration of her own dilemmas always served to reassure her as to both her acting ability and her responsible agency as a citizen of a rhetorical country.

Just as she was finishing the requested bouquet, she pricked her right hand on a rose thorn; her finger bled in almost comic profusion. To distract herself, Nomanzi turned on the shop's radio system, tuning it to KBZT-FM with the hand not wrapped in paper towels. The radio asked in song to be taken to the river, to be dropped in the water.

A gray sedan of Bavarian make pulled up in front of the shop. Its windows were mirrored. A black man in half-livery emerged from the driver's side of the car, approached the shop.

Nomanzi saw the moment he opened the plate-glass door that he was Xhosa. Casting her eyes about the shop with exaggerated theatricality, she turned up the radio.

"I've come to pick up the flowers for Mrs. Ellery," the man said, looking closely at her. With his hands he made a writing motion. Nomanzi slid a pen and a pad of paper across the counter toward him.

He wrote: "It is lunchtime for you now? Our cousin is weary of feeding the birds. He has a message for you."

She said: "I hope this is the arrangement Mrs. Ellery had in mind."

"Yes," said the man without looking at the flowers. "It is the arrangement."

Nomanzi left the blossoms behind when she closed the shop. She left the radio on without quite knowing why.

At the car, she moved to open the passenger door in front, but the man, glaring at her, opened the back door for her instead. She got in. The car slid into traffic the way a fish, momentarily detained, might rejoin its school.

"The plans have changed," said the driver, glancing at Nomanzi in the mirror. His collar had ridden up over his jacket on one side, a white cotton triangle dog-eared at the jugular so that the pretense of livery began to seem farfetched. "Everything is different now."

"Why would things be different now?" she said carefully. "Besides, I thought I was the one left to come up with a plan."

"Yeah, Cousin. You and your father."

"My father?" They were speaking Xhosa. She stared at the fold of flesh at the driver's neck. "But of course, as you have surely been told, my father knows nothing of this."

Which is exactly when it struck her that the car's silvered windows left her not only invisible to the passing public but also vulnerable to her undefined back-seat situation. She hit the switch on the armrest to her right; when the lozenge-shaped pane descended with a hum, she relaxed and ran it back up again. "How did you know where to find me?"

The man shrugged. She noted the semicircles of perspiration soaking through his jacket. "When our older relatives have reasons to tell us things, then we listen."

"So this is all coming from Command?"

He made a half-frown. "This car is very dirty because of the ashes from the fire last week. Would the lady mind if we stop at this car wash?" He pointed to a concrete bunkerlike building just off the boulevard. Even from the traffic light at which they were stopped, the water roar of the car wash was distinctly audible—a cataract in the desert.

Nomanzi understood. She nodded.

"Just sign here," said the messenger. "I'll fill in the time."

Jabez propped the package—a narrow cardboard box about the

length of a man's arm—up against the studio wall. He signed the voucher. Boris, who had roused himself for the messenger's arrival, settled back onto the floor with a thump.

Hearing Laurel pronounce his name so startled Jabez that he fumbled the pen in returning it. She had come up behind him without a sound. "Laurel! You just about made my kid an orphan, sneaking up on me like that."

"I've got to find Michael right away," she said. "I know you can help me." She was pale, and her breath came to her with an exaggerated evenness that suggested she had prepared herself for the long haul.

"Well, sure, Laurel. I mean, I'll do what I can." On a video monitor behind her, the tape he had freeze-framed upon the messenger's arrival quivered with the image, in magnetic analogue, of a pickup truck apparently leaping through the display window of a jewelry store.

"Why, that must be the made-for-TV that Mikey lent you his pickup for," said Laurel, walking past Jabez to Michael's office. "When's it gonna air? I'm just dying to see it."

By the time Jabez caught up with her, she was running a finger through Michael's appointment book.

"Laurel, I—"

"That's okay, love bunch. I know there's no made-for-TV." She patted his hand absently. "It says here he's supposed to be making a delivery of foam rubber boulders across town about now. That sound right?"

"I guess so. We made up a batch a few days ago."

"I bet you did." She surprised him with a smile whose half brilliance seemed half genuine. "So." She slapped her haunch in mock enthusiasm. "Hot damn. Let's go."

"Us?"

"I'd like a little company on this road picnic. You know—the consolation of a friend of the groom? It's in the tradition."

Jabez, pulling at his beard, trailed after her toward the door. "Laurel, baby, now calm down a minute. First, we've got like zero chance of getting there the same time he does. Second—"

"C'mon, Boris. We're going for a ride."

"Second, whatever's going on—or *not* going on—I mean, it can't be anything you're going to settle in the middle of the—"

"Bring your package too. We'll need presents." She tossed him the package he had just signed for. "Looks like flowers, and you know how flowers are always appropriate."

Boris all but knocked Jabez over as, wagging his tail and barking, the dog squeezed between him and Laurel to follow her out the door.

So, by means of what seemed a supremely bad edit, Jabez suddenly found himself in the passenger seat of Laurel's green station wagon. She started the engine; in the back seat: Boris. Jabez stared mournfully down at the package he still held in his hands.

Standing on the inner sill of the studio's near window, catching the full glow of the early-afternoon light, was a full glass of orange juice. Jabez couldn't remember pouring it.

I'm dead now, he thought, staring at the glass and getting matters precisely wrong. The juice glowed. The tires spun. Then he and Laurel were gone from that place.

MICHAEL [*In voice-over*]: This damn pickup. I can't believe the fucking generator already— [*The engine starts.*] Okay. [*Calming himself*] Okay.

[*Looks irritably at his wrist. Remembers that his watch, which no longer works, remains on the bench in his desert home.*]

So what the hell time did she *say* she'd be done? [*Rubbing his jaw*] Of course, there's no reason why she *should* tell me everything. How much can you know about someone you just met anyway? But that *guy* . . .

RADIO: At KBZT we've got the spirit. So *you* get the sound of the city of angels.

MICHAEL: Where the fuck am I going? [*Peers at digital-display clock above a bank he passes.*] It's too early to show up at her place. No keys; I'd look like a detective or a rogue real estate agent. Why didn't I tell Laurel last night? Now there's all this Geneva stuff to cope with, Sylvia's father, car bombs, gut-shot orange juice. God*damn* it. Enough to make you weep. [*Glances in rear-view mirror.*]

Okay, okay—pass me, asshole. I'm a deadhead, right?

[THE MAN IN THE CAR BEHIND HIM *roars past.* THE WOMAN IN THE PASSENGER SEAT *fires up a plastic butane lighter to its maximum flame, which, in the car's open draft, is like a curved orange finger. She displays this finger to* MICHAEL.]

"So we'll see you at the station tonight," said Glen, as Sylvia reapplied her lipstick—a semisaturated red the same value as her eyes' lilac.

"Sure." She peered into the rearview mirror of her car. Her lips were where the words came out. "Except now I'm back to audio only. Don't forget."

Glen grinned. He was wearing dry clothes but still looked faintly absurd. "Voices in the night," he said. "That's us."

Whereupon she waved to him, released the clutch, and got herself out of there. The traffic picked her up as smoothly as a hundred careful hands.

She realized then that she already regretted making the videotape. She couldn't think why she'd agreed to it.

Deals, she could hear her father intoning, *are made in privacy. Whatever is acted out in public is calculated to protect that privacy.* He would be pacing as he spoke. *The real work, the part that matters, is invisible.*

Caught at a stoplight, she made as if to take a cigarette from her bag, then halfway through forgot what she was doing and found her gaze rising of its own to follow something that had swept past the windshield—the wipers, she thought at first, imagining her knee had inadvertently struck the dashboard control. But it was not the windshield wipers, it was a shadow cast by a passing bird—a golden eagle, in improbable fact—and as Sylvia watched, the creature rose with the majesty of its kind to take perch high on a billboard that itself towered high above the busy boulevard. Depicted on the billboard, and partially rendered in startling relief, was a craggy, sunlit mountaintop, upon one ledge of which sat two real men dressed as explorers.

A coming attraction, a major motion picture, a wonder of nature.

The eagle emitted two shrill cries that sounded nothing like laughter. The men appeared not to hear.

On Sylvia's dashboard, a small red eye warned her she was nearly out of fuel.

"Boy, you some kind of fucking gringo bastard, man."

Both Nomanzi and her compatriot were fairly sure the epithet did not apply to either of them, but it was disconcerting to see a man walking toward them and shouting. They got out of the car.

"*Maracón!*" the man cried over his shoulder. He was struggling to get out of a beige jumpsuit that bore the name of the car wash on its back. Hard behind him came a younger-looking blond man with a sunburn.

"Sorry. We'll be operating in a minute," he told them. "Pablo here has been dipping into the till, and I'm giving him a goodbye party."

Nomanzi saw the man who had driven her to this place relax and withdraw his hand from inside his jacket. She shuddered. She had not guessed that her contact with Cousin would be carrying a gun.

"Is our cousin well?" Nomanzi asked in English, while they waited for the manager of the car wash to return.

"Oh, you know: with so much work, it is difficult." In tone, the black man's answer contained yet another warning: Wait, it said; Not yet, it said. Nomanzi again had to suppress a wave of irritation: as if she, *she*, did not know what was at stake.

In the middle distance, a few more Spanish imprecations; then the manager reappeared, a little redder in the face, it seemed. Nomanzi's driver got back in the car and, as the manager waved him forward with a traffic cop's rolling gesture, eased the car to the brink of the car wash tunnel. The manager hooked the chassis's underside to the steel-link conveyor belt; the black man debarked, leaving the key in the ignition.

"Some days you just feel like blowing up the whole damn country." Both Nomanzi and her contact nodded carefully, uncertain which country the red-faced man had in mind. "Anyway," he continued, addressing Nomanzi, "you want any of the extras?" He pointed to a sign that offered rust inhibitor, polyglaze polishing wax, a chassis bath, and super sealer by Tortoise Wax.

"No, I think we'll just have the regular wash," answered Nomanzi.

"Right." He threw the mechanism before him into gear, and the car began to inch forward. "Catch you in the stretch."

So that Nomanzi and her still-anonymous contact began strolling down the glassed-in gallery that, running adjacent to the back of the car wash, yielded poignant views of water raining down upon the vehicle, of huge roller brushes preparing to fit themselves to its contours, of exhaust vents and gridded drains.

"Well, my nameless friend."

"Call me Mlomo."

" 'Mouth.' You are witty, Mlomo. But we have little time. What has changed? What is it you wish to tell me?"

"Our cousin is hoping you can tell us. The order has come down to cage the birds until we receive further word. He is willing to do this, but the risk is very high, and he will need help. Why have our plans been interrupted?"

"This is the first I have heard of it—"

"You have been seeing the papers?"

"Of course."

"Something large is being prepared. Even a blind man can read through the headlines: German Trade Embargo, Suspension of Public Assembly, Car Bomb in Geneva. And now we are told that the rockets that just a few days ago were so essential to our struggle are 'temporarily unnecessary.' "

In his voice Nomanzi heard a tension that shaded toward anger.

"Surely your father has confided in you," the man went on. "You must tell me what you know of these events."

"I have not spoken to my father."

"If the purchase and transport of these rockets is meant to serve as a diversionary move—"

"You have already told me things of which I was unaware."

"If we are to be of maximum effectiveness, if we are to play our role convincingly—"

"Then perhaps there are further things of which we must be satisfied to remain unaware."

The two nonacquaintances, coming to a halt in that improbable gallery of glass and concrete, exchanged a determined look. To trust and not to know, to know and not to trust—there could be little choice. And the waters rained down upon the sun-warmed metals of the car being hauled through the concrete tunnel, so that there rose about Nomanzi and Mlomo a scent of summer shower in dry terrain—half metallic to the nose, half organic—each atom of the descending fluid delirious with hopefulness: ocean to vapor to flesh, the waters from the waters. A temporary flood: *Don't you see that I am that I am and will always be so?*

With a tremendous whirring, roller brushes gripped the sides of the car and spun. Soapy water fell in a stream.

"You'll need a place—a safer place—to nest the birds, then," Nomanzi offered.

"Yes. It is essential."

They resumed their former pace. It had become necessary to speak into each other's ears, because of the tumult, so it was not always clear whether their facial expressions referred to what had been said immediately preceding or to what would next be said. It passed through Nomanzi's mind that this circumstance was not the worst metaphor she had ever encountered for history.

"I'll arrange it," she said. "A neutral ground—neutral for us—but safe."

"How soon?"

"By the end of the week."

Mlomo pursed his lips. To be too quickly satisfied, to leave this rendezvous without having learned what he clearly suspected was being kept from him: Nomanzi saw he was making the errors of personal interest—of pride, even—for which she had earlier chastised herself. Unless—and she had to force herself to consider the possibility—he was not, after all, who he said he was.

"Mlomo. It was you on the phone yesterday?"

"We are not to speak of that."

"You told me it was not useful for me to become a 'bioscope star.' What if I told you it is not useful for you to carry a concealed weapon in a city where you might at any moment be arrested for that alone?"

Mlomo threw her a quick look but said nothing. Beyond the glass, the revolving brushes withdrew, and a sudden monsoon of rinsing waters rained down upon the car being towed through the wash.

"A storm trooper? Is that how you imagine I see myself?" Mlomo eyed her again. "It is a precaution only. Who can be sure what will happen?"

Accepting the answer as a partial reconciliation, Nomanzi touched his shoulder with her hand.

"I will do as I have said," she told him. "As soon as I can prepare things, I will call you as before."

The pair turned briefly to watch a team of Spanish-speaking wash attendants scrub the car's interior, empty its ashtrays, vacuum its floor. A change in skin tone, in the cast of their uniforms, and these men might just as well have been agents from Security, methodically searching the car for fingerprints, contraband leaflets, firearms, a bomb.

Mlomo turned back toward Nomanzi long enough to give her a wry smile, the first she had seen from him.

"When you next need to speak to your father," he said, "you must tell him our car is now as clean as the one that was outside the American consulate, eh?"

It was a bold probe. Nomanzi forced herself to smile. "I will tell him you said so." Less than fifty yards behind them, behind the car wash, the newly unemployed Pablo used a crowbar to prize the top off a steel drum. He peered into it. Swearing to himself in Spanish, he tipped the drum over and began rolling it toward the body of the long building.

MICHAEL [*Still at the wheel of the pickup; still in voice-over*]: Okay, okay. I am losing my fucking equilibrium. [*Strikes the undersmile of the steering wheel with the heel of his hand.*] I have breakfast with some asshole who claims to be my—who claims to be Sylvia's—who tells me . . . no, I'm losing it completely: this guy actually told me he was dead.

RADIO: And when this kiss is ohv-uhhh . . .

MICHAEL: Unless he meant . . . [*Close-up of* MICHAEL'*s face shows him realizing what we have suspected right along: that he,* MICHAEL, *is already so bound up in what is coming to pass that any version of outraged incomprehension has long ago ceased to be a useful strategy.*]

WINDSHIELD: Ker-splat!

MICHAEL: Shit!

GOLDEN EAGLE: I liked it better when I was an omen. But gravity? Not mine to worry about. *Worry* not mine to worry about.

[MICHAEL *frantically starts the windshield wipers as the cars around him begin honking in irritation at his diminished speed. The* EAGLE *executes a slow, gliding pivot off one wingtip and, leaving the billboard far behind, heads upcanyon toward his natural nest. Tonight, he will feed.*

[*At the intersection,* MICHAEL *stops to survey the possibilities. He sees what he needs. He turns right.*]

"Wait a minute!" said Laurel, executing a little hop in the driver's seat and glancing over her shoulder. "That was him!"

Jabez, who had sighted Michael's pickup by chance a block earlier, heard the involuntary note of hope in her voice. *Why me?* he thought. *Why do I have to watch this?*

"Am I okay in back?" asked Laurel, her glossy black hair pinwheeling out in alternately directed swirls as she surveyed the onrush of traffic.

"Yeah, Laurel, you're fine all over." Jabez sank lower in his seat. He wished for the company of his wife, his son.

Pulling a tight U-turn, Laurel set off in pursuit of Michael. It was the anticipation of surprising him that, against all reason, had caused the note of hope to enter her voice a moment earlier. It was the desire to compress to nothing the time and space still intervening between her and that moment of surprise that now possessed her utterly, giving weight to her foot upon the accelerator, giving pictures to her mind.

Pablo tipped a second canister of ashes into the car wash's rinse tank. Then he put a case of Tortoise Wax in the back seat of his carapaced sedan and, hitting the horn as he pulled into traffic, sped away.

CAR WASH OWNER: Shit, am I glad to see the last of *him*.

MICHAEL [*Watching his pickup enter the car wash*]: Guy's trouble, huh?

CAR WASH OWNER: Well—
PABLO'S CAR HORN:

CAR WASH OWNER: —what's it sound like to you? I mean, gimme a goddamn break, "The Mexican Fucking *Hat* Dance"? Dumb. Just plain dumb. [*Shakes his head.*] You want any extras?

Slowing to a near crawl as she coasted over the speed bump at the gas station's entrance, Sylvia felt like an extra in a film whose script she had never seen. Car bombs, an uncle from the undead, an affianced lover who seemed more fully apprised of her fate than she. And now she would be visible across the nation's scan lines; the days of pure voice and music were done.

She fit the pump's nozzle to her gas tank, careful to dress it with the vapor-recovery gasket.

"Looks like you need a little body work," said the station attendant, eyeing the gash in the car's hood, the droop in its headlight.

"Yeah. I kind of had an accident."

"Fiberglass; you ought to fix it as soon as you can." He handed her his card.

"Thanks. I'll keep that in mind."

"We're twenty-four hours a day here."

"Great."

There was a rip as well in the gasoline pump's vapor-recovery gasket, so that fumes rose before her, corrugating the transparent air.

"Hey, your voice is really familiar," the man said. "Aren't you—um—um—"

Sylvia peered through the fume-rippled air that blurred her gaze to the establishment next door.

It seemed to her she was looking at Michael—at Michael, Nomanzi, and a black man she'd never seen before.

Stepping forward, she knocked over a bucket of suds: windshield cleaner. "Hey, I'm really sorry," she said. "I just thought—"

"You're that deejay, aren't you? Sylvia . . . Sylvia something?"

"No, you must've got me mixed up with someone else. What's that next door—a car wash?

The gas station attendant squinted inquisitively at her. "Yeah, that's my kid brother's place."

Sylvia handed the man a twenty. She righted the bucket.

. . . and it is then she realizes that the suitcase that is a radio is actually a bucket, and that she has been swinging it through the air in progressively wider . . .

MICHAEL: Misfires.

PREGNANT WOMAN IN NEWLY CLEAN BLUE FOUR-DOOR: Huh?

MICHAEL: I said, your engine misfires. Ought to have it tuned. [*The* WOMAN *smiles at him vaguely, a bottle of orange drink clamped between her thighs. She puts the car in gear and lurches off.* MICHAEL *turns to* NOMANZI.] I guess I'm next, after you. But where *is* everybody around here? Wasn't that the owner I talked to?

NOMANZI [*Indicating the car wash's office with her chin*]: The man he went off to get some change for us.

[MLOMO *affects to direct his attention to the still-dripping gray sedan, looking it over for streaks, scratches, imperfections—all the while keeping an eye on* MICHAEL.]

NOMANZI [*to* MICHAEL]: Yes. Here he comes now.

MICHAEL [*Looking at* NOMANZI *more closely*]: That voice! You're from where—the Caribbean?

NOMANZI: No. [*Laughing*] I am African.

MICHAEL: African! You know, it's funny: my friend Syl—"

MLOMO [*To* NOMANZI, *meaningfully*]: We will be late if we don't—

CAR WASH CHORUS [*From within the wash itself, in broken, no-part Hispanic harmony*]: Hey, man! What's that shit comin' outta those sprinklers? Looks like fuckin' *ink* or somethin' . . . *Mierda!* Turn the motherfuckin' thing off before that gringo's rig gets customized *completamente.* . . . Hey, *cholo,* it's rainin' black shit or somethin' in here—pull that stick, man! *Hijo de puta!* I got it all over me! *Pull that fuckin' stick, man!*

CAR WASH OWNER: Just unhook the goddamn thing and *drive* it out! Goddamn that Pablo—when I find him I'll fuckin' put a blowtorch to his—

"Michael!"

The sight of him—he has clearly failed just now to hear her cry his name—fills Sylvia with a tenderness so complete that in her breast it seems to speak to her surpassingly of the savagery with which she, he, all of them, appear content—indeed relieved—to live their lives.

In her flared nostrils, the scent of gasoline confirms this savagery. The sight, at her feet, of the prismatic suds from the spilled bucket confirms it.

She is wearing a blouse of sand-colored silk. Caught by the breeze, it billows, flutters, then is molded to her breasts and abdomen as closely as if it were another skin. Then it billows.

Sylvia, getting back in her car, decides to drive up over the asphalt divider that separates her from Michael and Nomanzi.

Boris remembers the Michael smell. He wants to see Michael. Almost exactly then, through the nose-streaked windshield, he does. He jumps into the front seat. This is the good feeling.

"Boris, your tail!" cries Laurel. "I can't see."

The dog is wagging his powerful tail back and forth across her face like a rolled-up flag as Laurel waits to make the turn into the car wash. "Jabez, could you . . . Thanks."

"Who's that up there with him?" asks Jabez, relieved it isn't Sylvia, whom he has not yet spotted. "And his pickup, what the . . ."

"Nomanzi?" says Laurel aloud. "It's Nomanzi?"

It is Nomanzi who first sees the pair of cars converging upon the three of them, and upon observing Laurel at the wheel of the flower shop's station wagon, she thinks: *There is the end of my job.*

Immediately she realizes the thought is irrelevant to her present situation. She catches sight of Sylvia in the other car. It becomes more than ever unclear to her just what her situation is.

Mlomo has pushed her behind him as a father might do a daughter in times of danger or stress. A series of sharp glandular alarms runs through Nomanzi.

"Sylvia!" Michael cries, his throat aching at the sight of her with something he knows despairingly to be love. "Are you okay?"

She gets out of the car. She neglects to close the door.

Mlomo reaches inside his jacket—a curiously tentative gesture.

"I'm fine . . . but . . . ." Sylvie's gaze is fixed on Michael. "What is everyone . . . ?" In a series of tiny glances, each fractionally shorter than the last, she is absorbing the diversity of motive and expectation animating this impromptu gathering of several of her life's chief players.

Mlomo's hand is still inside his jacket—the gesture losing its tentativeness by the millisecond. Nomanzi at last understands that he thinks they have been ambushed. She realizes as well that she has no reliable set of references for judging whether he is right.

"Enough, Mlomo," she says nonetheless. "I know these people. They—"

Laurel pulls the emergency brake, gets out of the station wagon, and begins running toward Michael. She is crying? Or her soul has turned inside out as easily as a hand, held palm up, simply turns—

"Over there, everybody. Please walk; your hands up." Mlomo indicates an area in front of Michael's ash-drenched pickup. He is holding a pistol of Czechoslovakian make, a weapon not properly familiar to him. The perspiration on his forehead and neck makes him feel extraordinarily at risk among these coolly dressed and demeanored people.

Laurel alone ignores him. She continues running toward Michael, who has only just now seen her. Mlomo looks at her in confusion, and although this unknown white woman is defying him, nothing about her defiance indicates that she is to be regarded as directly inimical to him, Nomanzi, or their plans. He grimaces.

"Michael, Michael, Michael." Laurel is in tears.

"I'm sorry," he says, taking her into his arms.

"You *must not move*," says Mlomo, attempting with his voice's measure to compensate for his uncertainty. He exchanges a fruitless look with Nomanzi. "Stand there, by the truck," he once again tells everyone else.

"Oh, Michael, Michael. You stupid bastard." The weariness with which Laurel speaks makes it seem for a moment as if she were alone with Michael. "Don't you see I would have done anything for you? Anything?"

Jabez steps out of Laurel's car, still holding the package she has placed in his keeping. He puts it down behind the car in order to raise his hands, indicate his good will. Boris comes bounding out of the vehicle, headed for Michael with a will unmixedly benign.

"Laurel. I've always loved you."

"But you're a piece of shit."

"Well, at least I don't think in TV sitcoms."

"No," Laurel answers. "You think in jack-off magazines. So why don't you go home and fuck yourself even sillier with that stupid blond cunt you've always loved too." Laurel whirls around upon him one last time. "She's nothing but a cunt."

At these words, Laurel pushes Michael from her and shifts her attention to Sylvia.

Mlomo appears newly confused: the attention of this weeping woman clearly carries more power than the Czech pistol that even he has almost forgotten in his hand. For the first time, he wonders if he may have been mistaken in producing the weapon. Perhaps these cars and their occupants have converged upon him and No-manzi by chance, or for reasons not involving them, even though the choreography is that of a textbook arrest. He wants to look at Nomanzi, but she has moved farther back. To look at her would be to leave himself at the mercy of the events before him—events that seem now to stretch unimaginably far: his children's children's children.

"So, Angel Voice," says Laurel, thrusting her face to within a few centimeters of Sylvia's. "Congratulations. You've found the love of your life!" Laurel lets loose a noise that might have been a laugh. "I mean, too bad all his taste turns out to be in his mouth, but at least it's not in mine anymore."

Sylvia can think of nothing to say but: "I meant no harm." She wonders if she is the only one disturbed by the unknown man holding a pistol aimed at them. She wonders, looking at Michael's blackened pickup, where the real harm in this situation might be located. Perhaps everything is going to glow soon?

"Meant no harm?" Laurel is repeating. Michael is focusing on the gun. What is Nomanzi doing there, behind the man so incongruously brandishing it? These perceptions and questions wander from one person to another in quite nearly the same fashion as does Boris, who lopes about, tail wagging, urging the commencement of any interesting human activity that might conceivably include a dog.

"Mlomo," Nomanzi whispers, "put the gun away. This has nothing to do with us. We owe Azania's future our loyalty and care."

Laurel is talking again about harm. "I'm really glad you're so reasonable, bitch," she says to Sylvia, "because one thing I'll tell you: the very *sight* of you makes me sick."

Michael moves to intervene, but Mlomo shouts at him to stay where he is. Mlomo senses that the situation, whatever it may be, is veering out of control, and he knows as well that once a weapon has been introduced into human affairs, its withdrawal can be quite as violent in effect as its unrestrained, even indiscriminate, use. It now alarms him that Nomanzi is not within his field of vision. He has a quick bad thought about the rockets, and even about her, but he pulls himself together. "Nomanzi!" he says.

"That guy," Laurel is saying to Sylvia, "you know, he's really something. A goddamn expert." Her spittle is flying in a fine crystal spray with her words. "It wasn't ten minutes after I met him that I started making little private excuses for him in my mind. Things like 'Oh, he can't help the way he is' or 'He's just a dumb animal and he really needs me because I'm the only one who knows it.' Dumb animal, shit; they don't come any smarter than him. But screw it, why am I telling you all this? He's your problem now. Which, if you ask me"—she turns away from all of them, removes her diamond engagement ring, and throws it as far as she can— "you aren't even half ready for."

But then her words are being swallowed by Michael's actions. He takes Sylvia's arm and backs slowly toward his truck.

Mlomo appears enraged. He has wasted something important, though he cannot say what it is. His shirt, sticking to his chest, confirms the uselessness of this expenditure. He wants to turn back in disgust to the sedan in which he and Nomanzi have arrived.

In fact, though, it is Laurel's car that starts up first. Jabez, appearing on the verge of unhealthy laughter, is at the wheel, backing the vehicle furiously up. As it runs over the cardboard package he has not bothered to retrieve, two shots ring out, and he seems suddenly to be backing the car down a ramp into the ground.

But the sounds are not shots, and despite all the confusion, everyone else present can see that Jabez has backed over the package he was previously carrying and that in so doing he has inadvertently slashed the station wagon's tires with the sword—recognizably Japanese in design and wrapped in orange blossoms—that the box contained.

Jabez looks as if he's just been told a joke he doesn't get. Michael is calmed by the return of his father's sword and is in the process of trying to expand that calm into a sphere that may include them all. He is holding Sylvia. And calm does in fact seem to be returning. The scent of oranges is soothingly discernible to everyone. Mlomo half lowers his gun.

Then the owner of the car wash returns, carrying something that resembles a stick of darkly polished wood. "Like I told them down at LAPD, like I told my wife: I been robbed too fucking many times." He says this to no one in particular. "One too fucking many times." As he gets specific, his eyes take focus.

He raises the stick of wood, which is not a stick of wood, as if he were some kind of nobly exhausted athlete. He aims the stick at Mlomo.

"Nigger," he says, steadying the sawed-off shotgun in his hands, "I'm gonna blow your brains out."

And, with a deliberateness that stuns even him, he does.

It was late afternoon before the police at the precinct house were finished taking depositions from Michael, Laurel, and Jabez. The car wash owner had been arrested, his bail had been set, his wife now sat in a pew regretting—but this is a different story altogether—the enduringly fatal beauty of automobiles.

Nomanzi and Sylvia were still being questioned—individually, in separate rooms, by a pair of officers who took increasingly frustrated turns trying to trip them up.

Part of the problem, from everyone's point of view, was that Mlomo had never announced a holdup, had in fact died without declaring in any way the reason for the gun in his hand.

Sylvia watched the slimmer of the two interrogating officers slam the door as, for the dozenth time, he left the little linoleum-floored room in which she and he had been conversing. His footsteps sounded briefly in the hall. She heard a second door open, then slam shut.

Another part of the problem, if you wanted to look at it that way, was that a routine computer check had revealed that both Nomanzi and Sylvia were daughters of diplomatic personnel.

Nomanzi had never been within the dead man's line of fire.

"Okay, Miss Lolombela," said the policeman who'd just left Sylvia, "let's take it once more from the top. You say . . ." He peered down at his notebook as if its scrawled contents had turned suddenly into live, disruptive organisms.

"I have told you what I know. Am I under arrest?" A diagonal splatter of Mlomo's blood had dried across the front of her cotton blouse, and Nomanzi was aware of the stain's stiffness as an imperative far stronger than the arguments that had been but awkwardly marshaled by the living man. "I want to know why I am being held. I want . . ." It was horrible to see again that a death might be more powerful than a life.

"You say that until today you had no acquaintance whatsoever with the victim."

"That is true."

"And that he arrived without announcement at your place of employment."

Nomanzi sighed. "I told you—and I am sure Laurel Westfall has confirmed it—this was not employment: I was minding her store as a favor for her part in finding me the house I am renting with Sylvia."

The detective looked at her. He made a show of putting away his notebook. "Miss Lolombela."

"What is it?"

"You're not under arrest. You're free to leave these premises at any time. But I think you may also, without realizing it, be in a position to help this investigation. So a detail that may seem nothing to you . . . well, I'm sure you understand. So if you'd just tell me once more, in your own words, exactly what happened."

Nomanzi swallowed. This was nothing. She could do this in her sleep, really. Unless this *was* her sleep. . . ? She had to play to Sylvia's role, whatever it was. All right.

"All right," she began. She let her fingertips begin tracing her collarbone. "I was in the flower shop, it was nearly my lunch hour. I was working on a phoned-in order when this man, this . . ."

"You say he gave you his name."

"He did, yes." Unless Sylvia knew about the rocket operation, this part was easy. "He told me his name was Dumane."

"But you don't think he was telling the truth."

"I didn't say that. I don't know. Surely your detectives . . ."

"Then there was a struggle. After which you agreed to go to lunch with him, whatever his name was."

"Officer: as you said, I am free to leave here." The anger came to her quickly; she had to remind herself to turn it into paced, conscious expression—into acting. She pulled the collar of her blouse together and puffed her cheeks. Then, in a pretense of absentmindedness, she unbuttoned one more button, widening her décolletage. "So far I have not left. Now." Looking into the white man's eyes, she saw that he, too, had an actor's reserve—and that she had nearly been taken in by it.

"Why do you speak about a struggle?" she asked. "There was no struggle."

"Okay. No struggle. Only, I've got to put something in my report about . . ." He feigned, or pretended with considerable success to feign, a kind of weariness. "About what? The flowers all over the floor, the radio you left on: that kind of thing."

"That kind of thing, yes; your men are very good. And of course if my intention were to lie to you, how would I not agree to the idea that there was a struggle? There was no struggle. I have a terrible temper, and I—" she laughed, giving voice to a self-amusement that was entirely genuine—"I was making a mess of the arrangement I was working on, so I decided to be done with it and start again. Before I could pick up the . . . I guess to you it's 'evidence'? . . . two ladies came in. They thought the flowers scattered all over the floor were art; they bought over a hundred dollars' worth of orchids. So I left things the way they were. For fun and profit."

"And the radio?"

"Well, I did agree to have lunch with this Dumane. Nobody knows me here, but in my own country I am a sort of television star, and maybe I was feeling a little homesick."

She glanced down at her lap and affected to wipe the perspiration from her brow. There was no perspiration. She tilted her head and forced her glance to meet that of the gray-eyed white man questioning her.

"This fellow had seen me go into the shop; he recognized me from my show. He said he was a driver, a chauffeur, and he asked me in my own language if I would have lunch with him. I hadn't expected to take lunch, and I don't know how safe a shop is in this city, so I left the radio on to make it sound as if there were people inside. You can check the day's sales records about the orchids, maybe even question the two ladies."

"We already did."

"Okay, yes. So you see."

"Have you known right along about Miss Walters and Michael Bonner?"

"Their affair? I learned about it today at the car wash. I don't know what other people knew."

"Did Dumane in any way warn you that he was in possession of a firearm, or that there might be some reason to be cautious at the car wash? And are you aware of any relationship between him and Miss Walters?"

"No, no, and no. But. It *has* occurred to me that this whole event, the whole thing with the gun, it somewhat resembles one of the scripts for 'Ilulwane.'" She gave him the payoff look. "That's my show. He would have seen that episode."

Her interrogator drew himself slowly up from behind the green metal desk that separated them. He placed his palms upon its surface, locked his elbows, and, leaning forward, built himself into a tirelessly interrogative triangle.

"Okay," he said, giving her the fast eye now. "Talk to me."

When Sylvia realized that since she was not under arrest, the door to the room in which she awaited the return of her questioner would almost certainly be unlocked, she spent some moments considering exactly what, from an adversarial point of view, she might currently be expected to do. Then she thought: *Fuck it.*

The door to the corridor opened easily. Standing in the painted cinderblock passageway, Sylvia was able to observe that the precinct lieutenant, a dapper man of Korean descent, maintained an office directly across the hall; that he seemed to prefer to keep his own door open; and that he was at present engaged in discussion with someone whom she judged to be his chief of detectives, a man dressed, with reverse ostentation, in carefully chosen plain clothes.

It quickly became evident to her broadcast-radio ears that what was at issue here was federal agents: whether to bring them into the investigation or to let them take, by their own inclination, whatever notice they cared to take—if there was reason for notice. The chief of detectives, when he caught sight of Sylvia across the hallway, was reciting in a tone of professional outrage the schedule of perversions and character flaws habitually exhibited by federal agents. The lieutenant, following his subordinate's gaze, rose then from behind his desk and gently closed the frosted-glass-paned door.

Sylvia reflected that the time had certainly come for her and Nomanzi, every secondhand diplomatic stratagem aside, to have some kind of serious talk.

Violence was not a method—or even an experience—that Sylvia eschewed on principle. She just hated hurt.

She sat down again in the straight-backed wooden chair in her room. She'd come to think of it as *her* room.

She had not closed the door. What she remembered was: *I must remember not to leave anything open.* What she no longer remembered was why.

Michael, in a move he considered strategic to the point of vulgarity, had been released simultaneously with Laurel. The two of them walked together down the concrete hallway, her arms folded before her, his own swinging loosely at his sides. Video cameras, mounted at the join of wall and ceiling, shot stills every three seconds of whatever was going on, so that she and he each felt they'd been forced to suffer in second take the irreversible enormity of their loss. Michael and Laurel did not even look at each other. Nothing was going on.

"Boris is with the desk sergeant," Laurel observed unnecessarily as she and Michael arrived at the desk. It was clear that she meant something else.

"You've got one fine dog here," the sergeant said. The man, himself near retirement age, had apparently been calling Boris "Old Buddy."

"Yeah," said Michael. "We're friends."

In the parking lot behind the precinct house, Jabez was waiting by the pickup truck. The tainted water that had rained down upon it at the car wash had dried into a jigsaw pattern of deep black splotches suggesting, in their overall effect, the hide of some exotic, nearly extinct animal. Michael handed Laurel the keys.

"I'll have to wait for Sylvia," he said. "Why don't you take the truck home."

"Where's home?"

"Laurel. Don't."

"You know what's weird, Michael? I actually worry about you now. As of today."

"What do you mean?"

"Well, I always thought you knew I'm a normal girl—choose the wedding gown, seat the relatives just right, that kind of shit. And probably you do know what I am, since I've never felt you didn't appreciate me. Okay, fuck: I've always known you love me, whatever else I said today."

"Laurel."

"But, Michael—you're two people."

Michael said nothing.

"And that must be just awful." She turned bitterly into the wind. Stripped of stratagem, she was, almost despite herself, thoroughly beautiful—to Michael, to anyone with eyes. She cried soundlessly.

"I'm sorry, Laurel," he said at last. "I didn't know love was this dirty. If I'd had any idea, I'd have—"

"Shhh." She turned to him, she put one hand over his mouth. "Don't." Jabez was already in the pickup's passenger seat; all the vehicle's windows were closed. "Not another word," she said to Michael. She pressed her lips to his in a kiss that was unexpectedly soft, wide, lingering. It seemed that it was he who broke the kiss, but an instant later neither of them was certain.

Then Laurel was gone.

Boris looked up at Michael with a fixity of gaze that Michael knew at once to have its origin in the sanctity of the dinner hour, already twenty minutes breeched.

A look of hunger was always unmistakable.

What Michael saw next, fifty meters distant, was William leaving the precinct house through a side door. The man was wearing aviator glasses. He was turning a corner that in a second's fraction would remove him from Michael's field of vision just as surely as a matte-screen maneuver might remove an unexpected passerby from a film's final print.

Michael hesitated, then bolted after him. He twice called out the name "William" without having the least idea if it belonged to anyone within hearing distance. Parked cars shot chromium points of light unpredictably into his eyes, and in an instant of sun blindness he banged his shin on a fender.

When Michael rounded the corner, William, or the man who called himself William, was nowhere to be seen. Some distance away, on the same side of the boulevard as the police station, an elderly man who looked to be Hispanic was mowing a comically small parcel of lawn with a huge power mower. Michael watched him until, turning back toward the police lot, he was surprised by the sight of a small boy, eight or nine years old, sitting on the precinct house's single step and gazing over at him.

The boy's jeans were torn horizontally at the knees—blue gone to thready white. He wore a green-and-white-striped T-shirt that was not tucked in. In his hands, he held a peeled orange. As Michael watched, the boy prized the fruit gently apart with his thumbs.

"Hey, kid. You see anybody go by here?"

The boy mimed deep concentration, shrugged, and, in his gradually given grin, revealed the crescent of orange peel that lay pressed between his lips and teeth—a jack-o'-lantern smile.

In the midst of once again rehearsing for the steady-eyed detective just exactly how she had come to know Nomanzi, and live with her, and arrive with such infelicitous timing at the car wash, Sylvia was interrupted by the click-and-swoosh of the door opening behind her. What she saw, when she turned, was the Korean lieutenant. He gestured toward the detective—one precise move of his hand—and the detective hastened from around the desk to confer in whispers with his superior.

Sylvia observed the detective's impatient grimaces, but he saw her watching him and drew himself in.

"Okay, Miss Walters," said the detective, when the lieutenant had departed. "You're out of here."

Sylvia stared at the man. "I've heard that before."

"Well," said the detective, "I can't say I'm exactly surprised."

He turned to leave. He paused, as if reconsidering. Then he left. And when he went he left the door open, so that Sylvia, looking into the space it framed, saw Nomanzi standing there with an expression of exquisitely controlled exhaustion upon her face.

"What did they tell you?" Sylvia asked.

"It was strange." Possibly what Nomanzi's features withheld was not exhaustion but nervousness. Sylvia moved forward; she leaned against the doorjamb to listen. "My—I mean, the man questioning me—he was in the middle of taking down my story, when another man came in and told him I was to be released. 'Highest levels. Get her out of here. Do it right.' " Nomanzi smiled with near wistfulness. "I have very good hearing."

They walked together through the precinct house to the parking lot out back. When Sylvia saw Michael leaning coiled against her wilted-looking sports car, some sixty meters from the precinct's back door, she calculated right then and there that even someone with very good hearing—someone like Michael—would be unable to distinguish at such a distance what she might be about to say to Nomanzi.

So she waved to Michael, slowed her pace. She caught Nomanzi's eye to indicate a kind of anticipatory emphasis.

"You know, Nomanzi," she said, "we've been models of diplomatic discretion. I'm sure we learned this from our fathers—don't ask too much, don't show too much, but never forget that every curtsy might just be a kind of desperate ducking. Okay. But now we have to talk. Not in front of Michael, not in front of Johnny and Chentula. Not with our fathers in our heads."

Sylvia paused, waved again. "Hi, Michael!"

"You okay, baby?" He was walking toward them.

"So it'll have to be later, Nomanzi. Just you and me. Okay?"

Nomanzi shot her a look that might have been a rocket. "Okay," she said. The two of them understood then that when the time came, there would be no shortage of conversation topics.

The inside of Sylvia's car was *full* of love. It was just a little unfocused.

Nomanzi was perched between Michael and Sylvia to keep them from feeling more than they could stand. Boris had squeezed himself into the space that passed for the sports car's back seat. Everybody was heading anywhere.

"That's his blood, huh," Michael was saying. He knew how stupid his words sounded, but he was driving, and so certain things were up to him.

Nomanzi looked down at the stain running diagonally across her blouse. She, too, felt the stupidity of those words. "Yes," she said. "He . . . can you say that a man exploded? *Was* exploded, maybe?" She was still staring down at herself. "When they say 'killed in cold blood,' it is not a true thing, because I . . . what I felt on my . . ."

Everybody observed a moment of incoherent silence.

"How come you two were released so late?" Michael asked after a while. "They give you a hard time?"

Sylvia pushed a strand of hair back over her ear. "Us?"

Michael pursed his lips to indicate that bravado was not the approach he had in mind at this particular moment. He had begun thinking about William again.

"A hard time." Sylvia was scared but ready. "No, I can't honestly say that a little aggressive questioning seems like much of a hard time to me these days."

"Maybe we don't want to talk about it yet," Nomanzi suggested.

"They'll assume we did anyway, so we can pretty well play it any way we want." Michael knew he must try to take the objective view, even if there really wasn't one.

"Do you think our stories jibed?" asked Sylvia.

"I doubt it," said Michael, "since we were probably all telling the truth."

Sylvia closed her eyes and let her head loll around against the headrest. "It was weird," she said, "the way they just interrupted themselves to let us go."

Michael glanced at her: her eyes were still closed. That William had probably intervened to obtain the two women's release particularly annoyed him because it could mean anything. There was a lot to talk about, and somebody had to start; it might as well be him again.

"Nomanzi. It's great to meet you; don't even think about thinking otherwise." Changing lanes, he realized he'd been checking the rearview mirror more than necessary, and he cuffed it out of kilter to remind himself of the objective view. Nobody who might have taken a notion to follow them was going to learn anything from this particular jaunt. "The thing is, though," he continued, "I can't help wondering why you were with that guy in the first place. How come he had a gun?"

Turning away from the others, Sylvia glared out at the right-hand side of the world.

Nomanzi sighed. "It was some fellow who used to watch my show back home. He spoke my language—" She shook out the silver bangles at her wrist as if they had suddenly become confining. "I mean, literally the language. Xhosa. He spoke it." She paused. "I was feeling homesick. He wanted to have lunch."

"Well, I guess he got it," said Sylvia under her breath. Sometimes she just wanted to cry forever.

"Homesick I can understand," Michael said, inclining his head toward Nomanzi, "but what the cops seemed most interested in— besides my domestic arrangements, I mean—is why this fan of yours never announced a holdup or anything, even though he was right there waving a gun around in front of God and everybody."

The phrase "in for a nickel, in for a dime" went through Sylvia's head. She realized why: they were passing a drive-in bank that sported a huge revolving sign in exact inflated replica of a U.S. ten-cent piece—flora-flanked torch on one side, profile of General Douglas MacArthur on the other. You could actually see every kernel in his famous corncob pipe. She wondered whether the authorities had yet contacted her father.

"I think," said Nomanzi, "that this man today was a—what's the expression?—a nut case."

"The guy was a nut case," Michael repeated tonelessly.

"I'm not sure. But. On one episode of my TV show something takes place that's a bit similar to what happened today." For the second time in as many hours, Nomanzi made a mental inventory of which videotapes she'd had sent over to Petra—not that she could really change her story now. "I've always thought that the scriptwriter stole the plot, which is really pretty awful, from your U.S. series 'Houston.' But I guess everybody does a lot of that."

Sylvia looked at Nomanzi. She had become aware, from a hint

of artificial brightness in her housemate's voice, that Nomanzi was lying. A fly flew in the window, and Michael shooed it away. And suddenly it seemed to Sylvia that Michael, strong though his intention remained, was listening to Nomanzi's story without the least skepticism. But openness and a willingness to listen are qualities that often elicit truth by the sheer rhetorical vacuum they induce. Right?

"Right," said Sylvia, turning a little too quickly back to the sights rushing by her shoulder. "Everybody does it."

"Anyway, this episode is about a fellow who's always fancied this one particular girl, even though he's too shy to say so, and then she becomes a kind of township celebrity—only for a little while; it's because this news team interviews her for European TV. 'How long have you lived in the township? Is it what you expected? Do you have work? A sweetheart? Why did you leave the homelands? Do you ever go back?' The usual stuff. And of course no one in the township ever sees the interview—it's not for broadcast *there*—but word gets around anyway. The way it always does." Nomanzi's lips came together in a pout suggesting that her own words and thoughts had momentarily diverged. "So then, when this fellow hears about it, he comes to see her."

"He realizes it's now or never?" Michael suggested.

"No." Nomanzi relinquished the pout. "He decides she needs protection."

"Does she?"

"Oh, in real life maybe she would, but in my country even the black TV stations are government-controlled, so the show's producer knew he had to satisfy the whites in Broadcasting if he didn't want to go back and shoot the whole thing over again. No, in the story it's hinted that the only real threat to the girl was the European news crew, who maybe exploited her naïveté a bit, who were probably just looking for someone to illustrate opinions they already had. You know."

"I'm assuming you play the girl."

There was a sudden flurry of traffic and road signs then—place names, directional arrows, advertisements—and Sylvia interrupted the conversation to inquire whether Nomanzi had left at the flower shop anything that might need picking up.

"No. But actually . . ." From her perch between the two front seats she put a hand on Michael's shoulder. "If you could let me off at my brother's hotel, that would be great. I'd really better tell him what happened, since they'll be calling him too."

"Turn here," Sylvia told Michael.

"Oh, they're staying at the Château Beverly," Michael observed as he negotiated the indicated exit. "I had breakfast there this morning."

The affability with which he imparted this information sounded a little strained, even to him, but he resolved to press on. "The rest of the band staying there too?"

"Johnny's there with Chentula, yes. They're sharing a suite." Nomanzi leaned forward and plucked her bag from between her sandaled feet. "The music company wanted to use studio musicians for the record, so the other guys in the band stayed home."

"What? No groupies, no accountants, no anxious managers in freshly pressed safari shirts?"

Sylvia cleared her throat loudly at Michael, but she needn't have worried; Nomanzi's mind was already elsewhere. "No," she said, rummaging through her purse for lipstick. "Nothing like that."

They swung up the hotel's long, sweeping drive with a grace that reminded Sylvia of an airplane banking. "So how does it turn out?" she asked Nomanzi. "Your story."

Michael stopped the car just past the entrance so as to avoid a blitz from the valet-parking backfield.

"Oh. Yes." She looked out across the lawn, where, as the day faded, a teenage Chicano was running an electric edger around a flagstone. "Well, this fellow who fancies the girl is made out to be a bit of a tragicomic figure, and the girl takes a liking to him. Not the way he'd hoped, of course, but he's so fond of her that just being around her makes him happy, y'know, and she's been a little lonely anyway since she left the homelands, so . . ."

The buzz of the lawn edger ceased, and its voice seemed to be taken up immediately by a chorus of cicadas. Twilight.

"So she takes him to a shebeen—like a bar, eh?, but not legal. And they begin to have a good time: it's crowded, there's music, all that. They dance. It's very innocent." Nomanzi's lipstick tube had found its way into her palm after all, and she looked down at it with some curiosity. Since the car wash, a surprisingly large number of objects reminded her of weapons or ammunition or blood. She slipped the top off this one. "But then the girl's brother comes into the shebeen. He sees what's going on and picks a fight with the other fellow, her fan. They go outside, some shots are fired, but when everyone rushes out after them, both men have disappeared." She shrugged. "It's left hanging that way."

The three of them were staring down at Nomanzi's lipstick. Brilliant red. Then she raised it to her lips, using the rearview mirror as reference, and over her reflected shoulder she saw the lawn boy standing nearby. He was smoking a joint.

"*Hola, muchacho*, she called. "You had a long day?"

He considered this. Exhaled. "*Puro* party time, *señorita*. But I lived."

Sylvia got out of the car to make way for Nomanzi. "So did we," she said.

Back at the house, Sylvia let her hair spill as matter-of-factly forward as if she'd been alone.

"I love you," Michael whispered, sitting down beside her on the edge of the bed. They had shed their clothes on the stairs, in the hallway.

"What did you say to Laurel?"

"Well, I probably said the usual things, Sylvie. But I hadn't met you then. How do you expect—"

"No, I don't *mean* bed talk." She shook out her hair so she could see him. "I know the police released you two together today. I know they meant you to talk, offer each other explanations, maybe reconsider." Sylvia opened her pale eyes wide upon his to be sure he listened. "If I were just curious I wouldn't ask."

Michael took a deep breath—an inverse sigh—and allowed himself to fall back against the mattress, sheets, coverlet. "I told her love was dirty," he said.

Sylvia's expression softened by stages into a smile. "You know that?" She ran her fingertips slowly up the inside of his thighs. "I knew you knew me, but I didn't know you knew that."

She had unthinkingly turned her torso to follow the direction of her fingers' caress.

"Neither did I," he answered, pulling her up to him.

They kissed.

The press of their bodies seemed to both of them so much a matter of violence and single-mindedness that a great amount of time and room—can it really be true that time and room are the same thing?—opened elegantly before them.

"We're optimists," Sylvia said. "We talk and we fuck."

He watched her close her eyes, rise up astride him, and lower herself down upon his cock.

Once, in the course of developing his career, Michael had agreed—favor for favor—to read a film script written by the niece of one of his associates. The story concerned a scientist who had accidentally hit upon a compound that, when placed in solution and used as eyedrops, conferred X-ray vision upon the subject. The scientist experimented upon himself; the solution proved addictive, its effects cumulative. While initially the man was troubled by nothing more serious than the insomnia of someone who can see through his eyelids, he shortly found that the ceilings and floors of his apartment building, the bodies of his friends, all things sealed by nature or artifice, had given way vertiginously to his sight. His world dissolved in secretless transparency.

Although the film script was amateurish and unsalable, it had disturbed Michael thoroughly.

Now he saw from the flare of her nostrils that Sylvia was about to come. Bringing his hands' strength to bear on either side of her hips, he gentled the course of their lovemaking. Then he raised a hand to part her hair. "You're wearing that earring," he managed to say. "The one I found."

"This earring . . ." Her margins were losing definition, but in an exertion of will she drew her hair back one last time to show him the three-sided stone. "It's not what I thought. I mean, it's not part of a pair. It's extra."

The word "extra" glistened.

"I don't understand," Michael said. "It's just an earring, right?" A trickle of sweat ran suddenly from his temple into the hair at the back of his head. He'd left everything open.

"Well," she answered. "What if it isn't?"

Cupping her ass in his palm, Michael rolled her gently over and beneath him. What if what wasn't?

And so she poured, like a sudden storm.

In the lobby of the hotel where Michael and Sylvia had dropped her off, Nomanzi executed a slow 360-degree turn, as if deciding at leisure how she might amuse herself next. There were fashion magazines on the coffee table, and she picked one up. When she had ascertained that she was still unobserved, she ambled over to the telephone booth in the far corner of the sunny, half-open room. She was hips. She was capable.

Although it was possible to worry about the stain on her blouse, in this town bloodstains could no doubt become fashionable too.

She fed the phone a quarter and dialed.

NOMANZI: It's me.

THE OTHER VOICE: Yeh, yeh, baby. [*Switching to Xhosa*] I used to call you "Cousin."

NOMANZI: Call me what you like. Mlomo is dead.

THE VOICE, LESS OTHER: Mlomo, you say! Mlomo, oh! It is very bad?

NOMANZI: When is the death of a patriot—a comrade—not bad? [*Likewise switching to Xhosa*] But if you mean the other thing, is our plan compromised—no, not exactly. No. He got his message to me. I am in a position to understand it further, although, as yet, no. We were all questioned by the American police, but we were—I speak of myself and the daughter of the American diplomat Paul Walters—released I think by higher intervention. My story is very strong. The police will now be watching me, but I know that in this country there is a great division between . . . polices.

VOICE: You have changed.

NOMANZI: I have Mlomo's blood even now—his very blood—on my clothes. I saw him die.

VOICE: Do they know who he is?

NOMANZI: He carried no . . . [*almost laughing*] no ID, no passbook.

I told them he said his name was Dumane. I told them he had recognized me from TV. I said he wanted to have lunch.

VOICE: Dumane. Good.

NOMANZI [*After a deep breath*]: I must know that you were sure of Mlomo. Of Dumane.

VOICE [*Pause*]: We were sure. Yes.

NOMANZI: Then I must speak to my father.

[*A silence of deeper register passes. It is clear that in the wake of this silence, questions trail. It is equally clear that these questions cannot be asked.*]

VOICE: We must be flexible but not foolish. For example: whether you should continue to be involved in the nesting of our birds—

NOMANZI: You know that delivery of the birds has been postponed.

VOICE [*Too quickly*]: Yes, yes. [*Recovering*] And I read the American newspapers.

NOMANZI: So you see why I must speak to my father.

[*Static. Distance made audible. A flamboyantly long-haired young man carrying an open bottle of vodka strides diagonally across the hotel lobby, then bounds up the corner staircase, two steps at a time.* NOMANZI *notices that the back of his green T-shirt has the word "Static" emblazoned across it in letters so angular that she can only think they are meant to be threatening.*]

We must find out what is at stake if we are to know how to proceed, Cousin.

VOICE: Yes.

NOMANZI: I will call you.

[*From over the telephone, in the far acoustic background,* NOMANZI *can hear a television speaking to itself.*]

TELEVISION [*Sotto voce, but with great enthusiasm*]: —Making it 116-115 here at the Dome with just seconds left to play. Folks, *this* is basketball. The Warriors crossing midcourt now—Johnson to Riggs, back to Johnson, double fake left, and now the give to slam-dunk Abdul. Look at that drive, in on the paint, up—"

VOICE: We'll be waiting for your call, Cousin. As patiently as we can.

[NOMANZI *turns around just in time to see the hotel desk clerk flip on a row of TVs—picture without sound—that hugs the wall above him like a frieze. An enormous flying black man in shorts*] *and tank top is throwing a basketball down through a hoop with such force that, as she watches, the clear plastic backboard above shatters into a million tiny fragments.*]

"What I meant," Michael called to Sylvia, who was in the bathroom but had left the door open, "is that you can't really bank on anything Nomanzi says right now, so you just have to stay alert to the interest rates." Still in bed, Michael watched Sylvia emerge from the bathroom, a lit cigarette in her hand. She was naked, fragile-looking. "Nomanzi is a professional," Michael added. "But I can still tell when she gets interested."

"I don't know what I believe yet," said Sylvia, lying down beside him again, "and I don't know who she is. So why don't you tell me about your breakfast meeting."

Turning over on his stomach, Michael spread his hands out palm down upon the sheets before him and examined his fingers mournfully. He wanted to know the truth of things, but he was coming to see that probably the truth meant very little once it had entered the hearts and minds of men and women.

"Okay," he said, "William. The guy is definitely impressive. Full of innuendo and high-concept anecdote. He made it clear that the point of his visit was that I ought to doubt everything about you. He said I should ask you if you think your father is really in Geneva." Michael raised himself up on one elbow to look at her. "So I'm asking you."

"Did you see the papers today, Michael?" She was making a small to-do out of having dropped her cigarette and was energetically brushing the ash off the sheets.

"Yes."

"Okay. Then I'll tell you: it's not a matter of believing he's in Geneva or not. I've already talked to him. He's in France."

"My first state secret."

"Your first real proof that I've decided to trust you."

Michael laughed. He wasn't as exhausted as he'd thought.

"What's funny?" she asked.

"I've just had an idea. Some things probably aren't relative."

"You mean this guy kept up his story about being my half-uncle."

"Convincingly. With details."

"Shit."

Recognizing, in his newly regained vigor, that this was one of those moments when you could press on or not press on or just sort of drag on, Michael looked pointedly at the way Sylvia was holding her cigarette. Misunderstanding, she put it out in a teacup on the galvanized-steel nightstand. "Any left-handedness in your family?" he asked.

"Not that I know of. Why?"

"This guy's left-handed."

They both knew what was coming next.

"What's your father doing in France, Sylvia?"

She shook her head reflexively: no. Yet she knew at once that in the time it had taken her to turn her face from left to right and back again, a whole generation of loyalties, hopes, ambitions, even kinds of love, had fallen away in grace and pride. The effect was exhilarating, but it also required getting used to.

"I don't know anything else about this stuff. You know who my father is. It's national security. I'm told the minimum." She was touching her own ribs, counting them.

"Sylvia, we have to look out for each other now. And all this violence, threat, and harassment is obviously a little much for both of us. So—" He kissed her on the cheek. "Speak to me."

"Did this William character say why he did what he did?" she asked very quietly.

Michael drew a hand through his hair. "The guy said he'd been working for certain interests but that now he'd changed sides. These certain interests are in Washington, and according to him they are responsible for my film being canned. Also according to him, whatever methods they used to do in my pet project had an unspecified influence on his 'changing sides.' Note: not *because* they did me nastiness but because of . . . I think his exact words were: 'the way it was handled.' "

The briefest of silences. Long enough, however, for Michael to realize that he had for some time now incorporated the sound of nearby freeway traffic into his notion of silence.

"Did you know about this?" he demanded.

"No," she said. "I didn't."

"How about these, then?" he responded. From under a magazine on the nightstand he produced the two hundred-dollar bills and the explanatory fold of paper that William had left behind after their breakfast encounter. "Familiar in any way?"

The cry Sylvia was only partially able to stifle was like the sound of a silk dress torn by a careless movement at a dinner party: it was hard to know what to do about it. She snatched the two bank notes from Michael's hand, tore them into tiny pieces, and, walking over to the window, threw them out into the night. The slip of paper she inspected, then laid carefully on the nightstand at the left side of the bed—her side. She sat back down upon the sheets and turned to Michael.

"Okay," she said. "I'll tell you everything I know."

Afterward, they listened to the freeway for a long time. When Michael opened his eyes, he saw that her hair had been cried upon. She smiled sleepily at him.

"I think we're frightened now," she said.

There was a white-painted wrought-iron settee on the lawn outside the hall in Compiègne where the fission bomb talks were being held. On the morning after the day that the American President had publicly refused the white South African offer of a joint investigation into the Geneva car bombing, Heinrich Bloch strolled toward this settee. The sky above him was, for all its blueness, made practically transparent by the immaculate rise of a single cumulus cloud. Bloch sat down.

The American President's statement had made it possible for Bloch to avoid disrupting the previous day's talks, but the results, even as theater, had not satisfied him. There had been too much bumbling, too much wasted time. He crossed his legs now and, leaning back in the settee, felt the loneliness of a man who considers himself unreasonably separated from his dreams. Abruptly, the face of a woman he had known at university flashed through his mind. She had, in this image, placed her head between the jaws of a stone lion—a statue—and she was miming terror, her tongue thrust out in half-scream. He could not remember where this had happened— was there a photograph of it?—but he knew from the look of her lips that they had been lavishly kissed, and by him, and he knew it was to lovemaking that he and she had later returned. Had he only taken up this other, more private challenge, then he . . . Then what? This was a useless thought. That he must make use of. He recrossed his legs.

It was Walters he had expected first to approach him for more private consultation. That it had instead been Lolombela had initially confused him, then alarmed him, then shown him how to proceed. He knew that the connection between Walters and Lolombela had begun in a political sympathy that had pointed the way to a possible friendship. Clearly, they had taken up that friendship. As had, it seemed, their respective daughters. His own informants had quickly discovered that Lolombela's daughter was said to be engaged in weapons smuggling, but this knowledge seemed to Bloch of little use until he knew whether Lolombela himself was involved in the scenario. It was for this reason that Bloch had let drop to Lolombela—in mock-jocular inquiry—the fact that the African man's daughter was sharing a house with Sylvia Walters in Los Angeles.

A mottled brown hare sprang suddenly into Bloch's field of vision and, in a series of loping zigzags, disappeared across the lawn's far corner.

A stone lion. A kissed woman. A hare crossing open ground.

The force of nature.

Bloch himself had given little thought during his life's course to what the human part of nature had decided to gather, rather oddly it seemed to him, under the rubric of "nature." How could a thing's part name the whole? And yet over the past few days he had seen on the countenances of his colleagues the vivid mixture of glee and unease with which men might contemplate what Paul Walters had so adeptly termed "the unleashing of the forces of nature." As if gunpowder were not compounded by nature from nature. As if love were not. Bloch leaned back to see the sky.

It would be several hours before he could call Petra with his plan's pieces solidly in position. How much, he wondered, did she suspect? She was not entirely pleasantly clever.

Squinting eastward then, he sighted Lolombela, crossing the wooden bridge that spanned the gully separating the forest from this lawn. Bloch looked at his watch: 8:16. Lolombela was early.

"Good morning, Herr Bloch."

"A beautiful morning, Mr. Lolombela. Please join me"—he gestured to the seat beside him—"in appreciating it."

Lolombela sat. He had come to take less and less pleasure in the playfulness that sometimes passed among Europeans for a component of diplomacy, but he had, as a matter of professionalism, continued to observe its rules. "I have forgotten my notebook, Herr Bloch. You must tell me which microphone to speak toward."

Bloch stiffened slightly. "There are no microphones." He forced himself to relax, then laugh. After all, at least in this matter he was certain of his ground. "There is you. There is me. A moment ago there was a startled hare, but it is the nature of alarmed animals to be quickly gone."

For part of a second they both realized that in speaking English together they were acknowledging in the most unconscious way the history of the decades since the Second World War—or, perhaps more nearly, since the First. French was, however sentimentally, still the language of diplomacy, but when English had become the international language of aviation . . .

"Heinrich."

"Yes, Joseph."

"I am not an uncooperative man. You know what my commitments are, both as an individual and as a representative of my nation." He tilted his face toward the sun—not so much to warm himself as to savor the full import of the things to which he was unswervingly bound. He wore a blue suit of summer-weight wool. "My fear at this point, Heinrich, is that the three of us—you, Paul Walters, and I—may become excessively subtle. The needs of my people are not in any way subtle: they are the needs of men and women who have been deprived of their most basic dignities and yet have determined in their very souls to obtain those dignities nonetheless—for their children, for their children's children, whatever the price. We will worry more about the world community when we join that community more formally." He turned to look at Bloch. "This is obvious."

"Agreed."

"And yet." Lolombela rubbed his thumb and forefinger against his cheekbones. He knew he was now—or would be soon—at the crux of negotiations. "While I do not wish to personalize the issue of the fission bomb, I must tell you what you no doubt already know. I have meant all that I have said: I believe this weapon's greatest power *is* rhetorical; I do not support a test detonation at this time."

"Again we are in agreement, Joseph. This is why the three of us are speaking."

"Then why have you asked me to meet you alone this morning? Without our American colleague?"

Bloch removed a handkerchief from his breast pocket as if he were about to sneeze. He was not. Instead he unfolded and refolded the square of linen in the manner of a man unfolding then refolding a map. "I wanted," he said, restoring the handkerchief to his pocket, "to know your opinion of Paul Walters's authority to make policy—whether you believe he still holds his President's full confidence."

It was immediately evident to Lolombela that this explanation was a lie and had already been jointly recognized as one.

"Heinrich. I know you have no children. Forgive me for asking, but was it always your wish to be in this way unencumbered?"

"If wishes were horses then beggars would ride."

"I do not understand."

"It's an English proverb." Bloch stood. "How odd that we speak English to one another."

"I believe," said Lolombela, "without question that Paul Walters holds his President's confidence. That he has the authority to make policy. And that though he is a diplomat, he is also a statesman."

Bloch had begun to stride thoughtfully back and forth in front of the settee. "His daughter and yours—they are old friends?"

"No, Heinrich. They have just met. You must be frank with me if you have suspicions. We are here on this lawn alone."

Bloch continued to pace, began stroking his chin.

"Well. Then I must speak first, Heinrich. I know that your republic has acquired from Norway that nation's entire supply of heavy water. Is that the term—heavy water? I know that Norway is the only known natural source of such water and that your scientists have been attempting to use it in making a fission bomb."

Bloch had ceased his pacing, ceased his nervous self-caresses. He found himself, quite simply, staring at Lolombela.

"I know also that your scientists have not met with success,

Heinrich. It is possible that I am the only one of the three of us
here to appreciate the chance this temporary setback may have
afforded us. I am even reasonably sure that the Americans themselves know nothing of your efforts in this direction."

Bloch understood that he was being paid back in mixed coin for
having meddled—however discreetly—in the political ménage Lolombela's daughter and Sylvia Walters had, with whatever purpose,
assembled in Los Angeles. No doubt it was time to offer an abashed
but appealing grin in the American manner, but Bloch knew he
did not have it in him. A lock of hair fell across his forehead; he
brushed it back. "Naturally," he said, "I don't know what you're
talking about."

"Of course. It does not matter." Lolombela himself stood and,
folding his arms across his chest, began to walk only half mock-
processionally around the white settee. "What matters is that today
we agree upon a course of action. Then what matters is that we
carry it out."

"But we have already agreed upon this course, on what we must
do."

"Too subtly?"

Which is where Bloch found his footing. "Yes." He walked around
the inertly elemental piece of lawn furniture to face Lolombela
down. "Too subtly."

"Then we must be blunt. One last time. Together."

Sparrows hopped about in the grass, seizing insects with their
beaks.

"Yes," said Heinrich. "It is now."

So they rehearsed once again the points of the plan they had
agreed upon. That Walters would allow Bloch's people to leak to
the international press news of the fission bomb, that Bloch would
rally support throughout Europe against the weapon's detonation,
that in an elaborately choreographed diplomatic exchange the haz-
ards of a test detonation would be acknowledged and a widely
disseminated computer simulation would in the end be substituted.

"By which time," Bloch went on, "the fission weapon will be
firmly installed in the Azanian deserts, its photograph known to
every schoolchild across the globe."

"And it is your belief that an image alone—the image of this bomb—will cause the whites in my country to come to their senses and yield to free elections?"

"That and the concerted pressure of the German Federated Republics, the United States of America, and the emerging nation of Azania. The pressure also of world opinion. A shared sense of justice."

"Justice."

"I use the word in its diplomatic sense."

Lolombela sat back down. "Heinrich." He caught the pacing man by his elbow, and in the two men's sudden stillness, in the perfectly penetrating look that passed between them, an odd moment of fellowship was given them, and recognized by them, and left open for them like a pasture into which they might later wander, for whatever splendor or use.

"If you had been successful with the heavy water," Lolombela said, "this would be a different kind of conversation. It would be one in which you did not care that my daughter and Sylvia Walters are sharing a house. It would be a conversation in which the English word 'justice' "—he grimaced—"could not be relevant. In any language."

Despite this quickened confrontation, the two men took possession of the metaphorical pasture they had glimpsed. It surprised them. And yet, after all, it was their pasture.

Bloch sat beside Lolombela and sighed. His sigh was not at all theatrical. Or diplomatic.

"We all three of us have our different motives for involving ourselves in the plans we are outlining," Lolombela said. He pretended to strike his own forehead. "I speak like a neophyte, but perhaps it is not wrong to speak in this way."

"Perhaps not," answered Bloch.

"We all wish to gain what we can for our peoples," Lolombela continued. "It goes without saying. At the same time I believe we have an obligation to be forthright with each other about the largest matter: that we have so far agreed that any actual test detonation of the fission weapon would have the direst consequences for geopolitics, for our children, for the future."

For Bloch, the word "children," just uttered, pulled itself out of his insides as if he were the woman with whom he might have had his children. But the time was past. If it had not yet been, it was not to be. Bloch suddenly foresaw, with an odd distance, his own death, and he was chastened.

"Even if we had been successful using the heavy water method," he said, his eyes closed momentarily against the sun, his thoughts having settled maddeningly again upon the girl at university, "we would not have authorized a test detonation. I am certain."

"I will believe you."

"I know also about this element uranium, to be found in the Southwest American desert, to be found as well in the Kalahari of Southern Africa. A kind of poetry, the Kalahari—excuse me, it has always been a treasure of the world—but that it should be the site of man's birth and the potential site of his demise . . ." Bloch passed a hand across his face. "We must all be a little humbled."

"The English word 'humility' is not a diplomatic term."

The two men looked at each other, took time's measure, and broke, first one, then the other, into laughter.

"No," said Bloch. "It is not."

They continued to laugh until the time to cease laughing was obvious. That their eyes would then meet was also obvious.

"I've lately spoken," said Lolombela, "to my daughter. You must never bring her into our conversations again."

"The arrangements I have made," Bloch answered, "are not less personal."

"I believe you. But I insist."

"You have my word."

"We have no other coin, and of course I take your word. Your English word."

"Thank you."

"The readiness is all."

"As long as we are in English—yes, *Hamlet*, good. I take that too."

"Thank you."

It was then that, nearly simultaneously, the two men saw Paul Walters crossing the bridge that led toward the place that had till now belonged to them. His footsteps on the wooden planks reminded Lolombela of a drum's tattoo heard distantly across a savanna. The association saddened him.

"You know," Lolombela said, turning to Bloch, "I noticed how often this bench—or what is it, this thing we are sitting on—how often it has been painted. You see? The edges are buried under paint, rounded by it. And so I asked the innkeeper: 'Why is this?' And you know what he said to me?" Lolombela made a laugh. "He said, 'Don't sit there on a cloudy day.' So I asked, 'Why do you say this thing?' And he answered—"

Paul Walters, already offering them a cursory wave, was so nearly upon them that Lolombela was clearly being given the choice of finishing the anecdote as he had begun it, or of including his approaching colleague in its perhaps not entirely incidental denouement. The man Lolombela had decided to become at that moment lowered his voice to show that what he was about to say was of no intended consequence, and he prefaced his words with a laugh that he understood to be the sound of irony in the first world. He said: "The man said, 'That bench, lightning strikes it at least once a week.'" Lolombela arched his eyebrows in amused resignation. "This place we are sitting. It is struck."

And then so was he—with an unexpected suddenness—by the fear he saw in the Northern man's blue eyes.

The fear had nothing to do with lightning.

"You are both so sociable this morning," said Paul Walters, stopping before the two men. His hands were hooked affably into his pockets.

"It is always said," Lolombela offered, "that it is the Americans who are earliest to appointments."

"But today I'm the one who's late." Paul Walters sat companionably down, looked companionably at his watch. "Didn't you tell me eight-thirty, Joseph?"

Lolombela glanced at Bloch. The exchange had the character of a communiqué.

"Eight-thirty," said Joseph Lolombela, as if it were the name of a person, someone possibly dear.

For a time, no one said anything. The official negotiations were to begin at nine.

The cumulus cloud was blowing apart in a slow, faintly cinematic fashion.

"Has the innkeeper told either of you gentlemen yet"—Paul Walters turned his face to the sky—"about the lightning?"

. . .

Petra's office: many shades of white and cream, many textures.

Michael. Nomanzi. Entering the light-soaked room with the visible weariness of those who have lately been reminded that it is always possible to be violently surprised.

Petra, dressed in cotton florals and rising from behind her desk in greeting. "I really appreciate you coming by," she said. "I mean, I heard about what happened yesterday." She shook her head. "Was it, like, really horrible?"

"Yeah," said Michael after a moment. His eye fell upon the crystal hummingbird that hung at Petra's window. "It was."

"Nobody knew this man," said Nomanzi. "Or what it was he wanted with me." Her course chosen even before the police had arrived, her phone call at last put through to her father: she felt the coolness of a temporary destiny. The story she had given the police would make only the clearest of demands upon her. It would, for now, allow her the most latitude. It would suffice.

"This town." Petra turned briefly toward the window. "I could tell you how it's changed."

Michael gave her a quick look. "I could tell you how it hasn't."

Nomanzi stood up and turned away from the two others. "Anyway. Right now we are here. All three of us." She turned around again. She wasn't sure what was in her face.

"Right," said Petra. Swiveling into action, she offered her guests naturally carbonated mineral waters in several conformations of bottle and bubble, she told her phone to hold its calls, and she thought once—but once only—how Bloch, the fruitfulness of whose money they were about to consider, would without the slightest doubt sell her, his life's intermittent love, down any old river at all if he could that way achieve even a portion of what he wanted in the world of men and maps. Granting herself this last private moment, she could not help smiling: the great man was really a boy after all. And business, it soothed her to think, was finally only business; it was her husband she adored.

"Right," said Petra. "We're here. I think we can do good things together."

"We're a strange combination," Michael allowed. But he was nodding slowly. "Do we have backing?"

"Yessir. We got backing."

"Studio?"

"I hate to say it," said Petra, "but for now you've got to trust me on that."

Nomanzi's glance had grown temporarily stony. She stared at Petra. She realized that there was no way now to know whether Mlomo had been strategically maneuvered into the circumstances that had given birth to his death; indeed there was no real way to know if he had really been who he had said he was. But certainly nothing here—nothing in the West at all—was entirely what it appeared to be. Perhaps in the end it was true: she had lived here too long.

The diamond studs at Petra's ears were, Nomanzi realized only now, of the same cut and size as the single stone she had seen Sylvia wear.

"Now the thing here," said Petra, eyeing them levelly, "is not to scare ourselves into doing the wrong picture. We want a comfortable fit is what. Something unlooked for."

Michael understood what he was being asked to do. Insofar as the business at hand was about motion pictures, he was being apprised that in exchange for finding a star vehicle for Nomanzi, he would be given an unusual measure of what, for lack of a better term, was normally known as artistic control. Well, good. Okay.

Naturally he no longer believed that the business at hand was primarily about motion pictures.

Nomanzi, at that moment, had almost the opposite thought, though for the same reasons. Feeling instinctively that she ought to conceal both thought and reason, she began tracing and retracing her collarbone with her index finger—a kind of flirtation. "You'll want me to play an American, then," she said.

"Well . . ." Petra seemed to relax. "Not necessarily."

Along part of one wall there were bookcases in which semibound screenplays were stored, their open spines parallel not to the rise of the wall but to the shelves, so that they composed successive piles rather than anything like a library. Nor did they fill the cases: at the end nearest Nomanzi was a space in which an ivory-and-ebony-squared chessboard had been set up; its sculptural playing pieces, in recognition of one of Petra's earlier projects, were ebony on both sides of the board and, except for the direction of their gazes, indistinguishable, one tactical force from the other. Nomanzi lifted the queen nearest her, inadvertently knocking down in domino fashion half the corresponding second rank.

"I have been thinking about a story," said Nomanzi. She turned the queen over in her hands as if it were the story itself in chrysalis form. "A true story of my people."

She intercepted a glance between Petra and Michael. Holding up the chess queen as puppet surrogate, she went into a voice that might have been the purest down-home Delta. "Don't y'all worry now, there be plenty of room for white folks' box office in anything we gon' strut on out there with; she may be fun, Miss Nomanzi, but hell, she ain't no fool."

Petra thought: *She's* funny. *Can we use that?*

Michael thought, for the thousandth time: *Sylvie, Nomanzi, their fathers—can it be they used me?*

Nomanzi thought: *I am my use. It is unique to me. I mustn't forget to be everything I am if I want to discover all the uses of me.*

Nomanzi placed the black queen, without releasing it, on Petra's desk. Petra smiled. Nomanzi began to speak.

All of this is true.

It had been previously arranged, with the help of meaningful looks and solitary strategic wanderings into the kitchen, that after Michael and Nomanzi's meeting with Petra, Michael would drop Nomanzi off at her and Sylvia's house, then return to his studio. It was understood by all that there were discussions to be had, and that a certain delicacy of comportment would be necessary. It was likewise understood that while fear was a factor in these maneuvers, it could only be disregarded.

Not until Nomanzi opened the front door of her rented American house did she realize that she still held Petra's black chess queen in her hand. She put it down on the first flat surface she encountered.

"Nomanzi?"

"Yes. It is me."

"How'd it go?" Sylvia appeared from the kitchen, holding a dish towel and a bottle of cold-water-wash product.

"I told them I was grateful to the Academy for the award, and that without my mother and father none of it would have been possible." She laughed, then approached Sylvia and gave her a kiss on the cheek. "No, seriously. I think I have it. And the story line's my own idea. And Michael would direct."

The recitation's cadences released Nomanzi's pleasure more fully, and she performed a small dance of celebration, her arms fully extended above her head, in a gesture of voluptuous silliness. "My name in lights."

"Oh, Nomanzi, that's just great."

They both knew about the kind of light that lit up names, and neither of them held it in very high opinion. Still, the celebration was genuine.

Nomanzi froze her pose. Then dropped it. "Those things outside."

As if by stage direction, the two women began walking together toward the sofa in the living room.

"Yeah." Sylvia's forefingers slowly hooked her hair back over her ears. "Those are compacted bales of dead flowers held together by black steel bands." She glanced at Nomanzi as they sat down. "I guess, like, there must be some little daily inventory loss in the flower business."

"You mean she . . . after yesterday . . . ?"

"They were just out there." Sylvia sighed. "What the hell. Say it with flowers." Then she laughed and shook her head. "Or, you know, don't say it at all."

Which was when the nature of the time these two women were spending together changed completely. Still sitting, they drew themselves slowly upright. A beat taken. A look exchanged.

"I've spoken to my father, Nomanzi. Have you spoken to yours?"

"Yes."

"How're we gonna figure out what they know? How're we gonna figure out what *we* know?" Sylvia leaned precipitously forward to pluck her packet of cigarettes from the coffee table, but she ended up just touching them, her fingers at electric rest as if an impromptu form of Ouija were about to commence. "I'm not even going to bring up the matter of literal truth," she explained, studying her motionless fingertips.

Nomanzi looked where Sylvia was looking, drew Sylvia's arm back by the crook of the elbow, and said: "As far as I know, our meeting was innocent. Our fathers set it up, yes. But most of my wants are selfish ones. No doubt I am spoiled. My country is not."

"Our fathers are in France," said Sylvia.

"Yes."

"What happened yesterday . . ."

"It is withdrawn."

"A death? Withdrawn?"

"Yes. A death. A given possibility of death."

"Do you know what is being negotiated in France?"

"No. But you do."

"In a way."

"Tell me."

The Immobility Artist moved. Wherever he was.

"Nomanzi, a lot has happened. I've never seen anybody killed before. I know you've seen a lot more than me, but I'm not as sheltered as I may look, and I know the kind of things we've got to begin to say here, even if it's only to keep the cops away."

"The cops, eh! Too late for that! You saw how we were released."

"Yes. Okay." She drew a long breath. "So what were you really doing with that man yesterday?"

"I was trying to make myself useful to my country. Now I will have to do that some other way."

"Was it weapons?"

"What point to speak about a thing that never happened?"

"In France—"

The phone warbled once, twice, then strangled on the first note of its third appeal.

"In France," Nomanzi prompted.

Sylvia slumped. "We have only the stupidest reasons to trust each other."

"Yes. That's what trust is."

"Really? You think that?"

The sound of traffic passing on the nearby interchange suggested winds blowing across an uninhabited planet.

"Just don't use me anymore. Don't use this. If we—"

"No. But the same for me, Sylvia."

"Right." Sylvia was still staring at the phone. She tried to collect her thoughts. Kristen's activities wandered unexpectedly through these thoughts, but Sylvia quickly decided only to note their appearance, to draw no conclusions, to deal with the business all too obviously at hand.

"I think we're being too careful," Sylvia hazarded.

"But exactly! We have too few choices left to be interesting about them." Nomanzi lifted her left arm to let her bangle bracelets rattle down it. "Okay. Maybe I was going to help get some aid to my people. To my country. But it was called off because of France. Because of what's being decided there." Cocking her head, she asked: "Do you really know what's being decided there?"

Sylvia remembered the conversation with her father—the one that had taken place in the dark, the week before, in Zack's kitchen. She remembered how little attention she had paid to the actual import of what her father had been confiding to her; she remembered, with shame somehow mixed with filial love, her own tears. She considered possible applications of the word "betrayal."

"Yes," Sylvia said at last. "I really know."

A learned reserve on Nomanzi's part. An attempt at expectancy.

Sylvia stood. "I don't know who you are."

"I don't know who you are."

Sylvia began walking back and forth in a little area before the sofa. "What you want me to tell you might come to nothing for either of us. I know without asking you anything else that we're default diplomats. Like with computer, 'default'? Like with daughters?"

Nomanzi sat attentively, her hands folded in her lap.

Sylvia waited until she saw that the other woman would wait her out.

"Okay," she said then. "My choice, as the local expression goes." She stopped pacing. "A weapon."

An inward part of Nomanzi previously unknown to her just fell away. "What kind of weapon?" she asked, when she was able to strip her speech of the merely personal.

"Does the phrase 'the power of a thousand suns' mean anything to you?"

"In my country it is always considered better to have sons than daughters."

Sylvia pouted in momentary irritation but accepted the ploy. "Suns," she said. "Like daylight."

"No. I don't know about this."

There were ways to consider this statement the truth. In the interest of continuity, Sylvia tacitly decided to do so.

"From what I understand," said Sylvia, "this 'weapon' could blow up the whole fucking world. Or anyway a few of them could, exchanged in the heat of the moment. So everybody's getting together to decide whether to test one or not. To get the big picture, right?"

Nomanzi nodded. She had no idea what was going on.

A shaft of light coming through the artfully tipped living room window showed them there was dust—gray-white dust—in the air. The dust was swirling very slowly.

"So that's all that I know I know," said Sylvia, putting a hand over her eyes. "Which I guess means you can call the police now. Or the nuthouse. Or—"

"Or what?"

Sylvia dropped her hand from her brow. "Or you can forget I ever told you any of this."

Two hours later these two women were asleep, still dressed, their arms around one another on the sofa.

The phone rang.

"Sylvie."

"Kristen! God."

"In that order?"

"I'm cursed."

Nomanzi stirred, yawned, and departed for the kitchen.

"No curse," Kristen said. "Just family."

"Well," said Sylvia, considering the way of what she thought to be the world, "I've been trying to tell you this for the longest time, but you're the younger sister."

Sylvia switched the phone to her better ear and felt very much the older sister. "Tell me something startling and new; I've aged lately."

"Yeah, I've heard that this age thing is going around, but maybe it's mostly imagination, don't you think? Perspective, probably."

"What are you really doing, Kristen?"

"We have no secrets."

"National security."

"Personal safety?"

"Right."

"I think I'm getting fucked. In a nice way. On a regular basis."

"In the Bahamas?"

"Well, yeah."

"We know about the Bahamas, right? On a family basis?"

"Sure." Kristen switched the phone to her better ear. "You and I know what a free zone is."

And they both knew about silence. On a family basis.

"So, Kristen, who's this guy you're with?"

"Well, that's what I called about, actually. His name's Philippe."

"You called to tell me his name."

"No, I called to tell you"—she swallowed audibly—"that I'm going to marry this man whose name is Philippe."

"Kristen! Jesus, I mean, congratulations and all that, but—no, oh, that's what you say to the man, isn't it? Shit. Just . . . don't you think . . . ?"

"Don't I think what?"

Sylvia's heart flew open like a badly hung door in a storm. "I'm sorry. I was going to say something about timing. But I'm obviously no expert."

"You're my sister. I love you."

"I love you, Krissy. You know that. I want you to be happy."

"I've talked to Daddy," Kristen said, "and he's mentioning things about car wash incidents."

Sylvia glanced toward the kitchen, where Nomanzi remained. "It's okay here." From the other room, the kettle began to sing, first in one tone, then in a second. "Don't worry."

Kristen laughed. "We're quite a trio, huh? The Walters nuclear family in its present state?"

"Yeah, we are." Sylvia laughed too. "You tell Daddy you're getting married?"

"Sure. You know I'm very traditional in this kind of situation. Besides, I figured that after Geneva it was faster to tell him than to get him to have an EKG. QED: he's obviously in the best of health."

"This Philippe—he's very rich?"

"No."

"But you've been traveling all over the place. I don't mean to pry, but what does he do to pay the credit card statements?"

"We're both dipping into savings. And I . . . I sold the Balthus drawing."

"Oh."

"Philippe does real estate. It's just a down period for the business right now."

Because she believed the suspicious mind was a crippling thing, Sylvia again resolved, a little guiltily, to follow through on her plan to take Petra out and have all their jewelry reappraised. For insurance purposes.

"Anyway," Kristen went on, "we were thinking—Philippe's family's in Paris—that maybe it would be fun, if you could get away, for all of us to meet in Paris for the wedding."

"It's that soon?"

"Well, it could be. If you and Daddy and . . . everything. It's not going to be a grand affair."

"Sounds like you're doing that part already."

"Yeah." She giggled. "How's yours going?"

"So far so good." Sylvia tried to yawn, but she'd lost the knack. "And of course I'm coming to your wedding, Kristen—whether it's in Paris or Sumatra."

"Oh, Syl. Thanks."

"Hey." Sylvia sat up. "Did Daddy tell you what he—what they're negotiating in France?"

"God, no. I don't want to know that kind of stuff. Do you?"

Nomanzi had sashayed silently into the room and was now seating herself on the sofa opposite Sylvia. She was looking everywhere else around the room and sipping tea.

"No," Sylvia told Kristen. "I don't really think I'm suited for the role of diplomatic attaché."

"Bad for the skin."

"Exactly. The skin."

"Okay. So I'll call you tomorrow?"

"Great."

"Same time, same place?"

"Seems the best bet. Oh . . . ." Sylvia leaned forward. "Best wishes. *That's* what they say to the bride."

"Are you sure it's not 'silence, exile, and cunning'?"

Sylvia laughed. "Love you, Krissy. Talk to you tomorrow."

"Or is it maybe 'Tomorrow is another day'?"

Still laughing, the sisters hung up. Tomorrow was rarely another day—that they both knew.

"My sister," Sylvia explained to Nomanzi, pointing to the phone. "She's getting married."

"It is a great happiness to be married well."

"You've been married, Nomanzi?"

Nomanzi smiled. "No. I could not be here if I were married."

Sylvia watched a hummingbird study its reflection in the window to the left of Nomanzi's head. When the bird understood it was looking at a reflection—if it did understand—it darted off.

"Nomanzi, you never told me what your movie is going to be about. You said the story was your idea?"

Nomanzi leaned forward to put her teacup on the coffee table before her, so that at that moment she and the white woman Sylvia had placed themselves in mirror reflections of the same posture. They held it.

"I didn't tell you?" Nomanzi said.

FIRST-DRAFT SCREEN TREATMENT FOR "RIVER OVER THE SUN"

The film opens with the dawn awakening of a young black woman whom we'll come to know as Nongqause. The rest of her family sleeps undisturbed around her in the single-room circular hut that is her home. It is morning in Southern Africa, 1856. Nongqause arises, wraps herself in the from-the-waist-down blanket-skirt that signifies she is unmarried, and leaves the hut.

By the doorway are two metal buckets, obviously of Western origin. She picks them up on the run and heads out across the parched veldt. As the camera follows her progress, we see her pass a number of newly dead cattle, their hides still intact. Vultures feed upon one of these animals. The birds pay no attention to the girl's passage.

The cattle of the Xhosa, Nongqause's tribal group, are suffering an outbreak of lung sickness. It is believed that the English colonialists, who have steadily and bloodily deprived the Xhosa of their land, have used witchcraft to produce the calamity.

As she approaches the smoothly flowing light-brown stream that is her destination, Nongqause appears lost in thought. Although the chore of fetching the morning water is considered by her peers the most onerous of the various tasks an unmarried Xhosa girl may be called upon to perform, Nongqause herself does not mind it. She relishes the chance this chore affords her to be alone.

On this particular day she walks carefully through the rushes down to the stream's clay bank. Dipping one bucket into the water, she allows the stream's current to fill it; then she places the vessel beside her on the bank. As she is about to fill the second bucket, we hear a male voice address her from off-camera, using the most formal of her name's variants.

"Unonqawuza."

Terrified, she turns to find five men who, though dressed recognizably in Xhosa battle dress, are unlike anyone familiar to her. The tallest of them, carrying a spear, steps forward to speak to her.

He is, he explains, her father's dead brother. He has returned to the land of his people to help them regain what is rightfully theirs.

The witchcraft of the white men is upon the land, and it can only be countered by the full power of the Xhosas' own belief. What must be done is this: Despite the fact that the livelihood of the Xhosa depends entirely upon cattle, despite the fact that mealie corn is their people's single thriving crop, every head of cattle must be slaughtered, every ear of corn destroyed. Exactly one day after this sacrifice has been completely accomplished, two blood-red suns will rise at dawn; fat, healthy cattle will spring up in vast numbers from the earth; mealie meal will burst in great profusion from every unused bit of soil, and the white man—swept up in a relentless whirlwind—will vanish forever from the land of Africa.

The speaker instructs Nongqause to repeat to her father, a counselor to the Xhosa chief Kreli, what she has just been told and to bring her father with her to the stream the following morning. Snatching up the filled water pails, Nongqause hurries back home.

The next morning, she brings her father to the stream, and he immediately recognizes the spirit of his dead brother among the five strangers. There are now further instructions. Great kraals must be prepared for the reception of the new cattle so soon to appear in multitude; enormous skin sacks are to be made ready to contain the milk shortly to be as plentiful as water once was; huts must be strengthened so they may withstand the whirlwind that will sweep the white man into the sea. And, warns the spear-bearing spirit, those among the Xhosa who fail to obey these instructions will perish in the very same manner as their European enemies. After adding that all further communications regarding this matter will take place through Nongqause, the spirit spokesman leads his retinue back through the rushes and vanishes.

Kreli, the chief of this clan of the Xhosa, hears Nongqause's message with great joy. He summons the neighboring chiefs, explains what must be done, and the slaughter of cattle begins. The slaughtered cattle are eaten, great mounds of mealie corn are burned, the atmosphere is one of manically anticipatory celebration. The hides of two hundred thousand cattle are bartered with glee and abandoned to the hated white man for what now amounts to trifles.

Meanwhile, the British colony is regarding this agitated behavior with the greatest alarm. A young Scot, whom we will come to know as the Reverend John Brownlee of Kingwilliamstown, is particularly ardent in his efforts to dissuade the Xhosa from destroying their own livelihood. He meets with Nongqause, attempting to convince her to repudiate her story. She will not. It is widely believed among the British that the Xhosas' "infatuation," as they have come to call it, has been engineered by Kreli solely for the purpose of driving his people to war. Nongqause is unwavering in her belief.

At this time also, possibly because of her increasing notoriety—
although she is unquestionably an attractive young woman—
Nongqause acquires a lover. His name is Mlomo. Their liaison, in
accordance with custom—since this affair is not the prelude to an
arranged marriage—remains clandestine.

Mr. Brownlee, meanwhile, having failed to convince Nongqause
to stop the carnage, has nonetheless been successful at convincing
one of the Xhosa subchieftains, Sandile, to hold off ordering his
clan to comply with the sacrificial orders. On a certain morning,
on the riverbank, while fetching the water for her family, Nongqause is informed by the spirit of her dead uncle that Sandile's
obstinacy is a great obstacle to the fulfillment of the prophecy he
has made her privy to. She must reverse Sandile's opinion if the
events previously described to her are to occur.

Making no useful excuse to her family, Nongqause walks to the
kraal of Sandile. She makes her case. Sandile is aware of her involvement with Mlomo, says so, and she explains that as is custom-
ary in such situations, they have practiced *ukumetsha*—that is, she
remains technically a virgin. Sandile asks her if her father would
consider allowing her to become his, Sandile's, newest wife. Nongqause responds respectfully but willfully: it would not matter to her
what her father thought; she could not do such a thing. The two
then part stiffly and without further attempt at agreement.

Nonetheless, the next day Sandile gives the order to commence
slaughtering the clan's cattle, to begin burning down the fields and
silos of mealie corn.

Nongqause is told of this development by Mlomo the same evening, as they lie together in the bushes.

The following morning, at the stream, her dead uncle's spirit
expresses his satisfaction at Sandile's change of heart and at last
tells Nongqause the day on which the much-awaited miracles will
occur: one week later, February 18, 1857.

The activity among the Xhosa becomes frenetic.

In response, the British do everything possible to protect the
frontier from the anticipated attack—strengthening every post,
sending every available man forward. We see Mr. Brownlee helping
the wife of a colonialist fortify her house—boarding up the windows
and so on—but it becomes apparent from the conversation that he

does not believe that the Infatuation of the Xhosa is a military tactic on the part of their leaders. He does not believe there will be an attack. The woman's mouth is fixed, determined; she is unconvinced.

We see Mr. Brownlee praying in the crudely built wooden church that serves the area. He resolves to visit Nongqause one last time.

Arriving at the kraal of Nongqause's father, Mr. Brownlee is at first barred by Nongqause's mother from speaking to her daughter, but then, seeing that he means no harm, the not-so-elderly woman points out the spot where Nongqause is sewing sacks to hold all the milk that is soon to spring from the ground for the nourishment of all their tribe.

Nongqause at first ignores Mr. Brownlee, then, without a word, rises to her feet. She walks with him a short distance. They stop to talk.

Only now is it evident to us—from a gesture, a look, or a word on Mr. Brownlee's part—that he has developed affectionate, if not romantic, feelings for Nongqause; he is afraid he will not see her again. These feelings he quickly suppresses.

He tells her the British are preparing for war. He reminds her that the Xhosa have lost all such previous wars. He begs her to imagine what would happen to her people if the prophecies she has been entrusted with fail to come to pass.

Nongqause is adamant about the truth of the prophecies. After a pause, she announces very formally that she is sorry Mr. Brownlee will have to perish with the rest of the whites, but that is what will happen. She returns to the group of her sister workers, leaving Mr. Brownlee standing in the hot summer wind.

We now see, in a rapid series of crosscuts, the preparations on either side for the coming events—the British frantically consolidating their defenses; the Xhosa feasting upon their cattle in glad anticipation of the future.

Matters are in this condition when, on the evening before the expected miracles, a huge celebration begins among the Xhosa. There are dancing competitions, singing competitions, storytelling competitions—all this activity fueled by a seemingly endless "beer drink." Mlomo takes advantage of the extraordinary moment to approach Nongqause's father and announce his desire to take Nongqause as his wife. The older man does not appear indisposed to the request but is firm that the discussion take place at another time, in the traditional way.

As the night wears on, the celebration quiets down. By the hour before the dawn, the entire Xhosa tribe has fallen silent. They sit upon the ground, facing east. They wait.

When the sun rises as usual—it has no twin, it is not blood red— the silence of the Xhosa deepens. They continue to sit. When the sun sets as usual, the tribe's silence becomes that of defeat. They disperse.

Over the next several weeks, fifty thousand Xhosa die of starvation. Families disintegrate. Individuals disintegrate.

Some time after this disaster, Mr. Brownlee is driving a horse-drawn cart to the Cape Colony when he comes upon Nongqause walking alone by the side of the dirt road. He stops. They do not speak. She gets into the cart.

When they reach the Cape Colony, Mr. Brownlee finds Nongqause a position as a servant in the household of a young British man of comparatively enlightened views and obviously considerable means. We shall come to know him as Paul.

There is a piano in the house. It is an evident extravagance and clearly an utterly alien artifact to Nongqause. She touches it; Paul plays it. Brahms, perhaps. There is a daguerreotype of a young British woman atop the piano. Nongqause picks up the likeness in her hands because she has never seen this kind of likeness, then Paul takes it from her and places it facedown upon the piano's surface.

The two begin to have an affair. They love each other without discussing it.

Nongqause becomes pregnant. She does not mention it.

When it becomes obvious to Paul that Nongqause is going to have a child, they cease sleeping together. Still, it would be inaccurate to suggest that they have ceased being lovers. The child is born. It is a boy, very dark of skin. Nongqause and her child remain in the separate quarters allotted to servants.

The depopulation of Southeastern Africa resulting from the Infatuation of the Xhosa has allowed the British colonialists to settle peaceably upon land that is not theirs. It is suggested to Paul by the local commissioner that he annex the several hundred hectares that lie between his home and the Great Kei River to the north. Paul refuses.

One evening at dinner he asks Nongqause about her role in the Infatuation. She does not answer. He then asks if he might spend some time alone with their boy. To this request she assents.

Paul teaches the boy, whom Nongqause has named Mlomo, to shoot, to ride a horse, to tend the cattle. It is clear that Paul feels affection for the boy, but also clear that he feels puzzlement at the course his own life has taken.

Nongqause comes unexpectedly one night into the master house. Paul is sitting by the fireside, reading. When he looks up, Nongqause tells him that their young boy doesn't know Paul is his father and must never know. She leaves without Paul's having uttered a word. It is obvious from his distraught stare that he has had no inkling that this was the case.

The boy grows into an adolescent. Neither his mother nor his father seems to age. They resume sleeping together.

Paul keeps a pistol behind the books on the lowest shelf of his living room bookcase. One day, while Paul is in town, Mlomo pulls the largest volume from the shelf—it is a complete Shakespeare—and discovers the pistol. For a moment we see him holding the two objects, one in either hand: he is weighing them as if he were a balance. Then he returns these objects to their previous locations and quickly departs.

In his bedroom Paul has always kept a small mahogany box that is filled with keepsakes from his marriage to the woman whose likeness remains facedown upon the piano in the living room. One day, while Paul is in town, Nongqause lingers longer than usual in his bed. When she rises, she opens the mahogany box, which she has always known to be what it is. From the various mementos of a Victorian marriage, she picks out a single diamond earring, triangular in cut, set as a stud. She puts it under her tongue in a furtive gesture and returns to her quarters.

Time passes.

There is another drought, another episode of lung sickness among the cattle of the area. Paul's cattle are proportionately stricken.

Nongqause and Paul, without any direct discussion of the subject, decide that she and Mlomo will move into the main house.

The political climate between the Boers and the English of the area is becoming newly difficult as it ceases to be primarily military in character. We feel this shift only atmospherically, but it causes Paul to withdraw still more deeply into his unconventional household.

One evening we see Nongqause alone before a mirror. She is holding up one of Paul's wife's frocks before her. The effect is—and not only by its cultural dissonance—flattering. Nongqause herself remains, or has become, beautiful. She frowns, however, throws the garment down upon the bed, and leaves the room.

In the study, Paul is at his desk, writing—his memoirs perhaps? a letter?

In the living room, Mlomo, nineteen or twenty by now, is seated on a couch. The room is lit only by the firelight from the hearth. Mlomo is staring at the volume of Shakespeare in the bookcase opposite.

We see Nongqause pacing in the hallway outside the bedroom.

We see Mlomo get up off the sofa.

In his writing, Paul comes to a full stop. He lights a cigar and, leaning back in his chair, begins rereading what he has written.

Nongqause pauses, as if having heard something that we have not, then begins running down the candlelit hallway. In her wake, several of the candles are blown out by her passage.

Mlomo opens the door of Paul's study and levels the pistol at him. Paul, not exactly bewildered but not exactly convinced, rises to his feet and lifts his hands somewhat above his shoulders, as if about to climb into the air. Mlomo is shaking, but after a moment's hesitation, he pulls the trigger and shoots Paul dead. In falling, Paul grasps the grandfather clock that stands in the corner behind him. It topples with him, its somewhat overly crafted hands thus arrested at 8:16.

Nongqause stands in the doorway; on her face, a mixture of horror and confusion.

Her son turns to confront her. They look at each other for a time, both of them as breathless as bolting animals. Then she extends her arm fully into the space between them, opens her palm, and shows him what it holds. It is the earring.

She gives it to him.

They leave the house together, on foot, with only a few belongings.

Time passes.

Nongqause now appears considerably older. She is obviously back in the land of her childhood. She is carrying a pair of buckets down to the river.

Very briefly, we see Mlomo—looking perhaps ten years older, but very "town" (not "country"). He is sitting at a makeshift table in a makeshift dwelling. Surrounded by the people of his nation, who appear to be listening to him intently, he is speaking politics.

There is a still briefer shot, perhaps from remastered documentary film—of Louis Botha addressing the (entirely white) Colonial Conference of 1907 in London. Shockingly, he greets the imperial assembly in Afrikaans, the tongue that is to become the language of apartheid.

The year's date appears in white numerals superimposed upon the image: 1907.

Freeze-frame.

"Really?" Nomanzi continued, still looking at Sylvia. "I never told you my great film idea?"

"No, Nomanzi, you didn't."

"Oh, well." She picked up the teacup and took a sip. "There'll be plenty of opportunity for that. But in the meantime, do you think it's getting too cool to use the whirlpool bath on the roof here?"

"Never."

"Good. So I'll tell you the English translation of my name instead."

Sylvia smiled uncertainly and stood up.

"Nomanzi means," Nomanzi concluded, also getting to her feet. "It means"—heading toward the kitchen with her empty teacup. "Well, the closest translation would probably be—" She stopped without turning around. "Mother of Water."

"**W**here's Michael?"

"He's over there at the water fountain. You got the tickets, Petra?"

When you are at an airport, much of your time is spent keeping track of where things are.

"Right here, Sylvie. The travel agent delivered them to my office yesterday: you, me, Michael, Nomanzi, Johnny, and Chentula. We stop in New York for a couple of hours, get into Paris about noon their time. A day's layover, and on to Johannesburg. No problem. If it's all this easy, we might as well start making reservations for our post-production vacation."

Sylvia chewed her bottom lip. She walked a little ways into the terminal's many-minded crowd, then she walked back. "Petra."

"What is it?"

"You know that after what happened at the car wash, we—I mean Michael, Nomanzi, and me—" She was losing track of what might be the diplomatic way to approach this situation. She put her hands on her waist. "Don't you think it might be better if we leave from a different airport: San Francisco, maybe?"

"You're telling me the police told you not to leave town."

Sylvia nodded. "Although they probably meant, you know, the country."

Petra nodded. "Okay. I'll see what time the next flight north leaves. Just so we make our connection in New York."

There was a small commotion near passport inspection. A man dressed as an orange—he wore a swollen plastic replica of the fruit from neck to knees—was passing out samples of freshly squeezed juice. The security guards were ignoring him.

Michael, back from the fountain, put his hands on Sylvia's shoulders from behind. "Whatever he is, he's here," said Michael.

"So what do we do?" Sylvia whispered. She turned toward him with the smile of someone who was simply going to Paris with her lover.

"We give it a shot," replied Michael. "Because we're here."

"Right. Because we're here."

Petra was pretending to look away.

"Petra," Sylvie said, "let's just, you know, do it."

They were cleared immediately.

In the skies over North America, Chentula spoke to Nomanzi. "What you told me about this man at the car-washing place—you say you do not know him, that he was just a man who saw you on television. I do not believe this."

Chentula's forearm lay upon the padded armrest between his seat and that of his half-sister. Compressed air hissed down upon them. Nomanzi placed her hand upon the widest part of his forearm.

"What do you believe?" she asked.

"This man was your lover."

"No," she said, before she could stop herself. So that her reply was too convincing for her to pick it up afterward as a possible lie. She sighed and withdrew her hand. "He was not my lover."

Chentula affected to look out the window at the Great Plains, invisible from this height.

"He was . . ." Flight attendants were rushing by carrying compartmentalized meals. And a feeling of placelessness buzzed dully through the cabin, as if all the senses could be put in a holding pattern, or in the no-smoking section. Thoughts, though, were another matter. "He was a patriot," Nomanzi said.

When he turned to look at her, Chentula's face was impassive but alert. Of the dozen conjectures racing through his mind, he would shortly select one as the most probable. He would believe in it. He continued to gaze at his half-sister without speaking.

Across the aisle, Michael was laying bare the protein section of his meal with a fork. "Did we get all the equipment through?" he asked Petra.

"One plane has already landed in Cape Town. The second is leaving today."

"Good. Where's everything being held?"

"I'm not sure."

"Not sure."

"We take risks, don't we?"

"Yes, we do."

"So it's that kind of situation." Petra unwrapped the miniaturized steel flatware that accompanied her meal. There was an illustrative eloquence to the gesture. "Because it's that kind of location."

"Okay, but I was also thinking about Johnny and Chentula." Michael inspected the neutral-natured food with which the airline had provided him. "The band checked all their equipment through with us, and they're supposed to give a free concert almost the moment we get to Azania."

"Everything will be there," Petra answered. "If we are."

"And we'll be there." But he did not relax.

Sylvia, whom Petra, after a series of screenings of unknown pictures on which Petra had worked, had hired to do sound for the South African film, was waiting her turn at the toilet when Michael got there. In return for her agreement to serve as prime-time video deejay, KBZT management had agreed to give her a paid leave of absence.

An enormous, scentless man—impeccably dressed in Italian clothing—emerged sideways from the toilet cabinet directly behind Michael and Sylvia. The man did not look up from the travel guide to Baltimore he appeared to be reading.

"After you," said Michael to Sylvia.

They entered the stainless-steel bathroom together and closed the door.

"That guy—didn't he seem sort of . . . extraterrestrial?" said Sylvia.

"Locking the door turns on the light," said Michael. "How weird."

"Michael," Sylvia said. "Michael."

"Yes."

"I'm pregnant."

"I know," he said.

"You know?"

"There's a taste."

The light was very ugly, but Michael and Sylvia—just exactly then—were very beautiful. They both noticed this incongruity.

He kissed her.

Without really thinking about it, she began unbuckling his belt.

"We'll marry," he asked.

"Okay," she answered, tossing her head. "I mean, you know. . . .Yes."

He lifted her by the waist so that she might sit upon the sink's ledge.

She lowered her brow to look at him, and her hair cascaded down.

"I can wear underwear or not," she said.

"Mm-hmm," he said.

"I'm not," she said, drawing his cock into her, beneath her skirt.

Michael's own underwear rested somewhere down about his knees, caught in the open throat of his peeled-back pants.

"Is this," Michael inquired after a time, moving his lips from her neck to her ear, "the much-discussed compromising position?"

"Please, Michael. Don't be an idiot."

"I didn't mean us." He saw her eyes were closed.

"And don't stop what you're doing," she said. "Please."

"I could never stop."

"Michael. You know that I love you!"

"Yes."

A little speaker in the washroom asked all the passengers to return to their seats and buckle their seat belts.

"Too late," whispered Sylvia as she began to come. "No seat belts."

Little biscuit-shaped bars of soap spilled from a dispenser near Michael and Sylvia's shoulders. Turbulence. The soap clattered softly onto the tiny floor.

Ever since they had left the city of their angels, both Michael and Sylvia had been aware, without ever having consulted each other, that the two events they had agreed to be part of—Kristen's wedding and Petra's film—were almost undoubtedly something other than what they appeared to be, but that it didn't really matter what those events were until the cast involved knew why they had lent themselves to them.

Photons of light, abbreviated in spectrum, zinged about the tiny room.

Sylvia, leaning back, put the flat of her hand inadvertently on the push-top of the faucet behind her, releasing a controlled jet of water whose sudden rush startled both her and Michael for an instant.

MICHAEL: [*Raising his face, baring his throat*]: I didn't . . . uh . . .
    that with water . . . Oh, right; you're the sound person. [*Half
    laughs.*]
SYLVIA: Well, I guess we are playing this one by ear. Michael?
    Aren't we? [*Kisses his throat.*] Aren't we?
WASHROOM SPEAKER: This is your captain speaking . . .

When the plane, after refueling in New York, landed at Henri Pétain Airport in Paris, the notion of private conversation among the six travelers had been temporarily discarded. They stood expectantly together upon the glassed-in conveyor belt.

"I'm sure Kristen'll be here," Petra offered after a while. "You only get married three or four times in your life; it's an event."

Upon reaching the airport's main concourse, Michael, Sylvia, Johnny, Chentula, Petra, and Nomanzi discovered another event in progress. A hundred and some dozen people of various ages were marching about the triple-story space, chanting in French and brandishing picket signs. Some of the signs bore the name of Heinrich Bloch.

Petra paled, but just a bit, and drew her gauzy black scarf more closely to her neck.

"What is it they're saying?" asked Johnny.

Sylvia glanced at Petra, then answered, "It's a demonstration. They're protesting our— I mean America's—development of that fission bomb thing."

"I saw about it in the papers," said Chentula.

"Well, we all know it's not real," said Johnny. "Just political steroids, eh?"

The women said nothing.

The airport was very large.

"I'm seeing this German guy's name all the time," said Michael. "On the signs and stuff. Heinrich Bloch?"

A short silence ensued. Sylvia said: "He's the one who's leading the resistance to—oh, come on; I'm sure you've read all about it."

A young Frenchwoman in clothes of American design but Gallic fit offered Petra a leaflet. When Petra stopped to receive it, Nomanzi bumped into her from behind. They apologized to each other. The leaflet was in French. The speech was in English.

"My comrades, we must unite against this atrocity, this fission bomb." The young woman threw her head back extravagantly to get her hair out of her eyes, to punctuate her polemic. "It is said the bomb could ignite the atmosphere—our air. An obscenity, is it not?"

"An obscenity," Sylvia agreed, letting her voice go broadly American.

The Frenchwoman appeared startled. Her hair fell back around her eyes. After fussing awhile with the clipboard and pen she was carrying, she thrust them out to Sylvia. "So you will sign our petition?"

Sylvia met her gaze. She seized what was offered her and signed. They all signed.

"La lutte," the woman said, looking the six of them over. A still moment. The crowd swallowed her.

"I need an orange juice," Sylvia said.

Petra swallowed. "Aren't there a lot of . . ."

"Police?" Michael said. "Yes. There are a lot of police here. Sylvie, what does Kristen look like?"

"Does the leaflet say who organized this demonstration?" Nomanzi asked.

"Kristen? She's sort of like me, only a little shorter and less fair."

"Fair?" said Michael.

"Sylvia!" said Kristen, emerging from the crowd. She was dressed in a ruffled skirt whose hem fell well above her knees. "Oh, I thought I'd never *find* you!" She took Sylvia into her arms, and

Sylvia felt immediately the odd confluence of their blood: because she knew even then that they would always find each other—siblings, sisters, comfort, candidates. It was the kind of embrace Sylvia needed. It was the kind of need she'd nearly forgotten about.

"I've missed you, Krissy."

"Syl-Syl. Everything is happening so fast."

"I know. But just so you're sure."

"I'm sure."

They took a step back from each other, absorbing what they saw.

"Is Daddy here?" Sylvia asked.

"He's booked on the four-fifteen from Geneva."

"Geneva!"

"Yes," said Kristen. "Geneva. Where else?"

Sylvia forced herself to brighten. "Oh, right, sure. God, I must be jet-lagged. And I haven't even introduced my friends." She inclined her head just a fraction; her right hand grazed the diamond at her earlobe. She had always known how to hide things.

"Hi, Petra," Kristen said.

"Oh, I forgot—of course you two already know each other." Sylvia regarded Kristen to see if she was noticing Petra's paired earrings in any way that might explain something. But Kristen's glances didn't work that way. "And Kristen, this is Johnny, Chentula, Nomanzi, Michael."

There was a surge in the crowd. The police discreetly herded the demonstrators into a more contained area.

"It's very generous of you to invite us to your wedding mass," said Michael, shifting his carry-on bag from one hand to the other. "The groom is very lucky, obviously. I'm sure he knows it."

"Thank you."

"By the way," Michael continued, "where is the groom?"

"Philippe? Oh, he's . . ." She did a very graceful mime of oh-he-must-be-here-someplace, and it became evident to all that she was aware her neck was beautiful. "Well," she said at last. "He'll find us."

The wedding benediction was to be held in a small church around the corner from a small hotel on the right bank of the Seine. In accordance with French law, the civil marriage ceremony had already been accomplished.

An hour before the wedding mass, several hours after the groom had indeed found his bride and her wedding guests within the airport, the phone in Kristen's hotel suite began to ring with annoying insistence.

Sylvia was pinning up her sister's hair. Kristen wore a white lace slip; Sylvia had bought a green slip but was wearing nothing.

"Do we have to get that?" Kristen asked, although Sylvia, leaving one hand atop her sister's golden hair, had already picked up the receiver.

It was their father calling.

He was calling to say he was going to be late.

"Daddy," said Sylvia.

"Syl, have you met this guy? Because really the whole thing seems a little precipitous to me, don't you know, even taking into account the way Kristen's always been . . . whatever she is: impetuous, rebellious. Of course, from the very day she was born, she—"

"It's fine, Daddy."

For a while Paul Walters just breathed. Then he said, "It'll probably take me an hour and a half to get there. Can you . . . ?"

"We'll wait, Daddy." Sylvia saw Kristen frowning at herself in the mirror and groping with the wrong hand for her eyeliner. Switching the phone to her other ear, Sylvia swept the compact off the vanity and handed it to her younger sister. "You're coming in from Geneva?" Sylvia asked.

"About an hour and a half. I'm bringing Joseph Lolombela. His daughter is with you, right?"

"Nomanzi? Yes, she's here."

Kristen turned fully around in her chair and mouthed the words *Should I speak to him?* Sylvia raised the flat of her free hand in the manner of a traffic cop.

"Good," said Paul Walters. "Joseph very much wants to see her."

"You know where we are."

"Pont Royal, rue de Bach."

"I love you, Daddy. Here's Kristen."

Right nearby was Kristen's dressing gown, draped over the edge of the bed. While Kristen began to explain herself in patient tones, Sylvia threw the cream-colored gown around her own shoulders and slo-mo'ed barefoot down the hotel corridor to Nomanzi's room.

She paused before the cherrywood door. Even through its calm density she could hear the tones of the argument taking place within.

When at last she knocked, Chentula answered.

"Sylvia." Over his shoulder, he said something further to Johnny, who stood gazing out the balcony window—something in Xhosa, a continuation, it seemed to Sylvia, of what she had overheard from the hallway. But of course she didn't know Xhosa.

"How are you keeping?" Chentula asked her in English. He was wearing a red-and-yellow football jersey whose warmth of hue seemed to amplify the smile of welcome that now, somewhat belatedly, appeared upon his face. "Come in."

"Thanks." She kissed him on the cheek in passing. "Hi, Johnny."

"Afternoon, Sylvia." He had already put on the closely tailored blue suit he had rented for the ceremony. On either side of him and of the parted windows through which he continued to gaze, gauzy curtains fluttered like scarves in the breeze.

"Is Nomanzi around?"

"Still in the bath, I think."

Sylvia touched the back of Johnny's head as she went by; he leaned forward to put out the cigarette he'd been holding.

"Nomanzi, it's me," said Sylvia through the bathroom door. Then, taking the muffled response from inside to mean something like "okay," she opened the door just a crack, slipped through, and locked it behind her.

Nomanzi was in the tub, soapsuds nearly to her shoulder.

"How is Kristen keeping?" said Nomanzi. The bathroom tile was an oddly acid shade of blue. Nomanzi was staring at the part of it directly above her toes.

"Kristen? Oh, she thrives on moments like this—pops them like pills." Throwing open the small refrigerator, Kristen withdrew two frosted glasses and two tiny bottles of sweet vermouth.

"The boys are quarreling," said Nomanzi.

"I heard them. What about?" She handed Nomanzi one of the filled glasses and sat down on the toilet seat, beside the tub.

"Oh, it's what we talked about, you and I—or really what Chenny and young *Baas* John have been reading about: this fission bomb thing." She sank a little lower in her bath and took a sip of the red liqueur in her glass. "I didn't repeat anything of our conversation to them, but I think the scene at the airport made the politics of it—how is it?—more concrete."

"What's the problem?" Sylvia felt herself grow a little shaky, and to steady herself she reached out to touch the towels atop the steam-heated rack to her left. *Japanese restaurants,* she thought without realizing it.

"Johnny does not believe in the bomb—an American trick, he thinks—but he does believe Azania can use this ruse to draw more committed European support." Nomanzi closed her eyes and let her voice turn singsongy to indicate how wearisome she found such a debate. "Chenny believes the fission bomb is real but of no importance to the future of our nation, whose problems must be solved without outside interference." She negligently lifted one long leg to inspect the pearlescent toenails that she had come to think of as the most inconsequential and therefore the most enjoyable of her secret vices. "Of course, they have each written songs today about this fission thing, and that is what they are arguing about."

"Well, probably," said Sylvia, having swallowed her drink in a single gulp, "they'll have more ways to think about it an hour and a half from now, when our fathers, yours and mine, show up here for the wedding mass."

"My father, Joseph Lolombela, is coming to this hotel?"

Sylvia looked at her and nodded. "I just found out."

Nomanzi rose from her bath in a cascade of bubbles. "There will be press."

"I doubt it—this is all kind of last-minute—but, sure, you never know."

Wrapping one of the heated towels about her torso, Nomanzi removed another pair of one-trick liquor bottles from the undersized refrigerator. She handed vermouth to Sylvia and, pouring vodka into her own glass, sat down on the edge of the bidet. Her fingers, now at her chin, were very long.

"Does Chenny know?" she asked after a time.

"Not from me."

"You see, Chentula is my half-brother, but it is my mother, not my father, that we share, and when my father and I were forced to leave my—"

"I know this part."

Nomanzi paused. She would not have known, if asked, whether she was at that moment pausing as a daughter or a friend, but when she rose to turn the bathtub's hot-water tap completely open, she knew exactly why she was doing so. And when she resumed her perch on the edge of the bidet, beside Sylvia, she said, looking at her:

"Steam."

Perfect makeup, perfect dresses.

There had been demonstrators on the ribbon-width sidewalk outside the hotel, but because the protesters had been given the original hour of the wedding benediction, the police had ample time to clear them away. And when Paul Walters and Joseph Lolombela pulled up to the curb in the pearl-gray limousine with which French security had provided them, the only real on-site agitation was in the hearts and breath of their daughters and themselves.

"Joseph," said Paul Walters, laying a hand on his colleague's shoulder as they entered the hotel lobby.

"Ten years, man. My own daughter."

"But she's here today." Both men were wearing morning dress. Neither felt comfortable in it. "And so are you."

"Yeh, man. Okay." He smiled at the American. "Mutual accord."

They approached the desk while the French security guards who had accompanied them roamed embarrassingly about the lobby in filmic imitation of their profession.

"I'm Paul Walters," Paul Walters told the concierge, who indicated he was already aware of this fact by putting on his glasses and appearing elegantly confused.

"My daughter," Paul Walters prompted, "is having her wedding mass at the church around the corner in half an hour."

"Oh, yes, yes, yes. Of course." The concierge relieved himself of his glasses and his confusion. Premier étage." He looked at Joseph Lolombela. "First floor up, the dining room. *Pour les photos.*"

"Well, really, my dear man," said Joseph, leaning on the desk and into the most comically English English he could summon up, "I'm here to deliver croissants to my daughter, Nomanzi Lolombela—that is, if she's here? I'm not quite sure. It is always difficult to tell with one's daughters."

The concierge blushed to a degree that made literal the implied exchange about the difference in their skins. *"Pardon, monsieur,"* he said, stepping over to the hotel register and running a finger quickly down the list of guests. "I will phone upstairs to see if your daughters have left their rooms yet. One moment."

Three of the security men, apparently bonded for life to their sunglasses, left the area to inspect the first-floor room in which the wedding party was to gather for photographs just prior to the event. The two other bodyguards squeezed themselves into the elevator after Lolombela and Walters, pushed the button for the eighth floor, and made themselves as discreetly absent as possible for two men carrying semiautomatic weapons.

"Ce mec at the desk said what room?" asked Joseph Lolombela.

"Eight sixteen," Walters answered, adjusting his tie in the elevator's minuscule mirror.

The security men peeled off to either side in the eighth-floor corridor. Walters knocked on the designated door. Sylvia: Sylvia Walters, dressed in green, cream, and white, her hair in a chignon and her heart in helical ascension: it was she who threw open the door.

"You're here," she said, taking a breath and a slow-eyed look. "You're really here."

"All you need to track the big cat," he said, invoking one of their routines from her girlhood, "are nerves of steel, the persistence of stone, and superhuman cunning." He took his daughter into his arms. "These are my areas of expertise."

A tension Sylvia had not till then been aware of drained from her body in a single long sigh that nearly ended with a sob. "I've missed you so much, Daddy."

"You look wonderful, Syl. Just wonderful. How's the bride?"

The bride was in the bathroom.

Joseph Lolombela, still standing at the threshold, stared past both Paul and Sylvia Walters to the gracefully draped figure whom he recognized, despite the years of separation and self-recrimination, as his daughter.

"Nomanzi," he said. "It is you? The bioscope star?"

"Yes, Father." She did not move. "It is me."

They were speaking English, as if to dissipate the shyness that each felt at accepting this moment of nearness from a world that had so arbitrarily legislated their separation.

"You have your mother's grace, her beauty." Joseph Lolombela found himself smiling. "I would recognize you anywhere."

"Perhaps because I have my father's pride," she said. "That is something you would recognize even here, eh?" She, too, had begun to smile. "In a Paris hotel?" They were walking toward each other, their smiles giving way to laughter. "At somebody else's wedding?"

Which is how, after ten years, they came to embrace.

Sylvia knocked twice on the bathroom door, and her sister's voice rang out quickly, excitedly, in response. "Is that you, Daddy? Oh, I'm so glad you're here. I'll be right out."

Saying nothing, Sylvia rejoined the company. Although the suite was not small, and the creams and gold tones gave it a still airier aspect, Sylvia was reminded of the airport, congested with intention. *A roomful of crowded people*, she thought, watching Nomanzi and Joseph Lolombela give increasingly fluid voice to the conversation each of them had maintained in radio silence during the years they'd been apart.

"Oh, Daddy," Sylvia said, her eye having then fallen elsewhere. "You must come meet Madame Grandet, Philippe's mother."

The suite's door flew open, and Petra sailed in. The bathroom door flew open, and Kristen sailed out. Uttering a small cry of no particular import, Petra opened one hand over the mirror-topped vanity, deposited her earrings, lipstick, and compact right there, then swept unencumbered into the bathroom.

Kristen threw herself into her father's arms.

"My ears are ringing," she said, pressing the side of her head to his chest. "When you married Mommy, did it make your ears ring?"

Paul Walters laughed. "Something rang," he said. His hand, which had been about to touch her carefully arranged hair, was corrected by his eye and instead came to rest lightly upon her throat. "I think it was the bell, the one that tolled for me."

"Ding, dong."

"Other way, to tell you the truth."

"Dong, ding." They both laughed.

Sylvia, who had scooped Petra's earrings from the surface of the vanity, glanced toward the bathroom, then drew the point of one diamond stud across the dressing table's surface: in its wake, a six-inch-long furrow carved in the glass the way a figure skater's blade cuts the ice beneath into opacity. She quickly set about repeating the test with the other earring.

"*Vous êtes Monsieur Walters?*" said a trimly cut woman seated near the room's window. She was dressed in a black-and-brown-checked suit; she had been leafing inattentively through an Italian fashion magazine.

"I am," said Paul Walters, approaching her. "And you are no doubt Madame Grandet?" He bowed to her formally and kissed the proffered hand. She smiled to indicate that she was indeed Madame Grandet and that so far all was well.

"Our family was very relieved," she began in English, "to hear . . ."

Sylvia tilted her head to remove from her earlobe the last of the tricornered diamonds, the one Michael had found in her garage. When she had it in hand she drew it, as she had the others, across the vanity's top. She stared at the results: three matched furrows of glass dust in perfect parallel. The stones were all genuine.

". . . that you were not harmed in Geneva." Madame Grandet stood without fuss, placing her magazine upon the seat she had just vacated.

"Thank you," said Paul Walters. "Public service has its moments of surprise, although in general one's daughters are more startling."

"And one's sons!" added the groom's mother, letting her hand come lightly to rest on his forearm. A tiny gold cross quivered in the cup of her collarbones.

"*Salut, tout le monde, salut!*" said Petra, emerging from the bathroom. She was attempting to look inclusive, but she walked without hesitation to the spot where Sylvia's father stood. "You are Paul Walters; you must be. And I am Petra König." She shook his hand. "I have heard so much about you."

Sylvia, having just returned the supernumerary diamond to her ear, understood that something bad was going to happen before too long. And why was Petra acting more and more European with every passing minute?

"It is a pleasure to meet you, Petra König."

"How nice that you were able to get away for the event, really super. Are your colleagues . . . I guess it was a general recess? The papers . . . well . . ."

"I hear you're the producer of this new film, the one starring Joseph's daughter? Sounds good, sounds very good." Paul Walters, almost inadvertently, caught his daughter's eye. "I've got all my fingers crossed." He reengaged Petra's gaze. "Of course, I don't really know what the film's about, but production is everything these days, I'm told."

"I recognize your daughter in you," Petra said, in a near whisper.

"Thank you," said Paul Walters in a voice lower still.

"Did Heinrich—"

"Sylvia," said Paul Walters, putting his arm delicately around his daughter's shoulders as she arrived by instinct at his side. "I'm so happy to meet your friend Petra—may I call you that?—at last. She was telling me a little about the film."

"We're all very excited by it," Sylvia answered.

"*Et maintenant, je comprends,*" said Madame Grandet, stepping back into the conversation but addressing herself unmistakably to Paul Walters. "The mystery is solved."

"The mystery?" he replied.

"It was you who sent all these flowers."

There were Belgian tulips, it was true, in pressed-glass vases placed here and there by an aesthetic intelligence that had left them prominent to sight but just out of the way of elbows and skirts. The hotel staff, no doubt. It was a good hotel. However, it was not Paul Walters who had sent the flowers, and he apologized for having failed to do so.

Petra was putting on her earrings.

Those in the room who happened to be watching her were reminded by the intensity of her self-regard in the vanity's mirror that they were all about to be photographed. This knowledge added a note of artificial gaiety to events that were running just fine on adrenaline alone.

"Chentula will be there," Nomanzi told her father. "Right now he's with Johnny, the groom, the rest of the men."

Joseph did not attempt to appear surprised. "I will be glad to see him."

"I don't think he has forgiven you for leaving."

"It does not matter." Lolombela removed a handkerchief from his breast pocket and wiped the sweat from his brow. "I love him as my son. I love him as I love you, and as I love the woman who was mother to you both."

Nomanzi, drawing the moment out by turning her glance sociably away from her father and adjusting her closely wrapped turban, said in English: "I, too, love Chentula." Her turban was cotton of midnight blue, with a pattern of alternately oriented white commas. "We've begun to understand each other."

Lolombela took the cue immediately.

Kristen, looking at a watch so tiny as to be nearly indecipherable, said: "Everybody, we have to go downstairs in a couple of minutes for the photographer."

Lolombela answered his daughter in Xhosa. "Chentula, you say."

"Yes."

"He knows about what it was you had planned with Cousin?"

"No, in that way it is not so. But . . ." She allowed her fingers to take interest in a bottle of perfume on the dresser beside her; she decided, upon sniffing its contents, to streak her neck with the golden oil it held. "I had to tell him enough so that he could work out a story that would not make a lie about him or me."

Lolombela squeezed his daughter's shoulder.

"Or about what will be our country," Nomanzi added, returning the perfume bottle to its place upon the dresser. She turned to face her father. "Is that how much you've told me about your talks in France?"

In the short silence that ensued, it was possible to hear Paul Walters, his voice assuming a respectful register, express his interest in meeting Michael, the director of Petra's current picture, the young friend of his elder daughter.

"What I have told you," said Lolombela to Nomanzi, "about the negotiations . . . of course we know, eh, that there are no negotiations of the kind you mean?"

"I know there are no important negotiations in Geneva," said Nomanzi in English.

"So," her father continued, still in Xhosa, "I, too, have worked out stories that do not make a lie."

"Everybody, everybody!" Kristen was saying.

"And so, Father, the story that there will not be a test detonation of this—what is it?—this fission weapon . . ." But just then Nomanzi saw the little cruelties of age in her father's grayed temples; in the almost negligible misfocus of his moist brown eyes; in the desire expressed, upon his barely parted lips, that she understand him.

It seemed to her that what she understood, as little as it was, might for now suffice. "My father," she said.

"I have not lied to—"

"My father," she repeated, "although I have tried, I have never come to love my country more than my mother, more than Chentula, more than you, more—I must say it—more than myself." She looked down, and what she saw were her shoes; to her shame, she admired them. She looked up. "I will not cry." She found her hand going to his. "That is where my betrayal stops. And it is there that it will always stop. It is the largest part of what I have to offer."

People were moving festively about.

"My daughter," said Joseph Lolombela, "I would recognize you anywhere."

The wedding photographs.

A photograph is said to be "taken"—presumably from the lives of the people whose images are, by means of light, darkness, silver, and dyes, in innocence preserved.

The dining room on the hotel's first floor was painted a dusty rose; its moldings and wainscotings were cream.

"I am Philippe Grandet," said the sharp-featured young man who was, to the vertigo of Paul Walters, technically already married to his daughter. The two men were shaking hands.

"I'm," said Paul Walters. And his picture was taken several times.

"Daddy," said Sylvia, looping his free arm through hers. "Who are these people walking around in sunglasses? They don't seem like ordinary—"

"It's okay, darling." He turned back to Philippe Grandet. "I know that you will take good care of Kristen. I know that you know she is a treasure."

"I love your daughter very much, Monsieur Walters."

"Good," he answered, looking hard but not unkindly at the young man. "So do I."

Although Paul Walters could not remember how it was he had come to know that the russet-haired young man facing him had lost his own father several months before turning six years of age, the thought made him sad in a way that he knew, still more sadly, to be selfish. Walters did not wish to speak to the father of his daughter's husband; he would have avoided the moment, would have hated it had it occurred, would have certainly cut it short. Yet he knew that the world he was all but helplessly bequeathing his daughter, her husband, their children, was one that would make the elaborated innocence of a photograph—and after all it was no doubt through photographs that Philippe had reinvented his father—seem itself quaint, finished, an occasion for charmed laughter.

"Oh, good! Here's Chentula." Sylvia sidled forward, knowing she had something to say but uncertain beforehand what it would be.

"I'm in love with Michael," she told her father. "Isn't that weird? I guess I must have been saving myself for divorce or something." She lit a cigarette.

Paul Walters saw his daughter through a bluish curl of tobacco smoke, and in his mind he saw as well a sudden card-shuffle of images, themselves smoky at the edges, of a young man whom it took him half a breath to recognize as Sylvia's former husband, Zack. He had liked Zack, and so he was compelled to wonder, hardly for the first time, if life's beauty was not in fact to be found in the array of missed chances it offered.

"I'm glad," he managed to say to her, "that you've inherited your mother's ferocious tastes."

Someone was trying to pin a boutonniere to his lapel. What kind of flower was it?

Joseph Lolombela held out his hand to Chentula. What kind of script lay in the lines of his open palm?

The photographer was saying something stupid to Kristen. What language was it in?

Michael put his left hand gently on the small of Sylvia's back. "I'm Michael Bonner," he said to Paul Walters, offering his other hand.

And then: *Light.*

THE BRIDE AND HER FATHER [*He, a head taller than she, appears to have been instructed by the photographer not to look at Kristen—in any case, he has inclined his head somewhat awkwardly away from her. She, for her part, looks toward the camera in the manner of a woman who has learned how to be photographed. There is an accidental flare in the picture's upper-left-hand corner, where an overly silvered, partially disguised elbow pipe has caught the light. At the picture's center, Kristen's first three fingers, slipped beneath her father's lapel, have created enough of a curve to give the jacket a shadow's depth.*]: When you were a baby, Kristen . . . / *When I was a girl . . .* / When you were a daughter, daughter of mine . . . / *When I became a woman . . .* / Although I became an old man, this man, I never stopped loving you . . . / *When I became a woman, I understood that you would never stop.*

THE SECURITY AGENT WHO HAS REMOVED HIS SUNGLASSES [*Oddly, it is the cowlick sprung from his scalp's crown that reveals the depth of his dignity. He stands at a slight angle to the camera—visibly, he is surprised to be photographed—but he has turned his face parallel to the plane of this pictorial record, and on his features can be read: irritation (verging on anger), embarrassment (at what he must have considered a mild dereliction of duty), sudden professional interest (in the photographer), simple pride, a sense of his own age. On his shirtfront can be read: a breakfast of croissants and blackberry jam. However, it is his eyes—they are blue—that speak.*]: Okay, my friend. Now I will have to pay attention to you, and we both know that will be very, very boring. No doubt you, too, would rather be at home with your wife, but because you have—*merde, alors!* I promised Marie I'd pick up some wine for tonight, and now the shops will be shut. [*His hand shields from all eyes the shoulder holster he is wearing.*] *Tant pis.*

JOSEPH AND CHENTULA LOLOMBELA [*Shaking hands. Their features are noticeably tense, but even more noticeably searching—fixed in the camera's spasm.*]: It is us? Shaking hands like white men? If we laugh, what part of us will be laughing? [*Pause, half astonished, half suspicious. Though of course all of this is a pause.*] We have become men to each other?

THE BRIDE AND HER SISTER [*Embracing*]: Remember when we used to read the Sunday funny papers together? Wasn't it a blast? Oh, to be lovely young girls again—not knowing we were lovely, not knowing we were loved. Our radios were just naturally *on!* But we're something now too—right?

JOSEPH AND CHENTULA LOLOMBELA [*Turned at a just-opened-book's angle to one another, with their near shoulders almost touching, the two men appear to be addressing a third party, outside the photo's frame; they are speaking simultaneously. The third party, in fact many thousands of miles away, is the older man's wife, the younger man's mother. Joseph has raised one hand to his jaw, giving himself an aspect of dignified shyness; Chentula has forced a smile.*]: Hello from Paris, France! This is how we look right now, probably not to each other, but who can ever tell a thing like that! Nomanzi is here too. She is coming home to you and Azania to begin making a Hollywood film, so you will see her soon. Africa is never very far away. The reason we are dressed this way is that we are about to attend a wedding. (The bride is someone we have just recently met, but this is hard to explain.) We don't know why they are taking photos before the wedding—it must be a tribal custom revived for tourists!

Are all our cousins well? Are you? Do you have enough to eat? To drink? Do we look like strangers to you?

We have read about the Emergency Laws. You must watch yourself—as before, it is the children who must now lead the adults in our struggle.

We are running out of space, so we must end for now.

We think of you and our suffering land always.

This is our love.

THE GROOM [*Having placed one hand atop the back of a curly maple side chair, he stands at a three-quarters angle to the camera, his own back straighter than the chair's. In the upper-left-hand corner of the photograph can be seen a portion of the nineteenth-century portrait whose subject's posture he has unconsciously imitated.*] All of this that is happening . . . [*He is visibly inhaling.*] It is happening to me.

THE BRIDE AND GROOM: All of this that is happening, it is happening to us.

THE GROOM AND THE GROOM'S MOTHER: All of this that is happening, it confirms how much better it is to be my age than his / *my age than hers.*

Our age?

NOMANZI [*She has clearly anticipated the approach of the photographer: her eyes have met the lens with an actress's preemptive expertise. In fact, she has allowed herself to drop the canapé she has been holding (it is now suspended in the lower third of the photo's emulsion); she has tossed her head enough in laughter to blur the printed figure of her turban but not the flash of her eyes, not the half-translucent edges of her brilliant teeth. She has, in pure reflex, thrown open the palm of her hand to catch the falling canapé.*]: You are a camera, and because of all that I am, all that I have seen, I am suspicious of you. But part of what I am knows also that I and all my people were taught by the first sight of a South African passbook to fool any cold eye, any simple record.

THE BRIDE'S FATHER: Joseph's daughter. Yes. And of course she would be made of sterner stuff even than Joseph, because she sees how close the public dream he's spent his life pursuing has at last . . . how close it now . . . *A man without children always ages badly.*

Wily old bastard. Not even old. Hardly a bastard.

Christ almighty, I hope he's put a damper on this half-assed arms-smuggling business. We can still bring off this whole thing with Bloch if nobody breaks rank at the last moment, and if Sylvia . . . as long as she— Goddamnit, look at these guys. How's anybody supposed to trust security agents who all look as if they're Jean-Luc Belmondo?

MICHAEL AND PETRA [*They are turned fully toward each other in what could easily be taken for a publicity still of supporting actors in civil conversation. The bias of Petra's haircut allows one diamond earring to stare unflinchingly back at the camera. Michael has reached his left hand coaxingly out to cup her bare elbow. No one would mistake these two people for lovers, but neither would it be easy to overlook the unspoken complicity with which they hold their bodies so carelessly in grace.*]: Sometimes we go to the weddings of people we barely know, and sometimes we make movies without asking too many questions. You probably wonder why. *Because that's entertainment!* is why.

JOHNNY [*His spirits obviously restored, his carriage exuberantly erect, his right thumb thrust upward in salutation to someone (it is Chentula) outside the camera's field*]: Yeh, my brother! We are Africans. And when we get home, when we plug in our amplifiers for that concert—but definitely, man, a bloody perfect idea, that free concert, you were just right: the people's challenge has to be seen, isn't it. Isn't it? Emergency Laws. Right. And be heard too!

We'll show them what Emergency Laws can be, ay?

THE BRIDE'S FATHER: My daughters. Their lovers. Their friends. Children next, I guess.

When I got married, nobody told me life was a long emergency. Okay, so it's not the kind of thing people rush to tell you. Still, by the time I figured it out, the only person who might have forgiven me for taking so long to get the news—but hell, I probably married her because I knew she knew.

Since I've always recognized power, except maybe when I'm wielding it.

God, I miss her.

Now, Joseph, man. You better be with me on this fission bomb thing, because the whole situation looks to me to be getting just a little bit rank.

THE BRIDE: I am the bride.

THE GROOM: She is my bride.

JOSEPH LOLOMBELA: Of course it is because Paul does not trust Heinrich that he insists we return to Compiègne the night of his daughter's wedding.

OUTSTRETCHED HAND OF SECURITY AGENT [*Nearly, but not quite, covering the camera lens*]: Just because my upper stories have a fantasy life doesn't mean I'm off duty. No doubt you can read palms? *C'est bon.* Because now, my friend, it is you who are off duty. I do not joke.

WILLIAM [*The photo, perhaps because of the security agent's intervention a second previously, is so badly overexposed that the image itself—William leaning in a corner, watching the guests and biting into the slice of orange he has fished from his eau mineral—is barely legible. He seems nearly transparent, drenched in light, permeated by it. Transfigured.*

He is an afterimage.]

The church, a beautiful anomaly, was set at a seventeen-degree angle to the sidewalk before it. When approached from the east, it offered its Neo-Romanesque facade in a dignified but unimposing welcome. When approached from the west, where the small slice of space created by the structure's canted siting had been filled with a carefully tended garden, the church seemed more naked in its invitation, but no less welcoming.

The wedding party approached on foot from the east. Dusk was deepening to night. From around the western corner of the block, where they had been lying in wait, an American television crew came rushing over to Paul Walters. The lighting unit made the near darkness horrible with luminescence.

"Do you, sir," began the newscaster, who upon seeing Paul Walters recognize him with undisguised disgust was forced to draw breath, and so to pause.

Paul Walters kept walking.

"Do you, sir," continued the newscaster, hurrying in unseemly fashion alongside his prospective interlocutor, "believe that there is any connection between this afternoon's attempt on the President's life and the car bomb that destroyed the U.S. consulate in Geneva last week?"

This time Paul Walters stopped. He knew nothing of any assassination attempt, but he also knew that given his movements during the last few hours there was little chance that he could have been informed of one. If there had been one. Which there almost certainly had, judging by the commotion. He began walking again. He felt heavily the lightness of his younger daughter's presence by his arm, in this unholy light.

"All responsible men," he said, "all responsible women, wish with all their hearts for an end to the violence that can turn public representation into private tragedy, whatever the context." He yearned to look at Kristen but remembered, for her sake, not to. "As citizens of the nations of this earth, we know that our politics must sometimes conflict, but life is no less fragile a thing than honor. And I've—" He glanced at the church gate. "I'm sorry, that's going to have to be all, Tom. My daughter is about to celebrate her marriage." He faced the man down. "I don't have any more for you tonight."

The latch on the church-fence gate had been so many times repainted that it briefly defied Paul Walters's attempt to open it.

It was then that it occurred to him that of course this whole assault interview was going to be entirely redone in edit, so that maybe he did after all have something else tonight for this pissant newscaster.

Walters paused long enough to be sure the cameras were on him. Then he turned toward the newscaster, gave a 180-degree smile of the it's-tough-but-somebody's-got-to-do-it mode, and leaned forward to whisper into the newscaster's ear. "Tom."

"Yes, sir."

"I don't like to be the one to tell you this, but your hairpiece is taking the breeze a little badly; you probably want to look after it. I'll have to talk to you later."

As the newscaster cut the lights with a gesture that has at other times meant cutting a throat, Paul Walters opened the gate and, with his younger daughter on his arm, led the wedding party into the church.

The electric lights inside were dim, but there seemed to be a considerable number of lighted candles in the nooks and side altars of what was after all not a very large church. Above the altar was an interpretation of the Ascension—rendered in fresco and given the treatment, disconcertingly enough, mandated by the academic precepts of late-nineteenth-century Philadelphian art. It was undeniably engrossing. Odd.

"Joseph," said Paul Walters. "Do you have a moment?"

The priest, having greeted the principals, was now instructing the bride and groom in their choreography.

"Paul, man. You've noticed how we're beginning to have our best conversations in Christian churches?" He put a hand on his colleague's shoulder blade and guided him down a side aisle. "It's not what I would have expected for us, but if it works . . ."

"How much did Bloch know?"

"That would be hard to say. What I know I just learned. What about you?"

"You know me better than that. And you also know exactly what, if I'd let that so-called media person ask me a second question, he would have come up with."

Joseph Lolombela laughed. "Yes, yes, Paul. This media person: 'Excuse me, sir, but there is a widely held opinion that in the U.S.

government's upper echelons only you and the President oppose test detonation of the fission bomb. Do you suppose, sir, that there would be any connection between,' et cetera, et cetera."

"I thought your daughter was the one with the knack for voices." It was becoming necessary for the two men to slow their pace in order to avoid being drawn prematurely into the priest's obviously elaborate instructions. In fact, they stopped midway down the side aisle and faced each other like two fathers discussing the marriage of one daughter.

"I doubt it would surprise you," Walters began, "to hear I've become kind of uneasy about Heinrich. Not that I think he has any but the usual ulterior motives—the kind either you or I might have and, for that matter, in the interest of our nations probably do."

The sound of the church's organ, highly regarded throughout the *arrondissement*, hurtled startlingly against the wall above the two diplomats' heads and briefly reduced the men to sly chuckles.

As the triad chords faded slowly from the organ pipes, Paul Walters turned to face his friend and colleague, his possible adversary, and assumed his most deadpan of demeanors.

"Excuse me, sir," he said, with a half beat of mimicked deliberation, "but there is a widely held opinion that in age's upper echelons a man whose younger daughter is about to be married is entitled to forget everything he ever knew about life and retire into what for lack of a better term we might call his manifest destiny." He saw, but ignored, the priest's distant gestures of summons. "Your feelings?"

Joseph Lolombela's laugh was like a complex stew coming slowly to boil: it took its time. "Paul, man. My feelings—" For a moment he lost control, and his laughter bubbled over. The two men were diplomats in arms, and arm in arm they turned and walked back up the aisle. At the back of the church, they stopped.

Joseph became solemn. "My feelings. What I feel is that you have just shown me how to be more cunning than I have yet been. In addition"—he touched Paul's chest with his index finger, but he also let it fall away with enough melodrama to give the joke point— "in addition I must tell you that what I have just learned I will probably at some time use against you."

This time it was not necessary to laugh, though both men were amused.

"I'm flattered," said Paul Walters.

"Okay: Heinrich. Yeh, he is a certain kind of problem, but also he's obvious, man. He's—"

"Trying to make his move."

"Yes. In his way."

The church bells began chiming. Both men looked up. The priest was walking toward them.

"I haven't seen a newspaper today, Joseph. Have you?"

"No."

"Well, I think they were selling them right there on the corner, and if we hurried we could—"

"Monsieur Walters?" The priest, an unnaturally tall man whose height was given annoying emphasis by a head of perfectly white, nearly gaseous, hair, advanced importunately upon them. "*Un instant pour parler?*"

"*Mais bien sûr.*" Walters looked again at Lolombela. "Joseph," he said.

At the priest's words, Joseph had turned on his heel and begun measuring out his own doubts and ambitions in paces whose deliberateness seemed poignantly erratic in comparison to the stones upon which he walked. By European standards, the church was not old.

"Paul. You know, my daughter is a very brave woman. I have just learned this in my heart, as we would say in English. Heart." He walked quickly again toward Paul Walters, even as the priest was walking back down the aisle. Most people seeing Lolombela's approach would have assumed a fight was about to take place. Paul Walters had no such illusion, and his arms remained at his sides and his eyes remained on a man whom he had just come to love completely.

"Your daughter is without price, Joseph."

For each man, a breath. From the church's altar, preparatory whispers of the kind that are never truly preparatory could be heard reverberating against the church's masonry. So many lives had been through this small space. So much whispering.

"Paul, man. One time—do you remember?—when we were finishing out the Azania Agreement, you said to me that you were about to be . . . I think you said 'unpardonably frank.' Those were the words?"

"Yes, I remember. It was about how the U.S. was going to have to delay the news of our agreement so that we could . . . Yes, I remember."

"And we both knew, even as you said those words, that for me it would be treason to believe whatever you were about to say." Lolombela was staring, it seemed, at Paul's boutonniere. "Yet: we also knew it would be very stupid of me not to listen to your words. So you spoke."

Paul Walters caught sight in the candlelight of Kristen gesturing urgently from the altar for him to join her. He raised a hand and nodded encouragingly. He saw in the pleased, proud lift of her chin the fiercely lived pleasures of his own wife—how long dead? He turned back to Joseph.

"Now it is I who must be unpardonably frank," said Lolombela, taking his friend by the elbow.

The walkie-talkies of the French security agents who were now ranging about the entrance, vestry, and rectory of the church clashed in a high-budget way with the cascades of yellow, orange, and red flowers that surrounded the altar. Watching from his pew, Michael was reminded of an unedited rock video.

Watching Michael from the back of the church, Sylvia was reminded that she was pregnant.

Watching Sylvia from a few feet away, Kristen was reminded that it was Sylvia who had confided to her that when your whole life flashed before your eyes, it was really in the form of a picture, not a story.

Watching Kristen watch the picture, Petra had an intuitive moment, which she purposefully disregarded as unprofessional, although she knew it was not in the least uninteresting.

Watching her wristwatch, Madame Grandet stepped slowly forward and made a smile.

What Kristen was wondering, all searchlight smiles aside, was how it could be that life had arranged itself so that she, at the moment of her wedding, was foundering in an outtake that featured her fucking Wyatt—was that his name?—in Sylvia's garage in L.A., in America, at the end of the twentieth century. She remembered a diamond falling in avalanche fashion in some kind of half-assed excuse for the dark. She remembered that the stone's fall had been a flash of light.

She touched her dress.

She remembered that she was getting married.

"Kristen," said Sylvia, with a tenderness that surprised them both.

"But you cannot expect me to carry a guest list with me to my son's wedding mass!" Madame Grandet stood very close to the security guard who had just addressed her. She tried to modulate her hiss into a whisper. "And in any case there will be very few of us: we will all know each other."

The security agent was troubled. A computer check had revealed that the wedding photographer had twice been fined for selling privately commissioned snapshots to the press.

"Please, madame. If you see a stranger here, in the church, you will point him out to me or one of my men?" He popped a lozenge of chewing gum into his mouth.

"Yes, yes, of course."

The man nodded assessingly at her, then turned away.

The bridal couple had chosen a virtually unknown piece by Saint-Saëns as a musical prelude: its initial chords were major, but soon the music fell deceitfully away into minors.

"Did you know about the attempt on the American President's life?" Lolombela asked his daughter in Xhosa. He was seated in a pew between Nomanzi and Chentula. Security agents sat behind them.

"No," said Nomanzi. "Like everyone else these days, I get my news by the television crews, eh?"

Chentula said something no one could hear because the organist was allowing himself a near crescendo as the music resolved itself into its original majors.

"That's if anyone really believes somebody tried to kill the old bugger," said Johnny. He was seated to the right of Chentula, his arms folded across his chest in vaguely principled resistance to his own good time.

"Can you stay an extra day?" Nomanzi asked her father. "I could, y'know, become temporarily very ill from something I ate and then join the crew on location twenty-four hours later. There's a clause in the contract."

Lolombela looked at his daughter as a man might inspect a room in which he has just been invited to make himself at home even though the room in no sense belongs to him.

"Nomanzi." He had to look away a moment before continuing. "On my way here today I thought, 'But it's terrible. I've let them take my private life from me just as surely as if I'd stayed home and been arrested, sentenced, and shipped off to prison.'"

The music had stopped. A white-robed acolyte had entered from the vestry and begun swinging a censer before the altar.

Lolombela paused. Then, laying his pale palm gently against his daughter's cheek, he said, "I understand now that it was a stupid thought. I have seen you, heard what you told me in that hotel, and, yes, I have been given back more than I gave." He let his caressing hand fall slowly to his lap. "I want you and Chentula— and the children you each will have—to have the opportunity to be selfish."

From the back of the church, a walkie-talkie shot a fuzzy burst of no-voice sound into the air. The instantaneity with which this electronic stutter fell to silence startled the wedding celebrants more than had the noise itself. For a time, the only sound to be heard was that of human bodies shifting in fabrics.

Joseph Lolombela said: "So I cannot, this time, stay an extra day."

At the back of the church, Sylvia took her sister's hands in her own. "You look wonderful, Krissy."

Kristen smiled. An old routine: "As good as when I lost my virginity for the first time?"

"Can you get me a newspaper?" Paul Walters whispered in French to the security agent by his side.

"*Je m'excuse, Monsieur l'Ambassadeur, mais*—" The agent, who had seen to it that the photographer at the hotel had been detained for questioning, decided now to switch to what English he knew.

"I have been told—yes?—not to leave your side." In a mix of determination and embarrassment, the man stroked his nonexistent mustache with thumb and forefinger. "*La bénédiction nuptiale*— the blessing of your daughter's marriage—it is to commence at any moment."

"Yes."

"We have made arrangements for you and Monsieur Lolombela so you may leave by the rectory door immediately after the mass." He shifted his eyes to indicate the direction of departure. Walters looked instead at the dark glasses the man was holding in his bony hands.

"Daddy, are you ready?" Kristen asked her father.

It was a question he had always feared hearing from his daughters.

"Yes," he said, touching his tie. "I am."

Walking down the aisle in her role as *demoiselle d'honneur*, Sylvia remembered that she had very recently felt that something bad was soon to happen. She knew, as well, being a woman to whom regret of any kind was alien, that enough bad things had happened for her to have been possibly retrospective in her premonition. Anyway, she liked the music of Buxtehude, to whom she now paced her steps. The certainty of the man's music confirmed the uncertainty of real time.

Having glanced at the lectionary insert next to the prayerbook before him, Michael had discovered that the flowers at the altar had been donated by "*une bienfaitrice anonyme.*" After searching his memory, he had decided that Laurel really couldn't, for all her virtues, be thought of as beneficent. Nonetheless he quickly scanned the church to be sure she wasn't there.

Paul Walters, escorting Kristen toward the altar and her husband, silently berated himself for not having run a discreet security check on Philippe Grandet. And since when had incense begun to smell like oranges?

I was already pregnant when that happened at the car wash, thought Sylvia.

After a while, when the music had stopped and other things had happened, the priest said, "May the Lord send you help from this holy place, and from Zion may he watch over you."

He said it in French, the language of diplomacy.

What Lolombela was wondering was, first, had the TV cameras caught a shot of either himself or Nomanzi during the media ambush outside the church, and, second, was the network's research team devoting any of its expensively misdirected time to the days-old incident at the American car wash.

"Father," said the priest, extending his hands from his ghostly white vestments, "by your power you have made everything out of nothing."

After an initial hesitation, Nomanzi had joined Lolombela in kneeling whenever the liturgical language of prayer was invoked. Chentula and Johnny remained steadfastly upright in their pews.

Michael forced himself not to scan the back of the church again for what it now seemed to him he had observed while ascertaining that Laurel was not in fact in attendance. Besides, the word "father" had begun to distract him for whole minutes at a time whenever he heard it, whatever the context. What did it mean, for example, to be the "Godfather of Soul"? Had the priest really said that?

"And made mankind in your own likeness," the priest added.

Which is exactly when the fire department of the City of Paris arrived and, after bowing in sulky unison, proceeded directly to the vestry, where a fire had indeed broken out.

There were titters among the celebrants.

Paul Walters was sitting in the front pew, beside Sylvia and Michael. By leaning forward, he could see the fire's reflection in the polished wooden walls of the vestry at his extreme right, and he was immediately relieved: the flames reached no higher in relation to a man than might a house pet, happy to see its owner. The priest was still intoning the lines of the blessing. Walters reached out toward Kristen, who, with her husband, continued to kneel at the nuptial prayer rail directly in front. Then he felt the hand of the security man touch his back.

Glancing toward the flickering vestry, Michael whispered to Sylvia, "They're playing our song again."

She cuffed him lightly.

The priest's voice trailed off. The captain of the fire crew approached the pulpit, crossed himself, and with a coil of canvas hose slung over one shoulder, began speaking to the father in low tones.

The security agent was whispering in Paul Walters's ear. *"Pardonnez-moi*, but it would perhaps be more prudent if you and your family waited with us in the courtyard outside."

From the vestry came the sound of a fire extinguisher discharging itself in luxuriant abundance.

Although there was no danger, absolutely no danger—the priest emphasized this point by smoothing the air before him with his hands—the celebrants would be conducted into the church's courtyard until *les braves pompiers* had finished ensuring the safety of this house of the Lord.

Sylvia looked over her shoulder. Another security agent was leaning across Nomanzi to whisper into Joseph Lolombela's ear. Kristen and Philippe were already being conducted around the chancel to the small arched door that opened upon the cobblestone courtyard.

The church shared its courtyard with three private residential buildings, and when the wedding celebrants had collected within this architectural embrace, several upper-story windows opened in quick succession. Spectators. They had seen the fire trucks.

"But surely it's a good omen," a fatuous-looking woman was saying to Madame Grandet. "One of warmth, no?"

Kristen, who had taken her husband's arm and was sweeping with him about the boundaries of the courtyard, appeared to be enjoying herself hugely.

"How special is that effect?" Michael asked Sylvia, who was standing stock-still at the center of the space but looking carefully at everyone.

"I can't tell yet. I don't see anyone who wasn't in church."

Nomanzi, Chentula, and Johnny were conferring over to one side, and though they held themselves a little taut, they might just as well have been the international contingent at a university cocktail party.

"I thought I saw someone in church who isn't here," Michael said, "but: hey, what's going on in this place: is everyone at a different party?"

Those among the wedding guests, mostly friends and family of the groom, who had not till then discussed the attempt on the U.S. President's life, were now exchanging information in the lingua franca of fact-laden rumor.

"But how seriously is he hurt?"

"Two bullets in the arm and shoulder, they say: not very bad."

"Ha! But no government tells the truth at times like this."

"They say it was an American security agent who shot the President."

"No, an ex-policeman."

"Oh, I left my purse in the pew!"

"See: the firemen have already done their work. And now there is a dog here to make sure there is no bomb. It will be all right."

"At her wedding mass! The poor girl!"

"And after what nearly happened to her father in Geneva!"

"Excuse me, monsieur, but you asked me to tell you if I saw anyone here I did not recognize. He was over there, in the corner. I don't see him now, but he had a mustache and one of those shirts with . . ." Madame Grandet tapped her own shoulders lightly with her fingertips. "How do you call them?"

"Epaulets?"

"Yes, yes. Like a jungle shirt."

"Please show me where you last saw this man," said the agent, taking her by the elbow.

The smell of skillet-warmed olive oil drifted down into the courtyard. Other windows opened above. People leaned out upon their sills with an air of benign entitlement.

Paul Walters spoke soothingly to Nomanzi about nothing of consequence. He believed the fire was in itself a harmless stratagem. But on whose part?

"I am quite certain I saw this man," said Madame Grandet.

French or U.S., probably, Walters was thinking. But on the other hand, you couldn't discount Bloch.

"Yes, it is a very strange house," Nomanzi heard herself telling Sylvia's father. "But maybe it's more normal in Los Angeles? I had never seen a house that looks like an exploding flower."

In the courtyard, the priest felt somewhat unnecessary. He was standing in an envelope of dignity, but he was no longer certain whether this dignity belonged to him or to his calling.

Are priests actually *supposed* to look like ghosts? Sylvia was wondering as she elbowed Michael lightly in the ribs. An American in a pin-striped suit had emerged from the basement door of one of the courtyard's residential buildings. He was carrying a briefcase, and he was headed for her father.

"I am sorry, Madame Grandet," the security agent was saying, "but none of my men have seen the person—" His hand went to his shoulder holster.

Sylvia began running toward her father.

"No rain is predicted," a voice said in English.

The priest was momentarily nonplussed by the realization that he was gravitating toward the only other person dressed like him, and that this person was the bride. Insights did not come frequently to him anymore. He stopped to stare at Kristen.

Who turned to stare at him.

Paul Walters was surprised but pleased to see the American chargé d'affaires walking his way with a briefcase. A briefing was just what he needed.

The French security agent caught Sylvia by the arm. "*Ça va.* He's from the U.S. Embassy. I know him."

Sylvia stared at this Frenchman.

"You have a gun in your hand," she said.

He put it away. "One cannot be too careful," he apologized.

Her father was shaking hands with the man in the pin-striped suit. "Perry, I'm sure your invitation just got lost in the mail. It's good to see you."

"Same here, sir. And I hate like hell to get you at a moment like this, but Washington—"

"Do you know the man in the suit?" Michael asked Sylvia.

She shook her head. She put her mouth to his ear. "But I can tell Daddy does. It's okay."

"Right *now*, Perry?"

"I'm afraid so, sir."

Kristen was disagreeing *sotto voce* with the priest as to what might be the most graceful way of resuming the proceedings. She had not noticed the arrival of the man with whom her father was conversing.

Joseph Lolombela drew aside the French security agent clearly assigned to him. "I will have to speak to my embassy."

"Yes, Monsieur l'Ambassadeur."

"I am not the ambassador to France. I am a guest at this wedding.

My daughter and stepson are here." The man Lolombela was addressing reminded him, by the uselessness of his presence, of a badly installed air conditioner, specifically of one he had seen in an Azanian township more than a decade earlier. The memory infuriated him. "Well, man! What are you going to do about it?"

The fault in the Azanian air conditioner's installation had been that there was no electricity in the house it was meant to serve.

The security agent had begun to sweat.

"Kristen," Paul Walters said. He took his daughter's face between the palms of his hands. "Krissy."

"You're not."

"If there were any other way . . ."

"Damn family!" She threw her face free of his hands.

"Listen."

"No!" She began to cry. "Okay, yes. I'm listening."

"You're my daughter, and you know how your mother and I always lived: duty and instinct, the same thing. We lived this way out of love, but later we knew that you and Sylvie could live more strongly still, and that became yet another reason for our own love. I know what a wedding is, but I also—"

"There is a car at your disposal, Monsieur Lolombela. It will take you to your embassy."

"—know what a marriage is, and if I thought that staying here would guarantee anything more for you than what I'm—" He took Kristen into his arms. He was as surprised by the lightness of her body as when he had first held her as an infant.

"I love you," he said. "I'm proud of you. I see how much Philippe loves you."

"You'll have to call me," Kristen answered. "And Sylvie will never tell you, but you'll have to call her too."

"If I can't find you, the embassy," said Walters.

"When wasn't it that way." She kissed him on the cheek.

The priest had begun to look ridiculous to almost everybody, including himself.

Joseph was embracing Nomanzi. Quick words in each other's ears.

As Paul Walters approached his older daughter, as he drew her by the elbows into his arms, she said, "I don't think I know any secret languages, Daddy."

"Neither do I," he answered. "Take care of Kristen. I'll call you as soon as I can."

He and Michael shook hands.

When Chentula extended his hand to Lolombela, Lolombela brushed it away and embraced him. Possibly they had begun to understand each other. Johnny he embraced without drama, because in the short run little was at stake and in the longer run nobody knew.

"I am told . . ." announced the priest.

And what happened was that Joseph Lolombela and Paul Walters followed the American chargé d'affaires back through the basement door from which he had emerged. Parked outside the apartment building was a pair of chauffeur-driven cars. The Americans got into one, the African into the other. The television crew was nowhere in sight.

After a while, the wedding mass resumed.

"Perry," said Paul Walters. The two of them were being driven along a suitably circuitous route to the American Embassy. "I've got to know. Whose idea was the fire?"

The man smiled with a grimness too early known for his age. "Not bad, huh? We used the incense burner and a couple of choir robes. The moment I thought of it, I knew you'd appreciate it. Just from the craft point of view, I mean."

Despite his growing sense that all his carefully stitched together efforts were unraveling by the second, Walters could not suppress the trace of a smile.

It was true: he admired the craft.

His briefing took place in the U.S. Embassy's conference room— a formal place outfitted with the furbelows and gildings by which the French were always reminding themselves that once they had had an empire.

Paul Walters recognized on sight the four Americans in the room, and he nodded to them in greeting before sitting down. All four were from State. They seemed to want to know if they still had an empire.

"Forgive me, gentlemen," said Walters, indicating his now-incongruous wedding outfit, "but I have a habit of overdressing. Shall we proceed?"

The President had been wounded only glancingly—small-arms fire at medium range in a Tacoma shopping mall.

The suspect, unharmed, was in custody. As far as could be determined at this point in time, he had acted alone.

The suspect. A forty-one-year-old Caucasian male. American. No previous criminal record. He had worked for the Seattle police force for seventeen years before finding employment with a local defense contractor. His job there had involved a considerable amount of travel—to Washington, D.C., for example; to Southern Africa, for example. But to many other places as well.

The media as yet had no known access to this information, but of course the situation was certain to change at any minute. Speculative stories were already being aired by the usual people about possible links between what had happened outside the Geneva consulate and today's attempt on the President's life.

Walters glanced at the elaborately contained door-sized windows lining one wall of the conference room. "Can we get some air in here?" he asked, gesturing toward them.

The relief that seemed to ripple through the room at his suggestion—*we have nothing to hide*—was the first real indication Walters had received of how nervous the staff indeed was.

Someone opened two of the windows. There was a breeze.

"Thanks. Much better." Walters poured himself a glass of water. "I understand that I'm well known for my unorthodox methods, so I might as well live up to my reputation." He looked briefly in turn at each of the men sitting with him at the conference table. "How many of you gentlemen have children?"

They all knew that he knew that they all did. They acknowledged their paternity with smiles or impatient changes of posture. Three of the men were also thinking of their wives.

"Good." He drained his glass at a gulp. "My people and I will need three, maybe four days to finish what we're doing in Geneva, but we're well on our way to a successful outcome."

Of course, no one any longer believed he was coming from Geneva.

"So I have to ask a few pointed questions." He paused. "Because of my daughter's wedding mass, I've been a little out of touch the last few hours. I need your help. Who's officially in charge of the presidency at this moment?"

He was informed that the Vice President, who would be addressing the nation in less than half an hour, was officially in charge, but that the President himself was back in the White House and fully in command.

Walters leaned to his right to speak privately to the American ambassador to France, a man somewhat senior to him in age but a Foreign Service lifer in the conventional mode. "Can we get a call through to the President from here?"

"Painkillers," the man whispered back. "In a few hours, maybe. He asked that we get you back to Compiègne. Which is why all the cloak-and-dagger crap in the church."

"I figured. That and avoiding the news team."

But Walters thought: *And I don't even know where my daughter will be living after the wedding!* This recognition somehow translated itself into his saying weakly, but to the general group: "What about France? Are they tracking with us on this?"

"Worried about the German Republics," someone said. "There's a perception that Bloch's gotten out of hand."

Working men, working women.

Secret languages. Walters ran the thumb and index finger of one hand across his temples.

The year before Pearl Harbor, when Paul Walters was eighteen, he had been playing around in the family's front yard with a bow and arrow he'd been given by his stepfather. It was a birthday present. He had never much loved his stepfather, who had recently instituted a summer push-up program—a war was coming on, supposedly, and his stepfather was a colonel in the army. But Paul had loved the bow and arrow, and in fact it was because he was admiring his own newly enhanced biceps as he drew back the bowstring that his fingers had slipped and the arrow had hurtled through the unopened window of his stepfather's study.

His stepfather had been at work at the time, his mother at the

Army-Navy Wives Bridge Tournament—a fund-raiser for the European war effort.

"I assume you all know Policy on this," said Paul Walters to the four Americans sitting around the conference table. He poured himself another glass of water.

The young Paul Walters had run full tilt into his stepfather's study to retrieve the misshot arrow, only to discover that the top drawer that had till that moment always been firmly locked was half open, its key still partly turned in the cylinder.

"France is meant to feel reason to worry," said Walters, holding his glass as if about to toast his colleagues, "but as you all know, it has no real cause. The German Republics have agreed to their role. France must be reassured at the proper time. The time will be soon."

Even as he spoke these words, Walters saw again the black-bound book he had discovered in the drawer of his stepfather's desk, saw again its pages and pages of oddly shaped polygons—English words at some vertices, German words at others. A codebook.

"If there's any reason, though, that you guys think we ought to reassess . . ."

And heard again the not quite decipherable shouts of his stepfather, just then returning from work. Looking out the shattered window, Paul had discovered that these imprecations were being addressed to his half-brother, William, who had picked up the abandoned bow with the unfettered admiration and curiosity of a six-year-old.

". . . then let's do it right now."

The young Paul Walters had replaced the black book and hastened to the front yard with the arrow.

"Because briefing begets debriefing begets Policy, and that's why we're all here," said Paul Walters. Everybody laughed.

His stepfather had broken the arrow over his knee. His mother had prevented further punishment. He himself had allowed William to beat him three times running at chess that evening.

"I guess," said the youngest man at the conference table, "we all need to be advised as to how to handle press on this stuff."

"A mixture of official looks and plain old sense of humor. Shake

your head wryly every so often; throws them off the track completely. It's too American even for Americans."

After a pause, everyone laughed. They were being advised as to
how not to lose heart.

"Sir, if you could spare a minute?" Perry, at the sound of laughter
in the conference room, had opened the door and poked his head
in. He was addressing Walters. "If you've wound things up in here?"
Perry glanced at the American ambassador to France, who nodded
curtly in what was obvious acknowledgment of a prior agreement.

Walters said, "Sure, sure." He shook hands with his confreres
and in a private flash wished he could speak to the President as
hurt man to hurt man in a hurt world, but that was not why they
were in it, obviously. They were in it to raise morale.

"What's that with the basketballs?" Walters asked Perry when it
became apparent that the moment he'd just been asked to spare
was going to take place behind the closed door of Perry's office.

"That?" Perry actually blushed as he turned to regard the object
of Paul's comment. "That's art."

By the window, on a stainless-steel stand suggesting exercise
equipment, there rested a sizable aquarium filled to its brim with
water of unnatural pellucidity. Suspended within it: two basketballs.
They did not touch each other, they did not touch the aquarium's
bottom, they did not breach the water's surface.

"My wife bought it," Perry explained, walking over to the as-
semblage in a proprietary way. "Guy's a New York artist, but she
bought it in an L.A. gallery." He chuckled indulgently. "If there's
an expensive way to do something, my wife'll find it."

[Expletive deleted.]

[Unintelligible.]

Noting the almost total lack of ambient sound in Perry's office,
Walters decided it was at least a fair bet that their conversation was
being taped.

He approached the aquarium. " 'M.B.,' he observed. "In Magic
Marker on that ball at the left. That how artists sign their work
these days?"

"Beats me. I'm your basic philistine. Except I do know the artist's
name is Jeffrey Something, so those aren't his initials." Perry leaned

over to look in genuine respect at this cultural peculiarity. "My wife says maybe it has to do with the title of the thing."

" 'Venice,' " Walters read aloud from a laser-incised plaque affixed to the base of the aquarium.

"Michelangelo Buonarroti," said Perry, with the guilelessness of an encumbered man. "Get it?"

"Sure. That's probably it." Walters walked over to an upholstered chair in the far corner of the office and sat down.

"Perry, what're we really supposed to [unintelligible], because time is [unintelligible] just about now."

The space around them seemed to expand. Perry looked troubled. He mapped out a course by which he might amble over and sit casually down upon the corner of his desk. He followed that course without improvisation.

"People here are saying," said Perry, "that it was D.o.D."

"The Defense Department?" Paul Walters felt like a teacher trying to coax a pupil to confess to an infraction of which they were both already aware. " 'It'? Come on, man, speak."

Perry abandoned all pretense of sangfroid and began waving his hands about in a lost elocutionary manner. "You know—the bomb in Geneva, the President today, the fission thing. Right? It's not exactly a secret that Defense wants a test detonation. Whatever Policy says."

"So what are you saying?"

"The President wants the whole deal settled ASAP." The relief flooding over Perry's features even though he was trying to hide it was a beautiful thing to see. "There's a car waiting outside to take you and Mr. Lolombela back to Compiègne."

"Good." Walters decided the room wasn't bugged after all.

"Oh, and this." Perry took a videocassette from his top desk drawer. "We have a standing arrangement with those TV honchos to send their tapes back to New York via diplomatic pouch. So when we got the one of you outside the church, we just made a copy, demagnetized the original, and . . . well, this is the copy. Strictly FYI. No problems we can see."

Walters took it. "Good."

They stood.

And as if by effect of the earth's rotation—or maybe for the same reason that many people have fireplaces or televisions in their homes—the two men turned simultaneously back to the artwork aquarium by the windowsill.

The tension between them had been broken like an arrow.

"So what do you really think of that thing, sir?"

Walters studied it. After a moment he said, "Has a kind of pecker-headish aspect to it, if you want my studied art-historical opinion."

Perry laughed with real merriment, nodding. "Yeah. That's what I think too."

"Still. There's something I like about it."

"What's that, sir?"

Paul Walters saw he had his work cut out for him. He put his hand to his chin.

"It has balls," he said.

The limo waiting for Walters had been provided by the French. Lolombela was already in it.

"Joseph. We must have been given the same briefing."

A vigorous exchange of views between the French and American governments had ensured that a decoy limousine was proceeding even then to Henri Pétain Airport, where the late flight to Geneva was scheduled to depart in less than an hour.

"But one of us didn't have time to change his clothes," said Lolombela. He leaned back in the car seat as if it were a barber's chair. He closed his eyes and smiled. Walters still wore his morning coat; Joseph was again in his English suit.

"A shoddy thing, man—Bataillard's tactical people staging that fire drill to run us out of your own daughter's wedding." Lolombela opened his eyes, let his head loll sideways to engage his colleague's glance.

"Maybe we did have different briefings," Walters answered, arching an eyebrow and peering about the limousine with enough deliberation to remind Lolombela that he, Paul Walters, had not forgotten that the vehicle belonged to the French government and that had either he or Lolombela desired surveillance-free transportation it could easily have been seen to.

"No, Paul. The French are worried about Bloch, just as you said."

"The heavy water thing, what you spoke to me about in church . . ."

Joseph rolled his eyes theatrically so as in his turn to remind Walters that such conversation was by its nature weighty in price, never mind water. "The German project did not work. I'm sure that when Bataillard is informed of the failure, he will—"

"He must already know."

The chauffeur was a man from the Dordogne, and he truly did not give a shit about what went on behind the bulletproof partition separating him from his charges.

"He must know," Walters and Lolombela agreed, speaking untruly of Bataillard but truly for their nations' interests.

"Good," said Walters. He was saying that word a lot, and he recognized the repetition as a bad sign, so he produced the videocassette from his attaché case. "News of the day," he said.

Lolombela laughed voicelessly. "Your briefing was definitely different from mine, old friend."

"I've never believed in cultural relativism," Walters answered. There was a VCR fitted into the sphinx-shaped communications deck before them, and Walters fed it the tape. A storm of black-and-white static filled the monitor's screen.

"But what a hell of a way to leave my daughter after not seeing her for ten years." Joseph's eyes were focused intently on nothing. "I hope somebody realizes."

Walters hit the pause button on the VCR. He was professionally sensitive to the tone of voice in which favors are requested. "You'll see her after Compiègne."

"Maybe."

"The French would make arrangements, I'm sure."

"They're too busy, man. Everyone is."

The suspended swarm of video static, shivering slightly on the VCR, suggested to Joseph a vast civil conflict as seen by satellite. He thrashed restlessly upright in his seat.

"And why shouldn't they be, eh? A private matter is a private matter."

"Yes. Of course. But if the French can't manage it, I'm certain"— Paul directed his words to the limo's gray plush ceiling, because that would be the microphone place—"perfectly positive, in fact, that Bloch would never now pass up the opportunity to do Azania a favor."

Lolombela smiled and gave Paul a collegial punch on the shoulder.

Walters released the videotape from its quivering captivity. Wordlessly they watched the unfurling of the confiscated footage from outside the church.

When the screen offered up the background figure of the-man-who-looked-very-much-like-William-were-William-actually-alive, Paul Walters froze the frame again.

The limo hurtled smoothly through the night.

It was not until that moment that Walters realized he'd all along been expecting something just . . .

Like . . .

This.

Southern Africa. And this place was just another airport, in a way—fouled with hydrocarbons and badly skewed currency exchange rates. But it was spring in the southern hemisphere! At the preemptively named Winnie Mandela Airport of Cape Town! And there were flowers of good hope visible even from the runway: strelitzia, protea, sugarbush!

"Why are we holding our passports like this?" Sylvia asked Michael. They were sitting in molded plastic seats, on the other side of customs, in white-controlled South Africa, and they were holding their passports like tiny cocktail plates that they had at some earlier moment instructed their fingers not to spill.

"Holding them how," said Michael, without looking at Sylvia or at the midnight-blue booklet that certified his citizenship. He was watching Petra pace back and forth in the middle distance, her arms folded tightly across her breasts.

"Oh, for God's sake." Sylvia snatched his passport from him, paired it with her own, and thrust both documents into her purse.

Michael ignored this display. "Petra experiences anxiety," he said, letting his observation of her take a more contemplative vein. "I didn't know that."

"Michael, Michael, we all saw them haul Nomanzi, Chentula, and Johnny into that little room when they handed over their papers."

"But this is their country." He turned to her and blinked several times in a stylized imitation of earnestness. "They have to fill out more forms than we do."

"Okay." Sylvia released his wrist, which she did not remember seizing. "Done. I give in." She was wearing a black cotton cocktail dress, which had looked perfectly normal in Paris the previous night. "Just please talk sense."

"Okay," he said. A dark sweat stain was spreading across the front of his green-and-white-striped shirt. "Did you really believe Petra when she said there was nothing unusual about the pilot diverting our flight from Johannesburg to Cape Town?"

"I believe Nomanzi. I watched her face when the captain made the announcement, and I decided to believe what I saw there. Don't you ever do that?"

"Me?"

"We were going to fly here next anyway. The shoot's just east of here, whatever." She stirred uncomfortably in her seat. "Hey, are you hungry?"

"No."

"Me either. We've been eating funny."

"Travelers eat funny," he said. Probably he was really ravenous and didn't know it.

Petra continued to pace.

Another flight had arrived—its passengers mostly, but not exclusively, white. Having cleared customs, they weaved determinedly through the arrivals concourse: children, tired adults with luggage. Which is how Michael and Sylvia's view of the room where their friends were being held was momentarily obscured.

"Did you see that?" Michael asked her to calm things down.

"What?" she said.

He pointed past her shoulder. "That over there."

She looked. The billboard advertisement was for an American whiskey. A black couple and a white couple were depicted drinking in a futuristically appointed interior that suggested the living quarters of a starship. The four friends were shown dressed in bodysuits that differentiated them by sex (blue for the men, red for the women) but not race. The legend below—black letters on white—read: "Good taste doesn't change with the times."

"Wishful thinking doesn't anyway," Sylvia said.

"And if you had three wishes?" he said.

"You, me, and them," she said.

He put his hand on the back of her neck.

"I don't mean 'them' like in the advertisement; I mean"—she arched her back in an attempt to undo the twist in her dress that was chafing her breasts—"you know, the world." She almost laughed.

Chentula, Nomanzi, and Johnny—in that order—emerged from the metal-doored room in which they had been sequestered. Two brown-shirted agents from Security followed them two strides out into the larger space but stopped at the same kind of invisible boundary that certain insects observe. One of the officers removed his cap and wiped his brow. The air-conditioning wasn't working.

"There they are!" said Michael, catching himself just before he waved.

"Where?"

"Over there by Petra."

It's exhausting to be pregnant, thought Sylvia, struggling slightly to get up from her seat.

But Michael stopped her with a touch to her shoulder. "Maybe it's better if we let them find us," he said into her ear.

The crowd of new arrivals thinned out. A young black man was moving purposefully from one thickly flowered planter to another, feeding the soil with a comically large watering can. He wore a spotless blue-and-red jumpsuit. On his left foot he wore a brown moccasin-style loafer; on his right, a black combat boot laced with copper wire.

"I've lost track of Petra," Michael said.

"She's over at the car-rental desk," said Sylvia.

Chentula, Nomanzi, and Johnny strolled the lounge's perimeter, peering into the shops, pointing, smiling, exchanging what looked from a distance to be the most casual of remarks.

The light that poured through the canted glass ceiling of the arrivals concourse so reminded Michael of his own home that for an instant he ceased to feel like a traveler. Then he remembered that Sylvia was pregnant. Then the notion of traveling seemed irrelevant to him.

"Look," said Sylvia, leaning against his shoulder to indicate direction.

Petra, still at the car-rental desk, was offering a blossom of strangely tinted paper money to a half-young man in a red-and-blue jumpsuit. He was smiling, shaking his head, and stepping back nervously from the suitcase-laden wire trolley he had just delivered to her.

Michael put on his sunglasses and looked away. "Their luggage."

"So we're out of here," said Sylvia, closing her eyes.

And they were.

The airport was twenty-one kilometers southeast of Cape Town. Petra drove. Nomanzi sat in the front seat, on Michael's lap; the other three were in the back.

The conversation was noncommittal, and the radio was up. It said in English: "Today's executive supermen are more than just boy scouts with good teeth. They're an alternate breed, a new genetic force, a threat to the norms of menopause—"

Johnny said a few words in Xhosa, and Nomanzi leaned forward to change the station.

Looking idly out the window, Chentula said in English: "Coming home, I have back my appetite. Can we stop there?"

Petra glanced at him in the rearview mirror, got no indication at all where "there" might be. So she pulled over into the parking lot of the fried-chicken restaurant to her left. The architectural motif involved red and white stripes and the hideously enlarged image of a white-haired man with a white goatee; he wore black-framed eyeglasses and a black string tie.

Everybody got out of the car.

" 'Das vingerlek lekker'?" asked Sylvia. She was reading from the Afrikaans slogan that trailed across the sign in black letters from the mouth of the man-who-would-be-logo.

"Oh." Nomanzi stopped to look where Sylvia was looking. "Yes, that means—what is the expression?—'It's finger-lickin' good.' "

Michael saw the word "Kentucky" on another sign, which revolved atop the establishment like a weather vane. "Weird," he said.

Johnny and Chentula were already inside.

"Petra," said Nomanzi, turning in sudden privacy to her nominal employer. "I saw you were having a little trouble with the brakes on this car—excuse me, I know I can be silly about these things—but there's another rental outlet right next door, so maybe we should just change cars? To be on the safe side, I mean."

"The brakes? I wasn't having any trouble with—" But sometimes a steady-state gaze from a brown-eyed woman can have the authority of a solar flare. And what a producer did was produce. "Yeah, really, I didn't want to worry anybody, but now that you mention it, what we've got is sort of a spongy situation with those brakes—even if it *is* a Bavarian. So maybe while the guys are in there with the poultry . . ."

Nomanzi blew Sylvia and Michael a kiss, pointed at the car, and called, "We must make a quick trade-in. It's the brakes. Meet us over there."

The two women got into the Bavarian sedan and drove it across the thin sandy divide to the rental franchise. They were greeted immediately by two men of Indian descent.

"What was that about?" Michael asked Sylvia.

She shrugged. "I'm just the sound unit. As far as continuity goes . . ." She veered momentarily toward anger, then, just as arbitrarily, all the way back again. "Well, shit. You're the director." She was holding a black straw hat with satin ribbons dangling from its sides. She put it on and tied it beneath her hair, still gathered in a chignon.

"Hey, what's that?" said Michael, turning her by the elbow.

Behind them, to the north, the air had turned the color of dried earth, fired clay. It was a storm of topsoil loosed first by drought, then by the winds. It was a disaster.

Sylvia moved into Michael's arms. Her hat fell off and blew away, but she made no attempt to retrieve it. The two of them watched it roll across the sandy flats on its brim; occasionally it hopped into the air for yards at a time, like a tire in a TV commercial.

"Are we going to the hotel now?" Sylvia whispered. She felt like vomiting.

"Yes," said Michael.

Chentula and Johnny emerged from the fried-chicken franchise, each carrying a cardboard bucket filled with the specialty of the house. "Eleven different herbs and spices," explained Chentula as he bit into a drumstick.

Nomanzi and Petra backed a brand-new Japanese sedan into the parking lot. When everyone had gotten in, Nomanzi said: "Yes, this is much better." She turned around to address Sylvia in the back seat. "It just threw my concentration off when those Security fellows at the airport kept telling Chenny, Johnny, and me that our car would be ready as soon as it had been through the car wash." She was again sitting in the passenger seat, on Michael's lap. "They said, 'We know you would want your car to be just as clean as the one you had in Los Angeles.'" She smirked. "Even I don't scare that easily."

"Did they offer to fly us back to Johannesburg?" Sylvia asked.

"Oh, yeh," Chentula answered. He fished a chicken wing from the bucket in his lap. "But we didn't want to go."

"We can call Jo'burg when we get to the hotel," said Petra.

And as unexpectedly quickly as a train rounding a bend may encounter an oppositely bound train speeding down the tracks alongside it, the travelers found themselves looking out over a vast vista of improvised shelters. Some of them had roofs of galvanized metal; others had been constructed solely of twigs, cardboard, and plastic sheeting. Only a few women and children were visible.

"That's the middle kind," Johnny explained. "Not a showplace, not a squatter camp."

It went on for a long time, then ceased abruptly.

"That was its border," said Johnny. He poked around in his bucket of chicken without interest. "Its *legal* illegal border. The other boundary you can't see from the road."

"Johnny, man. You should show them the handbill they gave us in the Kentucky place." Chentula dropped a chicken bone into the bucket and began to wipe his fingers methodically on a paper napkin. "Everybody knows about our concert tomorrow; we had to sign ten or twelve of these fliers in there."

"At least that many," said Johnny. "One girl even had a T-shirt with our faces on it. We signed that too. It's a punch-up, y'know?" He handed the flier to Nomanzi.

BROTHERS AND SISTERS OF ALL AFRICA!
JOIN TOGETHER IN PEACE TO WELCOME HOME
SOUTHERN AFRICA'S #1 MUSIC GROUP
TSOTSI
AT THEIR OPEN-AIR CAPE TOWN CONCERT
ON THE LOWER SLOPES OF TABLE MOUNTAIN
("District Six")
OCTOBER 3 TUESDAY, 8 P.M.
"ALL OF US ARE THE SOIL OF AFRICA"

"What's District Six?" asked Sylvia. She'd been reading over Nomanzi's shoulder in the dim, dust-filled light.

"District Six," said Chentula to himself, as if he were speaking of an old lover.

"You see," said Nomanzi, "it used to be a very large 'Coloured' neighborhood—mixed race mostly, eh?—right in the heart of Cape Town. But when the government decided to make more relocations, it bulldozed the whole place down and moved everyone . . . well, you just saw where some of the people live now. And District Six, it is empty still: a kind of wasteland."

Petra turned on the windshield wipers against the dust.

"But then doesn't that make it a dangerous place to hold a concert?" Sylvia had begun to feel uneasy about Michael's silence. " 'Emergency Laws'? 'Riotous assembly'?"

"We figured it the other way," said Johnny. "If there are enough of us, right there in the city . . ."

"We'll all take care of each other," Michael said, when the silence had made a space. "That's what we're here for."

Near now before them rose the huge flat-topped mountain beneath which Cape Town proper nestled. Beyond it, the Atlantic Ocean. And despite the dust storms visible to the north, the sea was palpably near.

Petra turned up the car's air-conditioning.

The hotel into which they'd been booked by the airline was classified as "international," so it was okay for blacks to stay there too—if they were from overseas, or if they were famous, or if they were rich.

The lobby's carpet was done in a figure of linked infinity signs: black, white, beige.

The uniformed man at the reception desk was coloured. "So that will be rooms 119, 120, 121, and 122, missus," he said, handing Petra the keys.

Petra, who had not failed to absorb the lessons of the car-rental place, sorted through the plastic tag-ends of the keys. "Oh, that's so kind of you to put us right by the dining room," she said, "but I have this—I'm really sorry—I have this just unbearable insomnia, and I always do better on the upper floors?" The hotel was twenty-seven stories high. "Especially when I am about to shoot a movie?"

Music of no distinct character issued from no particular place.

"The lady would like to change rooms?" The man behind the desk was tall and lithe, stringy at the neck and arms like a runner. He cast his eyes lightly over the exhausted group. "A different floor?"

"Oh, that would be so super," said Petra. "Thank you. I know how inconvenient it must be to move all of us just because I'm . . ." She took the first knuckle of her forefinger lightly between her two front teeth and tried using her eyes.

"It's business," said Michael wearily. "You know, business? Like, we can't sleep?"

It was Nomanzi upon whom the desk clerk's gaze had come to rest. "You are her? 'Ilulwane'?"

Nomanzi thought for the thousandth time about attempting to explain that yes, she was the *actress* who played Ilulwane, but a meaningful nudge from Chentula dissuaded her from this bit of casuistry. So she nodded. After all, perhaps in a sense she *was* Ilulwane. She shifted her weight onto one hip. "I've just come from America, y'know, but when I get home again and meet people like you . . . it must sound strange, but it is only then that I really know why I do my work."

A shy curling smile spread across the face of the desk clerk. "We all must do our work," he said to her in Xhosa. Then, in English: "There will be four rooms open to you by the time you reach the twenty-seventh floor."

He handed her new keys, and she thanked him in yet another language.

"What was that?" asked Michael, as the elevator doors closed. Her eyes glittered with amusement. "Zulu," she answered.

Four rooms, then. One for Michael and Sylvia, one for Johnny and Chentula, a room each for Petra and Nomanzi. The carpet figure of the linked horizontal eight shape was apparently continued throughout the hotel, but it seemed to burst into hellish exuberance on the upper floors.

"Is that vermilion?" asked Sylvia, sinking to her knees to inspect. She was actually crawling across the room like a drunken anthropologist. "What I see here is a dull white, a dark blue, and . . . well, I've never been sure about vermilion."

Michael pushed a button that turned on both bedside lamps. "Sort of a reddish orange." He studied the carpet abstractedly. He turned off the lamps.

"Michael, I think I might"—she pulled herself softly up off the floor onto the bed and stretched out—"take a nap."

He was at the window. The sunlight outside so thoroughly suffused the noontime city skyline—an array of glossy high-rises spectacular against the mountains—that this luminescence seemed to emanate from the air itself. *A thousand suns, a thousand sudden—* Michael began to draw the curtains.

"No, darling," murmured Sylvia, her eyes almost closed. "Leave the drapes open so I know"—she was nearly asleep—"where I am."

He lay down beside her. The scent at her hairline was like that of early-morning seaside grass. When she rolled into his arms she had already begun to snore faintly.

After a while, Michael saw that sleep would not come to him. He disengaged himself gently from Sylvia, got up, and closed the door to the bathroom. He had never been able to stand the smell of commercial disinfectant, and here the ineptly concocted odor of pine seemed to him particularly disheartening. *Although probably there really are pine trees somewhere in this country,* he thought. Then he shook his head. He didn't really know anything about this country.

"What I *really* love . . . ," said Sylvia in her sleep. Michael froze. She tossed violently upon the bed, grasped a handful of cotton coverlet without waking, and said no more.

Michael walked once again to the window.

He had come to this place without expectation. What he felt for Sylvia was so exacting that he had from the first known it would be costly, but because he knew as well that what he felt was love, he had also resolved to ride each moment till it crashed. So far there had been no crashes. And he had come to sense the inadequacy of the metaphor—the sea's surf was only the sea's surf, the summer was only the summer, there were no special effects.

"Cali-fucking-fornia," muttered Michael under his breath. He closed his eyes for a moment but opened them almost immediately, and through the window what he saw was this:

Three quarters of a block away, on a rooftop maybe half a dozen stories below, stood a semicircle of black men, obviously rousted from the cinder-block shelter that rested like a shoebox behind them. One of their number had stepped forward to address a man who was even at that distance instantly recognizable to Michael— the gold-tinted sunglasses, the tricolor logo of the motorcycle T-shirt, the red high-topped basketball shoes: Chentula. The man to whom Chentula had just spoken was now making many gestures, responding volubly. The gestures began to resolve themselves into a single one—that of a man giving directions. He was pointing over his shoulder to the southeast; he looked twice in that direction for emphasis. At last Chentula removed his sunglasses, nodded in apparent thanks to the man, and turned away toward the fire stairs that would return him to the street.

This is a whole new ballgame, thought Michael.

Beneath his fingers, the elegantly grilled central air-conditioning unit kicked audibly in, sending a swoosh of frigid air up into the room. Michael looked down at himself; he saw that his sweat-soaked shirt had dried in such a way as to leave crusty white perimeters of salt like a topographical map of his body. He turned.

In her sleep, Sylvia had partially kicked off her underpants. They hung like a flag just past the bend of her right knee.

Sitting down upon the edge of the bed, Michael picked up the phone and dialed Petra's extension. Sometimes he just felt like chatting.

·   ·   ·

Immediately upon closing the door behind the porter who had brought her bags up to her room, Petra had commenced working.

First she had called her production assistant. He had flown ahead to Johannesburg a few days previously to make arrangements, but now she instructed him to fly down to Cape Town with the rest of the crew by the following evening. She also made sure that he knew how to do the sort of cost accounting that was required: this unexpected diversion to Cape Town, she reminded him, was an economy measure.

Then she had called the storage facility, which, she now saw, lay an uneconomical number of kilometers north of her present coordinates. Both of the cargo shipments registered in her name had arrived safely, she was told, and all three allotments of equipment had been sent to their respective destinations. *Three allotments?* she thought, since all she could inventory just then, with a hand over her eyes, on a bed in South Africa, was Tsotsi's musical equipment and the hardware she had sent over for the film. But it was Heinrich's money and her picture, so she decided for the moment not to get curious.

Finally she leapt from the bed, shed all her clothes, and peering warily into the bathroom mirror—because appearances, too, were part of her work—removed all of her makeup. She took two ice cubes from the wet bar, wrapped them in a washcloth, and lay back down upon the bed.

She put the cold cloth over her eyes and fell asleep at once. A minute later she woke again. She took the phone off the hook.

She fell asleep.

"Gentlemen," said Paul Walters, "our work here in Compiègne—" He glanced about the conference table at the faces of the men he was addressing and was momentarily struck dumb by the beauty of the fiction by which this meeting had been convened: that a man could represent a country, that a country could represent its people.

The conference table was composed of three long, thin refectory tables expertly joined at their width so as to compose a surface of undisturbing proportions.

Walters recovered himself, and immediately his optimism became professional in tenor. After all, he had sought public life; it had sought him.

"Let me just say that while the events of the past few days—both in Europe and in the United States—may have complicated our task here, I am convinced that they have in no way compromised it. Very possibly the opposite. We gathered here in privacy for a free exchange of views about a matter that will unquestionably change the course of history. As I have said from the outset, my nation does not wish to proceed without the consensus of its allies. And when I spoke to the President last night—"

He paused again. He had not in fact spoken to the President, because neither he nor his aides had been able to get a call through on the Chief Executive's private line.

Most of the newspapers of the world had that morning carried a photograph of the American President pitching horseshoes on the White House lawn. The pictures indicated that this man was a Texan, a man demonstrably unharmed by the attempt on his life. In a few informal remarks, the President had explicitly reaffirmed the authority of Paul Walters to represent U.S. interests at the newly expanded disarmament talks in Geneva, where, to facilitate the negotiations, Paul Walters had been instructed to maintain a seclusion from the press.

Paul Walters looked at his watch. "Well, I see it's nearly lunchtime, and we've been here all morning. . . ." The only man not watching him was Bloch, who had been doodling impatiently on his notepad. Lolombela continued to sit bolt upright in his oaken chair. A crystal vase of purple gentian blossoms sat at the center of the table.

The way Walters realized he had blinked was that the flowers' purple became orange in his retina's afterimage, and so reminded him of a dream he'd had the night before. Why William of *Orange*? But sometimes dreams were just dreams—isn't that how the expression went? He hastened once again to resume control.

"Our country's position," he said, "is this: First, that if the sentiment of the nations concerned is that there should be no test detonation of the fission bomb, then there will not be one. Second, if there is to be no test detonation, then the nations concerned will issue a joint statement explaining the reasons for our restraint and the nature of the weapon itself. Third, that a computer simulation of such a detonation, formatted on videotape, will be made available in unlimited quantitites to any nation requesting one. Fourth—" He was standing up.

He was making it all up as he went along, standing up.

He was angry, but he knew how to conceal it.

"Fourth—" He knew how to appear to relax. He knew how to let his shoulders go and he knew how to smile. "The United States feels we should think about this during lunch, make the phone calls we have to make, reconvene in the afternoon, and be out of here by tomorrow morning."

For a moment the translators and stenographers continued their work. Then there were hushed consultations. Then the envoy from Japan rose to his feet as Paul Walters had done.

Eisako Yoshida was a man of immense grace. He was also, as the jade cufflinks at his wrists attested, something of a dandy. "Your country's proposal is a provocative one, Dr. Walters," he said in English, "and at a moment such as this it is often only the unexpected that can lead us to the obvious." He directed a courteous smile at Paul Walters. "I would like time to consult with my government."

"*Moi aussi*," said Bataillard, without rising.

There was a general murmur of provisional assent, although everyone except Bloch continued to watch Yoshida. Bloch was now staring at Walters.

"May I suggest, then," said the Czech representative, struggling to his feet, "that we reconvene at three P.M.?"

A pause. Walters saw that Lolombela was watching Bloch. Then there was a great scraping of chair legs against floor, oak against oak, and the thing was done.

Back in his quarters, Walters changed his shirt. He decided against a tie. "Right now," he told his chief aide, turning away from the mirror to get his hairbrushes, "the best thing would be for you guys to keep trying to get hold of the President. I'm going to think this whole goddamn thing through one more time, and I have to be alone to do it. So I'm going to lunch. Then we can talk about how best to handle this afternoon session."

"Yes, sir, only—"

Paul Walters stopped. "Only?" It was becoming more and more annoying to see his aides look so nervous.

"Well, sir, State has ordered a bodyguard for you, and this guy—"

"Where is this guy right now?"

"Um, he thought he ought to check out the conference room— you know, just routine, but—"

Walters repeated his relaxation effect. He smiled. "Good. That's fine." He had always wondered why horn-rimmed glasses inevitably collected a matte-white patina at the temple pieces, and he had long known he'd eventually have to fire this man wearing them. "Only thing I'm a little worried about, though, to tell you the truth, is that weird-looking gadget stuck under the bathroom sink. It's probably nothing, but I guess this guy ought to have a look at it. So if you could ask him about it? Tell him I'll be waiting in the car."

"Ten-four, sir." The relief passing over the aide's features was horrible to contemplate. "I'll do that." The man pushed his glasses back up his nose, did a tottering about-face, and departed.

Paul Walters waited three seconds. *Of course, you never know who is firing whom in this business.* Then he carefully opened the glass-paned doors in his bedroom, walked over to the empty government-issue sedan parked on the dirt road behind the inn, sat himself behind the steering wheel, and drove away.

Three kilometers northeast of Compiègne, Walters found a restaurant whose appearance he liked—an inn on the edge of the forest, an inn with a terrace and a garden.

The maître d' seated him at a table that had been ingeniously cantilevered out from the trunk of an enormous oak. The tree's leaves had just begun to fall. Three of them were on the table.

"I'll have the rabbit with morels and rice," he told the waitress.

"Very fresh," she said approvingly. "Shot only this morning in Compiègne."

Walters smiled and returned the menu to her. It was really true that he had only wanted to eat alone.

Acutely now, as he gazed out across the sparsely occupied terrace, he felt the foolishness by which men had so consistently attempted to divide their public lives from their private ones.

"S'il vous plaît," he asked of the waitress as she passed. "A glass of white wine?"

She nodded briskly. But something in the abstractedness of his gaze affected her, and she paused. She smiled—not engagingly but with a slight crimp at the corners of her mouth that suggested sympathy or teasing reproof. She looped a lock of dark hair back over her ear. Then she said gaily in French, "There is no wine in all of France, but perhaps, if we are lucky, I will find you some." She laughed and disappeared.

And so he was at once chastened and cheered. Life belonged to the coquettish after all.

By the time his meal arrived, in the hands of a different waitress, he was in a far better mood. The rabbit was excellent. A breeze blew across the terrace, gently rattling the leaves of the tree above the table.

When he saw Bloch arrive upon the terrace, looking distractedly about for him, Walters realized that although this was a development he had hoped to avoid, it was not one that entirely surprised him. He waved.

"Please join me, Heinrich," he said when Bloch stood tableside, looking up at the ancient tree that towered above them. "I can be difficult to find sometimes, but I always enjoy your company." He peered down thoughtfully at his nearly empty plate. "Oh, yes. I recommend the rabbit."

"Paul," said Bloch, sitting.

"How did you find me?" said Walters.

"I saw you leave."

"Are we alone?"

"Ja, of course. I left the same way."

"So what'll we be talking about?" Walters inquired jovially, avoiding eye contact. He gestured to the maître d' for another menu and scanned the terrace with severely professional bonhomie: two couples in their twenties, an elderly man in love with his food. That was all. Returning his attention frankly to Bloch, Walters noticed that the man looked a little disheveled—his suit was wrinkled, his hair uncombed.

"Heinrich, I don't think you've been getting enough sleep since you've become the conscience of Europe."

The waitress offered Bloch a menu, but he declined. She crossed her arms and examined him vexedly for a moment before departing.

"We are not here for sleep."

"Of course not." Walters brought the damask napkin to his mouth, then leaned back in his chair. "How informal is this discussion?"

"As informal as a discussion between two men of good will in our—" Bloch drew a hand across his brow in frustration. "No." He picked three oak leaves from the table. He let them flutter to the ground. "I would like it to be a discussion between friends."

"Done."

"You know about my romantic liaison with Petra König."

"Yes."

Bloch might have been surprised by this answer. Yet Walters could not help feeling that the suddenness with which the man froze was a little theatrical.

"I see her very rarely," Bloch continued, "but for what it's worth to you, I love her. What is the expression in English? 'Angels come once only'?"

"Something like that."

"For me it is true."

"It sure as hell was for me."

Bloch drew himself forward in his chair. "Tomorrow some of my opponents in the German Republics will leak a story to the press about my relations with Petra König. Ordinarily, this would be a merely personal matter, but because I have involved Petra—without her knowledge, I assure you—in our arrangements regarding Azania and the fission bomb, matters may be changing faster than we anticipated. And I . . ." He dropped his glance in something like embarrassment. On the flagstones a few meters past Paul Walters's left shoulder, a thrush held part of a breadstick in its beak. Still holding the morsel, the bird inspected Bloch, first from one eye, then from the other. Nature. Bloch laughed silently to himself.

"This is a discussion between friends, Heinrich."

Bloch nodded: a gesture of submission. "Petra loves her husband," he said. "I don't want any harm to come to her. If there is a way to suppress the story—"

Walters waved these words away as if they constituted a bad

smell. "Petra also loves her work, Heinrich. And I love my daughter. And I know for a fact that Joseph asked you never to involve his own daughter again in what we're doing here."

The look on Bloch's face was one of incredulity mixed with a grain of admiration.

"We all did it anyway. Why? For the higher good, maybe? I hope so." Catching the waitress's eye, Walters mouthed the word "espresso," and the woman skipped away in a self-amused impression of servility.

"But since this is a discussion between friends," Walters continued, "I've got to ask you something. Are you telling me that you think things back home are no longer under your control?"

"No, I—" Bloch, who had been toying with his fork, brought it down slowly upon the white mesh table at which they were seated so that the implement's tines left it suspended upright like a misshot arrow. He let it stand. "Yes," he said.

Walters raised his eyebrows.

"It is an internal matter. My opponents at home do not understand anything about the fission bomb but that a test detonation would be a defeat for me. Their position is the same as that of the Soviet bloc, now that the press has had its . . . 'field day'? *Ja?* Okay, field day?" He twanged the fork into the table between them as if it were a catapult aimed at himself. "I have made a mistake."

"Politically?"

"No." He drew the deepest of breaths. He loosened his tie. "I have lived my life in stupidity and ambition."

Walters, who had heard and said so much across so many tables in the service of his country, his family, and—it now had to be admitted—his ego, was deeply impressed. Bloch was a genius.

"Heinrich."

"I should not have come here."

"But here you are."

To the side, in the terrace's middle distance and peripherally visible to both Bloch and Walters, a young woman was feeding her escort a forkful of what looked like venison. Half of it went down his shirtfront, and as the man disconsolately surveyed the damage, his lover laughed at him. Then she kissed him.

Bloch removed his jacket.

"All morning, Paul—" Bloch struck himself lightly on the forehead and winced. "Forgive me. I'm calling you Paul."

"Yes, you are. It's fine." Walters once again felt his own sentimentality draining through the basin of what would shortly become the real source of his authority. "We've been speaking alone."

"Paul, when I involved Petra König in our scenario, I did not myself realize the extent of what I was doing. I flatter myself that from the first I have understood how our arrangements here might change the world; I am very good at that sort of thinking."

Reaching behind, Bloch caught his jacket just as it was sliding off the back of his chair. Walters nodded in acknowledgment of this double deftness.

"But all morning, Paul, I watched you and Lolombela at the conference table, and I understood that I no longer knew what to do. I saw that the two of you had involved your daughters in our plan, and that you had always known the price. I have no children. I did not know the price." He grimaced, as might any man who had suffered an unforeseen indignity. "Of involving Petra." He waved away his own lie. "Of having no children."

"What are you asking?" Walters inquired as gently as he could. His espresso arrived, and as the waitress delivered it, she minced about in affectionate parody of medieval courtliness. Walters bowed to her; she danced away.

"Heinrich. If you want, I can see to it that the U.S. TV runs an appropriate number of news stories about the implausibility of your liaison with Petra König. If you want to know whether you, Joseph, and I are equally compromised by the ways we have used our private lives in the service of the plan we have agreed upon"—here Walters felt a flare of anger, but he was able after swallowing to even his tone of voice—"then I can assure you we are." Walters twisted a sliver of lemon rind into his coffee.

"What I am asking," said Bloch, throwing out his hand into the space between them.

But he could no longer remember what he was asking.

"You think that I've lost my country's mandate regarding the fission bomb," said Walters. "You're telling me—whether you believe it or not—that you may no longer be able to direct European opinion on the matter. You're asking me if I believe Joseph is unambiguously with us." Walters swallowed his coffee in two gulps, then, from the porcelain holder on the tabletop, selected a sugar cube. He unwrapped it and fell silent.

"Paul. You know that all three cargo consignments from the U.S. have arrived safely in Southern Africa: the film equipment from California, the sound equipment for this—what is it?—this Azanian rock band, but also . . . all the other matériel."

Walters had already popped the sugar cube into his mouth. "Sure, I know that." He chewed his sweetness slowly. "Did you think I wouldn't? Did you think, when I asked that this be a conversation between friends, that I wouldn't reassess whether we were friends or not?" Now he, too, leaned forward, hands clasped before him upon the table, eyes locked with Bloch's. "Did you think I might not have asked by what right you judge me?"

Bloch did not blink, although he knew that had he been a more truly private man he would have been frightened differently by now.

Walters held his colleague's glance, then turned softly away to laugh, as if in theatrical aside. "Did you think," he said, "that any man of state is really ignorant of the uselessness of his emotions, whatever the context?" A silence passed. "That's okay, Heinrich." He'd rarely felt himself so worked up. "I know you didn't think those things. So—what are you asking?"

"I really think it is Petra I am asking about."

"Then you should call her in Johannesburg."

"In Johannesburg?"

"Yes, they've just arrived there—the whole bunch."

"But, Paul." Despite himself, Bloch brightened. "They're not in Johannesburg. They're in Cape Town."

Still napping in their respective hotel rooms (Sylvia and Petra). Reclining uncomfortably bedside in a Masterlounge chair, a copy of *What's On in the Cape This Week* clutched in his hand (Michael). Gathered tautly around Petra's rental car in the hotel's underground garage (Nomanzi, Chentula, Johnny).

"But, Chenny, man," said Johnny, almost plaintively. "Be reasonable." He slapped the roof of the sedan and turned away.

The hotel's garage had acquired a measure of local celebrity by virtue of the tile mosaic that adorned its walls. The mosaic's subject was Vasco da Gama, taking a Khoikhoi spear through his shoulder after having arrived at the Cape in 1497. The mosaic's celebrity derived from the Portuguese explorer's unaccountable resemblance to Donald Duck.

"Look, Chenny." Johnny began to pace up and down beside the car. "If you run off half-cocked like this, you have about half a chance in hell of finding your mother before our concert tomorrow. And that's supposing your safari guide up there on the rooftop really has any idea where they relocated her."

Leaning forward, Nomanzi planted her elbows on the still-warm hood of the car and languidly cupped her chin in her palms.

"Phopho is never wrong about what he knows will matter to one of us," said Chentula. "They moved my mother—" He glanced at Nomanzi, who was studying the way the rental car's wax job partially caught her reflection. "They moved our mother from her place to Nyanga the day we left for California."

"Nyanga." Johnny stopped pacing. It was the black township they had passed on their way in from the airport. "Okay. And I guess your Phopho gave you a permit to enter Nyanga whenever you feel like it, too. I guess he arranged for Surveillance to go on holiday while you visit. I guess—" He appealed to Nomanzi. "Damnit, can't you see it's a trap to get him detained so there's no concert tomorrow?"

"I see what I see," said Nomanzi without looking up.

The garage smelled sweetly of gasoline. Chentula, very softly, peering softly away, said, "Over there, back to the left. You recognize that man?"

They both looked. It was the hotel desk clerk, now dressed in a powder-blue jumpsuit, vigorously scrubbing down the fenders of a Cheetah convertible.

Chentula had not moved. His eyes took no certain focus. "This man is on his lunch break. He washes fifteen cars a day, every day except Sunday. The same cars. He gets paid five and a half rand a month. That makes thirty cents U.S. a wash."

Johnny flushed as if he had been slapped. "What're you telling me, ay? If you think I don't—"

"No, no, man." For the first time since landing in Africa, Chentula

smiled. "You are my brother. I'm just telling you we're home."
He tossed the car keys to Nomanzi.

"We'll be back before dawn tomorrow," said Chentula, opening
the door on the passenger side. "Petra—it is she you should talk
to about our equipment. The setup for tomorrow's been taken care
of. The rest of the band is down by Crossroads. They know what
to do."

Nomanzi opened the driver's door and slid into the seat. She
blew Johnny a kiss in purposefully comic exaggeration, but then
she saw his face—its concern—and she blew him a slower, more
serious kiss. *What would it be like to sleep with him?* she wondered,
tucking the end of her lilac-dyed, faux-lizard belt back down the
front of her jeans. *I've never known a man with so much nose hair,
but I rather—*

"Okay," said Johnny. "I'll try to keep the upstairs crew from
panicking." A smile made its way across his face because he understood a female gesture as well as the next man, and because he
understood as well that the kind of resignation he felt was maybe
a variety of macho grace. "Don't be late." He knew when to turn
away and walk.

Nomanzi turned the ignition, and she and Chentula shot out of
the parking garage, into the sunlight. The Cape Town towers, to
the left and right, looked like a not-quite-matched set of false jewels.
Nomanzi took the main road out of town, back toward Nyanga.

"What did you mean, *sisi*, when you said that?" It had been years
since he had used the affectionate diminutive in addressing her.

"When I said what?"

"That you saw what you saw."

Nomanzi turned the radio on. She looked at Chentula and
laughed fondly. "I meant," she said, "let's go."

For several minutes after that, the movement of the car bound
them pleasantly together.

Nomanzi, following Chentula's directions, bore left, turned right,
turned left. The well-maintained asphalt highway gave way to a
shoulderless tarred road, which before long gave way to gravel,
then to sandy dirt. They were circumspectly approaching the township so as to enter it through what Johnny had referred to as its
unwatched back door.

The acknowledgment, unspoken between Nomanzi and Chentula, that they were not in the position to avoid taking chances drew them together as surely as did their half-shared blood. Likewise, the unasked-for intimacy of the connection put them half at odds.

"When was it you last saw our mother?" Chentula asked.

"I've forgotten. So long ago."

"I saw her last month." He threw her a glance. "Maybe you will be surprised."

"I am always surprised." She turned off the radio.

"Why so long that you have stayed away from her?" Chentula asked softly.

"You know, you know, you know what was the agreement: we were to lead our lives, we were not to give the whites the chance to make us into monuments or detainees, we were—" She found herself impatient to let the argument develop fully so it could at least be temporarily resolved. Rolling down the window, she thrust a loosely cupped hand out into the windy breath of her country.

"When engaged," she recited, "in the struggle for national liberation against settler colonialism, when *confronted* by the continued certainty of a racially divided society, when *required* by historical *necessity*—"

Chentula shook his head. The gesture began as a denial but tapered off into a nearly diaristic, punch-drunk nod. "No, *sisi*," he said. "*Sisi* Nomanzi. No."

They had passed into the township without incident.

"We're home," said Nomanzi, affecting a sigh.

Rows of matchbox houses—cinder-block walls supporting galvanized steel roofs—extended in draftsmanlike symmetry to the left and right. Nomanzi was trying not to be distracted by the way that the motion of the car made the side streets seem to fold diagonally behind her like fishbones.

"When I met your *tata* . . ." Chentula felt himself oddly revealed by this uncertain intimacy of address. "When I saw 'Joseph Lolombela' again . . ." The sentence had no finish. They both allowed it to rest.

A very young boy in a pom-pommed stocking cap and a blue jersey chased after them for several meters, then threw down the hand mirror he had perhaps been intending to sell them. In the rental car's rearview mirror, Nomanzi saw both the object and the boy's will to sell it break.

They drove for some time in a silence punctuated only by Chentula's occasional instruction to turn left, turn right, look for the next working water pump: these were the directions Phopho had given him. A brown haze composed of the countless cooking fires hovered over the township. And the streets, so nearly empty on the side of the settlement that bordered the highway, were here even in the day's heat thickly populated: by children in shorts, by dogs worrying bits of garbage, by women bearing home five-gallon buckets of water on their heads.

Nomanzi guided the car carefully through the township's sandy roads. But after a while, when Chentula had ceased issuing directions and the silence between them had begun to sour, she pulled up behind a tangle of chain-link fence and stopped. "We're lost," she said.

Chentula removed his sunglasses. The muscles in his face were as taut as the lines in an anatomical diagram. "No," he answered. "We're here."

It was as Phopho had said: all that distinguished their mother's new house from its architecturally identical neighbors was the eaves-high reach of dead brown thornbush surrounding it.

Nomanzi parked the car. There were no other motor vehicles in sight, and when she and Chentula had determined that they were not being watched, they got out of the sedan.

Their mother, Nozembe Lolombela, had till now been one of those the police had apparently decided to overlook—whether because of her first husband's exile, or because of her subsequent liaison with the mild-mannered man (long since dead of pneumonia) who had fathered Chentula, or because, the notoriety of her name notwithstanding, she had chosen to work unostentatiously as a charwoman in Cape Town, no one knew.

The windows of the house in which she had now been interned, elaborately protected by forged-steel grating, offered no sign of life. Nomanzi and Chentula walked up the tiny lawn of half-dead sea grass to the door. To the back and side, sand dunes were visible.

There was no obvious place to stop and prepare for whatever was to come, so Chentula reached out one hand and stayed Nomanzi

by the shoulder. "You must be ready," he said. "She has changed."
"Yes." Nomanzi looked down. "In the time since I . . . Yes."
"Her life before . . ."
Nomanzi felt his hand tremble. She lifted her face to the man
who was her brother. "You are right. I cannot know about that."
The sound of American music, somewhere behind them—in a
house? in a hand-held tape player?—forced her to search out her
courage. Nomanzi said: "And now she, our mother, lives here.
Here. Neither of us knows about that."

Chentula's eyes went liquid to hers. His anger was the anger of
a dignified man.

"Our mother cared for your father no less than she does for mine,"
said Nomanzi, laying her hand upon his.

The door was flung widely open before them.

What Nomanzi had not expected: that their mother, dressed in
a scoop-backed cotton dress, her hair bound in a modified *doek* of
black and gold, remained undeniably beautiful.

What Chentula had not expected: that the leverage his mother
exerted over him—it was as womanly as parental—could never be
extinguished: not by political circumstances, not by forgetfulness,
not by death.

"My neighbors," said Nozembe Lolombela, casting her eyes
about the house behind her in the national gesture of security
consciousness. "It is kind of you to visit me in my new home. Please
be welcome."

She drew her children into the little three-room house and embraced them passionately. "On a day like this," she said, disengaging
at last, "you'll be wanting a cold drink." Her eyes glittered. It had
indeed been too long.

But she has lost so much weight, thought Chentula, who had not
anticipated being the one surprised.

"They have qualified me for a garden in back," said Nozembe
Lolombela, beginning to pass into the room that, because she lived
alone, might with some effort of the imagination be considered a
kitchen.

"Please make yourselves comfortable in those chairs by the fence,
neighbors. I will bring us our juice."

It was only then, as her mother turned, that Nomanzi became

aware of the presence of two young men sitting in molded fiberglass chairs just inside the house's back door. The men were Xhosa. They wore black berets and T-shirts that across the chest bore a rainbow arc of English words too stylized to be legible to Nomanzi even had the men's arms not been folded menacingly before them. She glanced at her brother. As he touched her arm, she followed him past the men into the house's backyard.

A round steel table, thickly painted in forest green, stood crookedly upon the sandy soil out back. Unmatched lawn chairs of aluminum and nylon webbing were scattered around it in the attitude of their most recent sitters' departures.

"Those men," said Nomanzi, circling the table.

"Fourteen, fifteen years old." Chentula was already seated in one of the rickety lawn chairs. With his forefinger he began to scrape at a bit of thrush dropping welded to the tabletop by the sun. "Men, yes. It should not be so." And yet his tone held no obvious rancor. "They are young."

"I could not read what was written on their T-shirts."

He looked up at his sister and smiled. "*Sisi.* We do not speak of this, you and I, but we are both still sending our mother money?"

Nomanzi sat. "Yes."

He looked down again. Again he picked without purpose at the white-and-purple bird droppings. "The shirts say 'Nyanga Motor Club and Safety League.' "

"She has hired bodyguards."

"Yes."

It was possible, from where Nomanzi and Chentula sat, to smell the sea.

"I am not yet used to this place," Nozembe called, emerging from her cinder-block house. "Please excuse my slowness." Upon the flat of her right hand and at the level of her ear, she carried a tin tray of cold drinks. With her other hand she gamely hauled her hobbled left leg forward. "When you have lived in the city so long . . ."

Nomanzi relieved her of the tray, and Chentula helped her into a seat. None of the doctors Nozembe had consulted over the past seven years had been of any help about her leg.

"Out here," she said, throwing a disdainful glance at the offending limb, "there are no microphones." Then she smiled as if in uttering the words she had made them true. Nomanzi began to be alarmed. "My children. I have thought so much about—"

"We have not stopped talking of you," said Chentula, intercepting Nomanzi's glance. "In America we . . ." But he faltered.

"Over there," continued Nomanzi, "we spoke often of how much you would laugh at the troubles Americans have invented for themselves, at how much—"

Their mother frowned.

A seagull wheeled high above them, and for a time its squawk was the only sound the three family members could agree upon. The bird disappeared.

"You have seen Joseph," said Nozembe.

A quick exchange of glances left Chentula with the role of respondent. "Yes, Mother. We saw him in Paris." From his back pocket Chentula produced a baseball-style hat. "Joseph asked that we tell you it goes well with him."

"It goes well with him," Nozembe repeated in English.

Chentula's hat said "International Harvester."

Nomanzi said, "He is working on new ways to come to visit you. He misses you."

Nozembe said: "I have loved two men in my life. You are their children."

All of these stories had been told many times.

From a spot somewhere beyond the house and across the half-made street on which it fronted, a dog began to bark with the monotonous regularity of the confined.

"We only learned today of your relocation," said Nomanzi, leaning forward. "A friend of Chentula's told us how to find you."

"Phopho," said Chentula. He removed his hat and inspected it. "He is of us. We must always protect him."

"Yes," said their mother. Her eyes still glittered. "But you saw Joseph?"

Because the question seemed so pointedly directed at her this time, Nomanzi reared back, and with her wrist she knocked her untouched glass of juice from the table. The accident remained unremarked upon by the two others. Chentula began to spin his hat awkwardly upon the point of one index finger.

"Yes, I saw my father," said Nomanzi.

"It has been many years now," her mother answered.

"Ten years."

"Does he seem the same?"

"Yes. He seems the same."

Chentula let the hat cease spinning, then with a casual gesture tossed it over his shoulder into the drought-dead khaki weed behind him. "He is not the same," Chentula said. "None of us are."

It was what they had all been waiting for, however unconsciously. Chentula stood. The lightweight chair fell backward behind him as casually as his hat had lighted upon the lawn's spiky weeds. He began to pace.

"You say there are no microphones here. Good. But it is not the microphones that are our enemies. If the whites had wanted to detain you, jail you—take you, our mother, away from us . . ." Chentula paused. He felt again the profound difference between "home" and "place"—*my home, my place*. His rage surged back upon him like a wave retrieved by the ocean that lay audibly within reach of this small patch of seaside grass and sand. "When they brought you here, did they hurt you?"

Nomanzi bit her knuckle and looked away.

"No," said Nozembe. "They did not hurt me. They did not question me." She seemed to be reciting a dream. But as if from a dream, she seemed then to awaken. "And if they did?" She laughed. "Have I not lived a life in which my answers to injury and interrogation have always been the same?" She drank down half her glass of juice and licked her lips with a somnolent anger that by its inwardness once again alarmed Nomanzi.

Chentula continued to pace—his eyes closed, his thumb and forefinger grasping his temples. His pain was as palpable as a headache.

"Mother," said Nomanzi, wheeling around. "Your answers have always been the same. And Chentula and I—your children—are also your answers." Nomanzi appealed to Chentula with her eyes, but his remained closed, so she continued. "And, yes, Chentula is right—none of us are really the same. That would be wrong. Because every step we take must be a step forward." She took her mother's face in her hands. "You taught us this."

Chentula picked up his chair and heaved it as far toward the ocean as the careless wind would allow. The chair blew back into the khaki weed and lodged there.

"You have seen Joseph," said Nozembe.

Nomanzi rose in startled recognition.

Now drained of anger, Chentula walked toward both of them. He had not yet seen what his sister had seen. "Which is the sin, my mother?" he said. "To fail the past or to fail the future?"

As quietly as possible, Nomanzi removed the two remaining juice glasses from the table. She poured their contents into the soil.

"You have seen Joseph?" Nozembe repeated.

And then Chentula understood what Nomanzi had already noticed: their mother had been drugged.

Nomanzi let the glasses drop discreetly to the ground behind her as if they were the playthings of children whose bedtime had come. She sat down again at the table.

"Have you been ill, my mother?"

"Ill? No, I am never ill. You know that." She laughed. "Me? There is no time for illness."

"So you have been taking no medicine?"

Nozembe, furrowing her brow, appeared confused. "But I have just told you I am not ill! Why would I take medicine?"

Her children looked at her. Then at each other.

Chentula said: "Do you feel like yourself?"

Nozembe looked at her daughter. *Was her daughter like herself?* She looked away. "I am not happy here," she said softly.

Chentula dragged a broken-backed chair to his mother's side and sat. "What is this thing: the Nyanga Motor Club and Safety League?"

Tilting her head in the attitude of someone fondly recalling a distant memory, Nozembe said, "Don't you know?" The glitter had come back to her eye. "Did we never tell you that story?"

"What story?" said Nomanzi. "What 'we'?"

To the seaward side of where they sat, the sound of a helicopter sliced off the conversation as neatly as a gardener's hoe might cut the edge of a lawn. Reflexively, mother, daughter, and son scanned the sky above them. Nothing man-made was visible in heaven. So they looked again uncertainly at each other.

Gradually Nozembe discovered her concern. She struggled to lean forward. "But Chentula, now that you are back you must go to Jo'burg, to your job."

"Yes, Mother. The day after tomorrow I will be a gardener again. But first the band will give a concert."

"Oh, yes. The band." She relaxed too quickly, but not insincerely. "Your father would be very proud of you. He always said that music . . . that politics . . ."

"What was it he said?" asked Chentula—pleased, desperate, proud.

Nomanzi calmed herself by running her hands down the front of her thighs. After all, she was the firstborn.

"Your father," Nozembe said to Chentula, again letting her eyes go to the faraway. "He was a man who knew—" She twisted in small grandeur in her small chair and giggled grandly.

"Oh, he was a man who knew."

Oddly, all three of them laughed.

"He always knew you would be a musician," Nozembe continued. "Yes, he knew that."

"He loved his steel-box guitar," said Nomanzi.

But Nozembe was not to be diverted. "And he was right," she said, continuing to address her son. "Now you are famous in the world, Chenny." She looked at Nomanzi. "Of course, your sister is famous too."

The thought appeared to confuse everyone. A silence ensued.

"But you were saying," Nomanzi prompted, "about these two men inside—the Nyanga Motor Club and Safety League. Do they stay here with you?"

"Oh, they go off, they rotate." She wrinkled her nose in an expression of distaste that seemed quite at odds with her first response to the inquiry. "It is a little too play-time military for me, but because of the Emergency Laws we decided . . ." She lost her train of thought. "Phopho arranged it," she said finally, as if no further explanation could possibly be necessary. "Would you like more juice?"

From the coast, very distant as yet, came the sound of the helicopter returning from shore patrol. Nomanzi nervously consulted her watch but found to her annoyance that it had stopped. *How could I not have checked the time since eight-sixteen this morning?* she wondered, staring at the watch's immobilized face, then shaking her wrist.

"When you mentioned that story," Chentula said, "the one you said Nomanzi and me have never been told . . ."

"A story?" repeated Nozembe in confusion.

"When I first asked about the Motor Club boys."

"My Motor Club boys? But there is no story about them; they have been in this place no longer than I."

The chatter of the patrol helicopter's rotor was nearer now but still far enough off so that when Nomanzi glanced at the sky, Chentula understood she was referring only to the vehicle's eventual arrival. "If they see the car," Nomanzi added *sotto voce*, "it won't matter if they see us. Ask about the juice, her food, who she sees."

Chentula, resting his ropy forearms upon his thighs, leaned toward Nozembe. "This afternoon, our Mother, we cannot stay long. We will be back. But we have come here to be certain that you have the things you need."

"Need?" said Nozembe, scornfully. And looked away.

"Your food. Who buys it? Who prepares it?"

"I buy my food at the Indian shop. And do you imagine that I hire a cook? Of course it is I who prepare it."

"Yes. And when they—" Chentula stared down at his red high-topped sneakers. The realization that his father would have been amused by such shoes threw him into the task at hand.

"When the *Gats* brought you here, the place was empty?"

"Oh, a little furniture; what you see." Then she smiled. "And three cases of fruit juice. Can you imagine? You, my children, are famous for your music and your acting. I am famous for liking fruit juice. It was that photograph they took of me after Joseph's trial, after he left. As if fruit juice can stop the course of history!" She chuckled.

Chentula and Nomanzi exchanged a look.

"Our Mother," said Nomanzi. "Please excuse me, but I am taking the sun badly. Perhaps if I could go inside and lie down for five minutes?"

Nozembe fluttered her hands in a scolding gesture. "Oh, yes, Nomanzi. Quickly, go!" She looked concerned. "An actress, you must take care of yourself. *Hamba!*"

Inside the institutional dwelling, Nomanzi greeted the Motor Club boys and told them she thought it might be better if they sat just outside the back door, where her mother could more easily sense the strength of their presence. They readily assented, and one of them asked Nomanzi to autograph his T-shirt. She rummaged around in her purse until she found a felt-tip pen, then signed her name across the chest of part of Azania's future. He smiled; they thanked each other. *Where had he gotten such a notion?*

As soon as the two young men were outside, Nomanzi saw the three cases of fruit juice on the floor, and the situation became obvious. More than three quarters of the liter bottles remained in their cartons, but the twist-off aluminum top of every single one of them had been broken open and resealed. Immediately, Nomanzi dragged the cases into what passed for the front yard and began pouring the contaminated juice into the soil. When she was done she noticed a group of small boys watching her from the middle of the potholed road. The varied tilt of their heads suggested to her the infinity of political disagreement, even among those on the same side.

"A shame," she said to them. "All this good juice gone bad with drowned silverfish." She shook her head. "A shame," she said to them. "But someday soon it will all be very different."

The children neither responded nor dispersed, and Nomanzi wondered whether perhaps they thought they were watching television. The idea depressed her profoundly.

She replaced the bottles in their cartons and brought them back into the house.

When she rejoined her mother and Chentula in the backyard, Nozembe said, "Chentula has been telling me of your success in America." She reached a hand out to touch her daughter's face. "We must make our country's way in many fields."

"Thank you, my Mother."

"And to speak selfishly, I am glad to think I will see much of you while you are making this"—she struggled for the American term—"this 'picture.'"

Nomanzi clasped her mother's hand, still flat across her temple, with her own fingers.

"Our Mother, you must drink no more of that juice. They will bring you more. But it is drugged. Promise us, your children. No more."

"Drugged?" She removed her hand and looked at it as if addressing her palm. "I am drugged?"

"This Motor Club," said Chentula. "They are reliable?"

"Yes." Nozembe let her hand fall to the table. "I am sure of it."

This time it was Chentula who gave a meaningful skyward glance. Nomanzi understood at once: for whatever reason, the Surveillance helicopter had again reversed its direction; the noise of its gasoline-fueled chop was fading.

"What does Joseph say of this?" asked Nozembe indignantly. She struck the green metal table with the authority of someone striking a gong. "I am drugged?"

"If it is true," Chentula answered, "how could he know it? We are being careful."

Nozembe examined her palm, which stung from the slap she had delivered the table.

"You have seen Joseph?"

Sister and brother rose as one.

"We must go," said Nomanzi. "We will see you soon."

"Or Phopho will be in touch with you," added Chentula.

Nozembe recovered herself. "Yes, my neighbors. Yes. You are so kind to visit." Without getting to her feet, she embraced her daughter and son fervently. "Please come back soon. You are always welcome."

"*Amandhla—*" Nomanzi whispered the first half of the Zulu slogan into her mother's ear. Nozembe seemed puzzled. She looked vexedly from daughter to son. Then her expression changed to one of weary confidence, even satisfaction. "*Awethu,*" she answered. And turned away.

In the car, when Nomanzi and Chentula had once again passed over the township line without difficulty, Chentula grew restive, then briefly violent. He smashed the car's glove compartment with the flat of his hand, splintering matte black plastic in several directions.

"Hell, *sisi!* She never told me what he said!"

Nomanzi calmed herself by an act of will. "What who said?" she asked, picking a fragment of plastic from her lap as she drove.

"My father!" He put his sunglasses back on and all at once felt pulverizingly exhausted. He looked at his sister in bewilderment. "She never told me what he *said!*"

Nomanzi herself could think of nothing to say. She touched her brother's knee. They drove the rest of the way to the hotel without speaking.

"Michael?" said Sylvia, stirring sleepily from her nap upon the hotel bed. "Michael, I had this weird dream." She opened her eyes. "My father was—" She sat quickly up. "Michael?"

But Michael was even then racing down the hotel's fire stairs as if he were training for a track-and-field event. There was a video camera at every other landing. He was beginning to understand what was on in Cape Town this week.

On the one hand, he thought, *how stupid can I be.* This is how a man runs down steps without stumbling. *On the other hand*—he counted steps with syllables—*how much time do we have?*

After looking to the left and right, he departed by the hotel's delivery entrance. Johnny was waiting for him around the block, at the coffee shop they had agreed upon obliquely over the phone.

"Yes," said Michael to the waitress, an English white. "Maybe you could give us the corner booth? It's kind of embarrassing to be doing business outside the office, if you know what I mean."

"Embarrassing?" she said, leading them off. "The stories I could tell you." She looked at Johnny. "Do I recognize you?"

"I don't think so."

She winked, seating them. "Not to worry. My alleged husband was a musician too." She handed them menus. "Just give a sign when you need me." She turned suddenly. "Oh." Looking quickly around to be sure she was unobserved, she whispered: "We'll all be at your concert tomorrow."

Johnny smiled at her and nodded. "Thanks," he said.

She blushed and departed.

"Sylvia's still asleep," said Michael.

Johnny nodded.

"Petra's phone was off the hook," added Michael, trying to get things to go somewhere.

"Right." Johnny was now sweating as profusely as had Michael at the airport. He turned his empty coffee cup upside down upon its saucer. "And Nomanzi and Chentula are away for a little while right now, so I thought we could talk a few minutes—just us, y'know."

Michael turned his coffee cup over too. "You got it."

"Well, straight out, I wasn't sure about you over there in America, but now I am."

"Okay," said Michael.

"No." Johnny shook his head and scratched at his beard with the impatience of a man trying to decide what language to speak while his thoughts collided behind his tongue. "I mean, hell, I know we didn't meet until the airport, when we were leaving America. It's just that here I can *see*—d'y'know? Probably it's the same for you over there."

Michael righted his coffee cup. "Nah, it's America over there. We wear sunglasses."

Johnny laughed. "Yeh, I've heard that."

"Not a rumor." Michael laughed too. Looking very hard at Johnny, he pushed his fork, in a series of little bumps from his thumb, slowly off the edge of the table. It clattered with birdlike brightness upon the linoleum floor. "What're we here for, Johnny?"

The waitress arrived immediately. She swept a clean fork from the adjacent table and deposited it at the side of Michael's placemat.

"We're ready to order," said Johnny to the waitress. "Got any specials?"

"Only the *babotie*." She dipped down awkwardly to retrieve the dropped fork. "But it's the real thing, done proper." As she stood, the left strap of her brassiere caught at her collarbone, while her dress fell partly off the same shoulder. She made no move to adjust her clothing, and the beauty of her restraint became by itself a rebuke to the two men, though she intended no rebuke.

"We'll both have the special," said Johnny, handing back the menus.

"Two specials, then." She noted the order redundantly upon her pad and was gone.

"The special must be good," Michael observed, to fill the silence in which his first fork was, in the minds of the two men, still clattering to the floor.

"Looked it, ay?"

Michael nodded gravely. "She looked it."

They assessed each other anew and smiled. A kind of recovery.

"Well, for whatever it's worth, I was always sure of you," said Michael, "and if we don't have that much time, let's just hit it— whatever it is we're going to talk about." He dropped his spoon off the side of the table without the least attempt at discretion. "Like, I already know something's up, because even though it may not be my country in the personal sense, I could see we got out of the airport too easy for my personal taste. So now what I wonder is—"

The waitress returned to pick up the spoon.

"Can't stay away from you, love," Johnny said to her, touching her back.

"S'okay," she answered over her shoulder as she left. "I like a lot of attention."

"What I wonder," Michael continued, watching her sashay off, "since I'm naturally curious, is who's being set up for what, when? Probably this is what we want to talk about? I mean, I've got a sense for fast, and this is getting fast."

Johnny sat back in his seat.

"Like, I'm thinking maybe it's the concert tomorrow?" Michael paused to spread his napkin across his lap. "Keep the principals in one place? Given the Emergency Laws? But *I* don't know shit; I'm out of my league." He affected to smooth his napkin, then, unable to restrain himself, looked up wickedly. "Hey, you got a thing for Nomanzi, right? I can see it. Does that figure in this, maybe?"

Johnny put a hand over his face and laughed. "You're good, man. You're too good."

"But I'm done," said Michael. He took a sip of ice water. "So where are Chenny and Nomanzi?"

"They're visiting their mother in Nyanga, just outside of town."

"Legal?"

"No."

"And Petra?"

"Doesn't know they're gone."

"When are they coming back?"

"Tonight, I hope. Before daybreak tomorrow anyway." He took a sip of his ice water. "Can't pretend it's not a risk—they've got none of the permits, and maybe you're right about the setup, but . . . intimidation only works if you show you're intimidated, ay?"

"Even if you feel intimidated, you mean."

"That's my way of thinking."

"Mine too."

It was a moment of peace. The waitress arrived with their meals and, recognizing the change of mood at the table, said nothing except that she hoped that Michael and Johnny were hungry. Indeed the portions were large. Indeed the men were hungry. They thanked her.

"Well, it's obvious to me," said Michael after a couple of bites, "that a whole lot more is going on here than meets the eye. My eye, I mean."

Johnny's own eyes twinkled. "I was about to say the same thing to you."

"Nomanzi and Sylvia," said Michael. "What's your take?"

"Diplomats' daughters," said Johnny.

"Right," said Michael.

They ate.

"How about Petra?" Michael added after a while. "I mean, fuck— she's got the cards."

Johnny nearly choked with laughter.

"You think I'm wrong?"

"No, I think"—Johnny waved over Michael's shoulder—"I think Petra's about five meters behind us and approaching fast."

Both men wiped their mouths with their napkins and stood to greet Petra. She had a small piece of pink paper clutched in her hand, and she didn't look quite awake.

"Hi, guys. I got hungry."

They hastened to pull up a chair for her, and she gratefully sat down.

"I thought maybe Nomanzi and Chentula might be with you. Everything okay?" She still held the half-crumpled slip of pink paper.

"Didn't they say something about going out shopping?" Michael suggested to Johnny.

"Yeh. Spring sales on . . . something like that."

"Oh." Petra slumped back in her chair. She glanced at herself in the amoeba-shaped mirror that happened to adhere to the wall directly across from her. "Just, you know, after what happened in the airport, I was kind of worried." She began to fold her hair over itself so it might look amusingly disheveled instead of just slept-on. "Darlings, could you order something for me—something maybe vegetable?" She pretended a pout. "I've just got to run off to the ladies'." She smiled and swept off.

When the waitress arrived, she asked Johnny whether he'd mind coming up front; the girls were dying for, well, an autograph or, y'know, something.

"You mean Chenny and me really have fans?" He got to his feet. "Can't waste a second, then. But maybe you could bring a yogurt for our lady friend? And hold the monkey gland sauce?"

Alone at the table, Michael turned over the hotel telephone message Petra had left behind.

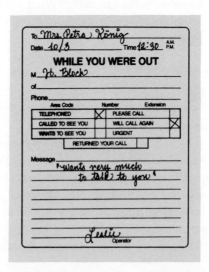

Lipstick traces, decided Michael, returning the note to its spot by Petra's place setting. *Skid marks.* He recalled the scene at the Paris airport—the demonstrators with their signs—and in a nonspecific way he felt confirmed in his intuitions as to how things were probably now going in the world.

From the far end of the restaurant, Johnny sheepishly made his way back toward the table.

Michael looked down at the fresh fork with which the waitress had provided them. It seemed like an extension of his hand.

He was very far from home.

"Hi. It's Sylvia Walters in 2711," said Sylvia Walters into the hotel phone. "I just wondered if there were any messages for me."

She had already tried Petra's room, Nomanzi's room, and the room shared by Johnny and Chentula.

"No, missus," came the reply. "There's nothing here."

She thanked the man and hung up.

Earlier, after having woken to discover Michael gone, she had fallen almost immediately asleep again. While it was uncharacteristic for her to return so easily to rest, she had come to realize that in all likelihood she was now going to have to revise her idea of what was, from anybody's point of view, characteristic. For example, she was still wearing a cocktail dress, and for some reason her underpants lay in the middle of the hotel room's carpet.

Everything reminded her she was pregnant.

She removed the dress, took a very hot shower, and afterward spread a pair of bath towels across the bed's pillows so that her hair could dry peaceably. There was a way of considering the world in which whatever came next might only involve the people she loved, but of course she'd been bred to realize that private life was a privilege.

Was she privileged?

She fumbled for the remote and turned on the television.

Whatever private life was.

"And today," said a woman with a large amount of oddly motionless blond hair, "what seemed to have been developing into a crisis turned into"— she widened her eyes for the camera—"a burst of sunshine."

The program cut to a shot of a young man standing in the desert. His skin had an attractively leathery quality, and he squinted engagingly at his viewers. "Just yesterday," he said into his microphone, "relations between this country and the United States seemed to be reaching an impasse. The American President's refusal of a bilateral investigation into the car-bombing of that nation's consulate in Geneva—a terrorist act for which a seemingly fictitious group here in South Africa has claimed credit—left officials in Pretoria baffled. This morning, however, a present arrived."

The man glanced over his shoulder, and the camera's eye flew with the obedience of a trained falcon in the indicated direction.

Sylvia sat suddenly up in bed. She turned up the volume.

VOICE-OVER: This tower is a solar power plant. It is made of steel, concrete, and solar receptors. [*Close-up of several sunburned white men at work in hard hats. The crew appears American— lean, tall, and thin-lipped. A winch is raising a large device to the tower's top.*]

SYLVIA: [*Hurling the remote to the bedside carpet*]: You fucks!

VOICE-OVER: It's a way to turn this drought to some advantage— and certainly we all agree that anything can help now—but more than that . . .

[*The picture returns to the newscaster, handsomely dissheveled in the desert wind.*]

NEWSCASTER: It's a certain indication that our allies are, however bumpy the road, still with us. [*Smiles.*] Robert Chisholm, reporting from the Kalahari.

Sylvia charged the television. She wanted to turn it off, but she wanted to turn it off with her body. Her thumb sufficed.

I've given up on fear, Sylvia told herself, as the room's buzzer buzzed.

She took a terry-cloth robe from the bathroom and, wrapping herself in its guileless density, answered the door.

There was no one there.

At first she was terrified, then she saw the large, beef-fed man standing with his two girl-children at the door of the adjacent room. He was once again pressing the room's buzzer. That was the sound Sylvia had heard. Smiling wanly, she waved at the children.

She closed the door and locked it. After a moment she sat back down on the bed's edge. A number of thoughts occurred to her.

One of them was that now she was really terrified, and that terror could induce a kind of calm.

She looked for a cigarette. But she looked for it without even moving her eyes.

"Paul, man! Where have you been?" Lolombela lunged angrily up the broken marble slabs set into the forest slope at the top of which Walters, just back from lunch with Bloch, had seated himself.

"I had to elude my aides," Walters called.

Flanking him, at the hill's crest: a pair of granite busts, giganticized women from whose breasts thin streams of water spouted vigorously into moss-covered troughs.

"A moment of solitude before the finale," said Walters, standing to greet his colleague. The conference hall was just out of sight behind them. The afternoon negotiations were about to begin. "Those guys are supposed to be working for me," Walters added, removing his pipe from his mouth, "but sometimes they get on my nerves."

Lolombela's brow was furrowed with suspicion, and under his arm he carried a newspaper.

Walters gestured to the spread-out newspaper—latest edition—upon which he himself had been sitting. "Sit, old friend. We'll talk."

After staring fiercely into the American's eyes, Joseph sat, and Paul sat down beside him.

"I wonder where Heinrich is," Walters inquired, relighting his pipe.

"He's back in his quarters, making phone calls."

"I didn't set out to have lunch with him or anybody," said Paul Walters. "But Heinrich found me."

Lolombela plucked a stalk of nearby grass and put it between his teeth. He appeared to relax somewhat.

"Our Heinrich seemed"—Walters turned to face Lolombela—"sort of upset to me. Have you spoken to him?"

"I saw him return. He seemed upset, yes. Distraught."

The sounds to be heard in a forest bower on an early-autumn

afternoon—birdsong, the buzz of insects, the touch of breeze-blown leaf against breeze-blown leaf—is calming to men and women no doubt because it is so easy to imagine that these sounds have preceded every human life and will likewise persist beyond the last of them.

A silence passed between the two men on the elegantly broken steps.

"For us, here," said Lolombela, "it will be decided this afternoon. After all we have said."

"I hope so too." Walters looked at his pipe. He loved this oddly half-shaped piece of briar, but now he saw that it was time to let it go. So he dropped it gently into one of the troughs given flow by the granite-breasted women behind them, and both he and Lolombela watched it dip and ride with absurd buoyancy into the stream below.

Joseph shook his head balefully.

"The equipment is in place in the Kalahari," Walters said.

"Yes."

"The tower is armed; you know we saw to that."

"Yes. We weren't sure before, but—" He sighed heavily. "Yes."

Walters sat a bit more upright. "Do you know that I was aware you weren't being straight with me when you told me it was Bloch who first approached you about the three of us having our . . . conversations? I always knew it was you who approached him."

Lolombela did not answer.

"Anyway, I did know." Walters laughed quietly. "Hell, it seemed okay to me."

"Protocol, man," Lolombela began. "I had—"

"Joseph—no shit from you now. I'm telling you, it seemed okay to me. And I haven't spoken to anyone about this, but I decided from the beginning that the only one of the three of us who might really want to see this bomb go off was Heinrich." He began to empty his tobacco pouch into the little stream of water passing by his side.

"What I hear now in your voice," said Lolombela, "is that you have trust in Heinrich Bloch but not in me."

"No," said Walters. "I'm sure about you." He took his tobacco pouch between two fingers and flipped it overhand into the stream as if he were dealing a playing card face up. "And now I'm ninety-nine percent certain of Heinrich too, because I see he's figured out that the three of us are stuck with each other, for better or worse."

"You spoke differently in Paris," said Lolombela.

"So did you," Walters reminded him.

There was a small bustle in the newly fallen leaves halfway down the slope, and both men caught a glimpse of a hedgehog making a hasty departure.

Lolombela frowned and nodded to acknowledge the irrelevance of whatever had happened in Paris. He tossed away the stalk of grass he'd been chewing. "But what made you change your mind about our German friend?"

"Funny you should use the word 'friend,' because that was part of it." Walters, picking up the piece of his own genetic coding that went with the word he'd just singled out, decided to go flat-out American for a moment. "Fella asked me if we could have a conversation 'just between friends,' and I said 'Sure.' "

"It was a personal matter."

"Yes."

"Petra König."

"Yes."

"So it was true about his opponents in the German Republics."

Walters saw that his tobacco pouch—a fine piece of Moroccan leather lined with nylon—had caught on a twig at the foot of the fountain. "Well, I don't know what 'it' is, but since you and I are also having a purely friendly conversation, I'd have to say, 'Yes, it is.' "

Lolombela heaved another enormous sigh. "In the press tomorrow, I suppose."

"Now of course I wouldn't really know about that. Probably it all depends."

The forest offered another silence. When it had deepened sufficiently, Paul Walters said, "You and I, Joseph—we *are* having a purely friendly conversation?"

"Oh, Paul, man, yeh."

"Good. Because there's one other thing I think you should know. And it was a surprise to me."

Lolombela was smiling. He had begun shaking his head in some form of relief.

"The whole Petra König crew—my daughter and yours, Chentula and this Johnny fella—their flight out of Paris was diverted from Johannesburg to Cape Town without explanation."

Joseph was on his feet in a second, his face seething. "But you know what that means!"

A falcon cried, or, no farther away, a set of radial tires screeched to a halt.

"Old friend," said Walters, standing now also. "You, Heinrich, and I have managed to remind each other that after all we're only men. Let's finish it up today"—he gestured with his chin back toward the conference hall behind them—"and then go on with the rest."

A falcon cried.

"Of course I know what it means," Walters added, vexedly pushing a hiker's discarded orange peel into the moss with his toe. "It means nothing at all."

When Michael returned to his hotel room, Sylvia was sitting on her legs in a round-backed upholstered chair. Nomanzi was sitting in a similar chair. The television was on, and both women were in bathrobes.

"We were kind of wondering where you were," Sylvia said, looking only once away from the TV screen.

"I was shopping," Michael said. He held three boxes. "Spring sale," he said.

A pause.

"But fuck it." Dropping the boxes.

Sylvia shifted her hips, extended her legs, and then with a kind of half hop was in his arms. "Darling," she said.

Nomanzi watched.

"I'm not feeling too good about this," Sylvia whispered into his ear.

"I love you too," said Michael just loud enough for Nomanzi to hear. He kissed Sylvia on the cheek and then disengaged from her embrace. "Anyway," he continued, "Johnny and Petra and I had lunch, and he mentioned that"—he directed his words toward Nomanzi—"that you and Chenny had gone shopping." Michael picked up the boxes. "Which seemed like a good idea to me. So—" He gave one of the gift-wrapped purchases to her. "I hope you like it."

Nomanzi received the package with the cupped hands that she had been taught as a child formed the gesture of graceful thanks. Later, she had been taught to satirize this graciousness. Still later, now, she found the gesture restored to her as her own.

She stood immediately and kissed Michael on the cheek. "You are very generous, Michael. Thank you."

In his pleasure and confusion, he handed the second box to Sylvia while saying to Nomanzi, "Oh, no, I was just trying to waste some time, and—"

"But Chenny and I didn't go shopping," Nomanzi continued, still looking squarely at him. "We went to visit our mother in Nyanga, that township we saw on the way from the airport. She has been relocated there."

Sylvia froze.

"Petra's the only one who doesn't know," Nomanzi concluded, even as she began to unwrap her present. "We didn't want to scare her."

"It went okay?" Michael asked.

"Oh," said Nomanzi, throwing the purple-and-green scarf around her neck. "It's beautiful." She walked to the mirror and began to arrange the scarf variously to accord with her own beauty. "Just lovely."

Sylvia's present was a nightgown, also lovely.

After a while, Michael put the third box, which was for Petra, on the dresser. None of the three looked at it again.

"You're the first person we've told," Sylvia confided to Nomanzi while Michael poured himself a drink. "But"—she looked at herself, dressed in her new nightgown—"I'm pregnant."

Chentula turned on the television in the room he and Johnny were sharing.

"Today," said a pink-skinned newscaster with tie to match, "the United States, in what was clearly meant as a further gesture of solidarity with this country, sent half its Sixth Fleet to the shores of South Africa."

Johnny picked up the remote and punched the channel buttons. There, suddenly, was Sylvia—wearing sunglasses and reclining in a lounge chair on what appeared to be a gigantic pool table.

"It's us," said Chentula.

"They're fast," said Johnny. He turned up the sound until it filled the room.

"Gentlemen," said Heinrich Bloch, rising to his feet at the conference table in Compiègne. "In a moment of historical necessity, we have proceeded historically." He paused for translations. He had known, even as he had cast the oak leaves from the table he had shared with Paul Walters at lunch, that if things went well he would want to deliver what amounted to the conference's benediction. And of course German was no more difficult a language than English.

Paul Walters reached out of habit for his pipe, then remembered what he had done with it.

"Even we," Bloch continued, "cannot know the full extent of what we have accomplished."

Lolombela was sorting nervously through the breast pocket of his jacket.

The Cape Town hotel boasted a nightclub in its subbasement, under the parking lot. In an unspoken concession to prudence, Petra and Nomanzi, Sylvia and Michael, Johnny and Chentula, had decided to dine in the hotel that night. Now, in an unspoken concession to boredom, all six of them were sitting at a table watching a cowboy-and-Indian act on the circular stage before them.

The Indians were all women dressed in body stockings and improbably scanty buckskin dresses with cut-out scoops for their breasts. The cowboys wore black or white hats and shirts that seemed to be made of red bandannas. The whole, all-white ensemble was lip-synching to the sound track of *Oklahoma* and writhing inexpertly over one another.

"Vegas," said Petra. "Only worse."

The waiters, however, were black. They wore sunglasses that

bore a line of tiny blinking lights—green and white in alternation—running across the tops of the frames.

"Weird," said Michael, ordering another round of drinks. "Kind of like traffic signs."

Sylvia intervened. "Nomanzi tells me," she said to Chentula, "that you two took a drive-by past the concert site today." Part of not drinking or smoking because you were pregnant involved introducing topics of conversation. "So what'd it look like?"

"They're really nearly done with the stage. Girders, wood beams, and planks; even got cloth bunting, y'know?" Chentula smiled. "They're really doing it."

On the stage before them, one of the cowboys produced a fair imitation of a six-shooter. When he pulled the trigger, it shot gaseous blue and yellow flames unconvincingly ceilingward.

Petra downed her drink. "Am I the only one who saw the warnings on TV to stay away from the concert?"

"Carrot and stick," said Nomanzi.

"It won't work," said Johnny. "District Six is ours tomorrow."

In the ladies' room of the club, Sylvia, after redoing her lipstick, turned to the elderly white matron sitting on the stool by the door. Sylvia explained that she was an American tourist thinking of taking the Kalahari package tour but that she'd heard the area was in the hands of revolutionaries "or something" and could not really be considered safe. She handed the woman a five rand note and continued to rummage through her bag, looking for her perfume.

"Oh, you mustn't believe everything you see in the world press." The woman stood, her tip already tucked away in the front pocket of her perfectly starched apron. "The desert is as safe as it's always been for man or beast."

"But what is this 'Azania'?" Sylvia purposely mispronounced the word.

"Like a political party, really," the woman continued, handing her a towel. "We are a nation of separate development, ay?" She sat back down upon her stool. "Separate ways for each tribe—British, Afrikaner, Zulu, Coloured, all of us." She brightened. "My husband and I would go on that tour in a second, y'know. He's always been foolish about the desert."

Sylvia snapped her purse shut. Minidroplets of sprayed perfume still hovered in the air about her. "Thank you," she said, smiling too.

"Mrs. König," said the man at the desk. "A message for you."

Petra, who had excused herself early from the gathering at the nightclub, stopped. It was another missed call from Heinrich; again no return number. She thanked the man and took the elevator up to her room.

Recalling that she'd decided not to become overly curious just yet, she tore the message slip into little pieces and flushed them down the toilet. Tomorrow or the next day would be soon enough to speak to him.

Lying upon the bed in only her underwear, she wondered whether it would maybe be a good idea to ask Nomanzi, Michael, and Sylvia to stay away from the concert tomorrow. She had an obligation to protect her actress and crew.

After a while she removed her brassiere, stood before the mirror, and tried to gauge the effect. She judged the effect okay to good. She removed her earrings and went to sleep.

"Block-building," said Michael, much later that night. He was asleep and Sylvia had been drowsing next to him, her bedside light still on.

Rolling toward him, she was at first confused by the bind she felt against her body. Then she remembered it was the nightgown he had given her. She touched his shoulder. "Block-building?" she asked him gently. "What about block-building?"

But he said no more.

"This man was the first for breakfast," said the captain to his waiter. "No one else! Even now there is no one else!"

It was true: the dining room of the Cape Town hotel—an orange-and-green expanse—was again empty on this early Tuesday morning.

"And this man, he asked only for a glass of orange juice?" the captain continued.

"Yes," said the waiter, making delicate shoveling gestures of appeal with his hands and afterward looking theatrically to the left and right. "I saw, he drank the whole glass down. He asked where was the men's room. I brought him"—it was the compelling evidence—"a menu!" The menu lay upon the table.

"Yes," said the captain in doleful agreement. His forehead was gathered in wrinkles of concern. Approaching the table, he picked up the glass. It was full.

The waiter, by classification a "Coloured," was easily fifteen years younger than his professional superior.

"Who is this man?" said the captain, himself a "Black" who had been reclassified as "Coloured" after several applications and a lengthy examination of his hair's texture by a "White" magistrate. "Where is he from?"

Sorting through his checks, although indeed only one was yet written upon, the waiter said, "Mr. William Waters. In room 816."

"Oh, Mr. Waters." The captain's forehead unfurrowed like a set of window blinds going suddenly down. "Then it is no problem. Not with this man."

"Not a problem?"

"He has paid his bill far in advance and asked us to take his expenses out of it."

The waiter again examined what was written on the check he held: " 'Mr. William Waters'? I am right?"

Clapping the man on his shoulder, the captain said, "You are right." He spied a young white couple entering the dining room, turned as if to greet them, and looked again at his waiter. "But why the orange juice is still full? You must have brought another one?"

"Yes," said the waiter, thinking of his job, thinking of his family, then scribbling another entry on the bill of Mr. William Waters. "I must not have remembered to write it up."

"Do not worry. Mr. Waters has paid in advance."

The waiter nodded gravely.

"Mr. Waters is a very good customer," said the captain, leaving to attend the new arrivals.

"I will not inquire how you arranged it," said Heinrich Bloch.

" 'It'?" said Paul Walters. The two men—the present negotiations settled—had run into each other by chance as they ambled across the lawn toward what was for the time being their last breakfast in Compiègne. They were going to be out of there on time after all.

"How you and your government kept Petra König out of the media."

"Oh, believe me, Heinrich; it wasn't just me *or* my government." He put a hand briefly on his German colleague's shoulder. "But I do believe that a friendly conversation deserves friendly consideration."

The statement not to test-detonate the fission bomb had, after some pointed but basically routine polemics from the Eastern European and Japanese emissaries, been signed unanimously. Walters was to be driven to Paris, flown surreptitiously to Geneva, where he was supposed to be anyway, and emerge with the American Secretary of State to read the agreement to the press in sobriety and hope.

"Were you able to get in touch with Petra?"

"Not yet," Bloch answered. "And you? You have spoken to your daughter in Azania?"

"No." The truth was a bit more elaborate: Walters had judged it imprudent to call her there on the day of what he foresaw would come to be known as the "Geneva Agreement." The day before, when he had counseled Heinrich to call Petra in Cape Town, he had seen no such danger. He remained convinced that there had been none.

"*Messieurs*," said Bataillard, catching up with the two men. "*Mes chers amis.*" He wore an elaborately tailored three-piece suit, and his manner was a bit formal for someone attending a celebratory country breakfast.

"Good morning," said Bloch. Then, switching to French, he added, "No doubt it is because of the quality of French mornings that we have come so far together here in Compiègne."

Bataillard smiled. "It will give me pleasure to think of it that way." He moved between the two men and put his arms loosely around their shoulders. "You know, I have not seen our colleague Monsieur Lolombela yet this morning."

"Nor I," said Walters. "But he never misses breakfast."

"*Bien*. It is only that I cannot be unaware of how barbarically he was taken from his reunion with his daughter in Paris." Bataillard released his colleagues without slowing his pace and inspected the skies as if it might indeed be true that it was in the sheer beauty of France that the world's good resided. "So if I or my nation can be of any help in arranging a more protracted reunion . . ."

Bloch stiffened a little as the three men continued to walk through the wet grass.

"I am sure Mr. Lolombela will appreciate your generous offer," said Walters in French, "and if we see him before you do, we shall certainly convey this message."

"Thank you," said Bataillard in English. Smiling reflectively, he bade the two men goodbye. "*Bonne chance, mes amis.* Certainly we shall meet again soon."

"*Certainement,*" said Bloch.

Paul Walters was in his quarters, packing, when his chief aide told him the President was on the line.

Walters and the President exchanged wry pleasantries of the sort favored by American men who have recently been made aware of their own mortality. The President congratulated Walters on the agreement that had just been concluded in Compiègne. Paul Walters could still taste a film of café au lait on his palate as he listened to these commendations, and he was forced to scrape his tongue against his teeth in order to respond comfortably.

Both men, each of them deduced, were in good health.

The President said there might be some problem with the Americans installing the tower in the Kalahari, although he personally doubted it. But maybe it would be a good idea to get to Paris a little early and talk in confidence with Perry at the embassy. Perry had been fully briefed. Then on to Geneva as planned, since you always have to beat the news media on anything like this one, a historical agreement, no question about that—hell, the stupid things you have to . . .

Walters made the various sounds of no problem, on my way, etc. The two men went on with a few pleasantries, this time regarding their families.

After a while, Walters hung up. Mentally he replayed the conversation he'd just had with the Chief Executive of the United States.

Things, Walters concluded, were much worse than he'd thought. He, Joseph, and Heinrich were being hung out to dry.

Three hundred and fifty meters away, in the crook of a larch, there was an abandoned thrush nest. A female cuckoo alighted upon it. In the spring, in keeping with the habits of her species, she might well have laid her own eggs in this alien nest. But it was autumn. She ruffled her chestnut-brown feathers in the chill and used the nest as a break against the breeze. It was time to fly to warmer terrain.

LOLOMBELA [*Regarding for the second time, and now with some irritation, the set of stag horns mounted above the fireplace in the quarters to which Paul Walters had been assigned for his stay in Compiègne*]: I have never understood the origin of this English expression, "cuckold." [*Reaches out to touch the point of one of the stag-horn tines.*] Why is the horn of an animal associated with faithlessness?

WALTERS [*Looking first at his closed luggage, then at Lolombela*]: Why is powdered rhinoceros horn considered an aphrodisiac?

LOLOMBELA [*Turning abruptly around to face his colleague*]: Have you felt at all this morning that perhaps our agreement here has cuckolded a world that has been even denied the privilege of watching us determine its fate?

WALTERS: Yes, Joseph. Of course. But I decided that in thinking that, I was being, for myself anyway, too sentimental. What I can contribute I have contributed.

LOLOMBELA [*Walking slowly to the window, his hands clasped behind his back*]: I have decided to return to Azania.

WALTERS: Bataillard?

LOLOMBELA: With or without his intercession.

WALTERS: The world cannot afford to have you jailed.

LOLOMBELA [*Smiling mordantly*]: You're kind, man. But the world can always afford to have someone jailed. It's what a *man* can afford that keeps the world in some small way honest.

WALTERS [*Smiling no less mordantly*]: You have always had one of the most complicated senses of humor I've ever known, Joseph. [*Pause. Walters, too, should be seen as thinking more than he's showing. Then: a softening of his gaze*] But don't go, old friend. [*Touches Lolombela's shoulder.*] Don't go yet.

The cuckoo, still sitting in the thrush's nest, turned its head nervously from side to side. It knew the time to fly was soon. It knew the time to fly was not yet.

And it was spring in Southern Africa, in Cape Town, one time zone to the east and many kilometers to the south of Compiègne! And it was late afternoon, a perfect afternoon, the afternoon before Tsotsi's evening concert, which everyone was technically forbidden to attend! But allowed to attend!

Whatever a time zone is, anyway. Or a kilometer.

"Darling," said Petra to the hotel manicurist. "Maybe another coat of polish? It's so"—she waved her fingernails about in the air before her face—"opalescent."

Since ascertaining that her production assistant and film crew had arrived safely from Johannesburg, Petra had grown more relaxed in her attitude toward that evening's concert. As far as she could tell, the TV warnings to avoid the gathering were no longer being aired, and although she had seen quite a number of troop carriers headed out in the direction of District Six, Nomanzi had assured her that this kind of military movement was routine, more a show of force than anything else. Besides, the local police had not made the least effort to stop young white volunteers from distributing handbills for the concert to anyone in town who would take one.

"Are you here on vacation, then?" said the manicurist, gently admonishing Petra, with a touch of her own hand, to keep her fingers still.

"Not really. Mostly work."

"First time?"

"Yes; I'm from Los Angeles."

"Well, you can't imagine how things have changed here over the last few years," the manicurist went on. "Like the Tsotsi concert tonight over on the mountain. Never would have seen that kind of thing two years ago. An' in a State of Emergency, d'y'know! I can tell you I'm going."

Johnny and Chentula had been out at the concert site all day,
except once when they returned to consult with Nomanzi about an
extra set of power lines for the lights and amplifiers. Petra had
overheard the words "for insurance."

"So you think it's safe, then?" Petra inquired.

"Oh, yes, it's all extra-organized." The girl started on Petra's
other hand. "Internal Security wouldn't have let it happen otherwise."

Petra studied the girl's long blond eyelashes thoughtfully. The
best thing might be for her whole contingent to go to the concert.
That way, if by some chance anything did go wrong, Petra could
keep all her principals together and arrange to get them out.

She waved her free hand negligently to hasten the drying of her
nail polish, and as she did, she caught sight of her watch: 5:45.

"I guess it's time to start getting ready, then," she said.

Upstairs, back in the hotel after a day of tourism, Sylvia and
Michael were also getting ready for the Tsotsi concert. They were
dressed only in blue jeans. Sylvia reclined in the Masterlounge with
a plastic cocktail cup of water in her hand; Michael paced back and
forth by the window.

"All I'm saying," Michael said, "is that it's one thing to enter
some kind of war zone when you're responsible to nobody but
yourself. But now we've got a third party to think about. He paced.
"So think about it."

" 'It'?" Sylvia had been quite sick that morning but had recovered
quickly. "If you even begin to think of our baby as 'it,' you'll see
special effects you've never dreamed of. And I don't mean from
me."

Michael wheeled violently around toward her. "Listen to me.
What about all those soldiers we saw today? What about all that
barbed wire?" They had taken a cable car to the top of Table Mountain, and in passing over—or rather by—District Six, they had been
surprised by the thoroughly military aspect of the concert site below. "Don't you fucking remember what you said? 'People are going
to get hurt down there.' Your exact words, I believe?"

Turning to face the television, he switched it on. She used the remote to turn it off. "I was making touristy remarks," she answered. "I was checking the ways of the world."

"The fuck you were."

Sylvia stood and approached Michael.

When she had his attention, though he had not turned to face her, she said, "Michael, we both know you're a dangerous man to love. I don't deny I've cultivated it."

She turned and he looked at her fully.

"Okay, I've cultivated it," she continued.

Michael watched her wander from him again.

"What I'm wondering now," she went on, "is whether you know that there's nothing I hate more than being protected."

"How could I not know that?" He followed her with his eyes, then his body. "None of this would have happened if we weren't . . ."

"Good," she said. "Good." Wandering.

The impulse to shake her into another kind of sense passed through Michael, but he resisted it. He put the impulse into his voice. "Where do you think we are, you crazy bitch?"

"We're in Cape Town, in a hotel." She made no move to escape his grasp. "We're two people who don't believe in having someone else protect us. So where we are is here. Now we're here; wherever we go next, that's where we'll be. Always like that."

The air-conditioning kicked in again. The chill caused Sylvia's nipples, just inches away from Michael's own bare chest, to pucker. It came to Michael that fear was a kind of modesty toward which both he and Sylvia thought they aspired when it was all too obvious that fear could have them any old time it liked.

"It was when I told you about this Bloch guy's call to Petra that all this evil shit really started between us, wasn't it?" he said.

Without warning, Sylvia commenced tearing at his bare shoulder with her teeth and fingernails. He crushed her body to his to stop her, then, grabbing a handful of her hair, slowly drew her head back so he could look at her. His love. His wife-to-be. The mother of their child.

"Yes," she said when they'd each looked their fill. "That was when."

The temper of their embrace changed utterly. She rested her head on the shoulder she had seconds ago attacked. She told him she loved him. After all, she was probably just shifting some of her protective feelings from her father to Michael. Otherwise why wouldn't she have told him how scared she really was? Otherwise why would her own fear have ceased to matter?

The fuck with it, she thought, plucking from her drawer a T-shirt imprinted with the logo of a commercially successful but talentless American rock band. The shirt's colors—black, green, and yellow—were the national colors of the purely rhetorical state of Azania.

"You know," said Michael, still rooting through his suitcase, "I'm looking for something in black, green, and yellow."

"You know," said Sylvia, as demurely as possible under the circumstances, "you already have her."

When he did a slow about-face to see what she meant, he discovered once again, but shyly now and with a depth of gratitude he'd not known before, that he did.

The phone rang. Sylvia answered.

"Hi, lovie, it's me," said Petra. "Nomanzi is here with me, and we thought we'd all go over to the concert together; I mean, if you two feel up to it?"

"Oh, yes. We're going." Over the phone Sylvia could hear ice cubes rattling in a tilted glass and the sound of Petra swallowing what would certainly be, as it always was in such moments for Petra, Scotch. "We were just about to call you."

"Super. Because"—Petra swallowed again—"Nomanzi's got it all scoped out about where to leave the car and everything. I mean, I've never really thought about parking *this* far east of the Hollywood Bowl, right? Plus, a bunch of the boys from the picture are coming along too, and this would be a great chance for everyone to get acquainted."

Boys? thought Sylvia. But what she said was: "When do you want us?"

"Anytime. Now." Petra's voice found its optimistic producer's register again. She paused. "What are you wearing, lovie?"

"Oh, you know: just jeans and a T-shirt."

There was another pause. "Maybe fifteen minutes, then. Okay?"

"You got it." It seemed to be the sentiment of the evening. Sylvia hung up.

"What'd she say?" Michael asked. He was standing before her in one sock. Sylvia giggled at him.

"She said," said Sylvia, rising to embrace him, "that she's never parked east of Pasadena before."

Petra's hotel room, when Michael and Sylvia arrived there eighteen minutes later, was faintly depressing to both of them. It was crowded with Americans whom Michael knew glancingly from his profession—indeed, he and Petra had hired them—but the sense of the gathering was oddly awry. After all, they weren't making a concert film.

Michael introduced Sylvia to some of the people she would be working with, then fell into a logistical conversation with Petra. Petra was wearing white jeans and a pearl-gray T-shirt of raw silk. Sylvia excused herself and sought out Nomanzi.

"How do you feel?" Nomanzi said.

"Strange," Sylvia answered. "But okay."

They walked, as if by prior arrangement, toward the bathroom. They entered it together and locked the door.

Nomanzi had spent much of her afternoon with Petra in order to calm her and keep track of her and be easily reachable. She had not seen the news report about the U.S.'s alleged donation of a solar power plant to White South Africa. She was the only woman in the present party who was wearing a dress, and she was also wearing the scarf Michael had given her.

Sylvia peeled down her jeans, sat immediately upon the toilet, and commenced to pee copiously. "I've always heard that when you're pregnant you don't do anything but pee," she said. "But I thought it was an old wives' tale."

Nomanzi leaned against the shower stall and smiled. "And now you know it is true—firsthand."

"No; now I know I'm an old wife."

They laughed.

"But I did hear something today, secondhand, that's kind of interesting." She glanced at Nomanzi. "I heard that Heinrich Bloch's been trying to call Petra here at the hotel."

Two women, daughters of diplomats. Two women who were for just a couple of minutes free of their countries and of any unchosen obligations.

The term "passing water" crossed Sylvia's mind.

"Well, then," said Nomanzi. "At least we know who else our fathers have been spending time with, eh?"

"I haven't spoken to mine since we left Paris." Sylvia stood, flushed the toilet, pulled up her jeans. "Have you?"

"No." Nomanzi walked over to one of the twin sinks and sat upon its ledge while Sylvia washed her hands in the other one. "The person who told you about these calls . . ."

"It was Michael. He saw one of the message slips the hotel had left for Petra."

"I don't s'pose there was a return number?"

"Nothing like that. Just that Bloch had called and would try again later."

"Yeh, yeh; diplomats, isn't it." Nomanzi looked over her shoulder at the impressive array of cosmetics Petra had deployed about the sink. She slipped lithely to her feet and picked up a jar of moisturizing cream. "Still, I don't quite see what it all has to do with us."

"Michael thinks his last picture—he was the special-effects artist—got killed by someone from Washington, and he's convinced this is all somehow connected."

Nomanzi began rubbing the cream experimentally into one dark cheek. "But how?"

"I don't know, but now there's this Kalahari business—"

Someone knocked on the door. "Are you *both* still in there?"

"What Kalahari business?"

Sylvia hurriedly dried her hands. "I'll tell you later." She started for the door. "Oh, but wait." From her pocket she pulled the third diamond earring. "I want you to have this."

Putting down the jar of skin cream, Nomanzi received the jewel. "But this is real, Sylvia. It must . . ." She made as if to hand it back. "No, you are very kind, but I can't accept this."

Sylvia closed her hand over Nomanzi's. "It's okay, it's okay. Just think of it as an extended loan. The other one is missing anyway."

"Probably they climbed out of the window," the voice outside the door seemed to be announcing to no one in particular.

"Here," Sylvia continued. "Let me put it on you." She did.

"Oh, Sylvia, I don't know what to say." Nomanzi looked at herself in the mirror, then turned and embraced her.

"Well, it's just for luck," Sylvia replied. "You're not supposed to say anything."

When they opened the door, Petra waved from across the room at Nomanzi. "Isn't it time, lovie?"

"Yes. We should go."

"Okay," Petra announced. "Everybody follow our car, and let's stick together, because it's bound to be, you know, just mobbed."

As Sylvia made her way over toward Michael, who was uncharacteristically pouring himself another drink, she got caught behind two exquisitely muscled young men from the lighting unit. One was talking animatedly to the other, who was idly shaking the ice in his empty plastic glass.

"No, really, you've got to hear this, it's just too priceless: If history repeats itself, once as tragedy, once as farce, what is it the third time?"

"I don't know," said his companion truculently. "What?"

"A Petra König Production."

Because the number of minor traffic accidents on the road back from Compiègne was unusually high but the verbal disputes that inevitably followed them were absolutely standard, it was not until shortly after dark that Paul Walters reached the American Embassy in Paris. He was not surprised that it was again Perry rather than the Ambassador who greeted him. In concession to the hour, however, the two men repaired to the so-called State Room, an elegant space impeccably fitted out in Louis Quinze furniture. At least here there would be no aquarium-bound basketballs to be inspected.

Walters accepted an Armagnac from Perry, clinked glasses, and observed to himself that the man looked unusually discommoded.

"Tell me, Perry," said Walters, "what else can possibly be up?"

The following things, it appeared, were up:

The white South African government had discovered that the "tower" (as Perry referred to it, out of either discretion or his own insufficient security clearance) had been erected in the Kalahari. A great point was being made of it on white South African TV, where newscasters referred to it as a "solar power plant, donated to the country by the U.S. in a gesture of solidarity." It was an unusually clumsy propaganda move on the part of the white government and almost certainly meant they had no clue as to what was actually going on.

At the same time, a great point was likewise being made in the white South African media of the U.S. warships currently off the coast of Azania (it was the first time Perry had used this national designation); they, too, were there in a "gesture of solidarity."

The announcement of the "New Geneva Accords," as they would be called, had been delayed until tomorrow morning so that Walters could be there when the American Secretary of State announced that the Western allies had, after careful consideration, unanimously endorsed an agreement not to test-detonate the fission bomb and so on as per everything he, Walters, already knew.

The U.S. would categorically deny any knowledge of a solar power plant in white South Africa, which nation, in any case, the U.S. no longer acknowledged. As for the American warships in African coastal waters, they were merely there as a part of a routine naval exercise, etc., etc.

Watching Perry pour himself another Armagnac, Walters noticed that the hand holding the decanter was trembling.

"Any harder evidence of Defense Department involvement in this thing with the President?" Walters took the opportunity to ask.

Perry glanced up quickly, overpoured his drink a touch, then replaced the decanter upon its silver tray. "Eyes only, but it's beginning to look that way." Perry turned his back on his colleague briefly and downed his drink in two gulps. When he faced Walters again, Perry would not meet his eyes, and Walters found himself concluding that he had just been lied to. The videotape image of the William look-alike came fleetingly back to him.

"Press?" he asked.

"Not on this one, thank Christ." Perry began rolling up his sleeves.

"What else, then?"

"Just this. Everyone back at State—and the President's really with us here, he really wanted me to give you the thumbs-up on this—they think it would be really useful if Joseph Lolombela were there for the Geneva announcement tomorrow. You know, to strengthen the Secretary's deniability position regarding all this white South African bullshit. Lolombela's presence, that's all."

"But when I left Compiègne, Joseph was talking about flying back to Azania." Once again, Walters had the impulse to reach for his pipe and recalled that he had discarded it. Okay, so timing was everything: then as now.

"I don't know where the guy wants to fly," Perry answered, "but right now he's waiting down the block in a gray rental Citoyen sedan. No driver, no bugs; we've had it checked out. There's a U.S. plane waiting at the airport to take you two to Geneva. Everyone's rooting for you. To convince him to go along with us on this, I mean."

Walters looked as calmly as he could at Perry. The man's hazel eyes held eagerness and fear in equal measure, and the flesh beneath them sagged with the weight of a hastily discarded sense of humor. He looked, in fact, like a ghost. Shifting in his chair, Walters reflected that somebody must have given the poor bastard a pretty hard time.

"Anybody tell you I can't drive?" said Walters.

"You . . . you mean . . . Well, what about—"

"Of course I can drive," said Walters, getting to his feet. "I'm a U.S. citizen." He put his hand on Perry's shoulder. "I just wondered if anyone had told you I couldn't drive."

Perry looked utterly defeated.

"Cheer up, bucko. It'll all work out. Now, anything else before I do the Le Mans to the airport?"

"Oh." Perry rummaged through the pants pocket of his suit and produced a slip of paper. "Yeah. Your daughter Kristen called, left a number."

Scanning the message, Walters saw that the international code was for Monaco. When he called the number, using the phone Perry had indicated, he discovered that he had phoned a hotel and that the newly wed Mr. and Mrs. Grandet were not in their room at the moment. So he reread the rest of Kristen's message: "We missed you, Daddy. I can't tell you how literally I mean that."

Perry was slumped in an armchair with his eyes closed as Walters hurried past him to seek Lolombela in the car he'd been told was parked nearby.

Obviously goodbyes were not in order.

"Shit," Michael heard someone from Petra's group say. "Anyone got a vid-cam, they best commence using it now or give it away to the lowest bidder."

It was true: the scene at Tsotsi's District Six concert was a bit more of everything than anyone concerned had imagined. Police with dogs rimmed the devastated ground that had once housed many people now removed to townships, and as if to set the terms of the game a little more clearly, shoulder-high tangles of barbed wire surrounded the police too.

"How many, Michael?" Sylvia said into his ear. "Just the audience."

"Week's box office of a hit movie in Westwood."

"No; seriously."

"Seventy thousand, maybe. A lot."

The opening act was finishing its encore. The stage was festooned with colorful banners, and the sound of the band, rebounding off the bulk of Table Mountain, was very loud indeed.

It was difficult for white Americans to know whether the situation was dangerous to them personally, since none of them had ever seen some fifty thousand nine hundred and sixty eight black Africans dance up and down in synchrony before. So maybe there were ten thousand white Africans in the audience as well. That only made the matter more complicated.

Sylvia said, "Food for thought." She realized she was hungry.

"All these lights," Petra observed, putting on her sunglasses. "This is what I call high production values."

Aha, thought Michael. *The lights.* But he realized he knew nothing in any real sense about what the fuck was going forward here, so he kept his mouth shut.

"This way," said Nomanzi. "There's supposed to be a place for us up front."

The crowd had begun to sing along with the opening band's finale, hitting the chorus on time, once in Zulu, once in Xhosa, once in English. Something about the spear that flies forever toward its target.

Sylvia noticed a white girl, no more than sixteen, jumping up and down in a pair of designer jeans. The label on the back pocket read "Freedom Brand Couture." Michael fell against Sylvia's shoulder for an alarming moment.

"You okay?" Sylvia asked him as he righted himself.

"Yeah. I just stepped on a rock or something."

The closer they got to the stage, the stranger they found their situation. The band was fronted by a chorus line of men in red jumpsuits who were performing dance moves that seemed a direct import from a Detroit that had vanished twenty years before, but the faces of the dancers held a concentration that was unmistakably other. Above them, a brightly colored banner proclaimed in spiky English lettering, "Azania, Africa: Alive!"

Michael bumped into two young men brandishing wooden replicas, obviously handmade, of Soviet-style automatic rifles. He doubted whether his mother, Russian-born though she was, would have understood the symbolism. He simultaneously realized he had begun to favor his hurt foot.

"Hey, look," said Sylvia. "That guy's selling ice cream."

"You want some?"

"Certainly not," Sylvia lied. "I mean, do you still believe that one about pregnant women craving ice cream?"

"No, pistachios is the one I still believe. Only I don't"—he craned his neck—"right now . . . see anyone selling . . ."

A substantial number of men in the crowd wore yellow hard hats. There were also schoolgirls in jumpers, university students in manifesto T-shirts, elderly white women with black sashes hung diagonally across their ample torsos.

"Here." Nomanzi herded her group into a small area that had been cordoned off with yellow nylon tape. As soon as the bunch of them had taken their designated place before the stage, Nomanzi ripped away both the tape and the poles that had supported it.

The gesture provoked scattered applause among those immediately adjacent to the reserved space, and the crowd pressed in past the discarded perimeters.

"There's Chenny," someone shouted.

Indeed it was true: Chentula and Johnny were walking about the stage, discreetly checking out a second bank of back-set amplifiers, returning periodically to the sound man, who was seated at his console all the way to the back of the stage, at the left.

"Isn't there going to be a break before Tsotsi comes on?" Sylvia yelled into Nomanzi's ear.

Nomanzi shook her head. "Permit law," she yelled back. "But just watch."

The first band had moved into a kind of call-and-response number with which the audience was apparently well acquainted: they sang the call as well as the response.

Michael noticed a dozen riot police, their helmets on and plexiglass masks down, standing atop the scaffolding on either side of the stage. They were each ostentatiously equipped with tear gas grenades, whips, and automatic rifles.

"Got a bunch of well-dressed cops here," Michael shouted into Sylvia's diamondless ear.

"What?" she answered.

He put an arm around her and kissed her on the temple.

The thing about special effects, he reflected, is that they're supposed to have the look of things without the substance. What you had here, with all these people and lights and music, was the substance. And substance always had its own look.

It further occurred to Michael that he was a slow learner.

"Who are those guys over there?" Petra shouted to Nomanzi. Several young blacks in green armbands and berets were walking watchfully about in the immediate vicinity of the stage.

"Volunteer marshals," Nomanzi yelled back. "The people's precaution." As the opening band entered an instrumental passage— keyboards, drums, guitars, brass—she began to hop up and down with the crowd. A subtle shift of rhythm was taking place. "Oh, I am so proud of them up there!"

One by one, the sixteen members of Tsotsi's expanded band—
all except Johnny and Chentula—wandered over to their instru-
ments and picked up their place in the music. The lights atop the
scaffolding shifted to form a circle of excruciating brightness near
the front of the stage. Observing a pair of white soldiers roll a man-
high coil of barbed wire across the nearest crowd exit, Michael said
to Sylvia: "If anything happens . . ."

"Nothing really bad can happen here tonight," Sylvia answered.
"There are just too many of us."

Michael bent down to loosen the laces on the shoe of his hurt
foot. He retied it with a double knot.

"More here than could fill Hollywood Bowl anyway," someone
behind Sylvia and Michael shouted to someone else. "On top of
which, there's no bowl here. Just, like, rocks and all."

An alleyway had opened up among the musicians at stage center,
and the line of male dancers had parted equally to the right and
left. They were bent over at the waist, backs perfectly parallel to
the floor, each of them doing a rotational watch-wheel kind of step
that had nothing at all to do with Detroit.

"What's 'Tsotsi' mean again?" Petra yelled at Sylvia. "The word,
I mean?"

Before Sylvia could answer, a pair of chiming guitar chords issued
from an unseen source at the back of the stage, reverberated off
the face of Table Mountain behind, and shot back out over the
crowd like magnesium flares. The audience roared, the two guitars
worked their chords out gradually into a filigree of notes that met,
meshed, bolted off in different directions, then chimed against each
other again like perfectly worked swords. Johnny and Chentula,
left- and right-handed respectively so that they faced each other as
they played, were walking slowly forward from the stage darkness
toward the spotlight circle at the front.

"Shit, man," said another of Petra's group. "They even got cordless guitars."

Chentula wore a many-colored shirt, olive-drab pants, and a
needlepoint skullcap of black, green, and yellow. Johnny wore work
clothes and leather leggings embroidered with the dried cocoons
of countless caterpillars. The two friends looked at each other as

they walked, taking their time with their stride but letting the music go further and further uptempo. Although they didn't smile at each other, they attempted no stagy scowls either.

A techy in a Tsotsi T-shirt ran in from the left and placed a stand-up microphone in the center of the spot, then retreated.

"Shit-fire," Michael heard himself say.

Without changing their pace, Johnny and Chentula walked into the spotlight and, at the end of the musical progression they'd been working, abruptly ceased playing. The rest of both bands played on. Johnny looked sternly about the audience, nodding to himself. Chentula remained impassive. A few measures later, the two men slowly took hold of each other's near hand, raised the double fist they'd made high above them, and after several further bars shouted with a single voice into the microphone: "Africa!"

The response was thunderous. "Africa!"

Johnny and Chentula spun away from each other and, bending over in the manner of the dancers on either side of them, addressed themselves with renewed vigor to their guitars.

The volume was such that had it not been for their lights, Michael would have failed to notice the three helicopters banking and re-banking overhead. They looked sort of innocent, like moths.

"Joseph," said Paul Walters, sliding into the passenger seat of the Citoyen that had been described to him.

"Hello, Paul."

Walters had some difficulty in finding the car, but the perfect posture and unswerving forward stare of the black man at the wheel were more recognizable to him than anything automotive.

"I don't know what you've been told," Walters began, "but I believe in you and I'm ready to play it either way."

"Either way."

"Both of us to Geneva, or just me."

Joseph, who had still not turned to look at Paul, began to laugh silently to himself.

"I'm speaking to you frankly, Joseph."

"Your people told you this car was secure?"

"Of course. But maybe my people would be wrong?"

Joseph turned to look at his friend. To the surprise of both men, there were tears on their cheeks. "My people looked this car over too, Paul. Nothing to worry about, they said." He reached into his jacket pocket and removed a sleekly designed machine no larger than a cigarette case. He handed it to Walters. "Only this."

It was a tape recorder, still running. Walters looked at the device as if it were some particularly perplexing bit of exotic fauna.

"Put it under the back wheel of the car," said Lolombela. "I'll run over it a few times. Then we'll go to Geneva."

Walters considered this. "What about Heinrich?"

"There's a phone in the back seat. I called the man, but Heinrich, he's tired too. He's on his way home."

"Home."

"Eh, eh, man—put it under the wheel."

Walters opened his door and did so. Joseph started the car, and when the destruction of the tape recorder had been satisfactorily accomplished, Walters got back in. They set out smoothly for the airport.

After many minutes Joseph said, "You know, man, I saw you notice me slapping my pockets at the closing session up there in Compiègne."

"Yeah. I was wondering what you'd lost."

"It was a commercial plane ticket to Cape Town. I'd already arranged for it. But as you saw, it was no longer with me."

"You really were going to go to Cape Town?" Walters discovered himself truly shaken. "Joseph." He turned halfway around in his seat to inspect his colleague. "What name did you use on the ticket?"

Joseph pulled fluidly onto the thoroughfare. "With Bataillard's permission," he said, glancing in the rearview mirror, "yours."

After a few seconds both men began to laugh.

"This whole city," Sylvia screamed into Michael's ear.

"What?" he replied. "I can't hear you."

She drew a breath and tried again. "This whole city," she yelled, jumping up and down with her arms around him. "It must be hearing this."

"Nah, baby, it's just they knew what was coming." He pointed vaguely to the helicopters above them.

Sylvia nodded exaggeratedly. "Me either," she said.

Since their arrival upon stage, Johnny and Chentula had not once let the music lag, although Chenny had exchanged his electric guitar for a guitar-shaped instrument with a keyboard across its face. He put on his gold-lensed shades, then moved with Johnny once more to the microphone:

> Spark is just a fire,
> Fire is just a light;
> Make a world of brightness,
> In the middle of the night.

"Hey," Petra communicated hoarsely to Michael, "who's that?" She made a subtle eyes-right in the direction of Nomanzi, who was speaking earnestly with a young man wearing a neon-blue wind-breaker and matching pants.

Michael believed he recognized Nomanzi's interlocutor as the man he'd seen Chentula talking to the previous morning, on the rooftop across from the hotel. But he couldn't be sure. "Petra, I'm new in the neighborhood."

She shrugged and decided to let it go. She adjusted her shirt.

"Hell of a concert, don't you think?" he added by way of compensation.

"When in hell," said Petra, shrugging her shirt back attractively across her shoulders, "do as the hellions do." She laughed at her own sally and slapped Michael on the back.

Woman's got guts, thought Michael of Petra. He shifted his gaze back to Nomanzi and Phopho, who continued to converse. The music softened by degrees—this, too, is all true—until only the two dozen hand-struck drums, amplified though they were, kept up the cadence that had been proposed by the audience's clapping hands.

Chentula advanced. He took the microphone from its stand and held it for a long time with his fingers. It was easy to see from far away that he did not let the mechanism touch his palm. The mike stand itself was spirited away by yet another techy. Chentula, using English words, addressed the crowd:

"We, Tsotsi, are home."

Johnny walked forward with a second microphone.

"This land belongs to all who live here," Chentula continued.

"All who live here," said Johnny, now shoulder to shoulder with Chenny, "belong to the land."

Another spotlight came on. After wandering slightly about the stage, its beam picked out the bass player, a thin black man in a porkpie hat and shades. He began to play.

"All men, all women, all their children," Chentula went on, "know of what we speak." The sound of the crowd and of the band had found a new equilibrium of deliverance and response.

The lights picked out another man on stage. He held a trumpet; he bowed to the crowd and began to play.

"This man has not been home in twenty-six years," said Chentula, but still he needs no introduction. Please welcome Mr. Miles Masekela."

Some burning things that had gone up in the air from the crowd floated down slowly as the man pushed the bell of his trumpet toward the microphone. Michael elbowed Sylvia and pointed to a detail of white riot police that was arriving atop the center of the stage with an array of what appeared to be tear-gas mortars.

"And we are all here for peace," said Johnny, in Xhosa.

"We are all here for freedom," said Chentula, in English.

"So welcome back one more of us," said Johnny as a brilliantly dressed woman in beads and *doek* walked forward, took the microphone handed her, and began to sing in a cascade of tongue clicks, glottal stops, and reined-in voice. "Aretha Makeba. Home again tonight after thirty-six years."

"Home!" the crowd roared back, momentarily drowning out the music.

A vendor walked by, displaying Tsotsi T-shirts on a rack improvised from lengths of plastic plumbing pipe. Barefoot children ran alongside him.

"You think things are about to get bad," Sylvia said to Michael.

"I don't know," he answered. "Like I told Petra—"

"Hey, how come all these white guys in the audience have walkie-talkies?" Sylvia went on. "In my experience, walkie-talkies—"

She need not have said another word, because at that instant all the District Six devices powered by electrical generators—the stage lights, the amplifiers, the musicians' microphones, even the little red, yellow, and green lights on the sound man's console—went absolutely dead.

"Michael!" screamed Sylvia in the darkness.

He had been wrenched violently backward into the crowd by the force of bodies streaming away from the stage. He thought he felt the grip of determined hands on his upper arms, but in the crush he could not be sure. "Over here!" he yelled. The hands, if they had held him at all, released him. He was reminded that his foot hurt.

"Where?" Sylvia called. She, too, was being swept backward by a shearing force whose intention seemed to her at once multiple and single. "I need you!"

Oddly, the music, though diminished in volume, had not ceased: the trumpet and drums continued, the singing was just discernible, and the hand-clapping from the audience, after faltering for a few moments, had increased in intensity.

"To the right!" Michael called to Sylvia. "The right"—he drew a breath—"of the stage."

In the darkness it was now possible to see that the lighted things cast up by the audience were leaflets that had been folded into the shape of paper airplanes and set afire. There were an increasing number of them, and with all the artificial lights out, they seemed by example to call attention to the stars above, astonishingly large and till now invisible to the crowd. Of course, there were still the helicopters.

Michael received a sharp blow across the cheek by what might have been an elbow. He struck back without success. Anyway, he reflected, the elbow probably just belonged to someone more skilled than he at fleeing. He made his way forward. "Petra!" he called. "Sylvia!"

Neither answered.

To his left, Michael heard a walkie-talkie crackle, and in the starlight he was able to snatch it from the white hand that held it. He zigzagged back off into the crowd, and when he felt himself hidden, he turned the device off. He regained his breath. His foot was no doubt only bruised, but stooping over for a moment seemed a useful stratagem in a semipanicked crowd. He retied his shoelace once again to allow for the swelling that had begun at his instep.

Sylvia walked around in the dark. At some previous moment, after the lights had gone out, she had been grabbed around the waist and had had the wind knocked out of her. But no one seemed to be interfering directly with her now. A great number of people were passing quickly by in what she could at the instant interpret only as random movement, and these people spoke a number of languages, none of which she was acquainted with.

Still, there was no tear gas, so probably things ought to be thought of as remaining in flux. She tried to draw upon her experience as a diplomat's daughter.

She was quite scared. Probably English was the thing for this kind of circumstance.

Making a fist around an imaginary microphone, she stood up straight and began speaking into it. "Arriving live tonight by satellite from Cape Town's beautiful District Six," she said as the crowd buffeted her about in a variety of directions, "this is KBZT-FM, Sylvia here, reminding you that if you could just die to fly, then you'd better dress to kill, because this fine night—take my word— is gonna be young for days."

She looked at her fist. She hadn't said anything in English after all, but really American was kind of soothing as a language. She let her fingers loosen.

Two white men who within her hearing had been speaking Afrikaans to each other turned to look at Sylvia. They approached her, and one of them said in English, "It would probably be best for your safety if you came with us." The other man placed something unpleasantly hard, something made of leather, against her breastbone. She looked down at it, then up at the men.

"Oh, I do doubt that," Sylvia said to them. "I mean, I'm a U.S. citizen not fully informed about how it is down here. But I'm a safety expert in my way, and—"

The surge of the crowd drew her, with a riptide violence so unexpected that it left her laughing, away from the white men who had threatened her with her own safety.

Several hundred meters to the east, Petra was speaking in reasonable tones to three policemen who were rolling back the barbed-wire tangle from across the crowd exit. She was flanked by a dozen or so unhappy Californians. "I just thought," she said, "if we could be of any assistance . . ."

The camouflage-garbed men she was addressing paid her no heed.

"Rocks," said one of the Americans behind her. "Now it's rocks." Someone else added, "I told you it was a dumb time to use your frequent-flier mileage."

The crowd had begun, in what was obviously not a fully thought-through strategy, to throw rocks at the helicopters circling above them. The rocks were raining back down upon the ground-bound audience below, and in a sort of attempt at response, the helicopters had turned on their searchlights.

"Where's Nomanzi?" Petra asked her production assistant. It was becoming difficult for Petra to avail herself of reasonable tones of voice.

"Nomanzi? Who's Nomanzi?" said the p.a. He was looking over his shoulder. "And what's this with the tires?"

Michael, far back in the crowd, heard the first of Tsotsi's back-up generators start up, then the second, the third, the many. On-stage, the lights came on too, then the amplifiers and microphones. He saw a number of young black men in the audience rolling automobile tires across the rocky ground. He saw Chentula take the microphone at stage center.

"Sylvia!" Michael called.

Somewhere in front of him he saw a white arm wave up, then, if he had really seen it, it went down—undulantly, with the look of languor.

"Brothers," said Chentula from the stage. "Sisters. We are here together for freedom and peace."

Michael saw that Nomanzi was onstage now, and he saw as well that after a small familial discussion Chentula handed the microphone to his half-sister. The music, such as it was, had trailed off some time before the power had come back on. Johnny stood discreetly out of the spotlight but unmistakably beside and with his friends. He had resumed his measuring nod, a gesture unbearably eloquent in its lack of self-consciousness.

"We are Africans here tonight," Nomanzi said, and the crowd settled down almost immediately. She was recognized. "We must conduct ourselves as one people." She was groping for time. "For the dignity and purpose of our nation; for our children, born and unborn."

"Ilulwane!" someone shouted from the crowd.

Toward the back of the audience there was a sound like a pistol shot, but it could just as easily have been a piece of wood shattering. The helicopter searchlights revealed that several groups of riot police were moving through the crowd; they held pump-action shotguns but as yet were aiming them at nothing but the sky.

"Ilulwane!" the cry went up. Nomanzi became confused. She turned to Chentula in silent appeal. He hit a chord on his keyboard guitar and spoke into her ear. "No Kentuckys," he seemed to have said, but she wasn't sure. "One more song?" she said.

"Ilulwane!" the crowd said. Her TV character's name had become a chant.

"Return to your homes!" said a thickly Afrikaner voice atop the stage's scaffolding. It was speaking through a bullhorn of astonishing power. "The concert permit has expired. Return to your homes."

Without a word, Petra hustled her party through the gate, and they all took off at a run.

"In fifteen minutes . . ." the bullhorn continued.

Sylvia saw one of the riot police who was passing before her stumble upon the rocky ground, fall, and, as he did, accidentally discharge his shotgun skyward. Above, a helicopter immediately sprouted a tail feather of fire. The vehicle peeled out of sight, but the flash of orange-yellow light it made as it crashed to the ground a kilometer and a half away lit up the sky.

Very shortly after, there were many fires in the concert space.

Sylvia watched as a black policeman who had been separated from his patrol was seized by the crowd. An automobile tire was placed over his head; he was doused with gasoline and lit afire.

"*Das vingerlek lekker,*" said a young black woman, twisting the bottom of her T-shirt up in a knot and turning away.

I've left everything open, thought Sylvia. She stared at the dying man long enough to consider how much a man or woman might hurt. When she realized that there were too many ways to think about this, she ran.

The tear gas canisters began to land among the crowd almost immediately.

In his hand, Michael discovered the walkie he'd snatched from the riot-control man previously. He could barely see it through his tears, but it came to him that there was gas in the air and that his tears were not entirely sentimental. He took off his shirt, wrapped it around his nose and mouth, and turned the device on. A cacophony of voices addressed him through it. Of course they weren't addressing *him*, but he understood the language of panic.

"You will die," an African voice said in his other ear, and Michael dropped the walkie. Another man grabbed him from behind, pinning his arms painfully against his back. Michael realized he was surrounded by a group of angry young blacks. "No undercover Security man can live in the Azania we are making."

"American," said Michael. "I'm with the band."

A tire was tossed over his head. Michael recalled that he was in love. How long had it been that he'd been coughing?

"You will die," someone else said to him. He was being thrown about so much that he didn't know to whom to speak. So he spoke to Sylvia: he cried out her name.

"Michael!" he thought he heard her say in response. "Over here!"

But of course everyone gets his last wish. No doubt Michael was hallucinating.

A woman with a half-gallon Diet Pepsi bottle stepped gravely forward and poured gasoline over him. "No, listen, you've got it wrong," Michael said.

It was then that he saw William, not two meters away. William, or the man-who-would-be-William-were-William-alive, was wearing black stone-washed jeans and an orange T-shirt. He engaged Michael's gaze with an expression verging on amusement. He began shouting.

"You bloody lot of Kaffirs! This is a white man's country! Can't you see?"

The group that had surrounded Michael wheeled about, transfixed by this unvarnished expression of racism.

"Can't you bloody well see that everything you have, everything you are, has been given to you by the white man?" He stepped forward. "We have brought you the only civilization you know."

Michael struggled to remove the automobile tire from around his neck.

"We brought you your own humanity."

A very young man with a "Lucky" brand beer cooler strode forward and splashed its gasoline contents over William. Michael succeeded in freeing himself from the tire's grip. He saw that no one was paying attention to him, but he knew also that he could not yet leave.

"You'd be nothing without us," William continued. "You'd still be walking around in blankets. You'd still be living in huts." He did not appear to be affected by the tear gas. "You'd still—"

A girl-child, her nose and mouth bound in surgical gauze, walked forward and threw a lit match at William. The match went out before it reached him.

"—be worshiping goblins."

Michael observed a young man next to him lean down to remove from the seam of his jeans a long metal thing that appeared to be a sharpened bicycle spoke.

"Stop," shouted Michael. But the man plunged the thing into William's chest, and it seemed, with the tear gas and all, that William had vanished. *Dead*, thought Michael, beginning to run.

Some time later, Michael was busy vomiting when someone tapped him on the shoulder. "Hey," said a choked female voice. "You smell all funny and"—he stood up—"you look kind of beat up."

"Sylvia." He realized dignity was beyond him, so he tried for something that might pass for a smile. "You okay?"

"Yeah, I'm fine."

"Everyone out?"

"Well, like . . ." She scanned the ground around them, her face covered in Nomanzi's scarf. "I guess that depends on what you mean by 'everyone.' Everyone on stage got out." She looked quite weary. She began to cough. "You've got a black eye."

"I do?" Michael touched his cheek, and it hurt. "Yeah, I do."

"It's time to move," Sylvia said. "Let's go."

They ran.

Several hours later, when everyone in Petra's group had been accounted for, when everyone in Petra's group had made it back to the hotel, it was morning. Sylvia was asleep in her clothes, and Michael was completely naked.

He turned on the television. "Hey," he said, laying a hand upon Sylvia's thigh. "Look at this."

Heinrich Bloch, Joseph Lolombela, and Paul Walters were being identified in white Helvetica type at the bottom of the video screen. The American Secretary of State stepped forward to a nest of microphones. "I consider it the greatest privilege of my service to my country," he said, "and what I hope will be my country's service to the world, to announce that the Atlantic–European alliance, in concert with its other allies—in Africa, in Asia, in this world's future—has come to an agreement to make no test detonation of the fission bomb at this time."

Sylvia sat up in bed and placed a hand over her right tit. "Jesus," she said.

Michael put a hand over her hand.

Three days later, at 0813 hours, Private Brant van Gelder of the South African Army gazed out from the established perimeter surrounding the solar power station that he had understood the United States of America had installed in the Kalahari, some kilometers south of the game reserve, within the borders of his nation. He saw no other human being in any place he could observe.

He sat down on a sandy rise, near a *kameeldoring* bush, and cursed. There was no reason to consider this anything but a stupid bloody watch, and he recalled again that he had earned it at cards the previous night.

In his mind he heard something his commander had said the night before. "Yah, for a gift the thing seems to have more electrical lines running into it than out of it." The man, drunk and in his underwear, had been referrring to the tower. "But so do my cards." He had stood up, paid up. "Van Gelder—morning watch."

If only, thought Private van Gelder, eighteen years old, *I'd studied hard enough not to flunk out before my matrics.* He was from Johannesburg, where he had a girlfriend whose bright blond hair turned from straw to silk under his fingers—even though they both knew she was too fast for him, and even though he had received no letters at all from her since he'd been reassigned to the South.

He touched his sunburned face.

Something near the tower moved, alighted upon its topmost rail. Moved.

Private van Gelder took his sunglasses off and removed his binoculars from his pocket. The thing upon the tower was a bird—of which there were none native to the Kalahari. It hopped farther along the rail of the grotesquely built structure.

Dead in an hour, thought van Gelder. *Not suited for this land.*

Private van Gelder had once visited Europe, where he had seen many things, including long-tailed birds like this one. *Thrush, is it?* he thought. *Cuckoo?* He stood up upon the grass-touched sand that was, by assignment, his turf.

The bird hopped along the tower's rail until it was perched at the center of the structure's bulk.

Put it out of its misery, thought van Gelder, taking aim at the bird through the rifle's telescopic sight. He released the weapon's safety.

His own head hurt him very much.

He had released the safety.

On a certain day in southeastern Africa, beneath a sky that held nothing of emergency or love, a girl-child of the Xhosa tribe went down to the river for water, and as she dipped her own filling hips to take the water jar from atop her head, she glanced with no specific intention at the place where the rushes grew the tallest, and in that helpless second, while the whole shivering world revolved, she reinvented *everything*.

The river behind her, despite the drought that had for many months plagued her land, flowed on like a smooth brown ribbon, rippleless. She placed the water jar on the bank beside her and continued to stare at what the rushes, like a half-drawn blind or a Western woman's clothes, simultaneously hid and revealed.

Part of the thing looked like a leopard, although there had been no leopard in this place for many years. Bending forward at the waist and taking one hand in the other, she stepped very slowly in the direction of the mysterious presence watching her from the rushes.

Eh-eh, Mother, she thought. *Now I will surely be killed.* Her real mother had once said exactly the same thing, but it had turned out not to be true: she had simply confused her first sighting of a single-engine aircraft with the arrival of God.

A pair of coupling dragonflies shot into her line of sight and hovered there, iridescent in the morning light. The girl-child shooed them away. And out of the rushes, one by one, stepped four strangers draped in leopard skin. The tallest of the men held a spear.

"Unonqawuza," he said.

The man was of commanding aspect, and she stared at him for the space of four breaths that might easily have encompassed the four stages of life a young Xhosa girl such as herself had been taught to expect.

But she answered, "Yes, Unonqawuza. Or Nongquase. That is how I am called."

"Your uncle is Umhlakaza."

"He is my uncle." She looked down, then fiercely up again. "As I am, you are a bad person to do these things, hiding in the rushes like an animal or *ichanti*. Why do you come here just to frighten me?"

A thin brown snake slithered in near-agony out of the eight o'clock sun and into the little shade provided by the riverside rushes. The snake hung about its sanctuary as if in weary synchrony with it. The man with the spear, indicating his companions with a sweep of his arm, said: "We have come here from the Land of the Dead to bring about wonderful events, events so wonderful they have never been seen before. Listen to what your ancestors tell you: We have come from the dead to save our people."

The girl's face was so perfectly unlined that when, as now, she frowned, the effect was of someone expressing not doubt but perfect belief. She began backing slowly away from the man.

It is impossible to exaggerate the beauty of her movement at this moment. Ankles, thighs, wrists, elbows, breasts—all at each instant plead their own newness, even as they helplessly boast of it. Her retreat is not a retreat; it is a tiny dance of absolute conscription. And in backing away from the four men—from the fixity of their stares, from their muscular torsos—she is drawing what they have said as fully into her as a woman does her lover in lifting her hips to him. A trickle of sweat runs suddenly from one faintly flossed armpit to her waist. The water jar, still unfilled, shatters against an egg-shaped rock beside it. The girl-child stops, but she does not look at what she has broken.

"How is this thing possible?" she whispers. "Where is the cleverness in it when the white man kills our chiefs and takes our land?"

One of the men who has till now remained silent steps forward, but the girl, as if emboldened by what she imagines he is about to say, rushes to continue: "Sickness has entered our cattle, and everywhere they are dying. The rains have not come. Our mealies and sorghum are as tiny as the fingers of my baby sister. Eh, fear of you has almost killed me, but it will be the white man who will be the end of us, because is this not his magic?" The strength that has come into her voice startles her. "*Is this not his magic?*" she says again, to listen to her own forcefulness. "And where, I would like to know, is the cleverness that is as strong as his?"

The snake does not move.

The man who has been about to speak stares very hard at Nongqause. "When the things we tell you to do have been done," he says at last, "then you will know the kind of cleverness we have— we! Our people alone! Because beginning from that day, there will be no more hunger, there will be no more sickness, there will be no more death. And on that very day—hear what it is we tell you— the white man will perish utterly."

The river makes a small sound, as if a stone has been dropped into it, and the girl makes a small sound, as if she has tried to catch the stone and failed. She is looking at the man who has just spoken, but she is thinking of herself. Not that the person-that-she-must-now-become doubts the truth of his words, but the very fact that it is she to whom these words are addressed has made her infinitely curious about the person she is. What qualities in her can have made this event happen to her, and to her alone? She looks from one man to another for the answer.

A sweet, suffocating smell of dried grasses passes over them. She looks from one man to another for the answer.

It is not they who have the answer.

She raises her face to the sun, which has some time ago but once again risen upon this part of the world where she has come to stand. It is still early morning, eight hours and sixteen minutes past what mankind has come to call midnight.

For the life of her she cannot remember her next line.

A second passes. Two.

Then the sky to the north, several hundred kilometers away, is suddenly illuminated with a brilliance that till now has been the province only of the sun upon the earth.

Reflexively, Nomanzi abandons the character she is playing, the character of Nongqause. There are two suns in the sky after all.

Michael, seated in the basket of the crane that allows him to frame the shots of the film that these people have gathered together to make, orders his cameraman to cut.

"What the hell is that?" he says, lowering his bullhorn and peering out at the second sun that has so suddenly doubled the sky's light.

Petra stares heavenward.

Nomanzi raises her hand to the diamond earring that she has not quite been able to keep from touching since Sylvia gave it to her in Cape Town. As her fingers caress the gem, she feels it dissolve between them. It really dissolves.

Nomanzi begins, from a place she did not know existed in her, to laugh.

"Sylvia Walters!" calls Michael through the bullhorn.

Nomanzi continues to laugh as she walks off the set. The sound she finds herself making is so completely compounded of bitterness, love, and hope that she knows already that there is no possibility of her continuing to work this day.

"Sylvia Walters!" Michael calls again.

At her console, in a tent to the side of the set, Sylvia stares down at her suddenly blanked-out controls.

Nomanzi, continuing to walk out alone into the sandy veldt, holds her now-unadorned earlobes as if they could guide her. There are tears running down her cheeks.

A woman laughing.

Is the sound of history.

A NOTE ABOUT THE AUTHOR

Ted Mooney was born in Dallas, Texas, grew up in Washington, D.C., and was educated at Columbia University, New York, and Bennington College, Vermont, from which he graduated in 1973. Since then his short stories have appeared in *American Review* and *Esquire*, and he has contributed articles to the Los Angeles *Times*. Mr. Mooney's first novel, *Easy Travel to Other Planets*, was nominated for the American Book Award in 1981. In the same year it also received the Sue Kaufman Prize for First Fiction from the American Academy and Institute of Arts and Letters. Previously the recipient of awards from both the John Guggenheim Memorial Foundation and the Ingram Merrill Foundation, Mr. Mooney currently resides in Manhattan, where he is a senior editor at *Art in America*. He is now at work on a third novel.

A NOTE ON THE TYPE

This book was set in Caledonia, a typeface designed by W. A. Dwiggins (1880–1956). It belongs to the family of printing types called "modern face" by printers—a term used to mark the change in style of type letters that occurred about 1800. Caledonia borders on the general design of Scotch Roman, but is more freely drawn than that letter.

Composed by PennSet, Inc., Bloomsburg, Pennsylvania
Printed and bound by Fairfield Graphics,
Fairfield, Pennsylvania
Typography and binding design by
Dorothy S. Baker